PRAISE FOR *Grace at Low Tide*

"This tender, good-hearted and moving tale of one Charleston girl's coming of age gives us what so many books these days don't: a character we can care about. Ms. Hart's evocation of the ways of Charleston society—blueblood and redneck alike— is right on target, her evocation of the landscape down here sure and certain. And of course she's made certain to include the three most important elements of any worthy Southern story: family, family, and family."

—BRET LOTT, best-selling author of *Jewel* and
A Song I Knew by Heart

"*Grace at Low Tide,* Hart's first novel, is a aromatic bouilla-baisse of Southern manners, island life, and God's redemptive love. Readers who loved Oprah's book picks will find this title in keeping with the best contemporary fiction."

—LYNN WAALKES, *CBA Marketplace*

"A delightful new writer! You'll love Beth Webb Hart."

—GAYLE ROPER, author of *Winter Winds* and *Spring Rain*

"*Grace at Low Tide* is a beautiful story of the power one young woman's faith can have. Beth Webb Hart perfectly captures the voice of a girl wizened too early by hardship, yet still essentially a teen at heart. Her struggle to find her way both within her family and out in the world will have you aching to see her succeed, and the lush setting of Southern island life is an education in an existence most of us will never encounter. A warm, wonderful book I'll eagerly pass around to my friends."

—ALISON STROBEL, author of *Worlds Collide*

Grace at Low Tide

Grace at Low Tide

BETH WEBB HART

WESTBOW
PRESS

A Division of Thomas Nelson Publishers
Since 1798

visit us at www.westbowpress.com

Published in Nashville, Tennessee, by WestBow Press, a division of Thomas Nelson, Inc.

WestBow Press books may be purchased in bulk for educational, business, fund-raising, or sales promotional use. For information, please e-mail SpecialMarkets@ThomasNelson.com.

Unless otherwise noted, Scripture quotations are from the HOLY BIBLE, NEW INTERNATIONAL VERSION®. Copyright © 1973, 1978, 1984 by International Bible Society. Used by permission of Zondervan Publishing House. All rights reserved.

Scripture quotations noted NLT are from *The Living Bible*, copyright © 1971. Used by permission of Tyndale House Publishers, Inc., Wheaton, Illinois 60189. All rights reserved.

Scripture quotations noted NKJV are from The New King James Version®, copyright © 1979, 1980, 1982 by Thomas Nelson, Inc., Publishers.

Publisher's Note: This novel is a work of fiction. Names, characters, places, and incidents are either products of the author's imagination or used fictitiously. All characters are fictional, and any similarity to people living or dead is purely coincidental.

Library of Congress Cataloging in Publication Data

Hart, Beth Webb, 1971–
    Grace at low tide / Beth Webb Hart.
        p. cm.
    ISBN 1-59554-026-1 (trade paper)
    I. Title.
    PS3608.A78395G73 2005
    813'.6—dc22   2004026279

Printed in the United States of America

05 06 07 08 09 RRD 7 6 5 4 3 2 1

ACKNOWLEDGMENTS

༄

Thanks be to God! And to the following: My agent, Rebecca Kurson, for her unwavering faith, and my editor, Ami McConnell whose direction made all of the difference. Thanks also to Deborah Wiseman, Amanda Bostic, and the entire Westbow Press Team.

I am grateful for R. H. W. Dillard and Jan Bailey who introduced me to creative writing as well as Gayle Roper and the Christian Writers Guild who opened the door with Westbow.

Much of this novel was written as part of my graduate thesis, and I would like to thank the following faculty at Sarah Lawrence College who served as my advisors: Linsey Abrams, Lucy Rosenthal, and Joan Silber. Thanks also to John and Carolyn Pelletier and Meghan R. Duckworth who put a roof over my head during those years, and Joe and Lynn Land, my employers, who allowed me time to write.

A special thanks goes to my beloved sisters, Peggy and Libby, and my sisters-in-Christ: Meredith, Lisa, Jeanne Anne, Holly, Amie Beth, Jenny, Amy L., and Amy W.S. Your ongoing prayer has made a profound impact on this book and my life.

Thanks to my mentor, Jean Corbett, who introduced me to the healing prayer ministry and to Dr. Thomas Hughes who served as my medical consultant.

I am deeply grateful to my parents, Betty and Joe Jelks, who have showered me with love, nurtured my faith, and provided an education in which I could pursue my desire to write.

This book is dedicated to my daughter, Frances, who daily fills my heart with joy, and my husband, Edward B. Hart, Jr., whose precious love buoys me in this and every pursuit.

Contents

Therefore we do not lose heart. Though outwardly
we are wasting away, yet inwardly we are being renewed
day by day. For our light and momentary troubles are achieving
for us an eternal glory that far outweighs them all. So we
fix our eyes not on what is seen, but on what is unseen. For
what is seen is temporary, but what is unseen is eternal.

—2 CORINTHIANS 4:16–18

Blessed are those who trust in the LORD . . . They are
like trees planted along a riverbank, with roots that reach deep
into the water. Such trees are not bothered by the heat or worried
by long months of drought. Their leaves stay green, and they
go right on producing delicious fruit.

—JEREMIAH 17:7–8 NLT

Mama and the Debutramp

"Fat is *not* the enemy," my mama says to me. She is sitting in her reading chair next to the sliding glass door with Easy the cat nestled behind her ankles. She sets the book down on her knee to look me over.

"So what is?" I say, grabbing one of Daddy's peanut butter bars out of the bread basket in the kitchen.

"Shouldn't you cover your arms?" she says. The creases on the inside of her black eyebrows deepen like the cracks in the ceiling above my bed, and a square pocket of skin forms at the top of her nose.

"Nope," I say, "that kitchen's hot."

She gives one steady nod and says slowly, "*Car-bo-hy-drates.*" Then she spreads her fingers out over the pages. "I wish your father would read this book."

"Love you," I say, and as I'm walking onto the porch she says, "Careful tonight, dahlin'. They're everywhere." She puts her hand on her chest and wheezes, "Those deer."

※

Mama likes to diet and study the Bible. About a year ago she joined this group called First Place, which she describes as a "Christ-centered weight-loss program." She drives all the way to St. Paul's Episcopal Church in Charleston twice a week to pray with her small group and weigh in. So far she's lost eleven pounds, but it's hard for me to tell.

Mama's got a funny shape. She says God took two different bodies, cut them in half, and sewed the opposites together. Her top, starting with her elongated neck, is noticeably thin—she's got bony shoulders, a flat chest, and a tee-niny waist. She's short and when she's wearing a long skirt, you'd swear she was little all over. But her bottom half is round, with pockets of flesh spread from her hips to her knees like bread rolls. It's like this: her wrists are pencil thin, but her ankles are as thick as potatoes.

Years ago at a beach party, I overheard my mama's brother, Uncle Bobbie, talking to my daddy while Mama (in her skirted two-piece) took some of the kids down to play in the surf. He said, "If only she was like a tube of toothpaste, then you could just *squeeze* some of her up."

Daddy looked at my uncle then back to my mama as she stood in the surf, leaning over to wash something out of my cousin's eye.

"Can't have it all," he said.

❧

"About time for work, eh?" yells Daddy. He is about twenty yards away, in the fish shed by the dock. He's slapping the dust out of the croaker sacks for the oyster roast as the tide empties out of the creek behind him, wide ripples of black water shaped like boomerangs hurling toward the sea. I can tell by how quick his bulky arms are moving that he's in a better mood than usual. It's two days before Christmas, and tomorrow the whole family—my brother, sister, and cousin—will be home. Family gatherings are one of the few events that make him happy.

"I'm off to work, Dad," I say.

"Mama says those deer are everywhere," he yells.

"Yep," I say.

"The last thing I want is another dent in the truck," he says.

I nod, and as I step carefully into the pickup, keeping my tennis socks from touching the layer of damp mud that is splayed across the door, he shouts, "DeVeaux," and I can tell by his tone that he's already irritated.

So I roll down the window and say sweetly, "Yes, sir?"

He walks toward me, dragging a croaker sack across the yard, his duck boots stamping the dark soil as he dodges the tire swing and shimmies between the tractor and the toolshed. He's gained about twenty pounds since last spring, much of which seems to have attached itself to his neck and cheeks. Now his eyes become two slits when he smiles and when he yells.

As he reaches the teahouse where the truck is parked he says, "Did you get the Orangeburg sausage?"

"You said you needed it by Christmas Eve," I say.

"That's tomorrow, honey," he says.

"I'll go first thing," I say.

"I don't want to have to ask you again," he says.

He turns his back and slaps the sack once, then he drags it back across the yard and throws it on the picnic table in the fish shed.

Daddy has been in a bad mood for most of my adolescence. (And you better take cover when that eerie half-grin spreads across his face, because that means he is about to blow.) Short tempers run in his side of the family, and sometimes when I get mad, I can feel my own temples pulse.

If you asked me what Daddy likes I'd have to say the sound of the television at a high volume and filling station food. He also loves to take off his pants before supper and walk around in his work shirt and white cotton boxers for the rest of the night. And he is often getting sick with gout in his feet so he can stay in bed all day with Mama waiting on him.

He used to love parties, dances at the Carolina Yacht Club, and oyster roasts on Wadmalaw Island. He was often hosting dinner socials at our home on Tradd Street in downtown Charleston, which ended with port cordials in the parlor where he would tell deer hunting stories and, if coaxed properly by guests, sing a few Gullah spirituals that Maum Bess, his nanny, taught him during the summers he spent at Rose Hill, a decaying sea-island cotton plantation that has been in his mama's side of the family since 1810.

Then he'd announce, "I ought to move out to Rose Hill and reacquaint myself with my heritage, feel the pluff mud settle like putty between my toes."

Mama would shake her head and mutter, "He's too much of a city boy for that life," then he'd end with her favorite song, "Faddah, Len' Me Your Walkin' Shoe."

❧

Truth be told, my father filed for bankruptcy five months ago. He had been developing a barrier island, Otter, which sits thirty miles south of the Charleston harbor, at the mouth of the North Edisto River. I can see Otter Island from the dock of the little caretaker's house on Rose Hill Plantation where we now live (Daddy came back to his heritage, but not the way he had imagined it), and occasionally on a calm day at high tide, my father will drive his johnboat out of the creek and into the Intracoastal Waterway where he'll circle Otter Island, counting the pink flags of the property lines: twenty-seven lots, ranging in value from $350,000 to $1,000,000, all of which have a 180-degree view of the Intracoastal Waterway or the Atlantic Ocean.

He borrowed the money to buy the property from his boyhood friend Dinks Edings, a local businessman who had made a small fortune by investing in the development of the Charleston Hotel and other sections of downtown King Street. "I believe this is the big one," he had told my mama and his mama, Mee Maw Rose, two years ago as he poured three glasses of sherry in the living room of our downtown home on Tradd Street, the only home I'd ever lived in until now.

I'm told that Daddy used to be a stitch. When he was nineteen and his girlfriends were making their debut, he coordinated a "Debutramp" ball where he and a group of his contemporaries rented out the Hibernian Hall and invited all the members of the Charleston Hibernian Society to view the male version of debutantes, fifteen well-heeled Charleston boys who, dressed in T-shirts and tails and black Chuck Taylor tennis shoes, strutted down the ballroom while the members of the club lined up on both sides of the aisle, chuckling in their tuxedos, their white gloves poised. When the debutramps made their way to the president of the society, Dr. Joseph Jenkins, who was seated at the end of the ballroom, they'd curtsy and lift their pants to their knees, revealing their hairy legs. Dr. Jenkins nodded in approval and led the gloved applause, which sounded like a hundred ducks flapping their wings.

Mama and Daddy got together up in Virginia during college. She was at Hollins, and he was at Washington and Lee University. His boys choir, Southern Comfort, went down to the ladies' school for a performance and Mama, who was the social activities chairman, greeted him at the school gates. They parked that very night on the top of Tinker Mountain, looking down at Mama's school in the valley. Mama was from Greenville, South Carolina, and she was rich ("a nouveau from the upstate" is what Mee Maw Rose used to say). Mama's daddy was a textile executive at JP Stevens and when she left for college he sent her off in the car of her choice, a baby-blue Chevrolet convertible, with a driver named Lawrence who carried her luggage into the dormitory.

Daddy passed for what they call a Charleston blue blood. He was the typical kind because his family fortune was dwindling and about all he had was a regular-sized house on Water Street (circa

1823) with the double front porch and the cobblestone driveway, a relative's name on a building here and there, and a lot of good manners learned at Mrs. Hillhouse's cotillion school. And, of course, Rose Hill Plantation, which is fifty miles out of town and across the Dawhoo River on a sea island called Edisto.

Mama and Daddy have two cardboard boxes filled with scratched-up 45 rpm records from their courting days. They say that in the summertime they used to park downtown at the Bayside Battery late at night with the radio turned up, take off their shoes, and shag down the sidewalk while the harbor lights blinked on and off.

Daddy's little sister, Aunt Eliza, who died in a boating accident off the Edisto River just before I was born, would steal their shoes, sneak into the car, and quickly reverse it out of sight just as my parents noticed the music fading. On these occasions, they would walk across the White Point Gardens to Mee Maw Rose's house on Water Street, their bare feet dodging the summer cockroaches that scurried in and out of the cracks along the road.

There are these old home movies of Daddy and Aunt Eliza that Mee Maw Rose used to show Virginia, Eli, and me when we'd spend the night at her house. We'd all pile into her bed, under the covers, and watch my father and aunt when they were barely old enough to walk, jumping naked over the sprinkler in Mee Maw's garden. Or riding their bikes barefoot down Water Street, waving to the camera before zooming by.

There is only one movie of them when they are teenagers and it's my favorite to watch, though nothing much happens in it. It is of the day Aunt Eliza went off to boarding school in Virginia for the first time and Daddy is driving her. He is thin and handsome, already a high school senior and number one on the tennis team, and just about to receive a scholarship to Washington and Lee University. He's got a crew cut and a broad smile, and he's dressed all preppy in an argyle sweater, khakis, and winter-white bucks. He is gracefully loading her luggage into the trunk and looking, every so often, out of the corner of his eye at the camera. Soon Aunt Eliza is beside him, her thick brown hair curled out and up around her shoulders. She's dressed in pedal pushers and a cardigan and she's looking excited, switching her weight back and forth. As Daddy comes up and puts his arm around her shoulders, she looks up at him, then looks back and mouths good-bye toward the camera. Then Daddy, his arm lightly on her elbow, walks her down the porch and into the car. He looks up just once with a grin before taking his own seat.

As they pull out of the driveway, Eliza puts on a pair of round, dark sunglasses and says, "Bye, Mama!" And then all you can see is the back of the car as it drives down the quiet street, their heads bobbing in conversation in the rearview mirror.

I like this movie because it allows me to see Daddy in a time when he had no burdens. When he was optimistic and capable and sure of himself. When his whole life was laid out before him like that highway to Richmond he carried his sister down, delivering her safely to school.

I used to imagine the rest of their trip to Virginia. I'd picture him kissing her good-bye at the door of her dormitory, and just as she starts to weep he says, "Sister, you are going to be just fine."

Just before Daddy declared bankruptcy, Mee Maw Rose passed away, leaving him all that she had: her home on Water Street and Rose Hill Plantation. But he had to sell it all right away in one last attempt to save his shirt. Within three months after Mee Maw's death, he had sold our home on Tradd, then her home on Water Street, and finally Rose Hill Plantation, which, as I said, has been in our family for more than one hundred and eighty years. He sold the plantation to a Japanese family, the Shuzukis, who live in Michigan and make cars. He arranged for our family to live in the four-room caretaker's house that sits on the creek, adjacent to the main house. That's where we are now, but Daddy says it won't be for long. And I'm hanging on to his words.

Daddy's job is to maintain the property, restoring the grounds and planting corn and okra to lure in the quail and deer. He's also supposed to take the Shuzukis on boat rides and teach them how to fish and hunt.

He arranged for Maum Bess, his nanny, and her son, Chambers, to have an official title to the property in the woods behind the plantation where they have always lived. He hired Chambers, who has been farming the fields for Mee Maw Rose since boyhood, to be his right-hand man.

"You're the agricultural consultant," Daddy said to Chambers. "But I'll hand my job over to you once I work out my next business venture."

"Yes, suh," Chambers said.

"We'll find a way out of this soon," he said to Mama and me the other day as he sent us to fetch the Shuzukis from the airport. "Don't you gals fret."

❧

Now, I grew up in the city of Charleston and life was just beginning to take shape for me there. I'd survived my freshman year of high school without getting in any trouble, the first in our family who didn't drink and have to go before a judge for the charge of possession of alcohol by a minor. My church had just gotten Bethany, the first female youth minister they'd ever had, and I was meeting with her and a group of girls for breakfast once a week and going to coed youth group on Wednesday nights. Sasser, one of my good old friends who is also the PK (priest's kid) from my neighborhood, had taken me into his confidence over the mysterious and much gossiped about breakup of his parents' marriage. He even got me praying, too, for the one request that seemed to permeate his every waking moment: that his mama would come to her senses and return home to him and his father. He has this vision that involves sitting around the dinner table again sharing the best and worst parts of their day as they had done for so many years.

So, I'm bored to tears out here on this dead island while I wait for Daddy's plan to get us back to town. Not to mention that the tap water tastes rusty and the pluff mud from the creek manages to find its way onto everything, staining my T-shirts and attaching itself to the crevices on the bottoms of my shoes. And then there is Daddy's temper, which has increased in its unpredictability over this last year. Mama and I have learned to navigate our way through him like a boat channeling a narrow creek at high tide, inching our way along in anticipation of the oyster-bed banks, their sharp shells poised just inches beneath the dark water.

But as I drive down the dirt road on my way to work at the restaurant, passing beneath the avenue of the gigantic, moss-covered live oak trees whose limbs stretch down to the ground like lazy fingers, even I have to admit that the sight of Rose Hill is grand. Sometimes, when I'm walking through the fields, I get stopped in my tracks and think that if it weren't for my neon Nike tennis shoes and my Cooper Hall Class of 1999 sweatshirt, the year could be 1820 and my great-great-great-grandfather Edmund Seabrook Rose could be on the dock, loading his steamboat with bales of superfine cotton.

Edmund Seabrook Rose built the main house, which sits on the edge of a wide tidal creek. It is made of white clapboard with a two-story front porch and an iron railing bordering the portico and the double front steps, with the name Rose molded across the ironwork where the steps meet. And some historians think that the house was designed by the same man who designed the White House.

Between the creek and the house is a garden with a multitude of walkways that are bordered with boxwood and Cassina berry trees.

Beyond the garden is the gall, a pond surrounded by palmettos and magnolias and azalea bushes that bloom in an abundance of pink and fuchsia each spring. Also on the property is a teahouse for dining and a ballroom where Edmund and his family hosted fancy dances in the golden days before, as Mee Maw Rose would say, the boll weevil and the Yankees invaded.

❧

Just as I cross through the gates and onto the dirt road that leads to the restaurant, I spot a group of marsh myrtle-berry bushes in the middle of a plowed-down cornfield to the right. I leave the truck running as I walk into the open field to pick up a few branches, which the waitresses can use as decoration for the plates at the restaurant where I work. When I reach the bushes I hear the quick whisper of gunfire in the trees ahead like a one-word secret. Christmas marks the last weeks of deer hunting season, and I picture the tall, camouflage hunting stands that Daddy hides in the pines around the open fields at Rose Hill. I quickly turn and run back to the truck.

Thing is, I can't deny that there is a hand on my life constantly steering me to safety. And I believe the hand is God's. But as I've told Bethany and Sasser, I have a sense there is this thick barrier that keeps me from fully knowing Him the way they do. I don't know what the barrier is or what I can do to remove it, so after a momentary blip of danger passes on the screen of my life, it is all too easy to forget about Him and His seemingly invisible hand. Sasser says it's like a kind of amnesia that I contract over and over again, and I need to find a way to wake up from it.

2

Sal's Lowland Cuisine

"Idle hands are a devil's workshop," Jeeter, the restaurant manager, says to me. He's leaning to the side, one hand on the vacuum cleaner and the other cupping a White Russian cocktail in a clear plastic cup.

Sal, the proprietor, looks up from the reservation book. He scratches between his legs and turns to me. "Tell Jeeter what a sissy drink that is."

I'm not in the mood for them so I just smile.

Then Sal says, "And tell him to get his mangy dog out of my restaurant."

Jeeter blows a kiss to Cocoa, his chocolate Labrador who has one yellow eye and one blue eye, then he shoos him out the screened door, shouting, "In the truck."

Sal looks me up and down as I climb the ladder in the wait station and pull out some napkins for folding. "So, what's up, lady?"

"Nothing," I say, without meeting his jumpy eyes.

"We gonna have fun tonight?" he says.

"Leave her alone, Sal," Suzanne, the head waitress, says as she walks in the back door. "Don't forget that she's fifteen years old, or I'll be the first one to report you to the police."

Sal grins.

"How many we got on the books?" Suzanne asks.

"One hundred twelve," Sal says.

"Holy mackerel," says Jeeter. Then he turns to me. "DEE-EEVO, I need you to whip the rest of that lettuce in the freezer and slice a bunky load of lemons."

"You're such a dork, Jeeter," says Suzanne and she winks at me. "You know, I can't believe you actually have a wife. That you actually found someone to marry you."

She turns to the mirror at the back of the dining room and twists her hair up in a bun on the top of her head. Then she stabs the bun with a gold hair tong to keep it in place.

"Shut up, Suzanne," he says, "before I stick you in section B where Dr. Halverson sneaks peeks at your backside."

"Put me wherever the tips are, Jeeter," she says as she outlines her lips with a pencil the color of mud. "I've got to pay for that Barbie playhouse Becky wants for Christmas."

Suzanne is a friend of my cousin Eli. She is twenty-two years old, and she has a four-year-old named Becky she raises on her own. Suzanne and Becky live down on the beach in an apartment above the Edisto Realty Company, and I babysit Becky occasionally.

❧

My title at the restaurant is busgirl, but basically I have to do whatever Jeeter tells me. I spend half my time in the kitchen making salads and desserts and biting off the mini-bottle caps for Suzanne's drink orders. Then Jeeter'll scream for me to get out on the floor where we'll clear the tables, wipe down the seats, and reset everything. Sal's is the only nice restaurant on the island, though we're located across from the campgrounds in a cinderblock building that used to be a gas station. The other two eateries specialize in the fried fish buffet, so we've always got a decent crowd. We serve wine and grilled tuna, stuff that costs more than five dollars a meal, and every plate gets a helping of finely ground grits that Sal buys from a special farm in Mississippi. Tosha, the chef and cleaning lady, cooks the grits with whipping cream and butter. She lets them simmer all day long and at the end of the night, if there's any left over, she'll set aside a plastic cupful for me.

Sal might say he owns the place, but Suzanne says his daddy really owns it. My cousin Eli, who is like an older sister, got me this job on the condition that I steer clear of Sal.

"He's a slime," she warned. "He's womanized two-thirds of the gals on this island. Not to mention the vacationers."

But Cousin Eli decided to take the risk because she knew I'd go crazy for sure if I had to spend night after night with Mama and Daddy in that tee-niny caretaker's house in the middle of nowhere while Daddy schemed up another get-rich plan. She ought to know, 'cause she's lived with our family since her mama and daddy died, and that was before I was born. So she talked to Suzanne and one afternoon in early October when I was checking the crab cages by the dock, Sal drove by in his speedboat, circled back toward the dock and said, "Okay, little lady, we got a job for you."

Sal is bald, though he has managed to grow a stringy rim of gray hair behind his ears that he ties into a little ponytail at the back of his neck. He drives an electric-blue Trans Am and he wears flip-flops and cut-off shorts all year long. When he makes his nightly appearances on the dining room floor, he puts on a pair of zebra-print pants and a white chef's coat (as if he does any of the cooking) and nervously turns a bulky gold ring that has his initials—S. C. J.—engraved on the face.

Once Suzanne asked, "Sal, what's the C for?" At first he said, "Cash," and then he turned around and said, "I mean, culture."

Then she whispered, "How's about coke?"

He took a quick breath through his nose with his nostrils open wide and said, "That's more like it."

Needless to say, that conversation made me a little uneasy, since I pride myself in staying away from stuff like that. Thankfully, the subject has not come up again.

❧

During the busiest part of the evening as the line gets long, Sal sends Jeeter to the reception area to deal with the customers who are hungry and drunk. Sal helps me clear away the plates and set the tables. We are always hurrying and he is always a half step behind me. When we enter the kitchen, barreling toward the bus bucket with our loaded trays, he puts his open hand an inch away from my hip and if I stop for a moment in the middle of our motion, he pats me there, where my back meets my side, and I know that I have got to keep on moving or else my shoulders will end up in his chest, the small of my back against the button of his pants, and he will be too close to me.

At the end of the night I'm sweating like crazy, so Jeeter puts a wet napkin that's been soaking in an ice bucket on the back of my neck and he pours a Budweiser into a Styrofoam cup, which he leaves on the counter and says, "For your ride home, DeVeaux. Careful driving."

"I'm underage," I say to Jeeter, handing the cup back to him.

"Oh, a Goody-Two-shoes, are we?" He hollers this in an effort to get the attention of the others, but they're too deep in their cups to pay him any mind.

"Just a law-abiding citizen," I say with a sanctimonious tone. *What do I care what they think? I'll be back in town by this time next year.*

Jeeter is singing the "Goody Two Shoes" song by Adam Ant. He's dancing in circles, sipping the beer that I handed back to him.

"Good night," I turn back to say to everyone else, but no one hears me. Suzanne and the other girls are making White Russians and flirting with Tanner Strickland, a local shrimper who usually drops by at the end of the night for some free food and drink.

Tanner brought Muddy Girl, a yellow Labrador who likes to roll around in the pluff mud at low tide. I watch Muddy Girl and Cocoa, who are having a standoff over by the dishwasher. They are leaving paw prints on the freshly mopped floor, but the glow on Jeeter's cheeks shows that he's too tipsy to care.

"Thanks for the help," Suzanne says to me, then, "Tell your cousin she better get over to see me as soon as she gets in. And she can bring that great-looking brother of yours, too."

As I leave I can see Sal in the back office with his hand on the knee of a short blonde woman from Powdersville whom he met in the restaurant last week. She giggles at him, then settles into a grin that she continues to hold as she takes a sip of her pink wine.

Tosha shakes her head in disgust and says, "Betta get on home now, gal, ya hear?" Then she lifts up her empty hands to indicate that she has no grits to give me.

I say, "Merry Christmas," and walk out the kitchen door, gagging at the stench of rotten food and liquor that emanates from the Dumpster.

Across the backyard I see Mr. Lumpkin, who owns the souvenir shop, which is also his house, behind the restaurant. He's pacing his front porch with a cigar in his hand, making sure that Sal's customers do not park on his property. He has a meticulous yard and garden that he accuses the restaurant customers of ruining every year. He keeps the hedges clipped around the no parking sign where his property begins, and he even has a rifle propped against the side of his porch to scare people off.

As he nods in my direction, approving my parking spot, I see Jeeter, who is running after me.

"New Year's Eve?" he says in a whiny voice. He's tilting to his left side with an unlit cigarette in his hand. "There's already 140 on the books."

"Why not?" I say, noticing a folded piece of notebook paper

underneath my windshield wiper. "It's not like I have anything else to do." *For now.*

After I leave the restaurant parking lot, I pull over to the side of the road, turn on the light, and read a note from Bethany, the youth minister from my church, who comes out to the island from time to time to see her aunt and uncle who run the bait-and-tackle store.

> The girls and I miss you at the breakfast, DeVeaux. See if you can get a ride to town on Wednesday night for youth group. I'll drive you back to the island if you need me to.
>
> You're in my prayers,
> *Bethany*
> (Deuteronomy 31:8)

3

Night Eyes

It's always pitch-black at night on this island. There are no street-lights or paved roads except for Highway 174, which leads to the beach. On the drive home, I keep an eye out for deer, 'cause I don't want to rankle Daddy with another dent in the truck before Christmas. Last week a doe darted across our dirt road at twilight and ran smack into the front of Mama's truck as she was coming home from First Place, bending the front grille and the hood at an inward angle before turning back and bolting off into the same woods she came from. Daddy took one look at the pickup and said, "We *can't* afford to get it fixed." Then he and I set out in the woods with flashlights and rifles to find the doe and put her out of her misery. We found a few bloodstains on the leaves and against one of the trees, but we never did find the doe. That night I dreamed that she stumbled into our yard and collapsed at our doorstep. And Daddy took one look at her, grabbed his rifle, and said, "Now that beats all."

As I press the gas over the mud holes, I can feel the soft dollar bills I just crammed into my pocket. I didn't count the money, but I have a feeling the waitresses tipped me out with a little holiday bonus. I look back and forth for those bright eyes as I pass my friend Tina's double-wide trailer home. The rooms are dark, but her porch is all lit up with blinking Christmas lights, and a plastic Santa Claus, a lighted bulb in his red belly, is tied to the side of the tin roof. A silver Corvette is parked in front of the house and it must belong to her mom's new boyfriend, some doctor from Walterboro who is teaching Tina how to drive a stick shift.

When I look back to the road, I pick up speed. Before I know it I am on the heels of this moving piece of darkness. I tilt the steering wheel in the opposite direction and when I pass, I begin to see the outline of a boy with skin the color of charcoal who is sprinting down the road. I look back in my rearview mirror and watch him leap over the ditch and into the pine trees, and before I know it he is gone. All I can see is the tracks of my truck in the soft dirt, tinted red by the rear lights. I wonder where that boy was going and why he was running so fast.

"Someone should tell folks around here to carry a flashlight," my older sister, Virginia, said one time when she almost ran down a black man who was hobbling on a cane in the middle of the road on a Saturday night. But now I'm thinking reflectors would do the trick. Just like the ones on the heels of my tennis shoes. Someone should give out reflectors to the boys and the deer and anything else that roams around here on this dark island where drunk men drive their trucks home at full speed.

Now I keep my eyes on the sides of the road again. If I can get home without hurting someone or something, I can do my part in keeping Daddy at peace this holiday. Maybe if I look up the verse Bethany wrote down, it will give me some direction.

This Thanksgiving just past was an awful event. Mama tried to make everything look like home. She set up the dining room table in the teahouse, polished all the silver and served oysters casino and a creek shrimp salad before the turkey. But Brother Will called the day before to say that he couldn't make it because his biology professor had invited him to present some kind of paper at a conference in New York, and his girlfriend's family invited him to spend the holiday at their house on Long Island. Then my mama's mama, Birdie, drank three Bloody Mary cocktails before noon and missed her seat as we were all sitting down for the main course. "My dear," said her date, Mr. R. T. Lancaster, a well-off widower from the upstate, "are you hurt?" When everyone was settled, my father gave a toast to our Mee Maw Rose, whom we lost to bone cancer last spring.

"To the late Elizabeth Rose DeLoach, the matriarch of our family," Daddy said. "Her absence leaves a void in all of our hearts."

Everyone was still for a moment and then Clayton Tankerslay, Virginia's kiss-bum boyfriend who is a labor lawyer in town, whispered, "What a woman."

At that moment I was remembering the Thanksgiving one year before when we were in the dining room of Mee Maw Rose's house on Water Street, drinking mint tea from her silver goblets. She was making the toasts, first to my father and the grandchildren and then to Maum Bess, who was leaning on the counter in the butler's pantry, measuring out the coffee to go along with the dessert. And, as always, she remembered her daughter, Eliza, and she would look back and forth between Cousin Eli and Daddy after she said Eliza's name.

So this Thanksgiving just past, I looked over at my father to say, "Shouldn't we remember Aunt Eliza?" but I didn't want to disturb him. He had this weird grin on his face that I hadn't seen in months. I think he was delighting in all the commotion his family made when they were gathered together.

Then, before I could say anything, my mother was raising her neck like a peacock and saying, "Won't you have a warm biscuit, Mr. Lancaster." And Virginia was telling my grandmother Birdie about the trip she took with her boss to the American Antique Show in New York. And Cousin Eli, who said she had run out of loan money in the middle of the semester and had been living off red beans and rice for a week now, was shoveling large pieces of gravy-soaked turkey down her throat and nodding to Clayton, who was telling her about the mallards he shot the morning before.

Just then a tap came from the window behind my daddy's head. It was Sagi, the little Shuzuki boy whose family just bought our plantation. He was pressing his face right up to the window, and when he saw all of us gathered around the table, he gave a large wave then turned quickly and ran toward the main house before we could respond.

My father turned around and looked at him and then back at my mother.

"I thought they were due in tomorrow?" she said.

Birdie cleared her throat.

"Son of a gun," Daddy muttered, "Thanksgiving Day and *they* show up." And then he said, "Excuse me, Birdie. Mr. Lancaster. Clayton." He nodded to my mama and said, "I'll be back."

But he didn't return until Mama was serving the pecan pie, and he came back only to say good-bye to our guests. Then he was off in the boat with Sagi and Mr. and Mrs. Shuzuki, who, though they had come a day early, still expected him to keep his appointment of carrying them over to Pine Island for a conch shell hunt.

When he returned home that evening, I went out to the dock to help him clean the boat. Four large, muddy conchs were laid out on the bow. Mrs. Shuzuki gets Daddy to clean and dry them, then she polishes them and uses them for bookends and door holders.

He nodded toward me as I stepped onto the boat, then he handed me a brush and said, "Thank you, honey." He hosed the surface off, and together we scrubbed all the mud and sand into the creek.

In the distance I could hear the Shuzukis' truck driving up and down the cornfields to inspect my father's work. Daddy just grunted. Then he crouched beneath the bow to get at some sand that was stuck in the rim. I spotted a line of mud on the back of his neck, and at that moment I felt so sad for him, and I wondered where things stood in his plan to get us out of here. I tried to create scenarios in my head that would speed things up: Maybe the shrimp farm he wanted to open next year with Brother Will would be a success and he could buy Rose Hill back from the Shuzukis.

Maybe Mama's brother could loan him some money. Maybe one of Mee Maw's paintings was worth more than we'd imagined, and we could sell it and move back downtown. But I knew in my heart that these scenarios were like fantasies, and that we might be here, like this, for a long time.

When he picked up the conch and began to scrape out its insides over the side of the boat he said, "So how was dinner?"

And I said, "No good without you."

With that, he turned off the hose, drew his lips into his mouth and said, "Let's go get some leftovers, sweetheart. I'll finish this tomorrow." I nodded, then stood up and watched him toss the conch he'd been cleaning into the creek. It drifted for a moment with the outgoing tide, then sank.

❧

Now, as I enter the gates of Rose Hill plantation, still looking out for deer, I pick up speed because I know every curve and mud hole by heart. A fog is rising off the cornfields and if I didn't know how absolutely boring this island is, I'd be afraid from all the gray and blackness.

I am thinking of Maum Bess, who says that the evil spirits start to come out of their hiding places and roam the land at this time of night. She paints the front door and the shutters of her house a neon blue to keep them out. She says you'll know 'em when you see 'em because their feet are turned backward and they never touch the ground.

When we moved into the caretaker's house, she asked Mama if she could come over and sprinkle some holy water and salt to cleanse the house from evil spirits.

"Yes, of course," Mama said. "We need all the protection we can get." So one afternoon when Daddy was out in the fields, she came over and prayed some prayers and made Mama and I follow her with a lit candle all around the outside of the house and through each room on the inside as she sprinkled water and salt and whispered in a language I could not understand.

"That's speaking in tongues," Sasser told me when I asked him about it on the telephone that night. "That's one of the ways the missionary prayed that day he healed me from the ringing in my ears. It's just a spiritual gift God gives to anyone who wants it."

It was true that Sasser had suffered from a ringing in his ears and migraine headaches for months after he took a mission trip with the youth group to Haiti. He'd been to the doctor dozens of times and even had an MRI, but no one could figure it out. Then one weekend his daddy invited an old friend from seminary, a missionary who was visiting family before heading back to China, to come over for supper. Sasser told the missionary about the ringing and before they sat down to eat, the man laid hands on Sasser's ears and prayed coherently, then spoke quietly in another language and during the prayer, the ringing stopped, and has not come back since.

"That man had the gift of healing," Sasser told me when he relayed this story one night in youth group. "It's another way to experience the kingdom of God in the here and now, DeVeaux. The disciples had it; it went hand in hand with the gospel they were sharing. Lots of people have had it since, and I pray to have it too. In fact, my heart burns to receive it."

So when I think of Sasser that is what I pray for him, "for his mama to come back home and for him to receive the gift of healing that his heart burns for."

❧

When I reach the caretaker's house, I park by the fish shed and stop for a moment to look at the lighted cedar tree that Mama and

I cut down ourselves over in the gall. She set it just in front of the windows on the back of our little house so that anyone passing by on their boat could see it from the creek. She learned how to decorate a tree from Dorothy Westbury, a famous Charleston designer who redecorated our house on Tradd Street when Daddy was making money developing strip malls in north Charleston. She wraps each branch from its edge to the spine of the tree so that every limb is outlined. This is the prettiest tree we've ever had because we inherited Mee Maw Rose's collection of Fabergé-replica egg ornaments, and Mama has spread them out on the ends of the branches where they can catch the light.

Walking toward the caretaker's house, I see my father beneath the fluorescent light in the kitchen. He is pouring himself a co-cola and spreading mayonnaise and peanut butter on slices of bananas. I stop for a moment and let the darkness surround me as I watch him. He is wearing his work shirt and his boxers and gray hunting socks with orange trim. He never could have dressed like this on Tradd Street, with all the neighbors and the carriages full of tourists looking into our windows. He balances his drink on his crowded plate, scratches his head, shuts off the television in the den, then turns and walks back toward his and Mama's bedroom.

When I enter the house, I take off my shoes and walk quietly down the hall. Daddy has left the door of their room open. Now the bedroom television is on and the blue light of the screen flashes on the walls of the hallway.

These floorboards are creaky enough to be heard over the eleven o'clock news report that booms toward me as I tiptoe to my bedroom. He presses the Mute button and calls my name: "DeVeaux."

I continue to creep, though I don't know why now that I have been found out, toward their room and peer inside.

He is tucked in beneath the afghan with the plate of bananas on his belly. His feet are positioned straight up like a mummy. Mama is snoozing beside him, still in her robe and slippers with a *Guideposts* magazine resting on her chest. Easy the cat is between them, curled up where the ends of their pillows meet and purring.

"How many did you have, honey?" he says as he pops a banana slice into his mouth.

"Around one hundred," I say, and at the sound of my voice my mother lets out a soft groan. "Hey, dahlin'," she says. Her black eyes close as quickly as they open.

Daddy rubs his tongue across his teeth.

"Make some money?" he asks.

"Think so," I say.

"Good girl; you make me proud," he says. "Done your chores?"

"Yes, sir," I say.

"Make sure and help Mama get everybody's rooms ready for tomorrow."

"Everybody doesn't have a room," I say, still wondering how we are going to fit six people into a two-bedroom house.

"I know," he says, then he notices Easy purring.

"How about throwing that cat out," he says. His eyes return to the television and he mashes the Mute button again, releasing the sounds of engines and sirens as the Live 5 news crew reports a fire in a mobile home on John's Island.

Mama twitches, then reaches out to me for a good-night kiss. I lean down and she pecks my forehead lightly, then she pets Easy and says, "My two surprises."

Before I fall asleep, I think about the way Daddy has started to call my jobs around the house "chores." Ever since we moved out of town he says, "Done your chores?" and he puts that old Charleston drawl on it so it wouldn't be mistaken for something a redneck would say.

When we lived in town he used to ask me if I had done all my homework, which he calls "lessons." He'd be standing in the doorway of my room on his way to bed, saying, "Done your lessons, love?" But he doesn't ask me about my lessons too much anymore. I think he is depressed about where I go to school. One month into this school year, they took me out of Cooper Hall, a fine private school for girls where I'd been going since kindergarten, and put me in this small, sort of run-down private school just over the island drawbridge. It's called Dawhoo Day, and there are only fifteen people in my grade. What makes him even more depressed is the fact that I was supposed to leave Cooper Hall last year and go off to St. Mary's School in Richmond and follow in the educational footsteps of my sister Virginia, my cousin Eli, my aunt Eliza, and Mee Maw Rose. But he couldn't send me. He could barely keep Will at MIT (and he has a scholarship that pays for half), and he dropped Eli's tuition at the University of South Carolina altogether, though I thought Mee Maw Rose had left specific instructions for Daddy to set part of the inheritance aside for her education. (I think Mee Maw had a hunch that he was headed for the poorhouse.)

When Mama questioned Daddy about Cousin Eli's tuition he said, "Her father, if he were still around, never would have been able to send her to college. I'd bet my life on that."

"But isn't there some way we could manage?"

"Of course not, Dee. You can't begin to comprehend the kind of debt we're in."

Mama said, "But your mother expected you to—"

Daddy cut her off. "My family money has been dwindling since the Civil War. There was no more money. You know that."

"I could sell the textile stock Daddy left me," Mama suggested.

"For Eli? A child who is not even our own? We raised her for fourteen years, Dee. It's not the end of the world for her to take out a few loans." Then he slammed his hand palm-down on the kitchen table, causing the salt shaker to wobble and roll on its side. He said, "You are going to sell that stock anyway. *I* need the money."

❧

The humid day in late August when Mama, Daddy, and I moved out to the plantation, I went and sat with Daddy on the dock. He carved circles in the planks with an oyster shell while we stared out at the black water as it poured into our creek from the ocean, and watched a gray heron in the marsh on the opposite bank, pecking at sand fiddlers for food. Then Daddy looked to the left mud bank and pointed to a low cage made of chicken wire that sat beneath an oak tree.

"See that?" he said.

"Yeah," I said.

"It's a cage for raising doves. When your mother and I were first married, I was trying to make a little money on the side by raising birds, so I ordered a shipment of baby doves from California."

"What happened?" I said.

"Well, your aunt Eliza came out here one afternoon. She must've been about nineteen and she was all wrapped up in those crazy Vietnam War protests, and was throwing the word *harmony* around a little too much for my taste. She'd learned that kind of fool talk up at Vassar where she met that ridiculous husband of hers. Anyway, she came out here during her spring break and when she spotted those doves she walked directly over to them, opened that cage, and set those creatures loose. All sixty of them."

I followed his lead and chuckled with him, though I wasn't sure what was funny.

He continued, "I happened to be out here that day, checking on them, and I came upon her: her skinny arms holding back the wire door, her bare feet gently knocking the cage, and as soon as one caught on, all of the others followed, and she lifted her arms up to the sky and said, 'Be free,' like she had just released the last prisoners of war."

He kept smiling and said, "I didn't have the heart to tell her that those darn birds had no idea how to survive in this swampy region. Most of them were probably nipped by snapping turtles or bobcats their first day out." He gently pushed the oyster shell off the dock and as it fell quietly into the creek he added, "I sure never laid eyes on one of 'em."

Then his throat kind of croaked and he put his hand, which had somehow gotten muddy though he didn't realize it, on my back, leaving a print that spread across my shoulders and did not come out in the wash.

"This is what they call hard times, DeVeaux," he said.

"Yes, sir," I said, thinking what I've always thought since I was old enough to understand that my cousin lived with us because her parents were dead. That is, it is possible to lose everything.

❧

Later that evening, as Mama was hanging the childhood portraits of Virginia and Will on the wall where there was a black spot from a gutter leak, she said, "We can't keep you in school," and the next day she drove me downtown to Cooper Hall, where we cleaned out my locker and turned in my tennis jersey. Then we went to a stockbroker's office where I sat in a waiting room drinking coffee with powdered creamer, while in the next room Mama was selling all the textile company stock that her daddy left her when he died. On the drive out of Charleston she started to weep, so I let her listen to her favorite Christian program, James Dobson's *Focus on the Family*.

"I hate this for you," she said. "As soon as we are able, we'll send you back to a good school."

"It's okay," I said, and I meant it. "I'm tired of Cooper Hall, Mama, and I sure wasn't looking forward to going to St. Mary's. When Cousin Eli went she started smoking and wearing Grateful Dead T-shirts, and before that Virginia went up there and got it in her head that she had to have a double-strand pearl necklace and a nose job, both of which she got by graduation, and she still isn't happy. If you ask me, all-girls schools, particularly boarding schools, bring out the weird in people. Maybe when we move back to town, I can go to a good public school."

Then she said, "DeVeaux, life with your father has *not* turned out the way I expected."

I wasn't quite sure what she was getting at, and I really didn't want to know. All I knew was that at that moment, I didn't feel empty like I thought I might. A new school, especially a run-down school, could have its advantages. For one thing, it could be easier. Maybe I'd read some of the books on the reading list, since I overheard Ms. Meyers, the vice principal at Cooper Hall, tell her secretary that Dawhoo Day is years behind. Or better yet, my chances must have increased for the spot of the smartest and/or the best-looking in the class. I'd never made a poor showing in either category at Cooper Hall or Mrs. Hillhouse's cotillion school, but Charleston is a town of beautiful people and my guess is that the competition at Dawhoo Day would be less fierce.

By the time we reached the island drawbridge, Mama seemed to settle down. She lifted the visor and let the afternoon sun heat her face, leaning forward to turn up the volume of the familiar voice that soothed her with its careful instruction.

And I just stared across the marsh for miles. It was at once brown and green as the sun beat down and the water rose.

❧

Now I can hear Easy crying outside my window. She's walking along the railing on the front porch (the front door opens into my bedroom, which is technically the foyer), her golden eyes trying to catch mine in the darkness. Mama and I found Easy the day after Hurricane Hugo hit the low country. We had driven from Charleston out to the island to see what kind of damage the storm had done to the plantation house. The day before the storm Mee Maw Rose asked Chambers to haul all of the valuables to the upstairs, and it was a good thing because when we arrived there was pluff mud and creek water as high as my waist in the downstairs of the old home. There were even shrimp jumping along the windowsills.

Mama was the first to enter the house. She trudged through the living room to the stairwell and climbed up to the second floor to see if the antiques and the paintings had survived. And there, on the bed where Edmund Rose used to sleep, was Easy, curled up in a little ball on the hand-embroidered bedcover. There wasn't a smudge of dirt or sand in the entire room.

So, Easy is an unplanned member of the family like Cousin Eli and me. "A surprise," my mama says about me, because I was conceived on a trip to Venice that she and Daddy took for their fifteenth wedding anniversary after they thought they were through having children. "A faux pas," I once overheard my father whisper to two couples who were seated in our dining room on Tradd Street for one of his socials.

I told Bethany about the "faux pas" during one of the Bible study breakfasts when no one else showed up. She stopped in mid-bite of her ham biscuit, pulled out a sticky note and her Bible, and wrote down these verses:

My frame was not hidden from you
when I was made in the secret place.
When I was woven together in the
depths of the earth,
your eyes saw my unformed body.
All the days ordained for me
were written in your book
before one of them came to be.
(PSALM 139:15–16)

Then she said, "DeVeaux, if all of our days are recorded by God, how could we be mistakes?"

"I don't know," I said, relieved to hear those words.

Bethany looked me straight in the eyes and said, "You are no faux pas. You are here because your Creator wanted you here, and He has an eternal purpose for your life."

It shocked me to consider that before I was born God had recorded the days of my life. It warmed my heart, so much so that I grabbed the piece of paper from her and put it in my billfold so I would not forget it. It surprised me from time to time when I searched for change to buy a co-cola from the vending machine at school or a carton of eggs for Mama at the grocery store.

When we moved into the caretaker's house, I took the verse out of my billfold and put it in the bottom corner of the mirror in my bedroom, and I read it sometimes when I'm having a bad day, and it lifts me out of the fog I'm so often in. As I fall into bed, I wonder if there is even a purpose in this downer of a chapter in which my family finds itself right now. When I talk to God I say, "I do believe that I'm not a mistake, so will You show me what You want me to do with this life I'm in?"

Then I reach for my student Bible that Mama bought me after confirmation and look up the verse that Bethany wrote on her note to me this evening: *"The Lord himself goes before you and will be with you; he will never leave you nor forsake you. Do not be afraid; do not be discouraged"* (Deuteronomy 31:8).

I wonder if it is really true—if God is going before me, making my paths straight. I have a hunch that this is true, but it's so hard to let go into it. Before I ponder it fully, my spiritual amnesia sets in, and I work hard to fight it and the desire for sleep.

As I shut my eyes I picture the back of God, with a great machete in some sort of tropical forest, cutting a path before me to walk safely through. When we were confirmed Father Dan told us that ever since our baptism as babies, the Holy Spirit has been fermenting in us like grapes turning into a fine wine, and once the bishop lays hands on us, the bottle is uncorked and the divine wine will be poured out of us as we claim Christ as our Savior and minister in His name.

So maybe the path that the Lord is going before is in my heart. He wants my heart and the wine that's been in the making since I was eight weeks old. And though the thick and gnarly vines of this world are wound tight around it, He is cutting through them, and I wonder how long it will take for Him to get to me.

❧

In the middle of a dream Easy wakes me by clawing the screen outside my window. I open the window and let her in, and she settles herself in a ball above my hip, her lighted eyes hidden beneath her soft, gray lids.

In my dream I was with Cousin Eli on a mud bank at low tide. We were seining on a narrow creek like we have many times before, with Daddy and Will running the nets. As usual, it was our responsibility to drag the coolers along the banks and when it was time for Daddy and Will to pull the net up, we were supposed to grab the blue crabs and the shrimp that were flapping and scurrying across the mud and throw them into two separate coolers and ice them down. In the dream Cousin Eli, with a look of wonder, reached into the cooler of live blue crabs and allowed herself to be pinched. (She had actually done that one time in real life during blue crab season, but when she saw her blood she cried and Daddy popped her on the leg, and she didn't do it again.) In the dream, she didn't say a word when the crabs pinched her. She just took a hunk of ice and held it over her wound as we continued to drag the cooler beside the men. And she didn't do it just once. She did it four or five times, each time jumping back ever so slightly but also satisfied, as if she were about to reach some sort of peace pact with the creatures. In the dream, as usual, I was scared of the crabs. I had imagined their sharp pinch and was not about to test their claws that I knew would be my fresh dinner, dipped in melted butter, in a few short hours. I could not understand why in the world Cousin Eli kept going back to their painful clutch, but she did it again and again without saying a word, until Daddy noticed the stream of red running down her fingers and yelled at her to stop.

❧

Last month as Daddy and I were on the front porch of the main house, cleaning the windows, I asked him what exactly happened to my aunt Eliza, who died in a boating accident in a creek off the river. Mee Maw told me that she drowned, and I wanted to know how it happened. And what happened to her husband who died there too.

Daddy crumpled up the newspaper he was using to wipe the windows, turned to me and said, "They drowned. It was an accident. That's all there is to know." Then he started to wipe the glass again, slightly turning his back to me.

4

Good Neighbors and Bad Manners

The next morning as I'm brushing my teeth, I hear my friend Tina calling me from the porch like she's in a hurry. I walk out and see that she's got the Corvette parked right beside the house. The motor is running.

Her five-year-old sister, Baby Faye, is on her knees, squealing at a little brown box that has newspapers spread out on all sides of it. Baby Faye is dressed in a black leotard and thick ballerina stockings the color of children's aspirin, which are on backward, the seams snaking their way up the fronts of her plump little legs. Her hair is in two thick, frizzy braids with green and red bobbles at the top and the bottom. Once Suzanne told me that she thinks Baby Faye has black blood in her because of the thickness of her hair and the richness of her skin. It's the color of café au lait.

Tina's skin, on the other hand, is so pale it's translucent; blue diamond-shaped veins line her knobby knees. She's got her stringy yellow hair pulled tight, twisted up in a ponytail on the right side of her head. She's wearing a Walterboro High School wrestling team T-shirt that belongs to her half brother. When she sees me, she cocks her bony hip to one side and flips her ponytail back. "You know about this?" she asks.

I shake my head no, then kneel down and look inside to find a six-week-old puppy with curly red hair licking his backside.

I say, "It's a Boykin spaniel. This is the best kind of dog."

"Hunting dog for your brother," Tina says. "Surprise from your daddy."

"How do you know?" I say.

"Chambers said he bought her for Will, but he'll send it to a trainer in a few weeks and she'll be ready to retrieve by the time Will graduates in May."

My brother, Will, is some kind of a whiz when it comes to biology and water life, and Daddy wants him to open a shrimp farm down here when he graduates so they can go into business together and make some money to get us out of this mess. They've talked about a plan to take part of the Rose Hill land and irrigate it, and lately Daddy has been scribbling figures on a little yellow notepad about how to get the financing. This puppy must be Dad's idea of sweetening the pot for Will, a lure of his own.

Just then, Chambers walks onto the porch with a basket full of magnolia limbs.

"How 'bout dis here dog?" he says to me.

I pick it up with both hands and hold it against my chest, and it sucks my hair with its bare gums.

"You'll get plenty uh time wid it, Miss D.," he says, "but now I's got tuh take it up to de teahouse so your brother don't catch a glimpse uh it."

I hand it to Chambers, who picks up the box and carries it to the teahouse.

Baby Faye holds her mermaid dolls up for me to see. One is a blonde and the other is a brunette, and they both have silver seashells over their breasts and hot pink fish tails. Tina says, "Let's go for a spin before your daddy gets home."

"Where's Mama?" I say.

"She's over in the gall cutting some limbs off the magnolias. Then she's going to fix up the big house for those Chinese people," Tina says.

"Japanese," I say.

"What's the difference?" Tina says.

"I'm sure there's a lot of difference, but I don't know enough to tell you," I say, shrugging my shoulders. "Did Mama see you?"

"No, Chambers told me."

Tina, Baby Faye, and I drive down to the beach with the sunroof open. We park at the pier and walk out to the end where the gray waves smash against the pilings. The sky is like one big cloud and there's not a soul in sight. Tina cups her hands over Baby Faye's ears and tells me that she made out with her mother's boyfriend's son last night.

"Let go," says Baby Faye, who is holding both of her mermaids in one hand. "No secrets, Tina," then she hits Tina in the hip bone with the heads of her dolls.

Tina licks her thumb and wipes a red mark off Baby Faye's cheek, then she pulls a half-empty roll of Ritz crackers out of her pocketbook and says, "Want to feed the gulls?"

Baby Faye grabs the bag from Tina and says, "Yeah. Yeah. Yeah." Then she takes a cracker, crushes it in her hand, and throws it up into the air. The crumbs hit the tops of Baby Faye's tennis shoes then fall through the wide cracks between the planks of the pier. Tina and I get her started by throwing a big piece to a gull who lands on the railing by the fish-cleaning counter. Once he starts cawing, two other gulls join him and in no time there is a group of eight hovering over Baby Faye, whose fingers are working furiously to crush the crackers and throw them up into the gulls' mouths.

Tina and I take a few steps back and sit on a bench at the other side of the pier.

"What happened?" I ask, partly curious and partly gearing up to tell Tina about the speaker who talked to the girls in youth group about abstinence after she had contracted AIDS from a former boyfriend during high school. (*Maybe this is why God has brought me out to this crazy island*, I think to myself, *to minister to Tina.*

Maybe if I get this right then He'll find a way for my family to go back to Charleston. Could this be the mission I've been sent on? And, better yet, the beginning of the story's end?)

"I don't know," she said. "Last night after we had finished watching *Fantasy Island* with Mama and Larry, Mama got him all fixed up to sleep on the couch. His name is Shane and he's nineteen; can you believe it?"

"You're kidding me," I say, thinking that Tina's family does the strangest things, but before I think of what to say next, she jumps in—

"After all the lights were out, and I was falling asleep, I heard this little tap on the door. The next thing I know he has one knee on the bed and he says, 'Tina?' and I say, 'Yeah?' and he says, 'Want to watch some TV with me?'"

As I try to picture the scene, I stare down the quiet beach and spot a middle-aged man in a wet suit barreling toward the ocean with a pink surfboard under his arm. From the surf to the horizon, the ocean is full of whitecaps, ideal conditions for catching a wave.

"Then what?" I say to Tina, who squeezes my wrist and begins to speak, but when she checks on Baby Faye, she sees that she is down to her last cracker and she pulls open her purse for some more but there aren't any.

"Dang it," she says as Baby Faye throws the crumbs from the last crackers up in the air, "I've got to talk fast."

"Hurry," I say, suddenly caught up in the moment and allowing my curiosity to overtake my attempt at ministry. "So what happened?"

"Well, the next thing I know we're lying down on the couch watching some hunting show and I say, 'Could you not sleep?' and he says, 'Yeah, I'm having trouble 'cause I know a pretty girl is only one wall over from me.' Can you believe he said that?"

"No!" I say, completely sucked into the romance of the story now.

What I like about Tina is that she is full of stories that are beyond my imagination. I think it's because she goes to public school where they show those videos titled *Safe Sex: How to Install a Condom* and *Highways or Dieways: The Consequences of Driving Under the Influence*, where a man gets a beer bottle through the back of his neck when he wrecks into a telephone pole while taking a swig. She's constantly showing me parts of the world I never knew existed, some good and some bad. I may not have had this kind of conversation until college if I'd stayed downtown.

"Go on," I say as Baby Faye picks up her mermaids and walks toward us, the gulls following closely behind her, flapping their wings inches above her head.

Tina hurries, "So all of a sudden we're kissing and he's some kind of a kisser, just like Mama says Larry is. His arms started to tangle with mine, but then I hear Mama get up and go to the bathroom and I say, 'I better go back,' and he quickly gets up and goes to the kitchen for a glass of water, and I head back to my room. Just as I'm falling asleep he taps on the door and says, 'Sweet dreams,' and I'll tell you, DeVeaux, I felt so good that I swear I grinned my whole night's sleep."

I chuckle and picture Tina's mobile home the way it looked last night when I drove past it, dark windows with that plastic Santa Claus tied to the television antenna, glowing from the inside out. I remember once when I was a little girl, coming downstairs in the middle of the night for a glass of water, and catching Virginia and one of her high school boyfriends making out on the living room sofa.

My mind starts to race with questions for Bethany. I know that kissing is okay and fornication isn't, but what about all the gray area in between? How am I going to minister to Tina if I don't know where she should draw the boundary lines? I'm interrupted from compiling my mental list of questions when Baby Faye pounds her fist on Tina's knee and says, "More crackers, Tina. Them gulls is hungry."

⅌

After the pier, we stop at the Exxon station so Tina can pick up a *Cosmopolitan* magazine for her mama and a bag of Skittles for our ride home. Baby Faye insists on feeding the green Skittles to her mermaids. She crams the discs into their fixed smiles and pretends not to notice as they fall to the floorboard.

On the way home Tina makes me read her horoscope while she wonders out loud what Shane's horoscope might be, and I feel guilty because when I was in grade school Maum Bess made me swear I wouldn't read horoscopes. She told me they are the work of what she calls the "hooch," which is this evil spirit she says breathes down your neck when he wants you. I asked my mama about this after she became religious a few years later and she said, "I agree. You can't let the devil get a foothold."

Now, I could count the times I've been to church and youth group on one hand since we moved out to the country, and I have a few hard questions for God about how things have been going for me lately. But I still have this dark image of Maum Bess's hooch, his hot breath burning my neck, and it frightens me to this day.

Then Tina says, "So can I come over sometime and stare at your brother?"

"Sure," I say because I'm used to having friends gawk at Will, and it's nice to have someone state their intentions up front. Tina lets her ponytail down and strings of her hair get picked up in the wind from the sunroof. I look in the backseat and see that Baby Faye is copying Tina by letting her hair down, only it stays tight on her head, braids in place. Baby Faye holds both the mermaids out the sunroof, and after a few seconds, she pulls them back in and examines their faces to see if the wind has blown their pink smiles off.

Tina slaps my thigh and says, "I know someone who thinks you're something."

"Who?" I say, laughing because she has a funny way of putting things.

"C. C.," she says, "my half brother."

Besides Baby Faye, Tina has two half brothers and they are both older. Her mother has been married three times and she had Baby Faye out of wedlock, but my mama has no idea about any of this or she wouldn't dare let me hang out with her.

C. C. works down at the marina filling boats with gasoline. Occasionally he works in the kitchen at Sal's restaurant washing dishes. He's real quiet and he goes out back to smoke cigarettes when it's slow. I guess he's sort of good-looking in a dirty, unshowered sort of way, but he's not *my* type.

"Well?" she says.

"Well, you know I have a boyfriend," I say.

Thing is, I've been dating John Henry Drayton off and on since the eighth grade. I met him at a summer tennis clinic at the Country Club of Charleston when I was still living downtown. He's a tenth grader at Christ Church School for boys and his family lives on Limehouse Street. One time he brought me pale pink rosebuds from his mama's garden. He wrapped the stems in a damp paper towel and a layer of tinfoil. Also, he was my dance partner the last semester of cotillion lessons at Mrs. Hillhouse's school. Together we practiced the waltz, and we demonstrated the proper way for a gentleman and a lady to handle the complicated business of getting in and out of a car. Whenever we were sitting down together in a room and I stood up, he would stand, too, his eyes following me across the room.

"Yeah, but he's all the way in town," she says.

"So what?" I say.

"So when do you ever even *see* him?" she says.

"Once a month or so," I say, "when I go to a dance or when the Christ Church youth group joins up with the St. Paul's group for a lock-in or something like that."

"DeVeaux, I think you need yourself a little island romance. Something where you *live*," she says.

I'm not living here for long, I say to myself.

"I'll think on it," I say to simmer her down, but I know I would never touch that greasy C.C. Just thinking about him makes me sick, especially when I picture John Henry Drayton serving me a ball in his white tennis shorts from the other end of the court.

❧

When I get home my older sister Virginia's BMW is in the driveway. She is in the kitchen with Mama, unwrapping all the Christmas presents from our friends and neighbors downtown. Virginia still lives downtown in a house on Wentworth Street with some of her sorority sisters from Vanderbilt. And she works four days a week at an antique shop on King Street so all of our friends send things to us by her.

When I walk in the door we all say Merry Christmas, then Mama wants to know where I've been.

"With Tina," I say, realizing I still have the *Cosmo* in my hand.

"You mean that little redneck girl that lives in a mobile home?" says Virginia.

I hate how Virginia just prances in here and calls my only halfway interesting new friend a redneck.

"Virginia, you try and live on this island by yourself, okay? I have to have some friends, and I like Tina. She's a colorful character."

"In what way?" Mama says, as if she's uncovered some sort of non-Christ-centered behavior.

"Her life is so different from ours," I say, then I put the magazine facedown on the counter and open a tin of cheese biscuits with a sticker on top that reads "Season's Greetings to the DeLoach family from the Jenkins family. We miss you!"

"What about that little Davidson girl?" Virginia says as she waves away the cheese biscuits, pats her backside and mutters, "Clayton says I need to lose weight if I want to fit into that Costa dress for the deb ball."

"Oh yes," Mama says, "Mary Margaret."

Mary Margaret Davidson is a sneezy girl who used to be in my class at Cooper Hall. Her father, the plastic surgeon who gave Virginia her nose job, moved their family out to this island after he had a nervous breakdown when he had to operate on a five-year-old boy who was hit by a UPS truck, his little nose and lips smeared across his face by the brown grille.

The Davidsons live in a two-story modern house with a spiral staircase at the edge of Blue House Creek, a deep-water inlet just below Rose Hill Creek, where Dr. Davidson sits on the porch most days reading mystery novels. They have a tennis court and Mary Margaret is always inviting me over to hit the ball with her. When her mother picks me up in their dazzling emerald-green Suburban, I am always amazed at how there never seems to be any mud or dirt in their car.

But I have to say, I'm different from Mary Margaret. I don't have nerdy friends, and I'm a decent tennis player. It is wrong to think this way, I know, but it's so natural that I can't stop it.

So I tell Virginia and Mama, "She was not my friend in Charleston, so why should she be my friend here?"

But Virginia has spotted the Fabergé eggs on the Christmas tree and has lost interest.

Mama has lost interest, too, and says, "Clayton says you've gained weight, Virginia?"

Virginia's shape is similar to Mama's, but she fluctuates from week to week. She does the best with what she has, a face shaped like an upside-down egg and highlighted hair the color of the sand dunes, which is so thin that she has to spray it every few hours to keep her bob in place. I have to admit, she usually dresses like a million bucks, fancy scarves and silk blouses and Italian shoes. But on a rare occasion she slips back into that frumpy, preppy look from high school and she'll wear something like a navy blue headband and an Eagle Eye sweater with whales stitched across the collar. When she realizes what she's done, she runs and sells the outfit to the Junior League's secondhand store.

"This tree is magnificent, Mama," Virginia says, and she walks over to it and begins to count the eggs.

"Do you think so, honey?"

Virginia has an eye for decorating and her opinion means a lot to my mama.

"Too bad there's *no one* to see it," Virginia says. "Now how many eggs do we have?"

"Eleven, I think," Mama says.

"That means we'll each get two when you and Daddy are gone, right?"

"What a gruesome thing to say, Virginia!" She is already irritating the heck out of me.

"They are collector's items, Little Miss Mobile Home."

Then Mama interjects, "Virginia, don't let your father know what the ornaments are worth or he's liable to sell them, too, and by the way, we were planning to give you yours when you start a home of your own."

"Perfect," she says.

"Yeah, Thunder Thighs," I say, chomping on the cheese biscuits, "don't get too greedy."

"When are you going to Augusta?" Mama asks, then she turns

to me to say, "Clayton has invited Virginia to Augusta to meet his family."

I raise my eyebrows in a "whoop-de-do" way and continue to chomp. Virginia is proud of her boyfriend, Clayton Tankerslay, and I think she even loves him too. She met him at Vanderbilt. He was in law school, and she was an undergrad studying art history. He's from Augusta, Georgia, and his father owns a car dealership called Tankerslay Chevrolet.

Thankfully, he's related to the Tate family of Charleston. This has helped him get a job at a successful firm in town as well as a membership at the Carolina Yacht Club. He must have serious intentions for Virginia because he works hard to make everyone in this family like him. Like John Henry, he jumps up each time Mama or I stand (though he exaggerates the gesture so we are sure to notice), and he's always cleaning Daddy's rods with WD-40 after they go fishing.

"Tomorrow afternoon, Mama," Virginia says. "We've been invited to Christmas dinner at his great-aunt Vee Vee's house."

"Well, you better not disappoint your father by leaving here too soon," Mama says, then she turns the magazine right side up, puts her hand on her chest and stares me down. "Are you reading this trash, young lady?"

Just then there is a tap on the kitchen window. Brother Will is standing there with a duffel bag thrown over his shoulder. I always forget how handsome he is until I see him. He has these dark, fuzzy eyebrows that match his hair and long, black eyelashes. His teeth are straight and white and he smiles a lot.

As Mama and Virginia go out to the porch to greet him, I see my father a few yards behind them. He must have let the puppy out without realizing Will was home, and now he is running to catch up with the little ball of fur before Will turns back to see it.

"Will," I scream from the inside of the kitchen window in an attempt to avert his attention. He looks back at me and places his palms up as if to say, "What?"

My mouth is full of cheese biscuit crumbs and all I can think to do is stick my orange tongue out at him.

"Look," Will says, pointing his finger at me from the other side of the window, "it's only been four months since DeVeaux left town, and she has already lost her manners!"

Mama shakes her head while I look beyond them and watch Daddy scoop up the puppy and stash it in the inside pocket of his camouflage jacket. He makes it into the teahouse before anyone notices him.

Then I open the cabinet beneath the sink and throw the *Cosmo* into the trash.

5

Greater Gifts

By five o'clock everyone except for Cousin Eli is gathered around the tree eating crab dip and mint-covered pecans. Will has built a fire, and Daddy has found *It's a Wonderful Life* on television. He has turned the volume up loud enough for me to hear it when I go back to the other end of the house to use the bathroom. I get annoyed because during the commercials he flips the channel and then forgets to turn back to the movie.

Then he mashes the Mute button and the interrogation begins:

"How are things at the shop, sweetheart?" he asks Virginia.

She straightens up in her seat on the couch. "The gallery, Daddy. Things at the gallery are going well. We just received the Lachicotte estate, and I'm helping Weston with the auction."

"So are you full-time now?" he asks.

"Well, not exactly," she says. "Weston promises by March."

"March? Good grief, honey, you've been there for a year now."

Virginia taps her navy blue flats on the hardwood floor and says, "Did I mention that I've been accepted into the Junior League?"

Mama says from the kitchen, "Congratulations!"

Daddy repositions himself in his chair and says, "That's wonderful, honey. You're following in the footsteps of Mee Maw Rose, Aunt Eliza, and your mother, who served the community through the League for years."

With this bit of good news he turns to Will, who jumps up quickly and says, "Who would like a drink?"

After Will takes orders, he goes over to the kitchen table where Mama has made up a wet bar with a bottle of scotch, bourbon, and red wine and little bottles of soda water. She has set out the crystal cocktail glasses and these little green paper napkins with gold rims that are left over from our neighborhood Christmas Day party last year. I can't believe she actually packed those napkins and moved them out here, but that's Mama for you. She's pretty resourceful for someone who grew up with a driver and a lot of money.

Daddy has a grin on his face like a party is about to start. Since Will is occupied, he goes back to Virginia.

"So what else is going on with my firstborn?" he asks.

She dips a cracker into the crab dip and says, "Well, Clayton has invited me to Augusta to meet his relatives."

"How 'bout that?" he says, turning to Mama, who is smiling at the cutting board on the kitchen counter as she chops celery.

"This isn't getting serious is it, honey?"

"Well," Virginia says, examining the back of her left hand, "it has been a year."

"Going in for the kill, eh?" Will says as he scoops ice out of the freezer.

"Hush," Mama says to Will.

"So you'll head to Augusta on the twenty-sixth?" Daddy says.

Virginia lifts a cracker from the tray, considers the dip, then puts the cracker back on the tray. "No, Daddy, actually we have to leave tomorrow morning. We've been invited to Christmas dinner at his great-aunt Vee Vee's house."

"Christmas morning!" says Daddy. He shakes his head and takes a big slurp of the bourbon and water that Will has placed on the table beside his chair. "You're gonna leave us in less than twenty-four hours? But we've got the whole family together for the first time in six months. Since Mee Maw died."

"I know, Daddy, but this is a big deal. You know?"

"I just can't believe you are leaving us that soon." He calls to Mama, "Can you believe this, Dee?"

"I told her you were going to be disappointed," Mama says.

Will winks at me as he sits down on the couch next to Virginia. He takes a swat at her hair, which is stuck together with a thick layer of hair spray. "Clayton gets really turned on by this helmet, I take it?" Will says.

She has to laugh and tells him to shut up. "So what about Will's sweetheart?" she says, deliberately changing the subject. "We're going on our fourth year here, right?"

Daddy clears his throat. He doesn't understand why Will has dated the same girl all through college. Her name is Ruth Rosenberg and she's from Long Island, which is where the Buttafucos are from. Like me, Daddy associates Long Island with the Buttafucos, and because of this Will says that we are closed-minded.

Will and Ruth met when they were paired up for an ichthyology research project in Alaska during their freshman-year spring break. One time I overheard Will tell Eli that their first kiss was by the "the glory hole," which is this pool in Alaska where the salmon gather to mate and die after swimming upstream.

Will brought Ruth down to Charleston last summer, when our houses still belonged to us. For one whole week I shared my room with her on Tradd Street, and she would wake me up each morning clamoring around the bed collecting fragile objects like a portable microscope, waterproof magnifying lenses, and an underwater camera, which she stuffed into a padded case that she carried loosely under her arm. She could have been an attractive girl— she was tall and slender and she had large breasts the shape of Nerf footballs, but Mama and I were shocked to see that she didn't shave her underarms or her legs (she wore a tank top and shorts every day), and she didn't wear a drop of makeup, not even a light shade of lipstick (not that I'm all into makeup, but a little touching up never hurt anybody).

Each day she and Will went to the clam farm where he has

worked since he was twelve. There she would sift her fingers through the pluff mud and bind bits of shells and dirt up into little Ziploc bags as he dislodged the clams one by one from the decaying ground.

"How is that young woman?" Daddy asks.

"Ruth," Will says, "is fine. She's just been offered a spot on a National Science Foundation research team that will fish a black hole at the mouth of the Rio Negro, which is connected to the Amazon River."

Mama says, "Now that's somethin'."

"She's *brilliant*," Will says. "I think she's going to take it. There's an estimated three hundred new species down there. It's the ultimate abyss."

"And how's Ruth's family?" Mama asks.

Daddy is tired of discussing Ruth so he mashes the Mute button, and suddenly we are bombarded with the angel's voice in *It's a Wonderful Life* trying to talk James Stewart out of jumping from the bridge.

I hear Virginia say, "And how's Ruth's mustache?" and Will has to laugh and slaps her hair-sprayed head again. "Softer than a helmet," he says.

Daddy looks back to the kitchen where Mama is basting the tenderloin, and he notices Easy, who has jumped up on the counter and is sniffing her way over to the meat. He presses the Mute button and says, "Look out for the cat!" Daddy dislikes Easy and never calls her by her name.

Mama picks Easy up and puts her down on the floor, but in seconds she leaps back onto the counter. Mama doesn't seem to notice. And I know she doesn't care. I've seen her let that cat take a flounder tail right off her plate when Daddy wasn't around. Daddy looks back to the kitchen again. "Dee," he says to Mama, "put the darn cat out before she ruins the meal!"

I jump up before he goes ballistic and say in a fake-nice voice, "I'll get her," then I go over to the kitchen, scoop Easy off the counter and walk out to the porch, closing the sliding glass door behind me. I sit down on the picnic table, look out past the muddy banks of the creek and the marsh to the pines of Otter Island. The sky is beginning to turn pink and I can hear the floating dock brushing against the anchor pole. The tide is low but it is starting to rise. I listen for the thrashing sound of the porpoises as they trap the fish against the muddy walls, but I don't hear them. They must have chosen a different creek to feed in today.

For the first time since our move, I am down. I am thinking about our house on Tradd Street and John Henry, Bethany, and Sasser. And how my best girlfriends, Louisa Townsend and Lesesne Murray, used to swing by and pick me up on their way to the midnight Christmas Eve service at St. Paul's. Ever since the spring of the eighth grade, when the bishop confirmed us, our parents allowed us to leave our family pews and sit together in the balcony with the rest of the youth group. Last Christmas Eve we sat behind Will and his friends Jack McCall and Preston King, who are about the two best-looking boys I know, and we kept leaning into them and sneaking long looks at their freshly shaved chins and broad shoulders while we whispered to one another about Lenora, the temperamental organist, who had just chewed out the ladies of the flower guild because the greenery around the choir section was making her allergies act up. She had refused to play until Father Dan had a sit-down talk with her. Even after that, she reluctantly made her way up to the organ seat just before the service began, and she cleared her throat, dramatically, during much of the sermon.

We watched the way the boys shook hands with their neighbors during the peace, and we couldn't help but relish the sound of their voices as they belted out the carols like it was some kind of a joke. During the confession of sin we heard Preston tell Will, "Say your prayers about our hunt, boy."

"Three bucks for Christmas, good Lord," Jack said, looking up at the ceiling.

The words they uttered and the gestures they made were like some kind of a promise to us, and we nudged and popped one another's stockings, as if to say one of our Christmas gifts was our present proximity to these three young men.

And then the ushers handed out the candles as they turned down the lights for "Silent Night," and I looked down at the congregation below. I saw the Rose family pew where the tops of their heads— Mama, Daddy, and Mee Maw Rose—were fading into the darkness.

Then I looked to the outline of Sasser, in his acolyte robe next to his father, reverently singing his praises to God, and I was in awe of his earnest worship, how he could put aside his earthly thoughts and focus on what this service meant—celebrating the birth of the world's Savior. And I knew that he would be back at church in less than six hours to serve at the sunrise service. He's always the one who gets stuck with it, but even so, he'd be singing the same songs and praying the same fervent prayers to the Lord: for his family, for the church, and for the gift of healing so that he could experience again that power he felt when the missionary prayed for him. As I made out Sasser's profile in the darkness, I promised myself and God that I would start coming to youth group regularly and meet with Bethany for breakfast like she'd asked me to several times that autumn, because I wanted what Sasser had. I wanted what I think is the greatest gift—that is, the gift of faith—and I still do.

❦

This year we decided to go to the midnight service at Edisto Episcopal, here on the island. Mama said, "Bloom where you are planted," and Daddy said, "No need to drive all the way into town when everyone has just arrived," but I know he doesn't want to go downtown so soon after declaring bankruptcy and all.

So Daddy planned a high-calorie, high-fat menu that Mama scoffed at, then he sent her off to the Piggly Wiggly where she loaded her cart with bottles of red wine and a beef tenderloin and packets of béarnaise sauce.

᳔

Now I look in the glass door, wondering if anyone else feels as down as I do. Daddy is sitting in the stuffed blue chair that faces the television. He has a tin of Christmas mix in his lap, and he's scooping handfuls into his mouth. Virginia, who is once again examining the Fabergé eggs on the tree, lifts her head toward Will and says, "How about another drink?"

Mama says, "Not too much. Church at eleven."

Through the darkness, I see a shadow moving toward our house. It is the slender frame of my cousin Eli, with two skirts draped over her arm and a shopping bag hanging from her wrist. She is dressed in white striped overalls like a conductor, and her thick brown hair is in a single braid, resting on her shoulder. She is humming as she looks out at the creek, unaware of my presence. I watch as she walks steadily toward me—my parentless cousin who occupied the small bedroom next to mine on Tradd Street, who had moved in there before I was even born to be raised by my parents.

I think of how as a child, I used to wonder what would happen to us all if something happened to *my* parents. On nights when they went out to their cocktail parties, I'd frighten myself by imagining their deaths on the streets of downtown. I'd see them being hit by a car or attacked by a crazed thief. I would lie awake in my bedroom with the window cracked, listening to all the footsteps and cars and carriages that went down Tradd Street, straining to make out the voices of my parents on their way home.

I tap at the door and say, "She's here," and by the time I say, "Merry Christmas, Eli," Will, Mama, and Virginia are behind me on the porch.

"Welcome home, sweetheart," Mama says as Will grabs the shopping bag out of her arms and kisses her cheek.

"Nice luggage, cuz," Virginia says. "Merry Christmas."

Daddy is hanging back in the den. He's awfully funny when it comes to Eli. The fact is, he has a hard time looking her in the eye. Mama says it's because she looks like his sister's husband, a man from Vermont whose name was James Flint. But I think her eyes are just like Mee Maw Rose's and Daddy's, too, a soft hazel with gold flecks.

Eli's skin is so tough by now she doesn't even seem to care about Daddy. She walks right on in the house and says, "Happy holidays, Uncle Billy," and he nods his head and says, "Same to you," and then, "Welcome." He takes another breath and says, "home." Then he says, "I'll be right back," and he walks onto the porch and out the screened door.

I think how strange it must be for Eli to come home to this little caretaker's house. Her parents died when she was five, and from then on she lived with us during the school year and spent every summer on this plantation with Mee Maw Rose in the big house so that Mama and Daddy could get a break. It was this very dock by the fish shed where her mama and daddy set sail one afternoon for a boat ride from which they did not return. She says she can almost picture her mama making tomato sandwiches on the dock and her daddy loading the rods into the boat, but she has heard Mee Maw Rose tell the beginning of the story so many times, each detail like a step-by-step recipe for disaster, that she doesn't know which part belongs to her memory alone. It's the end of the story that is never described.

ॐ

"*How* did they die?" I once overheard Cousin Eli ask Mee Maw Rose in her parlor on Water Street.

Mee Maw Rose, taking a puff on her floral pipe, said, "I've told you before, dahlin'. They just drowned."

"But *how* did they drown?" she asked. "*How* did they get from the boat into the water?"

"It's hard to say," Mee Maw said. "They must have been thrown out of the boat somehow. Maybe they hit a bank at high tide that was just beneath the water. Somehow they drowned. That's the end of the story, and that's as much as we need to know about it."

ॐ

"Aunt Dee," Cousin Eli says, walking over to the tree, "this is the prettiest tree I've ever seen."

"Thanks, sweetheart," Mama says. "I couldn't have done it without DeVeaux."

Eli nudges me in the back. "Sometime I want to hear all about the restaurant," she says to me, "and you better have kept up with your end of the deal."

"Don't worry," I say, "I'm steering clear." Then I whisper, "Of Mr. Grabby Paws."

"DeVeaux," Mama says, "I don't even want to know what you're talking about. Now help me set the table."

Virginia looks Eli up and down, remarking on her scuffed-up

boots, which are the same ones Mee Maw Rose bought her back in high school. By the time we all settle back in front of the tree, Daddy is standing at the sliding glass door with a little piece of darkness in his arms. Virginia jumps up to open the door, and Daddy bends down and lets the puppy onto the hardwood floor.

"Well, look at that," Mama says, looking at Will to see his expression. "Who do you belong to?" The puppy runs and jumps into Eli's arms.

"What do you think, son?" Daddy says to Will.

Will is beginning to understand, and he walks over to Eli, who hands him the puppy. He cradles it in his arms and lets it suck his fingers.

"He's beautiful, Pop," he says.

"He ought to be," Daddy says. "He's from Jerry Mountain kennels just outside of Atlanta."

"The best," Will says.

"That's right," Daddy says, "and they can train her to retrieve for a good price."

"Dad, he's beautiful, but I . . ."

"What is it, son?"

"You shouldn't have spent that kind of money."

"Of course I should have. It's an investment, a third partner in the shrimp farm, right? And not a bad duck-hunting companion, either. You'll need a dog when you move back here."

"I need to talk to you about next year," Will says as he puts the puppy down. "Tomorrow?"

"Okay, but I hope you're still considering going into the shrimp farm with your old man," Daddy says, looking straight into Will's eyes. And I realize now, this is Daddy's only plan to get us out of debt and on to a new chapter of our lives.

"I am, but I've gotten a couple of offers because of my thesis and I just want to . . ."

"Let me guess," says Daddy as he throws a fresh log on the fire, "the Amazon River."

"Actually, that is one," Will says, stepping back as a worn log crumbles into orange coals on the hearth.

"Oh, c'mon Will, that's not the kind of thing you want to do. That's for the academics," Daddy says, turning back from the fire. "These are the waters you know."

"Let's talk tomorrow," Will says.

As we are sitting down to dinner, the telephone rings and we can hear Mama say loud and enunciated, "The house is ready for your arrival," so we know that she is talking to someone in the Shuzuki family. Then I hear her say, "Yes, he is, but we are just sitting down to our Christmas Eve dinner. We've got the whole family here."

"Durn Buddhists," Daddy says as he cuts the tenderloin. "If they're going to live over here, they may as well learn the holidays."

Then he sticks the fork and knife into the beef and says, "Let me talk to 'em."

He takes the telephone from Mama, and we all sit down and serve ourselves but we don't eat until he comes back. Mama fixes him a hefty plate, which she sets at the head of the table as he hangs up the phone.

His fleshy cheeks are red and filling with air.

"Everything okay?" Will says.

"Everything hasn't been okay for a long time, son, but I'm getting used to it," Daddy says.

"It'll be better soon," Mama says, beginning her mantra. And I fear that she might break out into the refrain of "Tomorrow" from the musical *Annie*.

Daddy looks uncomfortable. He starts to unbuckle his pants so that he can have dinner in his boxers, but Mama whispers, "Please don't."

He buckles them back as Mama lights the candles and Virginia turns off the lights.

"Will you bless the food, honey?" Mama says to Daddy.

We all bow our heads and hold hands.

"Heavenly Father, thank You for bringing each member of my family safely home—Virginia, Will, DeVeaux, and Eli. Thank You for the gift of Your Son, and we pray that You would bless this food to the nourishment of our bodies—"

"Thank You, Lord," Mama interjects with passion, and I understand her need to do so because Daddy's prayer rings hollow somehow, as if he could say those words over and over and not glimpse the miracle behind them.

"In Jesus' name we pray," Daddy says, "amen."

We all say "Amen" and squeeze one another's hands for a split second.

I watch as Daddy covers his tenderloin with béarnaise sauce. He pours so much on there that you can't even see the meat.

Lately, I've noticed how Daddy kills the taste of food with sauces. When we eat boiled shrimp, he loads his plate with gobs of cocktail and tartar sauce. When we bake potatoes, he covers them with butter and sour cream. I know that he wouldn't eat this way if his mama were still here and if we still lived on Tradd Street, and for some reason this really gets to me.

As Mama offers second helpings, Daddy is going over the menu for the holiday. He says, "And tomorrow, before Virginia leaves us"—and he stares down the table at her with that face of disappointment—"we're having eggs and grits with red-eye gravy and my favorite Orangeburg sausage from the Orangeburg Meat Packing Company, isn't that right, DeVeaux?"

"Uh-oh," I whisper to myself, and the look on my face must give me away.

"Is that *not* right, DeVeaux?" Daddy says.

"Well . . . Are they open on Christmas Day?"

"Oh, child, how could you forget? What in the world were you doing all day?"

I shrug my shoulders and murmur through my clenched teeth, "I'm sorry, Daddy." Now I wish I could just go back out on the porch. My thoughts are screaming: *I mean, all that jerk can think about is food and taking off his pants. Tell me, who is the child in this room? I've been through a lot, too, haven't I? His bad decisions have harmed me as well, right?*

All eyes are on me, and I'm ready to spew venom, though I know I don't have the guts to do it.

I'm a wimp, I think as I watch my father dive back into his tenderloin. And I'm also a sinner, because I know I'm not supposed to dishonor him in my heart. Plus, it's got to be a super-sized sin to break one of the Ten Commandments on Christmas Eve. So I just shove my plate aside and call the puppy over to me. As he rolls over on his back I lean down and stroke him on the belly and everyone goes quietly back to their food.

Toward the end of the meal the telephone rings, and Mama picks it up before Daddy tells her to let it go.

"Hello, Ruth," Mama says. "Merry Christmas . . . uh, I mean . . . Happy Hanukkah, but I know that's over, so happy holidays . . ."

Will jumps up because he knows Mama will go on forever digging herself in that hole.

"Mama," he says, motioning to the phone, and she hands it over to him.

His smile widens at the sound of Ruth's voice. "Hey, I miss you," he says.

Daddy has the remote beside him on the dinner table, and he turns on the television to catch the news.

Mama starts to make the coffee and Virginia, Eli, and I clear away the plates.

Mama tells Eli to relax, and she excuses herself and walks outside. She's probably going to smoke a cigarette on top of the fish shed where you can get a good view of the moon rising. "It's a vice I just can't shake," she told me on Thanksgiving, and I know that must be true 'cause she's been smoking since she was my age.

"Dee," Daddy says, "let me talk you out of a slice of that pecan pie with a scoop of vanilla ice cream."

"It's coming, honey," Mama says.

Daddy gets the attention of the puppy and pulls him up to rest on top of his round chest.

"What are we gonna call you, little fellow?"

I hear Will say, "Let me go get it," then he comes back to the telephone with his laboratory case. He is feeling beneath the inside pocket and he pulls out what looks like an airline ticket.

"No way!" he says, examining the ticket. "How did you get that in there?"

He's grinning and balancing on the tiptoes of his hiking boots.

"Thank you, sweetheart," he says. "What a present."

He notices Mama and me watching him, so he takes the telephone into the utility closet and closes the door.

The creases on the insides of Mama's eyes deepen like two short knives. She groans and makes a wheezing sound from way down in her chest.

After a few minutes Will comes back out. Daddy presses the Mute button and says, "So how's Ruth?"

"She's fine," he says. "She says to tell you all happy holidays."

And then Will says, "I need to tell you guys something."

Daddy turns off the television.

"For Christmas, she has planned a ski trip to Utah with her family." He holds up the plane ticket for us to see. In little letters across the front it says "Fly the friendly skies."

"Oh my," Mama says.

"When do you go?" Daddy says.

"Tomorrow afternoon," he says and then the room is quiet. "But I'll be back the day before New Year's for the whole weekend."

We are all staring guiltily into our laps, and I feel sorry for Daddy because I know that Christmas is not turning out like he planned. He clears his throat, but I do not look up until he says with authority, "You know what?"

And now that eerie half grin forms between his cheeks. And we all have heard that voice before, and we know there is nothing left to do but sit back and receive our tongue-lashing. He stands and lets down the puppy, who is asleep by now but wakes up for a moment, crawls under the sofa, and begins to snore softly. Daddy looks around the room, and I can anticipate his angry words that will ricochet all over the walls of this cramped house like a trapped wasp. I imagine him saying, "How could you desert your family?" or "Doesn't anyone give a hoot about Christmas?"

But he doesn't say a word.

Instead, he heads quickly toward the Christmas tree in the corner of the room.

He sticks his long arms into the spine where Mama has carefully guided all of the lights. He seizes it, tilts it, then squats down so that it falls over his shoulder, this seven-foot mass of crystal and glass.

Each face winces at the clinking sounds of the ornaments as they swing back and forth on the ends of their hooks. I am watching the pearl petals of the flower inside one of the orange Fabergé eggs. Its bottom half is knocking between a blue glass ball and the white lights on an adjacent limb. The two ornaments straighten for a moment as he stands, staggers, and with a thrust of his hip slides back the glass door and carries the tree onto the front porch, ripping the plugs out of the wall and turning several presents upside down in his wake.

Without hesitating, he kicks open the screened door and pulls the tree through the narrow threshold. The bottom half catches for a moment in the doorway and he gives it one determined tug, then pulls it through, leaving a small collection of limbs and ornaments on the doormat and the steps that lead to the yard.

The tree bounces on his back as he bustles toward the creek. It lifts up, knocking the Spanish moss that dangles like tinsel from the live oaks. He dodges the tire swing, the rabbit cage, the grill, and the fish shed.

Then he steps solidly onto the dock that leads him over the mud and marsh grass and out into the creek where the tide rises at a steady pace. When he reaches the edge, he does not pause. He uses the remainder of his strength and hurls the tree into the rising tide.

He pants back to the house, walks through the screened porch and stands on the threshold of the sliding glass door, which is still wide open and letting in a creek breeze.

"That's Christmas for y'all this year," he says, then he walks off the porch and we can hear the dull sound of his boots stamping into the soft ground.

Now we hear the sound of his truck gnawing its way through the dirt on the road that leads out of the plantation.

Out of the corner of my eye I see Cousin Eli slide off the roof of the fish shed and walk toward the cornfields in the direction of Maum Bess's house. When I take a step forward the puppy screams. I have stepped on his toe. By the time I reach down to pick him up he has crawled back under the sofa where he licks his paw.

6

Christmas Day

Early the next morning there is a tap at the door. I look out my bedroom window and see the back of Mary Margaret Davidson's emerald-colored Suburban. Both of the back doors are open, and mud is streaked across the inside of the windows and smeared on the green interior.

Last night feels as distant as a dream. Daddy lost it worse than he ever has. And Will got so fed up with Daddy that he drove to Charleston to spend the night with a friend. And Eli disappeared as quickly as she appeared. She probably escaped to Maum Bess's and then on to Suzanne's. Christmas is spoiled for everyone.

"Anyone home?" the voice calls from the back porch. I roll out of bed and my feet slap the cold hardwood floor. Nobody else is making a sound, so I figure that I'm the only one awake. It's seven in the morning.

I leave my room and walk toward the sliding glass door and sure enough, there is Mary Margaret Davidson and her father, Dr. Davidson, dressed in dark-colored anoraks and yellow rubber gloves, clutching the spine of our Christmas tree, which is caked in pluff mud and dripping large drops of black water.

Now this is pretty embarrassing. *Some Christmas the DeLoach family has got going over here*, they must be thinking. *Some pathetic life DeVeaux lives now*, Mary Margaret must be thinking, and I picture her father waking her up at the crack of dawn to help him pull *our* Christmas tree out of *their* creek and haul it back over to *our* house while Mary Margaret's tree, which is color-coordinated in red ribbons and white lights and glossy balls, towers clean and dry above her tightly wrapped presents: a five-disc stereo, a pair of duck boots, and a 14-karat-gold tennis charm with a pearl in the center of the racket.

The heels and toes of their boots are covered in pluff mud and a piece of seaweed is strewn across Dr. Davidson's left shoulder. Mary Margaret's auburn ponytail is falling down around her pale neck and she sniffles, holds back a sneeze, and wipes her nose on the arm of her anorak as I open the door.

"Hi there, honey," Dr. Davidson says to me.

I nod.

"I spotted this around sunrise, caught beneath my dock," he says. "Does this belong to your family?"

I nod again and see that in her other hand Mary Margaret is holding an ornament I made when I was in second grade. It is an angel whose body is constructed in thin blue Styrofoam from an egg carton with my second-grade picture glued between the two wings. Mary Margaret must have an angel just like this one with her own picture. We made those together at Cooper Hall, just like the turkeys with their pine cone bodies and pipe-cleaner necks that Mama sets out on the dining room table each Thanksgiving. Mary Margaret looks down toward her muddy boots and hands the ornament to me.

"Where should we put this?" Dr. Davidson asks.

Virginia is behind me now. She says, "Just put it down right here on the porch." We are both in our nightgowns, and our feet are bare and starting to get cold.

He takes a long look at Virginia and I want to turn around and see if he's staring at her nose, one of his many successful creations before the boy in the accident whose face he could not bear to put back together.

"It's awfully muddy," he says.

"That's all right," says Virginia. "We'll take care of it."

"All right, Mary Marg," he says as he begins to lay down the tree, "be careful; there are still a few breakables on here."

They set the tree down gently and Virginia places her hand on my shoulder, not so much as an act of comfort but more as a place for her to lean her weight. "What a nightmare," she mutters and when Mary Margaret and Dr. Davidson stand back up she says, "Thank you so much, Dr. Davidson. We really appreciate this."

"Have a merry Christmas," I say and the words are frail, disintegrating in my mouth like cotton candy.

Dr. Davidson nods his head and they turn and walk toward their Suburban, Mary Margaret sneezing finally as she takes off her rubber gloves and waits for her dad, who is gently closing the back doors of their muddy car.

As they pull out of the driveway, Clayton's Chevrolet pulls in.

"Just great," says Virginia sarcastically, and her eyes look tired and her bare feet with her clear painted toenails are beginning to turn gray.

"Why is he always so doggone prompt?" she says, and she runs down the hall and into the bathroom.

Mama and Daddy must still be asleep.

"Merry Christmas." Clayton bounds toward me in a tweed jacket and a burgundy bow tie.

He is polished and spotless like everyone else in town, living apart from all of this mud that stains my clothes and slips beneath my fingernails. He is holding two packages of meat, and he can't let things unfold at the natural time so before he reaches the porch he's explaining his gift to me, venison sausage and tenderloin from a deer he harvested just last week. He has taken it to the Sammy Hudson Packaging Company, and they have cut and ground it up and sealed it tight with Clayton's name in the center of a silver sticker, Clayton Louis Tankerslay III. Below his name is the cut of meat and the weight.

"For your family," he says. "A present."

I'm standing on the threshold of the sliding glass door with the base of the tree in front of my bare ankles. It looks like a gigantic pine cone, its wide base reaching as high as my hips. In the screen of the porch door a red ball ornament is caught just below the door handle. It starts to sway when Clayton opens the door.

He steps back for a moment and lets the door rest on his tweed shoulders. Mud is on the door and all around the slick concrete floor of the porch.

"What the heck happened to your tree?" he says to me.

Virginia left me no instructions on how to present this and so I say, "Well, Daddy threw it into the water last night as the tide was rising, and it must have made its way down to Blue House Creek and landed at the Davidsons' dock, and they just returned it."

Clayton steps onto the porch and lets the door shut behind him and says, "Your dad threw a decorated Christmas tree into the creek?" His thin eyebrows are making these pointed angles above his pale brown eyes.

"Yes," I say, "he did."

"What in the world made him do that?" he says.

"Clayton," Mama's voice sounds behind me. I turn to find her in sweatpants and one of Daddy's camouflage rain jackets. "I need you to help me move this tree over to the toolshed before Billy wakes up."

Clayton motions, palms up, as if to say in a polite way, "I'm all dressed up and on my way to my great-aunt Vee Vee's house, and you want me to move a wet tree caked in mud?"

Mama takes off her jacket and throws it gently toward him.

"I appreciate your help," she says, and settles that question. Clayton puts his packages of meat down on the picnic table and walks around to the base of the tree while she walks around to the tip. I hold open the door while the limbs splatter mud against the screen and across the bottom of my nightgown and my feet. I watch as Mama leads the way over to the shed with Clayton gripping the trunk over and over as it slips in his hands like a live fish.

"Get dressed," Mama says to me as she walks back onto the porch to screw the water hose onto the spigot.

"You and I are going to try and save a few of these ornaments before the salt water destroys them," she says.

When I am throwing on a sweatshirt in my bedroom, I can hear her back in their bedroom, the muffled voice of my father moaning like he is at the bottom of a cave.

After Virginia leaves with Clayton, I meet Mama back in the toolshed and one by one we feel our way through the mud that has settled between and around the limbs, uncovering ornaments.

"Forget about the lights," she says early on. "They are replaceable."

We're looking for the Fabergé eggs and the ornaments that family friends made for us when we were young, many of them cross-stitched with our initials, date of birth, and some sort of caricature like a lamb with a bell around its neck or a child kneeling. We are looking for the handblown crystal balls that Daddy bought for Mama at the glassblowing factory on their fifteenth wedding anniversary trip to Venice when I was conceived.

When we find one, we take the hose, rinse it off, use a fingernail brush and then our fingernails to dislodge the mud in the crevices. Then Mama pats them with a towel and lays them on the newspaper to dry.

"Your father is coming down with gout," she says, placing a silver bell on the newspaper.

"That's convenient for him," I say to her. "What a jerk."

"Don't speak that way about your father," she says without flinching or taking the time to look me in the eye.

And I really am gutless. Sure, I can dishonor my father in front of my mother because I know she is missing a spine, but I would never utter such words in his presence. How pitiful I am, preying on her weaknesses at a time like this.

"You're right," I say to her. "Mama, I'm sorry."

Trancelike, she just keeps rubbing the mud off an ornament. Hoses it. Brushes it down. It is a flat silver ornament that has a frame in the center with a black-and-white picture of Aunt Eliza and Daddy when they were young. The mud has seeped into the frame and the tops of their heads are blurring together.

I used to think Mama was a saint to put up with all of his temper tantrums, but sometimes I wish that she would acknowledge his extreme behavior and say *something* to him about it. It's creepy how they treat each other after one of his fits. It's as if it never happened. She's either too weary to hold him accountable or just plain afraid of him.

"Ha!" shouts a high-pitched voice behind us.

We turn and find Sagi, dressed in an argyle sweater and holding up the new little puppy.

"For me?" he asks.

Suddenly, Mrs. Shuzuki is standing in the doorway of the toolshed. She is dressed in a silk suit the color of butter.

"Ha-lo," she says. "We are here now."

Mama and I are a sight with our hands and knees covered in dried mud.

Mrs. Shuzuki has a perplexed look on her face. "Accident?" she says.

Before we answer she looks as if she's just remembered something more important and says, "Oh. My husband say to tell your husband that we want boat ride round three p.m. noon. Okay?"

Mama is speechless. She looks back down at the tree like she's in a trance.

"Okay," I say, and Sagi walks over to me and places the puppy at my knees.

"For you," he says.

Then he heads toward the doorway where his mother grabs his hand. They turn and walk toward the main house.

7

The Ebb

After Mama and I salvage the ornaments that survived the ride down the creek, we strip off our boots and pants and hose the mud off our feet so we can walk into the house. We have spent all morning on the tree and recovered seven of the eleven Fabergé eggs and two of the six balls from the glassblowing factory in Venice, though I think the glass balls are ruined, scratched all over by creek debris and filled with mud. Mama hung them upside down in the toolshed in hopes that the mud will find its way out.

When the icy water hits Mama's toes, she holds her chest and quietly tries to catch her breath. She looks like she's having to work for air.

"All right, Mama?" I say.

"Yes, dahlin'," she whispers. "My lungs must have clogged up from working in the mud, but it's nothin' a shower and a cup of coffee won't clear."

Since we've moved out to the plantation, I've noticed that occasionally Mama is short of breath. Sometimes she is downright croaky, and when I come home late at night from the restaurant I can hear the muffled sound of her grasping for air, short gasps in her sleep beneath the sound of Daddy snoring, loud and clear, filling the dark house like a foghorn.

"You were a big help," she whispers. "Thank you."

Then she walks over and kisses my forehead, and I want to hug her since it is such a horrible Christmas Day and everything, but my arms are still covered in mud.

"I'm going to try and make it to the noon service at Edisto Episcopal," she says. "Want to join me?"

I hate to disappoint her by saying no. And last night, I'm ashamed to say, she went to the midnight service all by herself after the family scattered. But as I sat there and sulked, waiting for my dad to come home from his tirade and muttering from time to time in a bitter tone toward God, "What next?" I got a call from Sasser, who needed his own consoling. His daddy had bought a small, fake tree for their house and ordered Chinese takeout for their Christmas Eve meal, which they ate with plastic forks and paper napkins at the dining room table. He reminisced to me about how his mama used to make several loaves of pumpkin bread and pecans with candy coating to give to the parishioners and that her baking would fill the house with its sweet holiday smell all the days leading up to Christmas. She'd take him with her to the tree farm on Edisto Island, and together they would select the grandest tree they could find for their living room. And for Christmas Eve she'd make beef Wellington for dinner and invite one or two parishioners who she knew had no place to go for the holidays.

"If she's not back by next year," he said to me, "I'll learn to make it myself."

"The pumpkin bread or the beef Wellington?"

"Both," he said. "Not only does MSG give me a headache, but on Christmas Eve, it's pretty depressing." We both laughed.

Thing is, Sasser's mama, Ella, had run off with a historian named Jake Chandler who worked at the National Register of Historic Places in Washington, D.C. He'd come down to examine and restore parts of the rectory since it was on the National Registry. Sasser and his dad were oblivious to whatever was happening between Jake and Ella during his three-month stay in their carriage house, but by the time he left, she was gone with him, leaving a note to Sasser that said: "You're sixteen and a young man of faith. I know you'll be all right. Look after Dad for me."

She had also left Father Dan a note, but Sasser never knew what it said, and he wouldn't dare ask, though he imagined all sorts of things it could have said.

Sasser said he had no idea it was coming. The only clue of their connection was that she took Mr. Chandler to a few of her favorite antique shops and an auction in Savannah, where she bought a table that he took to the carriage house to restore.

Sasser says his dad ran kind of a tight ship when they were young and this exasperated his mother. But the biggest problem was just that his dad was never there. There was someone always sick or dying or having marital problems or getting married or having a baby and he had to be there.

❧

As Mama waits for my answer about church, I just can't help but picture those snitty older ladies that seem to exist in many southern Episcopal churches, with their insect-shaped brooches, who will walk over during "the peace" to ask me what the Father blessed me with this Christmas. And I really don't want to face Mary Margaret and the Davidson clan (avid Episcopalians!) who already know too much about how our holiday is going. Even as I think of these things, I realize what shallow reasons they are for not going and worshiping the One I am supposed to have claimed as my God and my Savior.

My hesitation causes Mama to say breathlessly, "It's okay with me, love. You do what you want."

It's hard to imagine these words coming out of her mouth with such ease. Mama used to spend all of her energy on Sunday mornings prodding me and the rest of the family out of bed for church.

For a few years she actually walked around the house with a cowbell, singing, "This is the day that the Lord has made," until someone pleaded, "Okay, we're awake." Once, when we were in the car, all ready for church and waiting for Virginia to make her way out of the house, I said, "Mama, why don't you just let those who don't want to go stay home?"

She smiled and said, "Because I won't surrender to the devil, dahlin'."

Now Mama looks deep into me with a sympathetic grin, and I see that there are creases in the skin between her eyebrows that used to only form when she was upset or perplexed. They are faint but visible, now-permanent indentions that have settled in without my noticing. And I wonder, *Has she surrendered?*

But below the worry lines, her charcoal eyes have the same spirited stir of her prime. I know this because I have stared for long periods of time at the portrait her father had painted of her the year she was crowned the May Queen of Greenville High School, in a white sundress with the pastel-colored ribbons of the maypole draped across her lap. The portrait hung for years above the desk in my grandfather's office, the corner office at the top of the JP Stevens Building, the only skyscraper in Greenville at that time. When Mr. J. P. Stevens would fly in from New York, he used to admire the portrait during company meetings.

"What a beautiful black-eyed girl," he'd say. "I've got a nephew at Princeton who would be pleased to meet a southern lady like her."

"She's my treasure," Mama's daddy would say. "It won't be easy to give her away."

When Mama's father passed away, Daddy inherited the portrait, which he hung in the lobby of his real estate office on Broad Street in downtown Charleston until he went bankrupt.

Daddy used to let me answer the telephone at his office when I needed a little extra money, and during those times I would steal stares into my mother's black eyes and wonder what her thoughts were at that age, so distant from what filled her mind now: keeping a house, staying on a diet, organizing prayer meetings. It was a look at her life before it was filled and spilling over with Daddy, and the family, and the Lord.

It was during the depression following her father's death that Mama accepted Christ. Virginia says she remembers the rainy spring morning that Sasser's mom, Ella, came by the house with a basket of warm bran muffins that we devoured in the kitchen while Ella said to Mama over coffee on the wet porch, "Don't you know that *God* is your Father?"

Mama looked up from her coffee and said, "I want to know it." Then she collapsed into Ella's arms and wept while Ella told her the gospel.

The story goes that the following Sunday at St. Paul's, a guest minister from a seminary in Pittsburgh asked the congregation to raise their hands if they knew that they were going to heaven. So Mama was among the handful in the congregation who raised their hands. She lifted it proudly, right there between Daddy and Mee Maw Rose in the family pew that the Roses have sat in since the early 1800s. This, of course, caused Mee Maw Rose's jaw to drop while her head filled with words like *presumptuous, upstate,* and *nouveau,* which she spouted out to Virginia and me from time to time as we sat beneath the portrait of Edmund Seabrook Rose in her parlor on Water Street, scooping spoonfuls of sugar into the china cups that held her tart tea.

Then she would nod to the portrait behind us and say, "That is a Sully, girls. He lived with your great-great-great-grandfather for four months in order to capture him on canvas. Did you know that Sully has several portraits in the Metropolitan?"

"No, I didn't," I would say, afraid to ask what "the Metropolitan" was.

Then Mee Maw Rose would say, "You girls know that I think your mama is a good person."

"Yes, ma'am," we'd say.

"But I do not want you to forget your heritage, which dates back to the earliest days of Charleston. *Your* veins flow with the blood of French Huguenots and English lords. You are a combination of some of the oldest families in this state."

We'd nod back, sip our tea, and wince when occasionally we felt a leaf in the back of our throats.

Now the portrait of Mama is stored in the back of the teahouse between Daddy's fishing gear and one of Mee Maw Rose's antique armoires, which contains clothes that still hold her scent.

❦

When I go to my room to throw on some jeans, I hear the steady sound of Daddy snoring. I look down the hall and see that he is laid out beneath the afghan in his bedroom, except for his right foot, which he keeps on top of the covers since it has gout in it. Once he told me that when he has gout, just the corner of the sheet when it brushes over his foot feels like one thousand needles are poking him there.

Other than his heavy breath and the sound of the shower, the house is quiet.

I open the refrigerator for a survey. It is packed with all the decadent meals Daddy had planned for the holiday: wheels of cheese, pepper jellies, a honey-glazed ham.

It's hard to look at those mounds of food that were meant for our feasting without being depressed, so I close the door. Who can eat now while my family is scattered across the low country on the most important day of the year?

Then I notice the holiday photos that Mama has put beneath

magnets on the icebox door. Mostly they are photos of wealthy, happy families who belong to the college friends of my parents. They live in charming places like Alexandria, Virginia, or Chapel Hill, North Carolina. I recognize the Kitteridge boys, Rivers Jr. and Hunter, from past photos. They are, like all their past photos, on their sailboat in the Annapolis harbor with their latest pet, a chocolate Labrador named Godiva. Then I recognize the Barnwell family on their winter ski trip to Vail, dressed in gold ski suits that shimmer in the sun, their youngest holding a snowboard that reads "Cliff Hanger" in black letters across the slick yellow surface between the footholds. The Barnwells vary their backdrops, but they usually have to do with skiing, whether it's a lodge scene where they are dressed in heavy wool sweaters in front of a blazing fire or action shots of their dismounts from the lift.

I have never met most of these happy, well-dressed families with their rosy cheeks and straight teeth. They send these photos and "brag and gag" letters every year, and every year I get to watch people I have never spoken to grow older and older. I've seen some of these kids go from training wheels to braces. They have names that remind me of rolling hills or meadows. Names like Brook and Fielding and Heath. They take adventurous vacations where they propel down a mountain in Yosemite National Park or raft in the white-water river at the bottom of the Grand Canyon. And their annual letters confirm their perfectly well-adjusted, upper-middle-class lives: high SAT scores, short-term mission trips, acceptances to Ivy League colleges.

Would you believe that I have been to only two states outside South Carolina? One is North Carolina, where for three summers I attended Camp Pinnacle in the mountain village of Saluda; and the second is the state of Virginia, where I attended Virginia's and Eli's high school graduation from St. Mary's in Richmond. Daddy says there is no need to travel anywhere since we live in the prettiest place in the prettiest state in the country.

When I walk out onto the porch, I see that the sun is starting to burn off the morning fog. I watch a rabbit that is standing still as a picture beneath an oak tree. I think, *What would the William Rose DeLoach family say in a brag-and-gag letter?* I have to smile when I imagine it.

It might read, "It's been an exciting year. Daddy declared bankruptcy and gained twenty pounds, and on Christmas Eve he lost his cool and threw the fully decorated tree into Rose Hill Creek. But Mama says, 'God is good,' for we recovered seven Fabergé egg ornaments on Christmas Day. The only problem is that if Daddy realizes how much the ornaments are worth, he may sell them out from under us."

Just then I hear Mama rustling in the kitchen. She is dressed for church, in a red suit with gold buttons. I watch as she secretly pulls the checkbook from the cupboard and rips out a check for the offertory and crams it into her patent-leather purse. She keeps stealing glances down the hall to make sure Daddy is not watching her. Mama believes in tithing and Daddy does not, although every couple of years or so when he's doing well he'll write a check so big that Mama says, "Do we even have that much?" And he replies, "Just mail it."

Whenever they have the discussion about tithing Daddy says, "We give when we can." And Mama says, "But it's God's command to do it regularly." And Daddy rolls his eyes and says, "Who supports this entire family?" And Mama bites her lip and says nothing.

As she scurries out the door she whispers, "Check in on your father after a while."

"Yes, ma'am," I say.

"And run by Maum Bess's to see if Chambers could haul the tree to the dump," she says.

"Yes, ma'am," I say as I watch her attempt to step into the pickup without ripping the straight skirt of her suit or getting mud from the door on the backs of her stockinged legs. *So much for grace in this wild place*, I think to myself.

After Mama is gone, I climb to the roof of the fish shed so that the sun will warm my bones. The johnboat is tied to the dock, gently bobbing with the outgoing tide, and in the distance I can see Otter Island, the spit of sand that sucked Daddy's money and our life as we knew it away.

The fact is, it is awful to think that your father is a shameful jerk. It is awful to revile him, down to his eating habits, his facial expressions, his gestures. I can even see it in Mama as she recoils when he reaches out to hold her hand during the blessing. Lately she actually flinches, as if a cockroach were trying to walk across her hand. I don't think he notices. I hope he doesn't.

Yes, I think as the sun presses gently down on my face, *it is awful to know that your father is desperate and not have the desire you ought to have to care for him because you are just so fed up and grossed out by him. Especially when you can recall that he hasn't always been this way.*

Though Daddy has been grieving his sister and financially stressed much of my life, I have some great memories with him. He was the one who taught me how to play tennis. In the late afternoons of my childhood, he walked me down to Moultrie Park and we'd hit the ball back and forth until the sun set. He'd even race me home when we rounded Tradd Street, giving me a one-block head start and occasionally letting me win.

As my brother, sister, and cousin became teenagers, abandoning our company on weekends, he'd rent movies and take me to the grocery store where he let me pick out my favorite candy and ice cream, which we gobbled down in front of the television on Saturday nights.

My fondest memory is of the time he came to visit me during my twelve-year-old summer at Camp Pinnacle. I had been there for three weeks and I still had two left, and I'd had an awful time. My counselor cried day and night because she missed her boyfriend, and I had to sleep below a fat girl named Sissy who sang the camp songs in her sleep. Also, I'd started my period for the first time, and when I went to the nurse she told me to stay out of the water for a week and gave me some maxi pads that were thicker than the camp life jackets.

Pinnacle was a five-hour drive from Charleston up in the North Carolina mountains, and Daddy made the trip all the way by himself to the midsession parents day because Mama was looking after Mee Maw, who had the flu. When I came out of the cabin to greet him, he stopped in his tracks with his arms outstretched. He gave me the strongest hug I can remember, then he grabbed my shoulders, looked me straight in the eye, and said, "DeVeaux, you're growing up."

We spent the rest of the day avoiding camp. He took me to the Applebee's in Hendersonville where we sat for two hours eating buffalo wings and nachos, while I complained about the camp conditions and said, "I'm too old to come back next summer." And he said, "Baby, I agree. You don't have to."

❧

Now the rustling noise of the wind blowing the trees behind me fills up my ears. The floating dock creaks against the pilings and three pelicans fly over me and out into the marsh. The world around me is dense and immobile, from the deeply rooted oak trees to the thick decay of plant and animal life, the pluff mud, which forms the banks and fills the bottom of the creek. I am surrounded by such solid layers of the landscape, but my family feels as unsteady as props in a play—two-dimensional and capable of collapse.

It's this instability that has gotten the best of Daddy. Instability and unplanned events are the things that will drive a man like my daddy crazy. He's spent all of his life planning and developing, always able to rely on the value of his family name and his heritage and his own strength. So he continues to be shocked and grows increasingly embittered when events over which he has no control come into his life—like Aunt Eliza's marriage to a strange Yankee man and their sudden death in the creek at his home, the gain of two more children: Cousin Eli and then me, the loss of his once-successful business, the loss of his mother, and even the way he wanted this holiday to turn out.

It seems to me that a man who loses control and does not turn to God in his time of need is sad and dangerous.

Now I think of one of Mama's sayings, "The heart follows the will," and so I concentrate on Daddy hard, and I ask God to give me the will to love him again.

During this attempt, Tanner Strickland and Jonas, his hired hand, drive up. They carry two croaker sacks full of oysters to the fish shed. Now I remember that Daddy was planning on having a family roast tonight. I stay perfectly still on top of the shed because I'm not in the mood to talk to them.

Then I hear Tanner say, "There it is, Jonas."

"Where?" Jonas says.

"Over there in the toolshed," he says, "like a heap of mud."

"Oh Lord, I see it," Jonas says. "So it is true."

"Must be," Tanner says, then he turns and walks back toward his truck, shaking his head. "Strange folks."

"Not strange, brother," Jonas says. "I tell you they problem. They rich folk in the poorhouse."

"What does that mean?" Tanner says.

"Rich folk gone poor," Jonas says.

"Poor *and* crazy," Tanner says as he steps into his truck. Then he says, "Let's get out of here."

But Jonas stands perfectly still for a moment, observing the trunk of the tree in the toolshed. He shakes his head back and forth like he's at a funeral.

"We've got three more deliveries, and I've got a deer hunt at dusk," Tanner says, "C'mon!"

As I lay on top of the fish shed, I hear Easy crying over by the screened door. It is her hunger cry and it wakes up the puppy, who has been sleeping in the shade beneath the tractor. They are both whimpering now.

Suddenly, I have a burst of energy that is a gift from God, and it allows me to get up and feed the animals and check in on Daddy, who is still out from the gout medicine. As I walk back onto the porch, I exercise my will a second time: I will not stand idly by and watch my family collapse. There are things I can do to help the situation.

❦

On my way over to the Shuzukis, I stop in the toolshed to check on the ornaments. I pick up a glass ball and rub my thumb across the scratches. Ever since my siblings left home a few years ago, I have made a ritual of picturing them all spread out across the country, like satellite dishes, tied to Mama and Daddy and me at the home station.

So I think of Will, who is in the air by now, halfway to the ski slopes of Utah where Ruth Rosenberg will meet him, braless and makeup-less, the soft dark hair above her top lip parted and making way for his kiss. Or Virginia, in Augusta, sitting at the

Tankserslays' dining room table, dressed in a tailored pantsuit with a matching silk scarf while she raises one of Great-aunt Vee Vee's crystal glasses, which she has already marked with the mauve from her painted lips. Then Mama, in church, singing "Hark! The Herald Angels Sing," her arm relaxed by her side but ever ready to announce, if asked, her reserved spot inside the gates of heaven. And, finally, Cousin Eli, stopped somewhere on this island, entranced by some creature she has spotted or just shooting the breeze with whoever is passing by. Cousin Eli is the only person I know who just sits back and lets the world come to her.

Then I wonder what Daddy will have to say for himself when he wakes up. What could his next words possibly be? He's usually good in justifying his actions after he loses his temper by explaining to us all how we, the family, forced him to act in the manner in which he did. But this act was such an outrageous one that I can't imagine how he could possibly pin the blame on us.

When I get to the main house I see Mrs. Shuzuki scurrying across the porch. She is throwing out the magnolia limbs that Mama placed as decoration in the fireplaces and along the banister of the grand stairway. She looks at me and says, "The red bugs live in these," then she throws them in the trash can.

Mama and Maum Bess say that the Shuzukis are too clean. "They might as well bathe in Lysol," Mama said one time under her breath, and I thought it might have been the rudest thing I've ever heard her say. But I'll admit that we all had a good laugh when the Shuzukis ordered faux logs and an electric lighter to be installed in the marble fireplaces in the main house. None of us could figure out how anyone could stand a faux fire in a plantation house. And who would want to alter the hearth where Rose family guests like Lafayette once stood for warmth? But Mrs. Shuzuki detests ashes. She says that ashes leave a thin layer of dirt on everything in the house.

"Can we help you?" Mrs. Shuzuki says on her second trip out, her arms filled with the knobby twigs and the large, waxy green leaves. She is holding her chin up, away from them. In the hall I can see the broom and vacuum cleaner resting beneath one of the walled chandeliers. At the foot of the grand stairway is a basket of cleaning supplies, jugs of ammonia-type cleaning fluids and various scrub brushes and rags. I can't believe that Mrs. Shuzuki is cleaning again after Mama just spent the past two days scrubbing that house up one side and down the other.

"I wanted to let you know that my daddy is ill. Too ill to take you on a boat ride," I say.

She throws the armful down into the trash can.

"Oh," she says, then, "Ohhhh, no. Mr. Shuzuki be very disappointed."

"But," I say before she flies back into the house, "I will be happy to take you."

"Mmm?" she says.

I point to myself.

"You?" she says. There are four wrinkles across her round forehead.

"Yes," I say, "I can drive a boat."

"Mmm," she says. She places two fingers over her top lip then jerks them away, probably remembering the red bugs and the limbs.

"I can drive a car, can't I?" I say.

She nods.

"Well then?" I say. "I can certainly drive a boat."

She pauses for a moment. She rubs her hands on her apron.

"If your father say okay," she says.

"He certainly says okay," I say. "High tide is at 3:00 p.m. I'll see you all on the dock at that time."

She turns, crosses the threshold of the old door, and walks down the hallway of the house. Her movements are quick but steady. There is a speed and orderliness in her that I know nothing about.

As I begin to walk away, Sagi comes running out onto the porch. He puts his head between the wrought-iron railing, just above the "o" in "Rose," where sea spiders have already rebuilt the cobweb homes that Mama destroyed just yesterday when she was preparing the house.

"Hey," Sagi says to me, "do you know what day it is?"

"Yes," I say, wondering if this is some sort of a trick question. "Do you?"

"It is the day of Santa and the baby Jesus," he says. His round cheeks nearly cover his eyes as he smiles.

"That's right," I say.

"So?" he says.

"So what?" I say.

"So what did Santa bring you?" he says.

I stop dead in my tracks, realizing that not even a present has been exchanged in my family. I haven't even had a chance to wrap the presents that I bought for everyone. I was planning to do that after supper on Christmas Eve.

Now Sagi has a concerned look on his face. "Did you get coal and switches?" he says. He looks worried. He is either scared or sad but I can't tell which.

I have to laugh and reassure him that I did not get coal and switches.

"No," I say, "I haven't opened my presents yet."

"Oh," he says. His eyelids begin to flutter and he rubs the palms of his hands together in relief. It's sweet that he's worried about my Christmas. I start to ask him the same question, a little unsure of how to word it in case they don't celebrate Christmas, but as I begin Mrs. Shuzuki walks back onto the porch with more limbs. She pauses to talk to Sagi in Japanese before she throws them off the porch and into the trash can. Her voice has a sharp tone with lots of grunts and one deep breath. Sagi quickly lets go of the porch railing and runs into the house. I turn to walk away, but I look back over my shoulder after I hear the pipes on the side of the house begin their muffled rumble. I can see the top of Sagi's head through the kitchen window where the sink is. He is washing his hands.

On the way back to the caretaker's house, I stop by Maum Bess's. I want to see how she and Chambers are getting along and find out if she has seen Cousin Eli. I have to cut through the gall and the cornfields to get to their house. Halfway through the cornfield, I spot the backside of a doe who is twenty yards down the row of corn. In a split second, she is gone. She has disappeared, quick and quiet, into the rows I just came out of. Daddy says the deer are all over these fields, crouched down in the thicker brush, waiting for the sun to go down so they can come out and feed.

There is so much here that I can't see.

As I step through the last row of corn, Maum Bess's house, which sits lopsided on cinder blocks at the edge of a small swamp, is in full view. The porch is screenless and the shutters are painted a neon blue. There are dried gourds strung on wooden poles around the yard. Suddenly, I realize that I have never come here by myself. I've always come with Mama or Daddy and we are usually just passing by, offering them some fish or game that Daddy has hunted down. And I've never actually been inside. Instead, Daddy, Mama, and I stay on the porch steps while Daddy tells the story of how he captured or hooked or trapped whatever it is he is bringing them for dinner.

Smoke is rising from the pipe chimney and I watch as it slips through the treetops of oaks and pines and palmettos and up into the clear sky. When I get to the porch, I knock on the thin wood of the screenless door but no one comes, so I open it and step into the porch then I go to the front door and tap lightly. There are purple and turquoise tapestries over all of the windows to keep out the evil hooch and his entourage of spirits. One of the tapestries does not cover the bottom of the window, so I bend down and look inside. In the center of the small, dark room I see Maum Bess, who is dressed in her regular blue bathrobe with a bright yellow and green turban wrapped around her head. She is sitting in a rocking chair by the woodstove, watching a Christmas service on a big-screen television, lifting her hands up to the sky.

"Best stay away from there, gal," a syrupy voice behind me says. "No tellin' what dat woman prayin' up." I can feel my heart pound before I turn around and see Chambers, who is walking down the dirt road between the cornfield and the house. He's dressed in a black polyester suit with a green tie and a sprig of holly in his lapel, and in his right hand he is carrying a white leather Bible. I am taken aback because I have never seen him in such vibrant colors. He usually wears a gray-green work suit in the fields, which blends in with the landscape.

"May the Lawd have mercy on you, Miss D.," he says with a smile. "I know it ain't been the best Christmas yours had."

"How do you know?" I say.

"E'body know," he says, and his grin is wide. "Can't keep a secret round here, when it floatin' down de creek."

I grin back at him, partly ashamed. I wonder what Chambers thinks of us, falling apart after Mee Maw's death.

"Yes'm," he says, "but the Lawd see everything and He merciful."

"That's good," I say. "We could sure use some mercy."

"Be patient wid your daddy," Chambers says. "He's had it tough."

"I know," I say, and I realize Chambers probably knows a lot more about Daddy than I do. He's known Daddy all of his life, from the time he was a debutramp and a stitch to the time Aunt Eliza died.

"What you need from me, sweet?" he says.

"Mama wants to know if you can go over to the toolshed and get rid of the tree."

"Yes'm," he says. "I'll get the truck and tote you over there."

I watch Chambers as he walks around back to his truck. He moves with grace, as steady and fluid as the flow of the creek. Chambers is not big or muscular, but he is sure-footed and at ease, equipped with a strength that comes from a source as down low as a deep water well. Once, when he was in town, I watched him single-handedly haul a piano into my house on Tradd Street after Daddy had thrown out his lower back when he and Will tried it hours before.

And Chambers is brave and calm in the face of danger. Once he was bitten by a cottonmouth in the attic of the main house, and he called clearly down the stairwell to Mee Maw Rose, who drove him to the hospital in Charleston as he sucked the venom out of his arm and spit it into a little Tupperware dish she set on his lap.

❧

When Chambers pulls around, I hop into his old burgundy Ford, and we head on down the dirt road to my house. His truck smells like soap and salt, but I can remember a period of months, years ago, when it smelled like liquor. That was during what Chambers calls the "lost days," when he would sit on the corner stool at Coot's Lounge, drinking bourbon and mistreating women. But the story is that Maum Bess prayed on him so much that one Sunday morning he woke up waist-deep in the Sea of Galilee instead of on his old mildewed mattress at Rose Hill, surrounded by men whose faces blended in with the sun.

According to the story, these men put their hands on him and prayed for the heavy light to enter into him, and the next thing he knew this heavy light *did* enter and brought him back to his bedroom and directed him out of bed, leading him, barefoot and all, down to the Mt. Zion AME Church, where a group of elders were waiting on him at the front door. The congregation, including Maum Bess, followed the elders as they walked Chambers on down to Steamboat Creek, where they covered his head with the dark water so that his sins could be carried away on the outgoing tide.

As Chambers and I pull up to the caretaker's house I say, "Oh, say, have you seen Cousin Eli?"

"Yes'm," he says, "she was at our house for a little while last night 'til her friend come and pick her up."

"Must have been Suzanne," I say.

"Don't know her name, Miss D."

"I'll find her," I say as I watch Chambers walk slowly over to the toolshed, lift up the tree, and gently rest it in the bed of his truck.

Before I know it, he is driving behind the toolshed and out of sight, carrying away the evidence of my family troubles like the creek carried away each one of his lost days in one swift motion.

8

Edges

In less than an hour the Shuzukis are on the dock. They have driven their new golf cart over to the caretaker's house and parked it beside the fish shed. This is the first time I have laid eyes on Mr. Shuzuki since Thanksgiving. He is a small man who wears his pants inches above his waist, and his torso is always slightly arched back when he stands in one place. He is dressed in a starched oxford shirt with blue jeans rolled up meticulously above his ankles and penny loafers with thick wool socks. Mrs. Shuzuki is in a pair of corduroy bell-bottoms with another one of Mr. Shuzuki's starched oxfords tied in a knot at her belly button. She's wearing a large, round straw hat like it was a summer day. Sagi is in bright blue overalls with a Detroit Lions baseball cap and fancy tennis shoes that have red lights in the soles beneath his heels. The lights flash with each step that he takes.

I stand in the middle of the johnboat and help them to their seats. Mr. Shuzuki sits in the seat across from me and Sagi sits with his mother on the inside of the bow. Before I know it the puppy has jumped into the boat, and Sagi is so excited that I figure I'll let him go with us.

"What's his name?" Sagi calls over the motor as we slowly pull out from the dock. I forget his question for a minute as we float by our house and I look toward Daddy's room to see if he's still in bed. He is. Then I spot a green and yellow turban through the trees outside Daddy's bedroom window.

Maum Bess takes one strong stare at me through the trees. Though she is yards away I can see her black eyes bearing down on me, requesting my secrecy. I turn back long enough to see her sprinkling salt on the ground beneath the window, then turn and disappear into the trees. I know she must be praying something for Daddy. And I hope that her prayers work like they did for Chambers, because nothing short of a miracle is going to clear up this Christmas mess.

"Miss DeLoach," Mr. Shuzuki screams over the motor, "watch where you are going."

I whip my head around and see that we are pointed in the direction of an oyster bank, but in less than a second we are back on track, safe in the center of the winding creek.

"Miss DeLoach," Sagi calls, "what *is* the puppy's name?"

"He doesn't have a name yet," I say, and my voice sounds feeble going against the wind, like I'm in the bottom of a well.

"Oh," Sagi says as his short black hair whips backward. He turns to his mother. "The puppy doesn't have a name yet."

She nods and repositions herself. She rubs her hands together over the side of the boat as if she is releasing some invisible grime, and even I have to admit the johnboat is not exactly clean. There are bits of shrimp remains and fish scales in the cracks of the floor, and the seats haven't been washed out for ages. This boat belonged to Will growing up and he spent hours on the bow, throwing the cast net for bait or cutting mullet up into small pieces, which he pierced with a hook before casting his rod.

Daddy used to have a Boston Whaler that he bought for showing property at Otter Island. It had cushioned leather seats and a center console to block the wind. The Shuzukis would have loved that boat because it was brand-spanking new and clean as a whistle. Since the Shuzukis have so much money, I think that *they* should buy a Boston Whaler to be carted around in.

The sun has burned off the fog that hovered over the island. After we wind through the marsh creeks of Rose Hill and

Steamboat, our vision screened by the tall, brown grass, we sputter out into the middle of the North Edisto River, taking in the full view of the Intracoastal Waterway and Wadmalaw Island, our cross-the-river neighbor where farmers grow sweet onions too large for me to pick up with one hand.

The puppy walks to the front tip of the bow, where he lets the wind lift his flappy ears. Sagi crawls toward the puppy, but Mrs. Shuzuki pulls him back and sits him in her lap. I spot two porpoise fins near a bank fifty yards away. I point in their direction, but no one even notices me because of the wind and the motor.

I cup my hand over my mouth and scream, "Where would you like to go?"

Mrs. Shuzuki shrugs and looks to her husband. Then her hat flies off her head, but I catch it in midair and hand it to her. She holds it down in her lap.

Sagi cups his hand and screams back, "I want to go find the alligators."

Mrs. Shuzuki scolds him in Japanese. Her voice is husky and she makes a grunting sound between phrases. I would love to know what she is saying.

I look over to Mr. Shuzuki, whose eyes are closed. He is slowly spreading his arms out and breathing deeply with his mouth in the shape of an O, as if he could inhale the whole scene and tuck it away in the walls of his lungs.

Maybe he's doing some kind of weird Buddhist meditation, I think to myself. If Mama were here she might feel uncomfortable. She might remind him that he is enjoying the use of a boat that belongs to a Christian family.

"Then can we go to Bohicket Marina for a snack?" Sagi asks in the direction of his father. His father does not move. The palms of his hands are open and facing the sky. His fingers are spreading out.

"Daddy?" Sagi screams, and a second later Mr. Shuzuki slowly opens his eyes and looks at Mrs. Shuzuki, who is smiling gently at him.

She talks to him in Japanese, but this time her voice is low and soft, even over the motor.

Mr. Shuzuki turns to me. He motions out to the water and grins. "Paradise," he says.

I nod and smile and look out onto the water and the surrounding islands. There is water and marsh and untouched land as far as the eye can see.

One time I saw the Shuzukis' other addresses in Mama's correspondence book. They have two other dwelling places and both are apartments, one in Detroit and the other in Tokyo, which is where they are originally from and where their extended family still lives. Their homes are numbered 31B and 54G, and I guessed that those places are houses in the sky, surrounded by strangers above and under and beside them, no more than a wall away.

I thought of them last week when I watched a television show about Tokyo. The camera panned the crowded streets of the city where twelve million people cram themselves into small apartments, their ears filled with the sounds of man-made movement—horns and screeching wheels and subway trains—as the threat of earthquakes and cyclones and fire trembles beneath the surface of their minds.

I guess that Mr. Shuzuki wants to tuck this scene away so he can pull it out when he is looking from his apartment down into the crowded streets.

"Can you take us to the marina?" Mr. Shuzuki asks me.

"Sure," I say, turning the wheel to the left as the flat aluminum bottom of the boat crosses the small waves of the river. In no time we are tying up at Bohicket Marina, where Sagi's dad takes him to buy a treat. Mrs. Shuzuki and I stay in the boat and I point at the birds that pass overhead and tell her their names: "wood stork," "osprey," "tern." No one is at the marina except for the man who runs it.

❧

On the ride home, Mr. Shuzuki hands out Tootsie Rolls and Gatorades to all of us. Mrs. Shuzuki puts her hat back on and lets Sagi crawl to the edge of the bow and pick up the puppy, who eventually falls asleep in his lap. Except for the hum of the motor, we are surrounded by quiet, and in a strange way I feel glad to be with them and in the boat and living on this strange island even though it is the worst Christmas Day I've ever had. I'm enjoying this because it's like I'm in another world in their company, or at least I'm seeing *my* world through *their* eyes. And I realize that my world *is* full of wonder. That God's glory is all around us.

Then I try to imagine what Daddy feels like when he is carting the Shuzukis around like this. I wonder if he talks to them like friends, sharing what he knows about his homeland, or if he just drives with his eyes straight ahead, answering questions with as few words as possible.

After we cross the river and head back into Steamboat Creek, I have an idea.

"I'm going to ride you all down to No Name Creek. You can almost always find a porpoise feeding there," I say to them.

"Great," Mr. Shuzuki says and he looks at Sagi. "We are going to see the dolphins."

"Are there alligators?" Sagi asks.

"Could be," I say, "but porpoises are nicer and better-looking than alligators."

"Okay," he says.

I have to be careful as I cut through No Name because it is a narrow creek with mud banks that are hidden when the tide is this high. I hug the land side of the bank because there are oyster beds on the marsh side and the tide is getting lower by the minute. It is a beautiful, cave-like ride. There are great oak trees whose giant limbs stretch out over the water. We wind beneath them, ducking slightly like we're in a jungle.

Suddenly, from beneath the cluster of trees, we hear shouts and hollers from the woods. It is hard for us to tell what kind of shouts they are. We all look at one another because we don't know if we should be concerned.

We are so curious that we stand up in the boat to get a good look over the bank. Through the trees we spot four tall men dressed in camouflage clothes and army-green hats with rifles in their hands. They are surrounding something or someone, but it is hard to tell what. To the left of the men we see a deer hanging upside down, tied to a tree by its hind legs. I can tell it is a buck because of the rack above its head. I count the number of antler points. Eight. A big one.

The buck has been gutted, sliced down the center, and blood is dripping off its neck and into a bucket. One of the men, the tallest, walks over to the pail and picks it up. He steps back into the center of the circle, which has opened enough to reveal a boy, younger than me, maybe twelve. The boy is shirtless, his bottom half cloaked in loose camouflage pants, held up by a thick leather belt, and brown hunting boots that reach his kneecaps. The tallest man dips his fingertips into the bucket of blood and lightly touches the boy's pale cheeks, as if they were Indians preparing for war. The boy, who has had a serious expression up until now, lets a half grin form in the corner of his mouth.

The Shuzukis look to me. My calmness keeps them quiet, but their faces are beginning to ask questions. I am not concerned because I know that this is a common ritual around here, practiced after a boy kills his first deer.

The hunters pause for a moment, then the tall man pours the bucket full of blood over the head of the young boy, who begins to shiver and rub his eyes. They all holler some more and one shoots his rifle into the sky. We watch intently as blood runs down the boy's head into the corners of his mouth and over his chin. It forms thin red fingers that streak his bare shoulders and reach down into the pits of his arms. Then it makes its way toward his belly button, and his camouflage pants begin to soak up the red excess.

I remember now that the last part of the ritual is to cut off the testicles of the deer and tie them around the neck of the young hunter. As I see the tall man walk toward the deer with a knife, I look at Sagi's frightened face. He is stepping from side to side on the bow and the red lights on the heels of his shoes flash at me like danger signals. Quickly, I ask the Shuzukis to sit down. Then I give the johnboat some gas and speed us out of sight.

As we get back to Steamboat Creek I explain the whole ritual to them. They nod and say, "Ooooh," like they understand, but I can tell that they are slightly disturbed by the way Mrs. Shuzuki keeps wringing her hands. As I talk, Sagi curls up beside her, grabbing onto her arm. And Mr. Shuzuki's face has turned a shade of pale green. He is taking big breaths through his nose. I didn't mean to spook them, and I learn a good lesson from this: Pick and choose which cultural experiences to show an outsider. And figure in the sensitive-stomach factor.

Thankfully, we run into a group of porpoises after we turn into Steamboat Creek. The three fins lift out of the water, one right after the other beneath the sun, which is on its way down, hanging in midair between the islands. The sound of the porpoise's air spout reminds me of the sound of a swimmer gasping for air as he speeds down the race lane. This nature encounter is more up the Shuzukis' alley, and before long Sagi has let go of his mother's arm. He is whooping and laughing and saying, "Look." So I lean over the boat and knock on the aluminum bottom and hope that they will come closer. (I've seen Will do this before.)

The porpoises actually turn and swim a little closer. One in the group lifts the whole front of his body out of the water so that we can get a good look at his face and body. "Show-off," I say, and it must be comic relief because we all laugh out loud.

Once, when Daddy, Will, Cousin Eli, and I were returning from a fishing trip, we happened upon a porpoise giving birth. We saw a large fin swimming in a tight circle and watched another porpoise lift a tiny porpoise to the water's surface. When we went home that afternoon, Will pulled out his *Sea Water Encyclopedia* and we learned that three porpoises are involved in the birth process. There's the mother, of course, and she is accompanied by a "midwife," a female who lifts the baby to the water for air just after the birth. The father porpoise, the third member of the party, stands guard by circling the birth mother and the midwife in order to keep any intruders from messing up the process. After the birth, the midwife stays with the family for a year. The four of them swim together in a pack until the baby is large enough to be on his own. Then they all go their separate ways.

I tell this to the Shuzukis and they are fascinated. Sagi starts to count the number of fins in the pack swimming by us. "I think there are four," he says. "I think I see the baby!" Really, I don't see a baby, but who could burst his bubble?

On the ride home, we take the opposite route back in order to avoid No Name Creek. This means we approach Rose Hill Creek from the north instead of the south, and it also means we have to drive by Mary Margaret Davidson's dock. Fortunately, no one is outside. The light of day is fading so all that I can make out is their Suburban, which looks as though they have already taken it to the car wash and it is, once again, spotless. Then I see the white lights of their own Christmas tree through the sliding glass door that faces the creek. The lights grow brighter by the second as the sun sets.

As we curve off Steamboat Creek into Rose Hill Creek, I can see my daddy in the purple twilight. He waves at us and hobbles across the yard and onto the dock to greet us.

He helps Mrs. Shuzuki out of the boat by reaching out for her hand and pulling gently up on her elbow. And it is hard to believe that he is still, in many ways, a gentleman.

"Your daughter did a wonderful job," Mr. Shuzuki tells him.

Daddy winks at me and we stop and let the Shuzukis go ahead and load up into their golf cart and drive off.

As he hobbles off the dock, he says to me, "I really appreciate you doing that, baby. You're a big help, you know that?"

"No problem," I say, pleased that my plan seems to be working already. Then I ask him if he wants to lean on my shoulder and he says that he would like that, and we slowly walk toward our little house where there is smoke billowing from the brick grill beside the fish shed. Mama is placing bowls of cocktail sauce and saltines on the table beside the shucking knives.

"How about some steamed oysters?" Daddy says to me.

Then I see Cousin Eli, who is piling more logs in the bottom of the stove. She waves to me and it is almost like my family is together again. I run over to her.

"Merry Christmas, cuz," she says. "Are you all right?"

"Yeah, are you?" I say.

She nods. "Yes."

"I don't know where you have been, but I'm sure glad that you're here," I say.

"Me too," she says. "Suzanne let me crash at her place."

"Have you talked to anybody?" I ask.

"Yeah, Will called me from the airport."

Will and Cousin Eli have always been close. "What did he say?"

"He's fine, and I think he feels a little guilty for leaving, but he said that he just had to."

"I understand," I say. "I just hope he doesn't give up on Daddy."

She brushes her hands off and whispers, "Well, that's not a hard thing to do these days, but you know he won't."

Before we can really talk, Mama calls to me from the kitchen, "John Henry is on the telephone for you, DeVeaux."

"The first batch is ready, girls," I hear Daddy say. "DeVeaux, can you give me a hand with them?"

"Tell him I'll call him back," I yell to Mama.

As we shuck the oysters, I take pleasure from the familiar feel of the gritty shell in the palm of my hand. I look over at Daddy, who is drowning his oysters in melted butter and then cocktail sauce. He closes his eyes with each bite, grinning.

It is at this moment that I realize Daddy is not even going to mention last night. I think he has decided to ignore what happened—true denial. This is a whole new phase for him. Maybe Maum Bess has prayed a block-out-anything-bad-in-the-past prayer on him to tide him over until she can lift him up to the Lord as she did Chambers, untangling him from the thorns of life.

"Oh, these are good," Daddy says to us.

"Yes, sir," I say back.

Cousin Eli is eating them plain and answering Mama's questions about her classes. She's a special education major, and next year she will student-teach at the Columbia School for the Deaf. With oyster muck on her hands she signs something to Mama that none of us understand, and Mama just laughs and says, "That's wonderful, honey." And I picture Cousin Eli in a room full of deaf kids writing a lesson on the board. I'm happy because I know that teaching will be a good life for her.

She leans over to me and whispers, "That was 'My uncle has a bad temper' in sign language," and we both chuckle without anyone noticing.

Eventually, there are tiny cuts on all my fingers from holding the sharp edges, but the salt from the warm water inside the oyster shell seeps out of the pinched cover, soothing them. To me, shucking is well worth the trouble and the cuts when the tight cover reveals a long, juicy bite like the one I've just gotten into. I cut the oyster out of the shell and suck it off the blade. The delicacy catches in the back of my mouth and slides gently down my throat.

Toward the end of the roast, I drive Cousin Eli back to Suzanne's house, even though Mama kept asking her to please stay with us while Daddy put more logs on the grill and said nothing. However, as we were walking to the car Daddy came up beside us as if he'd just remembered something and said, "Eli, you've got everything you need, right?" He looked her in the eye for an instant before his eye caught a rabbit that was frozen still just behind us.

Eli seemed relieved to be asked. She took a breath and said, "Well, it's hard, Uncle Billy. I'm out of loan money, and I've just been trying to figure out how to get by."

"What about your job at that restaurant?" Daddy looks back at her. Eli has been waiting tables at a fancy restaurant called The Gourmand. Once Mama and I went and had dinner there when we were visiting for her parents' weekend.

"Well, I quit that job. It turned out to be a bad scene, and—" she begins, but Daddy cuts her off.

"You know what we've been going through here," he says, looking around the yard and nodding to the caretaker's house. "These are hard times. Even DeVeaux is working."

I step up as he says this, irritated at him because I know that Eli wouldn't ask if she wasn't truly in need. All I can think to say is, "Eli got me my job, Daddy."

Cousin Eli still looks at his face, though he is looking away at the rabbit. She says, "No problem. I'll find a way to work it out."

"Okay," he says, limping away in relief. "You'll figure it out."

I am infuriated at him once again because I can remember so clearly all the times he gave money to Virginia and Will on their way back to school. I know times are tough, and I know he's done a lot for Eli, but it's like his heart has hardened toward her and I can't understand it.

I gain a spine and walk up to him and say quietly but clearly, "This isn't right. We've got to help her."

He looks at me hard as though I have just switched allegiances. "Stay out of this, child."

And before I decide on a response, he hobbles back to the shed and relights the fire.

❧

On the way home, Cousin Eli rolls down the window and says, "Christmas depresses me."

"Yeah," I say, "well, Billy DeLoach depresses me, and I'm going to talk to him again when I get home."

"Never mind that," she says. "I'm going back to Columbia tomorrow."

"You're leaving for school tomorrow?" I say, shocked.

"Yeah, I found a ride and I have to look for work."

"Already?" I say.

"Yeah, I have to get back, you know?"

"But you hate Columbia," I say, and I know this is true. Eli *hates* Columbia. She is only there because it is the cheapest university in the state. She belongs out here in the country.

"Don't worry, DeVeaux," she says. "I'm fine."

"But we haven't even hung out."

"I know," she says. "I'm sorry about that. I know you're shouldering a lot."

"Yeah," I say, suddenly angry with her, too, "and everyone is just taking off and leaving me here to deal with it all."

When we turn from the island onto the beach, the moon is set low, just above the sea, and sharp chips of moonlight are reflecting off the choppy waves. I can't believe it but I just start to bawl. My temples are pulsing and I am furious and sad, and I don't want to go back to that caretaker's house alone.

Quickly, I turn into the Edisto Realty Company and park beneath the sign. Suzanne lives in a small apartment above the company. Fluorescent kitchen lights spill out her open door.

"I am so sorry, DeVeaux," Eli says, rubbing my shoulders. "I know that things have changed a lot for you this year."

"It's unfair," I say as I nod my head in frustration. Though I know Eli knows all too well about life not being fair, I have to vent. "And I can hardly stand being around Daddy."

She looks up to the apartment and sighs. She whispers, "I know."

"What's going to happen next?" I ask.

She looks to me, then back to the apartment. She pats my knee reassuringly and says, "I'll tell you what is going to happen, DeVeaux, and I think you know it as well as I do. First, everyone will forget about this holiday and by spring life will be on the mend. Virginia is going to marry Clayton and get a real job. Will is going to graduate from MIT and bring Ruth down to South Carolina. And your dad is going to get a grip. He'll figure out some business plan, some scheme to make some money, and he'll get back on his feet. And when he does, they'll send you off to St. Mary's where you can learn about the rest of the world and figure out what *you* want out of life."

"You think?" I ask. "That by spring it will be better?"

I can hang on until spring, I think to myself.

"Yeah, I do," Eli reassures me.

"And what about you?" I say. "I worry about you now that Mee Maw Rose is gone. I know Dad—"

"Don't you worry about me, little cousin. I've been on my own for a long time now. And I'm fine."

Then Eli takes a package out of her backpack and hands it to me. "Just a little something," she says.

I tear off the wrapping paper and see that it is earrings that are bright and seem to be made out of paper. I rub my hands across them.

"I made them myself from Mee Maw Rose's *National Geographic* magazines."

"They are so cool," I say.

"Tape and scissors and glue and that's all there is to it," she says.

"I love them," I say. "Thank you."

Suzanne walks out on the porch with Becky on her hip and waves to us before she walks back inside. Then Cousin Eli hugs me and says, "I'll be in touch. But in the meantime, take care of yourself. This island is different from town. There are some real characters out here, so you'll want be careful like I've told you before."

"I will. I promise," I say, then I reach for my billfold and offer her the tip money from the last few times I worked.

"Don't insult me," she says. "I'm not taking money from my tenth-grade cousin."

Before I can force it on her, Eli gets out of the car, looks back once and waves, then walks up the stairs.

As I drive out of the parking lot and down the road, I see the back of my friend Tina walking down the sidewalk toward the beach. She is with a tall boy whose arms are wrapped tightly around her. I drive up next to them and beep my horn.

"Good golly, DeVeaux," Tina says, "you scared the pee out of us!"

"Sorry," I say.

"Did your mama tell you that I called?"

"No."

"Well, I did. I called three times. Is everything all right at your house?"

Tina is acting strange. Her posture is different, and it seems she is trying to act more grown up than usual. I suspect this is on account of the tall boy. And he isn't exactly friendly. He doesn't even introduce himself. If I didn't know Tina was country and all, I would find her behavior to be downright rude.

"Everything is fine," I say.

"My brother C.C. nearly wrecked into your Christmas tree on his boat ride home from work," she says.

Tina and the boy laugh together at my expense.

"Yeah," I say, "my dad pretty much flipped out, but he'll get over it."

"Hope so," Tina says. "Well, we're on our way to the beach, so I'll call you tomorrow."

"See ya," I say as I watch them cross the road in front of me and head over the dunes.

Before I leave the beach I look back in my rearview mirror and see Cousin Eli sitting at the top of the stairs that lead to Suzanne's apartment. She is smoking a cigarette, staring out into the moonlight.

Sometimes I have what I think are some good questions for God. And tonight, I want to ask Him, "Why would You leave a girl like Eli alone like this?" What I mean is, "What kind of God sends men with sun for faces to give Chambers the heavy light, but leaves my cousin an orphan with no grandmother and no family and no money to pay for school, just sitting there, covered in her own smoke and darkness?"

My tires scrape through the sand in the road as my questions hang like fog in the night air before me. Frustrated and confused I go on to say, "Even though it's Jesus' birthday and all, I am struck by what seems to be Your cruelness."

As I say this the car lurches forward, and I feel ashamed. Who am I to question the God of the universe? The God who has reached down into my life over and over again with love and protection. And there are countless other times He has done it that I'm not even aware of. My peon life that is a blip on the radar screen, and His thumbprints are all over it.

Mist is rising off the ground ahead, and I imagine all the layers of life bedded down in the thickets of the woods, hidden from my eyes. And I wonder how God answers questions. How He speaks. And if I am deaf to His voice.

What I know is that my angry words toward Him have pierced my own chest with guilt, and now I picture my heart spilling out into the blackness of this island night.

༄

I decide to go to youth group the Wednesday after Christmas at Bethany's urging. Chambers gives me a lift. He says that he has to make a trip to the Seed and Feed downtown, but I think he just wants me to be in church. As we pull behind the parental line of cars waiting to pick up the junior high kids whose youth group is just about to let out, I feel a little silly watching all the kids my age drive into the parking lot with their own cars. Chambers finds a way to get around the line and as we drive to the back door of St. Paul's parish house, I scan the lot for Louisa's and Lesesne's cars, but they aren't here yet.

The junior high kids come running past me—hyper and giggly as ever, decked out in their bright plastic jewelry and Barbie-pink blush, sucking Blow Pops and chattering incessantly. Half of the girls are still taller than most of the guys, and more than half of them are still in braces. They shout to one another before slamming the doors of their parents' minivans. Next door to the Parish Hall is Society Hall, where on Wednesday nights Mrs. Hillhouse gives cotillion lessons, and I can hear her shouting out waltz steps over the crackly microphone, "One-two-three, one-two-three, one-two-three." A horse-drawn carriage clomps down Church Street with a cart full of tourists snapping their last photos before the sun goes down, and I am thankful to be back in my church, in my city, where life is moving forward.

As I walk into the back door of the Parish Hall from the alley-way, I'm cradled by the familiar smell of the place—a combination of must and floor wax with a hint of flowers like a sweet-smelling school. There are a few curled-up leaves from a bouquet under the water fountain, so someone must have got married, or died, or had a nice luncheon in the Great Hall last weekend.

I go by the kitchen for a cup of water from the old sink, and I am struck by how much I feel at home in this place. I love the grimy kitchen and the cluttered closets and the leftover junk from events past—like advent wreaths, shepherd's crooks, Easter eggs, and party hats from the Back to Church School Party that takes place every September.

As I look from the kitchen into the Great Hall that adjoins it, I think of all the meals I've eaten here since I was a kid. Hot dogs in December on Christmas caroling night, pancakes at the Shrove Tuesday supper, and an endless supply of Kool-Aid and butter cookies every Sunday morning during church school and every summer during vacation Bible school.

I imagine all the fantastic forms the Great Hall took during those Bible school summers, from an Amazon rain forest to an archaeological dig in Egypt to a great whale, whose mouth we walked through each of the ten days of our summer fantasy, pretending to be Jonah, swallowed whole. I chuckle to myself as I imagine a whale swallowing me up, then spitting me out on the shore once I agreed to God that I would carry out His plan.

At this moment, I am full to overflowing with thanksgiving for this old place. I feel safe here and people have loved me here and God has made His way into my heart here by every cup of Kool-Aid that was poured and handed to me, every pat on the back from Father Dan or a Sunday school teacher, every silly song or relay race or pancake stack that warmed and filled my belly with its thick, sweet sugar.

As I realize what this church has meant to me, I feel as if God's Spirit is whispering, "My hand has always been on your life."

"I know, I know," I say back to Him. "Don't let me forget it, Lord."

I feel so light and joyful that the curmudgeonly organist doesn't even bother me when she grunts and shuts her door in anticipation of the older group of teenagers headed up the stairs to the youth room for another night of pizza, co-cola, and raucous worship.

I catch Father Dan shuffling up the stairs out of the corner of my eye and when I turn to look at him, I glimpse the weight of the world on his shoulders. I know from Sasser that his days are filled with funerals, hospital visits, and broken marriages, and it looks as though these forms of pain are pressing in all around him.

Sasser thinks that the weight of walking through tragedies with parishioners is one of the reasons his mother left. Because in a church, he says, there is always something. Something important that takes the priest away from home. You can't say to death or divorce or the parents of a precious sick child that you can't come see them because you really need to have supper with your family tonight.

"There can always be a kind of tension in a ministry like this," Sasser said, "but the Lord did protect us and gave us a lot of good family time together. Mama just let a bitter root grow in her heart, and its vines ensnared her.

"I think that's why they didn't have any more kids," Sasser said. "In a way, she felt like she was the only one home to raise me—giving her husband up each day to the church just steps from their home in the rectory."

Sasser's mama used to go with Father Dan to pray with people who were sick or brokenhearted, just as she did for my mama when her daddy died. But somewhere along the way she became weary of it all, and she stopped going.

Even before she left, Sasser had taken her place as the one to accompany his dad to the hospital or to the home where a loss had just occurred. He's seen a lot of heartbreaking stuff: a young mother dying of cancer even as she carried her second baby in the womb, a father of five who was hit by a car on his morning jog just yards away from the church, a ten-year-old girl who just didn't wake up one morning, and the list goes on and on.

As I watch Father Dan make his way to his office, I can tell that neither he nor Sasser will ever give up the call God has placed on their lives. No matter how much sorrow or tragedy or death Sasser's dad has to stare down the face of, he will always choose God and choose life, and I believe he will ultimately be blessed by that.

Something makes him turn around, and when he sees me making my way to the youth room he calls out, "That you, DeVeaux?"

"Yes, sir, Father Dan," I say. "Good to see you."

He leaves the key in the door of his office and makes his way toward me. He suddenly gets this little skip in his shuffle like the Holy Spirit has just refreshed him in an instant, and he will make the most of this next ministry opportunity. As he comes closer I see that his clothes look a bit wrinkled and there is a little brown stain on his suit lapel and I imagine it is the Chinese food he and Sasser ate for their Christmas Eve supper.

"I've missed seeing your daddy 'round town. How's he doing?"

"He's keeping busy at Rose Hill, taking care of the plantation and all."

"Will you tell him I asked after him?"

"I will," I assure him.

"And look out for my boy upstairs," he says, referring to Sasser. "This year has been hard on him."

"Yes, sir," I say. "But he's a strong one. Whatever happens, he'll be okay."

"Thanks, DeVeaux," he says to me, and he swallows hard like he is either about to choke or burst into tears. As he darts back into his office door before I have a chance to say good-bye, I see the frayed ends of his left pant leg where the hem has come undone and though it may be a sexist thought, I know that a man without a wife to look after him can become a pretty pitiful sight.

❧

The youth room is on the third floor of the church. It has become more orderly since Bethany joined the staff with Stu. Her predecessors were all males who were young-looking and acting, with a passionate faith and their eyes set on seminary.

But even with Bethany's feminine touch on the place, there are still ground bits of popcorn and coke spots all over the tan floor from years of Bible studies and lock-ins, and there is masking tape with remnants of a yellow streamer from a bygone party here and there at the tops of the walls. Old Bibles are stacked high behind the three lopsided couches that form a square with the large TV screen. The stereo blares Christian rock music from punctured speakers, the music spilling out the windows and over the great historic graveyard that leads to the sanctuary.

When I walk in Bethany gives me a tight hug and Sasser is right behind her. Stu is flipping furiously through a worn-out Bible, reviewing his talk for the night. Sasser pulls me away from Bethany, points to a chair toward the back of the room, and says, "Sit here with me." As I take my seat, Sasser loads a paper plate with pizza slices and we gulp them down as the rest of the gang trickles in.

"So how's it going?" I ask him. He looks a little disheveled, too, in an oversized pair of blue jeans and a long-sleeved T-shirt that must have originally been white but is now a pale shade of grayish blue. But his face is clean and his eyes are still full of that light and fervor that make up Sasser. When I see him I always think of a verse I memorized for a Tootsie Pop in Sunday school in fifth grade that reads: *"The lamp of the body is the eye. Therefore, when your eye is good, your whole body also is full of light" (Luke 11:34 NKJV).*

"I was a little discouraged until today, you know? I mean, I've been praying for eleven months now that Mama would come home by Christmas, and she seems as far away as ever."

"I'm sorry, Sasser," I say. "Did you talk to her at all over the holiday?"

"Last week she invited me to come up to D.C. to spend Christmas with her and Snake." (Jake is his real name—the man she ran off with.)

"She said, 'You know Jake is rather agnostic, but we can go ice-skating and tour the Smithsonian or the White House. And it might snow . . . Can you imagine that?'" he says, imitating her in a kind of singsong voice.

"So what did you say back?" I ask.

I said, "'First, I'm not going to spend one of the most sacred days of the church year in a place where little is sacred. And second, I'm not going to leave Dad here alone to preach four services in a row on Christmas Eve and Christmas Day only to come home to an empty house with a fake Christmas tree and leftover Chinese food in the fridge for supper.'

"Of course, I didn't say it that eloquently, DeVeaux. I'm just dreaming about how I could have said it," he says. "I guess I just said, 'No, I need to be here.'"

"So are you ever going to go see her?"

"I don't know. Dad made me call her back and tell her I'd come sometime, but I don't want to see it—her life there. I'm afraid it would tear me up.

"When I called her back she said, 'Come in March when the cherry blossoms are in bloom.'

"'I don't care about the cherry blossoms,'" I said to her.

Now I can't help but chuckle at Sasser's hint of resentment that his mama's strange new life would have any beauty to speak of in it.

"What then?" I ask.

"'I care about you, Mama,'" I said to her. "'When are you going to snap out of this and come home?'"

"Sasser," his dad had said, overhearing the conversation. "Don't speak to your mother that way." Then he grabbed the phone and said, "Ella, this holiday has been hard on him; maybe you should call him back tomorrow."

"I haven't talked to her since," Sasser says, crumpling up the paper plate and throwing it across the room into the trash can by the door.

"Nice shot, Sas," says Bethany.

"Well, you know," Sasser says, "Coach Watkins did ask me to try out for the basketball team."

And we all laugh at Sasser's expense because he's a little shorter than most of the guys in the room.

"So what happened today to make you feel better?" I ask.

"Well, I went to the White Point Gardens park by the water and prayed for a long time today. And I felt God's presence in a powerful way, and I just believe that He is preparing me for something."

"Like the gift of healing?" I ask, because aside from his mama coming home, that is Sasser's heart's desire.

"I hope so," he says, "but I can't say for sure. It's just that I knew He was there and He was real, and He has something in particular for me, and all I have to do is wait and trust."

"Wow," I say. "That's pretty awesome."

"I know," he says, looking at me intently with his bright eyes. "There's something for you, too, DeVeaux."

"You think?"

"I know," he says, and as I ponder this, someone turns off the music and Bethany begins her announcements. Stu puts on his umbrella hat and break-dances behind her to get our attention, and we all crack up when she pushes him over in midstride.

As I look around the room I see that Louisa and Lesesne are not there, and Sasser says they have not been coming for several weeks. Seems that is a typical trend among upperclassmen. We are forced to attend youth group by our parents through confirmation in seventh grade, then we are hooked and enjoy it and continue on through ninth or tenth grade. But when the pulls of the outside world of high school become too strong, with boys and parties and club after club, we abandon church altogether.

So tonight it's Bethany, Stu, Sasser, and I who are left, along with some nerds and basically shy people from Cooper Hall and Christ Church School. And there is one hilarious boy named LeBruce who goes to public school and is a true class clown. He has his own little monkey dance that he performs from time to time in front of the TV screen or on top of one of the small-group tables, and while Bethany and Stu can hardly contain him, they are happy he is here because the room is never quiet when he's present.

Bethany's announcement reveals that she and Stu are cooking up an irresistible plan to get the lost crowd (Louisa, Lesesne, and the rest) back. They are offering a six-week study about relationships that would include Bible study on the differences between the two genders, dating, and sex.

I think their theory is that if they can get the girls like Lesesne and Louisa to come back, then the boys will eventually follow too. John Henry Drayton and his crew haven't been back since confirmation. But I just don't get how Louisa and Lesesne could do without an evening of Bethany's friendship and Stu's hilarious antics. He makes faces in the corner while Bethany gives information about an upcoming Habitat for Humanity trip to Younge's Island and a lock-in at the ice palace with three hundred other teenagers from churches all around Charleston.

Stu pipes in at this one and says he promises to eat a live goldfish if everyone in the room signs up for the lock-in, and he'll pay our way into the next paintball war if we bring an unchurched friend.

"And I'll eat one too," LeBruce calls out, "if you bring two friends."

"You're on," Sasser says, and Le Bruce begins his howler monkey call and even the section of nerds can't contain their laughter.

"That goes for the relationship class too!" Bethany says.

After Bethany gives an opening prayer, Stu begins his teaching by handing us each a bar of soap with our name on it and flipping furiously through a little book that he's been reading titled *Simply Jesus* by Joseph M. Stowell. The sandwich board at the front of the room reads "A Clean, Fresh Start," and Stu instructs us on how to get clean and back with God. Like a bath, he says, it involves getting naked, but instead of hopping into the tub, we must come bare before the cross and repent for all the ways we have not only rebelled but missed the mark of God's will—our shortcomings and the dirt we have managed to pick up along the way. Once we do this, Stu reminds us, He will clothe us with the most radiant bathrobe that ever existed and that robe will be our ticket into the throne room of God, where we can meet Him face-to-face and live in fellowship with Him from this day forward.

"Who or what else in this world can do those things for you?"

Stu asks. "Who can forgive you, wash you clean, put on a super-natural bathrobe, and allow you into the throne room of God?"

"Jesus is the answer," he says. "Let Him drape you with the bathrobe of His righteousness. And here is the ultimate bonus, guys: Once we are wearing this bathrobe, we are guaranteed our resurrection from the dead. And that doesn't just mean life in heaven after we die, which is unfathomably awesome in and of itself, but it also means resurrection in our daily lives here. Resurrection from the little bits of death we suffer every day that come in all kinds of forms: cruelty, heartbreak, sickness, and pain."

Yep, that's me, I think, picturing the crushed-up sea life that makes up the pluff mud. *My whole world is framed with little bits of death.*

Then Stu gets personal and talks about a drug problem he had in high school and college, which we all knew about.

"I didn't deserve anything," Stu says, "but once I watched a close friend land himself in the hospital after overdosing, I got down on my knees and asked for forgiveness, and I got help from good people to work through my addiction.

"God infused me with His light and has given me the privilege of teaching you guys, some of whom are the age that I was when I first started using, and now I am your youth minister," he says, rubbing some beads of sweat off his forehead. "That is resurrection in the here and now, guys. And whatever pains you have suffered, it is there for you, too, if you choose to get naked before the cross, accept the bathrobe of glory, and walk into the throne room."

I love the image of putting on the radiant bathrobe and coming into God's throne room. It is something I can see in my mind's eye—the throne room. It is a warm and glorious place and I am just a tiny speck before it, but once the robe is on me I am notice-able before Him.

"Wow," I say, turning to Sasser.

"Don't get amnesia on this one, DeVeaux," he says, prodding my side.

"It's true," Sasser says, "that resurrection stuff. So many of the families we've watched go through tragedies have had a new life on the other side of their troubles, if they turned toward God."

"Maybe your parents' marriage will have a resurrection," I say to Sasser.

"I hope so," he says. "I'm just still in shock that it ever died."

After Stu's talk we break up into small groups to share our New Year's resolutions. I was in a group with LeBruce, Bethany, and a quiet guy from Christ Church School named Reese, who was slowly ripping open the paper on his bar of soap. We all wrote down our resolutions and shared them with one another.

This is what I wrote:

1. To start believing what I know in my heart is true about God.

2. To love my parents in this difficult time. Even my Dad, who is somewhat off his rocker.

3. To not be ashamed of what has happened to my family or try to hide it.

At the end of the night, Bethany and Stu check in with me. I tell them about the Christmas tree incident and they are distressed, then laugh about it with me.

"I just can't tell if my dad is a bad guy or a good guy anymore," I say to them.

"Yeah," Stu says, patting me on the back, "but DeVeaux, none of us are good guys, you know? Only Christ."

"I know," I say, and before I finish Stu interrupts: "I'm not say-ing that makes your situation any easier, and if you ever find that it is an abusive one, let us know. I'm just saying try to look at your dad through the eyes of Christ. Be merciful and patient with him. That might help."

Bethany drives me the whole fifty miles back to Edisto without the sigh that most folks would have given. We listen to some music and chat a bit about my worry for Cousin Eli and how to deal with that and when we finally pull up to Rose Hill, she looks in the backseat and pulls the box from last week marked "Christmas gifts from God" that they used at youth group. She tells me there are a few left and she wants me to take one. I pull one out and it has the words "Answered Prayer" in bold at the top of a red piece of construction paper with a candy cane taped to it. It's Christ's words from the Gospel of John: *I tell you the truth, anyone who has faith in me will do what I have been doing. He will do even greater things than these, because I am going to the Father. And I will do whatever you ask in my name, so that the Son may bring glory to the Father. You may ask me for anything in my name, and I will do it"* (14:12–14).

"So this is true?" I ask Bethany.

"I think it is, DeVeaux."

"But I've prayed for my family to not be so broken and for us not to lose our house, and that didn't happen."

Bethany looks out into the blackness and takes a big breath, and I know that she wants to get this explanation just right.

"The story's not over yet," she says to me, looking me straight in the face with her kind eyes. "Don't you give up in the middle of the story or forget all that you know is true."

"But *when* will it be better?"

"Only God knows, but I'm praying that by spring you'll have a new hope," she says to me.

"Spring?" I say excitedly. "You're the second person who's said that."

"Just have *hope*," she says, "and wait patiently on Him."

I nod and close the door, and as I hear Bethany's car make its way over the muddy ruts in our road I am suddenly overwhelmed by her willingness to drive me all the way out here at the end of a long night. Why does she take the time to care for me like this? And Sasser, too, for that matter? Other than my mom, no one has ever cared for me like this.

The puppy is out on the porch, chewing on one of Daddy's hunting socks, and Easy greets me with her coos, asking me to let her in. I see her two green pupils before I make out her body. The puppy whines when he catches my scent, and the dark sky opens up and it begins to rain. I stand in the rain for a moment, imagining that the Lord is washing me clean like the waters of baptism. Then I run into the dark house, where my parents are already asleep. I put my New Year's resolutions on the bedside table and pray that Bethany will have a safe trip home and that Sasser would get the gift of healing and that his mama's heart would change and that she would come back home to them.

By spring, I silently say to the Lord. *Let us be in a better place by then.*

9

JO

It took us three weeks to name the puppy. And since I seemed to be the only one who was disturbed by the fact that the puppy did not have a name, it was my job to find him one.

I settled on "Flounder." A good low-country name. I settled on this because one day when the dog and I were sitting on the dock, he jumped into the water after a school of mullet and came out with a good-eating-size flounder in his mouth. I brought the fish in to Mama, who laughed while she cleaned it and then fried it on up and served it for dinner with grits and corn bread.

Now Flounder thinks he belongs to me. He follows me around wherever I go. I get frustrated because he still doesn't respond to his name, but I keep calling him by it over and over, hoping he'll catch on.

Every night Flounder sleeps at the foot of my bed, on the opposite side of a space he leaves for Easy the cat, whom Daddy has grown to dislike so much that he throws her out each evening when he comes in from working the fields.

I secretly let Easy back in after I hear Daddy snoring, because I hate the thought of her roaming around in the frost-covered fields while Flounder yawns and stretches in the warmth below my feet. In the morning I let her out my window and Daddy never knows the difference.

Now it is the end of January, and it's downright cold. Daddy keeps a fire going anytime we are in the house because the heater doesn't work too good. And Chambers wears his gloves even when he's operating the warm gears of the tractor.

The Shuzukis are back in Michigan, but their presence cannot be forgotten as contractors and carpenters come to and from the plantation house, renovating and adding on. These workmen drive down from Charleston or up from Savannah, carrying thick glass for the panes of the new sunroom and screens for a new back porch. And once we saw some men unloading a hot tub that had eight seats and multiple jets. Mama and I were so curious about this that we went into the house after the workmen had gone and saw that the Shuzukis are putting the hot tub on the rooftop after they cut a hole in the slate that Edmund Seabrook Rose laid down himself in 1810.

A few weeks ago Mama and I ran into Duncan Bell, a famous resort architect from Greenville whom Mama used to date in high school. Duncan Bell has designed the most famous houses on Hilton Head Island. He has come to Rose Hill to draw up a new floor plan for the Shuzukis that, in his words, "will preserve the history of the plantation while creating a modern floor plan for practical family living."

Mama and I ran into him one day when our truck got stuck in the mud on the dirt road home. Duncan found us and drove us in his fancy car, a new car called a Lexus, to Walterboro, where he bought us a link chain at the Wal-Mart and tied it to his trunk and pulled us out of the mud.

The Lexus had heating vents in the backseat, and I turned them on full blast until my eyes dried up and it took me a few seconds before I could get a full blink. (Our truck doesn't have such great heat, either.)

Also, when we were in Walterboro, Duncan took us to a café called "Warm Your Soul," which sits next to the Wal-Mart. He took us there because Mama was having one of her wheezing spells and said that a hot drink would clear her up. I ordered hot chocolate, he ordered an espresso, and Mama ordered a kind of herbal tea for breathing of a brand called Zen. The package had a picture of a yoga position for breathing on the front, but Mama was having too much trouble catching her breath to worry about partaking of a non-Christ-centered beverage.

After Duncan pulled us out of the mud, our truck wouldn't start and he had to get the jumper cables out of his trunk and jump us. At this point, we were quite embarrassed. When he fixed us up, he walked from his car over to the truck. Mama rolled down the window and he said, "Are you okay, Dee?"

"Yes, of course," Mama said, and she didn't seem to notice the concerned look that he was giving her.

"Thank you so much," she said to him, then, "We better be heading back home."

Then he just nodded and said, "Take care." And I could only imagine how strange it must have been for him to see Mama in such a different lifestyle from the one she'd grown up in—a life with drivers, and cooks, and carefully pruned gardens, and brand-new cars that ran smoothly down the freshly paved Greenville roads.

Mama, of course, was oblivious to all of this. She just smiled and said, "One way or another, DeVeaux, the Lord provides."

And I hoped that she was right.

❧

Despite our periodic troubles with the truck, Mama gets out of Rose Hill when she can. She still attends church, Junior League meetings, and even the exclusive Charleston Garden Club, which she was invited to join because Mee Maw Rose was one of the founders.

Mama has accepted an offer to lead next year's First Place program at St. Paul's (even though she has gained five pounds since Christmas) because she says that it's important to stay connected with the Charleston community.

She often shows Daddy invitations they have received for

Charleston social events such as the Jenkins wedding or the winter ball at the Hibernian Hall. Daddy grunts when he sees them and says, "We don't have time to think about parties." But Mama continues to place the invitations under the magnets on the refrigerator, silent reminders of another life.

So we have good days and bad days during our first winter at Rose Hill and though Mama and I have never discussed it, we are both trying hard to make Daddy better. And on the whole, he seems to be in much better spirits.

At least two nights a week he suggests playing gin rummy with me. I always say yes and together we sit at the kitchen table, and he lets me win a game or two a night.

One time we were so cold playing gin rummy that Mama took two pairs of old gloves and cut off the fingertips so that our hands could be warm and we could maneuver the cards. We really looked like a couple of bums and we both laughed at the sight of us while the fire popped and crackled behind our backs.

Daddy had a good hunting day a few weeks back, which seemed to do him even more good. He shot a twelve-point deer right on the edge of the gall, and he and Chambers cut it up and sent a good portion of the meat to a halfway house in Ravenel that always needs food.

For days we ate venison: pot roast, spaghetti, meat and macaroni casserole, while Daddy speculated about how they might be cooking it at the halfway house. Mama commended him on being a good neighbor and an old-fashioned hunter-gatherer just like the Edisto Indians who were the original owners of the island, providing for his family and all. He liked it when she said this. I know because I watched his hand go under the table and squeeze her knee. She giggled warmly in return.

But I have to say that the most notable upturn with Daddy was the day after he recovered from the Christmas gout and started cleaning out the teahouse. That day he came across an old Sunfish sailboat that he has now set in the toolshed where he is fixing it up. It was the old boat that he and his sister, Eliza, bought together when they were young. In that boat they learned to navigate the waters before they were ever allowed to drive boats with outboard motors. They sailed it in front of the Carolina Yacht Club in the Charleston harbor and out in these Edisto creeks. He says they spent half of their childhood sitting on the hull, feeling out the wind.

The boat had been fixed up once before by Aunt Eliza just before her death. But it sat for too long in the water after she died because no one could bear to move it. Now it is covered with algae and barnacles that are difficult to get off, but Daddy spends hours each day trying. Sometimes it worries Mama that Daddy is pouring so much energy into something that seems futile and has so much to do with a part of the past that ended in tragedy, but her happiness that he now has a project and is being productive outweighs her worrying.

We do not discuss the Christmas tree incident. We do what we have to do to wrap the whole thing up: collect the ornaments, file insurance papers, talk to neighbors who inquire, but we do not mention it among one another or to the rest of the family—Will, Eli, and Virginia—who have all started the new year as satellites once again in their faraway lives, relieved, I presume, to be a long distance from the unrest at home base.

As for me, I have been working at the restaurant and going to my run-down school where I reread books and redo assignments I did years ago at Cooper Hall. On Wednesdays, Chambers makes up some excuse to come to town and gives me a lift to youth group and Bethany brings me home. And sometimes, Mama takes me to Charleston where I hook up with the old gang.

No one in Charleston seems to know about the Christmas tree incident, which means that the Davidsons really know how to keep their mouths shut. This gives me a new kind of respect and liking toward Mary Margaret Davidson, and sometimes I get the urge to call her up or invite her to youth group, but then I am repelled by her sneezy aura, and I just can't do it. I'm still as gutless as ever, I suppose.

Most every one of my Charleston buddies has a driver's license now and brand-new cars with cell phones and loud radios. I try to buy the CDs of their favorite music, but to be honest, the music hurts my head and makes me feel edgy. It is all screams and pounding. What I really like is country music, the kind they play in the kitchen at the restaurant.

Once when my Charleston girlfriends piled into my truck and heard what station I had the radio tuned to they said, "DeVeaux, you aren't turning country on us, are you?"

But I can't help it. I have been humming the Garth Brooks song "Every Woman," which Jeeter played over and over on New Year's Eve at Sal's restaurant. I had a great time that night, even though Sal was being sleazy by ordering a stripper from north Charleston. C.C., my friend Tina's half brother, ushered me out onto the back porch when the stripper came and offered me a cigarette, which I took and pretended to smoke, coughing my way through when I inhaled by accident. He said, "You don't want to be a part of any of that."

"You're right," I said. "I don't really want to smoke, either, but of all the teenage vices I suppose this isn't the worst one I could try."

C.C. grinned. "You're somethin' else," he said.

Then we just sat there by the Dumpster and commented on Mr. Lumpkin's yard next door. It had little yellow flags all over it where he is relandscaping and planting a whole new garden for the spring. All the lights were off in his house.

When the clock struck midnight, Jeeter came back to the porch and poured C.C. and me some champagne. As he offered me some, I put up my hand to protest, but C.C. stepped in for me. "You know she doesn't drink," he said to Sal, then he whispered to me, "And I don't want to be the guy you had your first smoke *and* your first drink with."

"Thanks," I said.

Then he walked me to the car where he gave me one quick peck on the cheek. He smelled like the kitchen, salty and soapy, and this smell stuck with me on the drive home in the darkness.

So maybe I am turning country and losing my manners out here, but I have to say that the Charleston folks are losing their manners too. It's funny how the same boys who went to cotillion with us for three years, presenting us to Mrs. Hillhouse as we entered the Southern Society ballroom and fetching us co-colas from the refreshment table during our breaks between the waltz and the fox-trot, are now acting like jerks. These same boys are now always talking about "hooking up" and "catching a feel," as if we had suddenly turned from "Miss DeLoach, Miss Townsend, and Miss Murray" into inanimate objects consisting only of legs, breasts, and other body parts, for which the boys have supplied names that turn my stomach. They no longer refer to us as young ladies or even girls. Now we are "party cats." How ridiculous!

On weekend nights, my friends congregate at the end of undeveloped cul-de-sacs in Mt. Pleasant neighborhoods, where they drink beer and go off into the woods or into the backseats of cars. If their parents are out of town, they will congregate in those houses and split up into bedrooms where they make out in the darkness all night, the boys counting the bases on their hands while the girls decide what to let them touch.

Once, my best friend Louisa Townsend went with Peter Jenkins, a boy we've known all of our lives, and hooked up with him in her baby brother's bedroom when her parents were at a church retreat. They made out so long on her brother's bed that the frame broke in two and Louisa came downstairs and cried to the girls, while Peter laughed and told the other boys in detail how far he had gotten.

When I discuss my frustration about the Charleston boys with my sister, Virginia, she says, "Don't worry. They'll be opening the car door again after they turn eighteen and realize that it's cool to be a gentleman." But then she frowns and says cynically, "They'll open the car door and then they'll still try and move to second base, and things will be even more confusing."

༄

My supposed boyfriend, John Henry Drayton, can't decide if he's going to be a jerk or not. He continues to stand up when I enter or exit a room, but whenever we are alone, he just moves real close to me and tries to kiss me, and the one time that I let him, his hands were all over me before I could say, "Boo." The whole experience was more clumsy than rough, but it infuriated me because it was all so goal-oriented, and therefore unpleasant and unromantic.

When I think about it, my feelings toward John Henry are stronger when I'm daydreaming with my girlfriends about him than when I'm actually with him. My idea of romance is walking by John Henry's house with Louisa and Murray and seeing his muddy sneakers sitting on his front stoop and having a discussion with the girls about where he's been to get in such a mess. Or driving by the horse lot in my Cooper Hall car pool and catching a glimpse of his jersey during junior varsity football practice, turning my head away when he looks toward our car. Or staying up late at Louisa's house, watching some heart-wrenching movie about lost love and imagining that it is John Henry and me on the grainy screen, saying good-bye to each other for the last time before one of us is consumed by cancer or gets hit by a car.

Maybe I'm a late bloomer, but the truth is I just don't feel like being pushed into some little brother's room when the parents are out of town to give myself away beneath Power Ranger sheets. I am almost certain that I am right in thinking this way, but sometimes I worry that I am falling behind my friends and their love lives, that I am missing something I ought to have by now—some passion for John Henry that hasn't yet surfaced.

Two encouraging things happened on this subject. First, I shared my thoughts with Bethany, and she had been getting the same report from other girls who were uncomfortable with all of the heavy making out going on at the teenage gatherings. So, Bethany is tweaking her earlier plan to get the lost girls back and combining it with a plan to keep the found girls pure through a study she's re-created for the month of February titled "Relationships." The study is going to outline what a godly dating relationship could and should look like.

Then I am relieved and affirmed when Louisa calls and invites me to a good old-fashioned slumber party. "Great," I say to her on the telephone, "just like when we were in middle school, huh?"

"Yeah," she says, and we laugh about the time we ate so much raw chocolate-chip cookie dough that we were doubled over in our sleeping bags with pain and had to take long trips to the bathroom.

So all week I look forward to some girl time without the pretense and anxiety that the girls have around the boys. *It will be nice*, I think to myself, *to have a simple night where the greatest stress will be the nervous glee of gossiping or the fear that we're running out of chocolate ice cream.*

Friday afternoon Mama drives me to Louisa's house on Gibbes Street and as we reach a stop sign near her neighborhood, I am suddenly aware of the sound of our muffler banging against the fender and the large dent from the deer in the center of the grille that is causing the hood to rust.

I peer around the manicured yards of the homes that line the streets, with their freshly painted piazzas and polished brass door knockers and plaques spelling out each home's historical significance, and it seems even the flower boxes are smirking at Mama and me, and I hope she will drop me off quickly so that none of my friends will see me in this junk mobile.

It is weird to sit here and feel the shame rising up in my face as the muffler drones on. I know that everyone knows what has happened to my family, but the sight of our truck in the middle of this pristine neighborhood is too much for me. It's not that I want a new car like my girlfriends; it just feels strange to know that suddenly my life is quite different from theirs, and it will likely remain that way. There are differences between me and my downtown friends that are too apparent to ignore in the bright sunlight of Gibbes Street.

Instead of a quick getaway, we get stuck behind a school bus on the corner of Louisa's street and a few of my girlfriends drive up in their bright cars in the opposite direction and wave at me as they walk toward the Townsend home, carrying their monogrammed overnight bags, their new car keys gleaming like mercury between their fingers.

It takes several minutes for the students to get out of the bus as we rattle and shake behind it. Then I realize that it is the bus for handicapped students, and they are bringing home Sara Baker, a girl who was once a kindergarten classmate of mine and was suddenly diagnosed with Reye's syndrome at the age of five.

I can remember my mother recounting the story of how Sara Baker had the chicken pox and a high fever and when she took the normal dose of baby aspirin, she inexplicably went into a coma. Days later when she came out of it, she appeared to have suffered severe brain damage and was never coherent again. I can still picture her cubbyhole at Cooper Hall with her finger painting of the

Morris Island lighthouse thumbtacked to the side and her bright yellow rain jacket hanging limp on the hook. They warned us at school that year about the disease that seemed to take over when children took aspirin for a virus and so when I got the chicken pox, and my fever rose, Mama made me take an ice bath three times a day until my fever went down. Ironically, I got pneumonia from the ice baths, and Mama had to rush me to the hospital where they gave me a shot that seemed as long as my forearm. It must have made me better because I was back in school the next week, where I learned that Sara Baker would never be back.

As she rolls down the bus ramp toward her mother, we see that she is dressed in clothes a kindergartner would wear, a smocked yellow dress with a white ruffled collar, thick white tights and tiny red leather shoes with gold buckles on each side. Her head is as large as a fifteen-year-old's, but her delicate body is still the size of a five-year-old's, and her feet are as small as the palm of my hand.

As I watch the bus driver come behind her and roll her toward the front door, I remember how my friends and I used to go to Sara Baker's house to pay her a visit when our mothers coaxed us, and every year until we were eleven we attended a birthday party for her. The only expression or sound she made during these visits happened right when we arrived. Her mother told us to walk up to her and say "Hello, Sara Baker!" and when we did, she would respond by throwing her head back and cooing, softly but joyfully, with a great grin across her face. Her mother said that was the only signal anyone ever received from her, but it was enough to know that she was in some way aware.

"Lord, that woman is a saint," Mama says as Mrs. Baker comes out to greet her daughter. She takes the handles of the wheelchair from the bus driver, kisses her daughter, and rolls her up the ramp onto the front piazza. Before I respond to Mama, before I say, "How come we don't go see Sara Baker anymore?"

the bus drives on its way, and my previous shame kicks in so fast that I jump quickly out of the truck, and wave my mother off so I can get inside before my friends or Louisa's parents come out to greet us in our hunk of junk.

As my body makes the mad dash away from the truck, my mind is still thinking about Sara Baker. I wonder why our mothers stopped making us go and visit her or why we never just decided to go for ourselves . . . to do something nice like that. I decide I will bring it up to my friends tonight, when we're deep into our conversations about life (an inevitability at slumber parties, which I adore). I'll suggest that after breakfast the next morning we go right over there and see Sara Baker, and show her and her mom that we are still thinking about them.

Mrs. Townsend throws open the door and welcomes me in while remaining on the phone with a client. She has just gone back to work as a real estate agent after twelve years of being a full-time mom, and Louisa says she's doing as well as Dr. Townsend, who is a heart surgeon at the medical university.

As I walk through the dining room and living room, I am struck for the first time by the beauty and extravagance of the Townsend home. Of course, I've been in it many times, but I guess I never really examined it until now. There are paintings with ornate, gilded frames on the walls, cream-colored silk draperies with yellow silk tassels that line each window, and in the dining room there are three antique bureaus with cases of china, crystal, and silver trays and goblets. Bernard, their black Lab since we were children, died last year, and I miss him coming up and licking my fingers, his black hair clinging to our clothes and collecting in the corners of the hardwood floors. In his absence, each corner of each room is clean and shiny, and part of me wants to take my shoes off and slide across it in my socks.

In the distance I hear the rumble of our truck as it makes its way down the street. My friends must hear it, too, because they peek out from the kitchen and gesture for me to come on in.

Louisa grabs me by the wrist and pulls me into the kitchen where the rest of the girls are drinking co-colas and eating M&Ms. The gang includes Lesesne Murray, Sally Sanders, Nan Rutledge, and Kendra Riddlehoover (a striking and promiscuous girl who floats in and out of our group, abandoning us for the class above when the opportunity presents itself).

After Mrs. Townsend leaves the room, Louisa whispers in my ear, "Kendra slipped the key to my basement to Dewey Mason, and he has five guys spending the night with him."

"Really?" I say, trying to mask my disappointment, because I know what is coming. *So much for a simple night with the girls*, I think to myself.

"So they're going to sneak out around 2:00 a.m.," Kendra says, confidently crushing an M&M between her teeth before leaning her alarmingly large breasts on the counter and looking off in another direction.

Sally giggles nervously and says, "John Henry is spending the night with Dewey too."

"Oh," I say and Louisa, still focusing on her adoration for Peter Jenkins, adds, "You-know-who will be there too." And I just can't believe that she is interested in him after how he treated her the other weekend—kissing and telling and laughing at her.

Instead of telling goofy jokes and having quality girl talk, the rest of our afternoon is spent strategizing about the night, predicting the sleeping patterns of Dr. and Mrs. Townsend and the route the boys will take through the alleys and backyards to reach the basement door.

Kendra Riddlehoover is in charge of the show. I suppose part of this is because she is more experienced than the rest of us, and the other part is because she is so developed and striking that the

girls are simply in awe of her. She has deep red hair that practically reaches her hips, and she was one of the first to wear a bra
back in sixth grade. Since that time her breasts have remained the
largest in our class, like grapefruit in an orchard of tangerines.
Boys are always staring at them, and she seems proud of that fact
because she usually wears low-cut, tight shirts that accentuate
them to the point that even the girls can't help but notice. She's
attended parties with upperclassmen from Christ Church School
and Wando High School, and one night at one of the cul-de-sac
parties, she drank six beers and kissed a Wando senior who is the
point guard of the basketball team.

With Kendra at the helm, there will be little of the kind of relax-
ing fun I was yearning for. Everything in our conversations is based
on the expectations of the night, and even when Dr. Townsend
overcooks our hot dogs and Sally, who is a little clumsy, spills
mustard down her new white sweater set, no one laughs or makes
a joke. And late into the evening, instead of talking about what
is really going on in our lives, we watch horror movies that
Kendra has stolen from her stepfather's collection, *Carrie* and *A
Nightmare on Elm Street* and *Friday the 13th*, each of which
makes me slightly nauseous.

At 3:00 a.m., in the middle of the third movie, just as my sleeping bag is warming up on the basement floor and I am no longer
fighting the urge to sleep, we hear a tap at the door.

It is the boys and they are laughing and making faces through the
basement window. Louisa hits my shoulder in excitement to rouse
me. "They're here!" she says, and she is elated. She's been in the
bathroom every hour to touch up her makeup and brush her hair.

As they open the door, Kendra takes her place in the entrance.
"Get in here," she says boldly to them, and Louisa stands just
behind her, saying, "Yeah."

The guys are loud, their lips glossy and their faces flushed from the cold and whatever they've been drinking. They sway from side to side, recounting a story of how Peter Jenkins ran into a mailbox on their way over, which caused an old man, Mr. Dunleavy, to come to the front door with his rifle. They tell this story over and over, making their places in between us on the sleeping bags, except for Peter, who is over in the corner flirting with Nan, and I can tell that Louisa is hurt and angry.

Eventually Dewey climbs into the sleeping bag with Kendra, and one of the other boys turns the lights off and the movie on.

John Henry guides me to a little storage closet beneath the basement steps where there are old cans of paints, garden tools, and a small stack of firewood. We talk for a little while about school and our families, then he leans in to kiss me. It is a sweet kiss at first, but before I can come up for air, he starts to grab me all over, and I pull away, annoyed.

"What's wrong, DeVeaux?" he says, a hint of frustration in his voice. He puts his hands on my shoulders, and though it's dark I can tell that he's got those worry lines on his forehead. "What is it?" he says.

"I don't know," I say, reaching back to the fire logs for balance, and all I can think about is a guest speaker that Bethany brought to youth group one night who lost her virginity and contracted herpes after the boy she was on a date with forced himself on her in the family room of her own house.

"The gray area between holding hands and fornication can become a dangerous, slippery slope," she had said. "So decide now what your boundaries are so that you won't slip or find yourself trapped halfway down the slope."

"I guess you're too pushy, and part of me feels like I'm just a means to an end."

"Huh?" he says, confused.

"Like you're using me," I say. "Like I could just be anybody . . ."

"Using you?" he says. "You're the only girl I've ever kissed. I've liked you since cotillion school in sixth grade. I've got your name written on the back of every textbook I've had for the last five years!"

"Well then, why don't you tell me that, instead of attacking me like some kind of wild animal?"

"DeVeaux," he says, groping for my hand in the dark. When he finds it he squeezes it and says, "We're growing up and I want us to be together in a whole new way."

"I don't want that, John Henry," I say gently. "I want to wait."

He lets out a deep sigh then runs his fingers through his hair. I can tell he doesn't like what I have just said, but he has a faint understanding of it and he cares about me enough to let it go. He pulls me close for a platonic sort of embrace, and when he does, he knocks over a shovel that is hanging on the wall behind me. I jump toward him to get out of the way and when I do this a few logs become loose and they roll under us, flipping us both over on our backs.

"Quiet in there!" Dewey laughs, but the sound of the tumbling logs was too great to ignore and in seconds we hear parental footsteps in the kitchen, making their way toward the basement door.

"My parents!" Louisa shrieks, and the boys run out of the house and through the yard just before Dr. Townsend turns on the light and walks down the stairs.

"Girls?" he says.

"Yes, sir," we call back to him.

"Time to go to sleep," he says wearily. "I've got to operate first thing tomorrow morning."

"Yes, sir," we say as he walks back up the stairs.

Kendra giggles conspicuously. "That was close," she says.

"Yeah," Louisa says, swaying mournfully from side to side. Peter Jenkins ended up kissing Nan instead of her, so she, Sally, and Lesesne, who is a little overweight and never seems to get a guy's attention, sat on the porch with Charlie Morrison and shared a flask of bourbon that he took from his grandfather's overcoat. After Lesesne and I put the logs back in place in the storage closet we see that Nan and Kendra have fallen asleep, and Louisa is curled up in a ball on the front step moaning. As we console her, we realize that her face is turning a pale shade of green so we walk her to the bathroom, where she gets sick once, then climbs back into her sleeping bag and tries to fall asleep, though I can hear her crying as I brush my teeth. She reaches out to me just as I climb into my bag. "Why didn't he talk to me, DeVeaux?" she says, and there is a pain in her voice that astonishes me.

I want to ask her why she likes him so much. After all, he's been nothing but a disrespectful jerk. I want to tell her there are so many other guys out there, and we are only sixteen, after all, and it is way too early for us to give our hearts away. But I know that she is yearning to be comforted so I pat her back and say, "Louisa, it'll work out if it is meant to, I guess."

"I hope so," she says between whimpers. "I really do."

"Why don't you come with me to youth group this week? The whole month of February is going to be about relationships," I say.

"I guess I should," she says. "Call me and remind me."

After she and the others drift off to sleep, I walk over to the windowsill and stare out into my old neighborhood where a few of the early morning lights are coming on. It is 5:00 a.m. and the Baker house is the first on Gibbes Street to stir. I see Mrs. Baker at the kitchen window making coffee, and I wonder when she wakes Sara Baker up and how they spend their Saturdays together.

Thing is, my friends and I will grow up, we will go to college, we will marry, we will have children, and I suppose that Sara Baker will still be there, sitting at her mother's table, in her nearly silent world. I might not have realized this, I might not have had an inkling of the pain of this had I not moved to the island, had

I not been hurt by our own situation, and it pleases me to think that I see things differently from before when I lived downtown— that I might be gaining something from my family's misfortune. Then one of Bethany's favorite Scripture verses comes into my mind from the study we did on Romans last year, and it soothes my heart: *"We know that in all things God works for the good of those who love him, who have been called according to his purpose" (8:28).* And I think of when the Old Testament Joseph said to his brothers who sold him into slavery, *"You intended to harm me, but God intended it for good" (Genesis 50:20).*

When Mama picks me up the next morning, I ask if we can go to see Sara Baker, and she is delighted. The next thing I know we're sitting in the Bakers' living room drinking co-cola and eating cheese biscuits as Sara sits in her wheelchair, quietly sipping her juice, staring slightly past us toward a corner of the room. We talk for more than an hour, and I tell Mrs. Baker about each of the girls in Sara Baker's grade: how Louisa is number three on the Cooper Hall tennis team, how Sally finally passed the driving test on her third try, how Lesesne is still taking ballet from Stephen Vineyard, and particularly loves point. She tries to persuade us to stay for lunch, but Mama needs to get back to the plantation because Daddy needs the truck. As we tell them good-bye, Sara Baker makes her soft laugh, and to me it is a lovely sound, full of unencumbered delight, and I have this urge to hug her good-bye, but I'm too scared, so I don't.

❧

The next week John Henry's parents catch him stealing a bottle of their gin from the liquor cabinet. They decide to send him off to prep school at Woodberry Forest in Virginia so that he can be kept in line and reach his full academic potential.

He acted like an 100 percent gentleman to me again the week before he left. On our last night together, he held my hand tightly as we walked along the Battery and he pledged to write each week and call whenever he came home. "I guess abstinence, like absence, can have its pluses," he said, and he gave me a soft kiss good-bye on my cheek that made me want another. "My heart is growing fonder," he joked.

That simple and sincere kiss is what I will try to remember when I picture him in his prep school dorm room, the Virginia snow freezing on the limbs outside his window. Thing is, I don't think he'll write me, or any of us for that matter. My hunch is that this is our last romantic chapter, and I think God has prepared my heart for that because I am fine with the idea.

❧

One day in early February when I come home from school, I see my uncle Bobbie, Mama's one and only sibling, sitting on the porch talking to Mama. He has driven up on a weekday from Greenville after he got wind of the fact (from Duncan Bell) that Mama is driving a run-down truck. Uncle Bobbie is a very busy lawyer at a labor law firm, and it is a big deal for him to cancel a day's worth of appointments to see about her.

He asks her what happened to all her father's textile stocks and when she doesn't answer he just pats her knee and says, "Don't even tell me, sister, just know that it is going to be okay."

He says that he has come down to take her to the Charleston Motor Mile and buy her a car. He will not take no for an answer.

"But I have to ask Billy," she says, "and he's gone to Walterboro with Chambers."

Uncle Bobbie says, "Look, I am not going to let you drive around in a car that keeps breaking down, with no heat and dents all over it. Billy will understand that, and if he doesn't, I'll talk to him." Then he shakes his head and says again, "C'mon, Dee! What would Daddy have said if he saw you living like this?"

At the mention of her daddy, who'd referred to her as "his treasure," Mama begins to submit by hanging her head low and nodding.

So Uncle Bobbie goes to Rick Hendrick's Honda and buys her a snappy white Honda Civic. This car looks ridiculously out of place in our yard, where it sits between the rusty tin roof of the toolshed and the crumbling bricks that line the chimney and hold up the back of the fish shed. The car reminds me of a cartoon character, wide-eyed and slick. It looks as if it might come to life and dance around our house like a Disney movie.

When Uncle Bobbie leaves, he hands me a crisp one-hundred-dollar bill, which also looks like a cartoon. He winks at me and says, "You sure are growing up into a beautiful young lady," and then, "You look after your good mama now, you hear?"

When Daddy gets home and sees the snappy white car and understands what has gone on, he is furious and throws his first tantrum since Christmas. He says, "I will *not* let your brother buy you a car." And then, "That car probably cost fifteen thousand dollars—if your brother wants to give out that kind of money, he should give it to us to get out of debt. You do not need a car!"

Okay, Lord, I pray before standing up in defense of the car, *give me the backbone I need without dishonoring him.*

"It might be good to have a car that we can count on," I say, looking cautiously toward my father. "In case of an emergency or something."

And I can feel him tallying up another check against me as he stares me down.

"Stay out of this, DeVeaux," my mother chirps in.

"Yes," Daddy says, turning his eyes back to her, "at least we can agree on that, Dee."

This happened a week ago and ever since then no one has driven the car.

☙

One night at the restaurant, Tina drives up to the back door in her mom's run-down Dodge Omni. This is the first time I have seen her drive anything other than that Corvette since before Christmas. I am out on the back steps by the Dumpsters, drinking a co-cola with Suzanne and C.C. while Jeeter's dog sniffs around my ankles, smelling Flounder and all of the other Rose Hill smells.

Ever since I helped them out on New Year's Eve, the restaurant gang seems to like me a little more, and they don't make fun of me any longer for choosing not to drink. They have all adopted Jeeter's nickname for me, "Devo," after that stupid '80s band that sang the song "Whip It." It cracks them up to change the pronunciation of my name like that.

Tina's eyes are on me as she steps out of the car and walks toward the back steps. "Come to the bathroom with me," she says.

So we go to the bathroom and turn on a fan so no one can hear us talking.

"If Sal had the money," she says, "he'd have a mirror in here so he could watch the gals."

"Yeah," I say, "I wouldn't put anything past him. However, I don't think he's quite that clever."

Tina nods. She has a funny look on her face.

"So what's up?" I ask.

She seems to be staring beneath the sink at a small, brown spot on the wall.

"Skipped my you-know-what," she says, looking back at me from beneath her pale yellow eyebrows.

"Huh?" I say, knowing good and well she isn't talking about skipping class because she does that on a regular basis with great ease. Suddenly, I'm confused.

"I'm late," she says.

"What do you mean?" I say.

"I haven't had my period this month, DeVeaux! For heaven's sake, do you have to have everything spelled out for you?" she says.

I wait before I say anything. I suppose I deserved that insult and yes, a lot of times I do need things spelled out for me. I'm not Miss Walterboro High Know and Do Everything.

Then I feel guilty and I say, concerned, "Do you think you're—"

"I don't know," she says. "I need to buy a test from the store. Will you go with me to get one?"

"Of course I will," I say, thankful to have a specific assignment in this situation and then it occurs to me: "So you and Shane were . . . *together?*"

"Yeah," she says. "New Year's Eve was the first time, and I didn't tell you on account of the fact that I didn't know if I should be embarrassed or proud. I was feeling mixed," she says, staring again at the spot beneath the seat. "Plus, I know you're into that church stuff and all . . . So when can you go to the store?"

"How about Saturday?" I say.

"Fine," she says.

"What if you are?" I ask.

"I'll get rid of it," she says, then looks away. "Shane knows about a clinic outside of Savannah that don't ask no questions." She does not look back at me for a reaction. Instead she turns away quickly and says, "See ya Saturday."

Then all I see is the back of her thin legs, the bottom of an acid-washed blue jean miniskirt and the thick pink tube socks around her ankles. She bolts through the restaurant and before I can catch up to her in the back, she has gotten the car started. I watch her putt out of the grass lot and onto Highway 174 while the winter moon hangs low above the marsh water and Jeeter shouts, "Devo! Set table 7 for ten!"

The rest of the night I'm in a state of worry and shock. I become so consumed by Tina's dilemma that I start the coffeemaker without putting a pot underneath the filter basket, and I even mix the cocktail sauce with the steak sauce by accident.

Thing is, my friends in Charleston are making out all the time, but I don't think they are actually "doing it." No, they are definitely *not* doing it.

I guess it just hasn't occurred to me that someone my age whom I hang out with could be pregnant. Then I start to picture the look on Tina's face and hope she isn't scaring herself to death.

Suzanne has a hunch that something is up, and she pulls me aside in the kitchen and says, "Everything okay, DeVeaux?"

"Yeah," I say.

"You know your cousin Eli is counting on me to look after you." She moves closer and whispers, "You and C.C. aren't . . ."

"C.C.?" I say. "No! We're just friends, Suzanne."

"Well, I was just checking. He seems like he has a little crush on ya, and I wouldn't want you to end up like I did, with Becky at seventeen," she says, then she considers this and adds, "Though it ain't like she isn't the best thing ever came into my life, it's just—"

"I appreciate your concern," I say to Suzanne, now consoling her by putting my hand on her back, "but don't worry about me. I'm fine." *But someone else isn't.*

At the end of the night, Tosha sets aside some grits for me and Suzanne's daughter in two plastic cups. Daddy is still up when I get home, and he is delighted when I share my grits with him. He asks earnestly about the night, and I recount stories of busing tables in minutes flat, and making four desserts at once, and he chuckles and says, "I'm proud of you."

At times like this, it's hard to believe he even has a temper.

He finds an old movie on the television and together we eat the buttery mush, sitting in our respective den chairs beneath a couple of sleeping bags, spooning large bites in the glow of the screen until we both fall asleep.

❧

Saturday I pick Tina up in Mama's new Honda. (I tell Daddy that I have a girl-type emergency and since Mama has gone to town in the truck, I don't see any way around not taking the Honda. He is so engrossed with the sailboat that he swats his hand in my direction and says, "Fine.")

Since Tina can't decide what to wear, I have to sit in the den of her double-wide and wait for her while Baby Faye entertains me first by playing with her oatmeal and then by making up a date scene between the Barbie and Ken dolls she got for Christmas. Once I thought I heard C.C. rustling around in his bedroom, but he doesn't come out to say hello.

When Tina is ready, we head on to town to buy a pregnancy test. Our plan is to go to the bathroom of Sears in the mall to take the test, since they have a powder room where we can sit and wait. Tina is dressed in a floral Sunday school-type dress meant for spring, and I am in blue jeans and my Cooper Hall sweatshirt.

On the way to town, we keep quiet and I notice things in the landscape I haven't seen before, like the ruins of a burned-out church just before the Dawhoo River bridge and then an enormous bra that has been placed around two large knobs in a tall live oak tree that sits slightly back in the woods. Someone has painted red lips and big black eyes above it.

I chuckle and Tina says, "You mean you've never seen that before?"

"No," I say.

And we both laugh and Tina says, "Pretty funny, ain't it?"

Suddenly I ask, "How does Shane know about these clinics?" That had been bothering me ever since she said it. I even called Sasser to tell him about it and he said, "Bring her to youth group, DeVeaux, and if she's in trouble, Bethany and Stu can tell her about some great options. There's this place that will take you in and help you, and there are great adoption agencies if she chooses not to raise the child."

"Well," she says, "he's used them before, I reckon."

"So he's a regular stallion," I say, shocked because it is an unlikely thing for me to think, much less say, like a line in a very bad movie.

"He's nineteen, DeVeaux," she says, a bit irritated. "It ain't like he hasn't ever been with no one."

"Oh," I say. "Yeah."

"He says he'll pay for half," she says, rubbing in the rouge she's caked on her cheeks. "And I'd just have to hit C.C. up for the rest. He's got two jobs and all."

"And there are other options, too," I say, "but there is no sense worrying about that until we know if it's true."

She looks at me and a smile spreads across her face as if she's just considered the possibility that she's not pregnant. She says, "You're right."

When we get to the Eckerd's drugstore I look over to Tina, who looks as frozen in the seat of the Honda as the rabbits at Rose Hill do when they spot me walking by.

"Why don't I go in and get it," I say. "I won't be as nervous as you since it's not for me."

"Okay," she says, handing me her pink change purse. "I don't know what it costs, but there's thirteen dollars in there."

When I walk in, I'm disoriented and embarrassed. *Get a spine*, I say to myself. *Your friend needs some help here.* I keep walking down the aisles, but all I seem to come across is bandages and hair spray and lawn chairs. Finally, I spot the feminine hygiene aisle and I stare down the rows of stacked boxes containing tampons until my eye spots condoms at the far corner and then HIV tests and finally pregnancy tests. I can feel the gaze of the pharmacist as he watches me from over the counter. I wonder why they put the incriminating stuff under his nose. But I shrug in his direction. I tell myself that there is no need for me to be nervous since this test is not for me, and he has no idea whom it is for.

I look over both of my shoulders, then I pick up a two-pack test and walk toward the counter.

❧

When we're in Sears I read the directions, and Tina goes to the bathroom to pee. Whenever I think of pregnancy tests, I think of Virginia describing to my parents how unbearably trashy her freshman roommate was—in an effort to have my parents pay for an off-campus apartment that she wanted to get with her sorority sisters. She said, "I mean, she left her pregnancy tests in the room for weeks at a time, and she would put her cigarettes out in them."

Mama put her hands over her ears and said, "I can't stand to hear this."

Daddy said, "Do whatever you need to do to get out of that situation."

And Virginia made her way into a plush Nashville condominium complex with an indoor elevator and a fitness center. What an opportunist.

❧

Since Tina and I have to wait five minutes for the test result, we decide to make up stories.

"Once there was a fisherman," I say.

She concentrates for a moment then pipes up, "And he gave up fishing in the summer to run him a parasailing business." (Tina's mother's last boyfriend owned a parasailing business on Younge's Island, and she used to get free rides, which she loved.)

"He charged twenty-five dollars to sail in the sky," I say.

"Lots of families came to see him during their vacations and he did right well," Tina says. "He made out so good that he got himself a house on the beach."

"Unfortunately," I say, "he was a widower, and he had no one to share the house or his money with."

"So he went out one night to Coot's Lounge to look for him a gal," Tina says.

"Only he didn't like the looks of most of the women who hung out at Coot's, so one day when he was taking parasail orders on the beach, he ran into this lovely woman in a tasteful bathing suit, the kind with the little skirt bottom, and he asked her out to dinner."

Tina says, "And she says that she would love to go so he took her to Sal's Lowland Cuisine, and he ordered a bottle of bubbly and—" All of a sudden Tina goes blank and looks at her watch.

"And they fell in love somewhere between the salad and the grits," I say, knowing that it hasn't been five minutes.

"They got married," Tina says, tapping her white heels on the linoleum floor.

"And she helped him run his business," I say, "and at night they walked along the surf and watched the sunset."

"What time is it?" Tina asks.

I tell her to count to sixty, twice, and we start to, but we are interrupted by someone coming in to use the bathroom. We quickly throw the test into the plastic Eckerd's bag and cross our legs.

Lo and behold, I see that the person entering the bathroom is a close friend of my parents from downtown, Cornelia Edings. Her husband was one of my dad's childhood friends and his biggest real estate investor. They are also Brother Will's godparents.

"DeVeaux, is that you?" she says, looking at my Cooper Hall sweatshirt and then looking at Tina with her unfashionable, out-of-season floral dress, her side-angled ponytail, and her distraught-looking face, which is even more pale than usual.

"Hello, Mrs. Edings," I say, noticing and recognizing her jewelry—the glaringly large diamond she has always worn on her left hand, and the heavy charms she wears on the thick bracelet around her wrist. "This is my friend Tina Woodward."

"Why, hello, Tina." She pauses for an appropriate moment, the charms clanging together as she raises her hand to her lips. "You must be a friend from the island."

"Yes'm," Tina says, straightening up and eyeing the Eckerd's bag.

"DeVeaux, tell me how in the world your parents are?" she asks. "We haven't seen them in months."

"They're fine," I say, smiling and remembering how I used to sit in Mrs. Edings' lap when I was little, during Daddy's dinner socials, and pick at the charms on her bracelet, which include gold silhouettes of her three children with their dates of birth in the middle of their foreheads, the Eiffel Tower, where Mr. Edings took her for their honeymoon, and a globe that he bought her on their tenth wedding anniversary, which has a different type of stone for every country they've traveled to together.

"Oh, please send them my love," she says.

"I will," I say as she walks toward a stall then turns back to wink at me and says, "What a wonderful surprise to see you!"

Since Tina and I look like we are up to no good just sitting there while Mrs. Edings goes to the bathroom, I grab the Eckerd's bag and say, "Good-bye, Mrs. Edings."

"Good-bye, DeVeaux," she says, and before the door closes

behind us I hear her say, "Do say hello to Mr. Edings, who is somewhere in the electronics section of the store."

Tina looks very anxious so I pull her arm over to the children's section where the Edings are not likely to be and I say, "Let's just wait a few minutes for her to go, then we'll head back into the powder room and see what it says."

"Doggone it," Tina says. "I can't stand this waitin'!"

"Calm down," I say, rubbing her shoulders through the puffy, waxy material of her sleeves.

We duck behind a rack of bibs when we hear the voice of Mrs. Edings calling to Mr. Edings, "The exit is this way, dear."

When he comes closer, I get a good look at him in his usual houndstooth suit and a brightly striped bow tie. The toes of his black wingtips are as shiny as bowling balls. Suddenly I think of how my daddy looked this morning when I left him. He was in the toolshed scrubbing down the boat, unshaven and dressed in camouflage, the cut-up gloves Mama made for him exposing the ends of his thick fingers while the clank and clatter of the construction workers reminded him of the metamorphosis taking place in his ancestors' plantation house just yards away.

Mr. Edings puts his arm around Mrs. Edings and we overhear her say to him, "I just saw one of Billy DeLoach's children in the bathroom."

"Which one?" he says.

"DeVeaux, the baby," she says.

"Of course," he says and his tone becomes lower, "and how did she look?"

"She looked scrawny and she was with a friend of hers from the island. A poor-looking child," she says.

"I can't say I'm surprised," he says.

"They must be truly down and out," she says.

"Honey," he says, "they're *ruined*. Billy went so deep in the hole over that Otter Island development, I don't think he has a *thing* left. And who would invest in his business again?"

"You better not," she says.

"Don't worry," he says. "Billy's an old friend, but he's a poor businessman. Overextends himself, takes too many risks . . ." And as I listen to their footsteps become lighter and their voices more muffled, my heart sinks for my father. And in a way I am grateful to now feel some of his sorrow and anger. If my friends thought of me this way, I suppose I would have a temper tantrum or two also.

My daddy's life must be at its lowest point, and I'm not sure what will bring him back up.

Have mercy on my daddy, Lord, I silently pray. *Don't let ruined be our family name.*

Ɛ

Back in the bathroom we see that the test is negative and Tina is thrilled. So thrilled that she takes me out to Hardee's, where we both get double cheeseburgers and chocolate milk shakes. I am so relieved for her that I forget for a moment about what the Edings said about Daddy, and together we sing out loud to Garth Brooks all the way back to the island.

Before I drop Tina off, I invite her to youth group this week and she says she'll go, but that I need to be right by her 'cause churches spook her a bit.

When I pull up to her trailer, C.C. is sitting on the porch smoking a cigarette and reading a Dr. Seuss book to Baby Faye, whom he holds gently in his lap.

"Wonder where those two pretty gals been?" he says to Baby Faye.

"None of your business," Tina says to him, then she runs into the house to change and call Shane.

144

"What's up, Devo?" he says.

"That's not her name, silly," Baby Faye says to him.

"I know, silly willy," he says to her, licking his finger and poking it into her ear.

Baby Faye looks at me and shrieks with laughter. "You sure are crazy, C.C.!" she says to him.

Just then Mama drives by in the truck. She rolls down her window and says, "Where in the world have you been, DeVeaux? You've been gone all day. Supper's ready; now come on home."

C.C. grins and Baby Faye points her finger at me and says, "Better do what your mama tells you."

❧

That night Mama fixes the last bit of venison in the form of a meat-and-potato stew. I feel obligated to tell Mama and Daddy about running into the Edings, and Daddy is startled by the mention of their names because they have been out of touch so long.

"What did they say?" Mama probes.

"Mrs. Edings said to send her love and that she wants to get together soon," I say, not sugarcoating it, just saying it plain out.

"It's been so long," Daddy says.

This is Mama's opportunity for community reconnection, and she is going to take it. She says, "Why don't we have them out for dinner, Billy?"

"Oh no," he says, "not now."

Though I want to agree with him because I don't think it's such a good idea, I'm afraid to chime in for fear they will both reprimand me. Hosting a dinner in the state we're in could be a downright disaster, but I'm too gutless to stand in the way of it.

"We can do an oyster roast!" Mama says. "Casual and fun."

He pauses, then stands up and says he is uncomfortable, so he takes off his pants and rests them over the back of his chair and sits back down in his boxers and starts eating again.

Mama moves in for the kill. She says, "Billy, do you know that someone at the Charleston Garden Club last week asked me if we were separated because she hasn't seen you in so long?"

Daddy is tense. He looks back at the fire, then down at his plate again. Then out of nowhere he agrees to have the Edings over next week for dinner. "But you call them," he says to Mama.

Mama plows into her food and takes a hearty bite. Delighted, she says, "Think how far this one deer has gone. Billy, you are a real provider, just like the Indians."

Now I try to be enthusiastic because even though the Edings can be snotty, I do think it might be good for Daddy to be around people, and almost anybody would do. I can't think of what to say so I just jump on the bandwagon with Mama and say, "Yeah, just like the Edisto Indians," and then, remembering a recent history lesson, I say, "Did you know that they traded this island to some English lords for two sets of beads and a knife?"

They consider this a moment and then both look down at their plates, now solemn. The only noise is their chewing and the light breath of Easy the cat, who sneaked into the house when Daddy wasn't looking and has hidden herself beneath my chair.

❧

In the middle of the night I wake up from a bizarre dream. I was in a dark room, like a basement, sitting by myself, but the door kept opening and closing and someone different was standing in the doorway each time. First it was John Henry and he was calling me "Miss DeLoach," the way he used to present me at cotillion. "May I present Miss DeLoach," he said, reaching his hand through the doorway to me. Then it was C.C. and he was calling me "Devo" and saying, "You sure are pretty for around here," while he pounded his new pack of cigarettes on the heel of his hand before unwrapping it. And once it was Dinks Edings, and I remember seeing the gray in the sides of his hair. He was in a fancy suit and he said, "Can I come sit down in there with you, poor and ruined little girl?" "No," I said to him fearfully, "get away from me!" as I pictured Mrs. Edings and her heavy charm bracelet that weights her wrist with the symbols of their shared history.

After I come to, I feel like my mind is being attacked with strange thoughts, and I remember 2 Corinthians 10:5: *"We take captive every thought to make it obedient to Christ,"* so I pray, "God, I give this weird dream to You. Give me a peaceful night's sleep, and don't let me out of Your will."

You are not ruined, His Spirit says to me. *And neither is your family. Have faith.*

I see that the cat has managed to stay in the house all night without Daddy seeing her, and now she is curled up beneath my feet where Flounder usually sleeps. I can hear Flounder outside whining so I go out to get him.

When I'm outside, I see that it's not Flounder who is whining but a scruffy old wild cat who is calling Easy from the back steps of the porch. "Go on," I say, and the cat wanders off into the fields.

Then I spot Flounder and see that he is snoring away beneath the tractor. "Flounder," I call to him. He doesn't stir. I keep talking until he recognizes the sound of my voice, which to him is his name. When he finally hears me, he comes running.

If there is one thing I've learned, it's that you can't wait this long to name something. It never quite sticks with you or whatever it is that needs a name. This reminds me of the obituary section of the newspaper where last week I read an article about a newborn baby who died shortly after birth. The article read, "An infant, daughter of Mr. Lionel Smith and Mrs. Shirley Rayburn Smith, died two hours after birth due to a heart problem. The funeral will be held . . ." But I remember being disturbed by the fact that the baby did not even have a name. They would have to think of one quick and scrawl it on the tombstone.

When Flounder and I settle back into bed with Easy, I think of Tina and the baby that was all in her mind and the clinic in Savannah where Shane sends his girlfriends whose babies, in their bellies, are to be broken down into unidentified bits and pieces.

10

Young Love

I pick Tina up for youth group around five in the afternoon, and she looks a little nervous because she's dressed again in that waxy Sunday dress with the floral print.

"It's casual," I say to her, and she goes back into the trailer and comes back out in some white-washed jeans and a well-worn sweatshirt of C.C.'s that says "Edisto Marina" on the front.

"I'm not sure about all of this going to church business," she says as she rubs some of her mama's cinnamon rouge onto her cheeks. "Never been, DeVeaux."

"Are you serious?" I say. "You've never been to church?"

"Nope," she says as she blots her painted lips on the back of a receipt. "Mama got spooked one time by some snake handlers that came through Edisto one year on a tent revival, and she told me she weren't going back again."

"Don't worry," I say, trying to hold back my chuckle. "There won't be any snakes at youth group. It's not that kind of a church."

"Yeah, Mama said it might be one of those highfalutin' churches," she says, crumpling up the receipt and stuffing it in her pocketbook. "If it's one of those places where they burn funny smells and stuff, I reckon that's just as weird as snakes, DeVeaux."

"No, Tina, it's youth group, and it's not even in the church. There's music and pizza, and I told you we'll be talking about girl-boy relationships. It's good. Trust me."

"All right," she says. "I'm comin' 'cause you want me to." Then she asks me to turn the radio to the country music station so she can relax to her favorite songs.

When we get downtown, we swing by Louisa's house to pick her up. I'm not near as self-conscious about my rumbling truck in the fading gray of dusk on Gibbes Street. Besides, I'm on a mission for the Lord, and that gives me confidence and peace no matter how loud or beat-up my truck is.

My mission is for Louisa to come back to youth group so she can have some perspective on her life and stop giving her pearls to swine like Peter Jenkins. And I want Tina to learn about the Lord and catch a glimpse of what a healthy relationship might look like. It will be awkward to have both she and Louisa, my friends from entirely different worlds, riding in my car and sitting together in the youth room of St. Paul's, but this message is for everyone, and they both need to hear it.

"Which one's your old house?" Tina asks while she gawks at the homes on Gibbes Street as we pull away from Louisa's.

"It's one street over," I say.

"Can we go by it?" she asks. "Some of these places are like mansions," she says with her nose to the glass.

Louisa laughs under her breath before checking the missed calls on her cell phone. She looks up just in time to see Peter Jenkins' house as we turn onto Meeting Street, and she stares up at his bedroom window on the third floor, where I know she has snuck up the fire escape to see him. The window is littered with stickers of rock bands that you just know his mother begs him to take down.

"Yep," I say to Tina, who is still waiting on an answer. "Let's go by it on the way home, okay?"

"Don't forget," Tina says, "I want to know where you lived when you was *rich*."

Louisa catches my eye in the rearview mirror from the backseat and gives me a kind of "Who is this country girl?" look.

I just put my focus back on the road and our route to church. I'm on a mission.

When we walk through the Parish Hall, we see that there are large laminated hearts made out of construction paper outlining our path down the hallway and up the back stairs. Tina is close to my side, but she's smiling at the hearts, and I can feel her get excited. Louisa is smiling too. "I can't wait to see Bethany and Stu," she says. "It's been months. Bethany is so cute. You just know she made these hearts, DeVeaux. Aren't they sweet?" (And it's easy to understand my brother Will's mantra: *Girls are so full of mush.*)

We're running a few minutes late, so we grab the last slices of pizza from one of the many boxes piled high with warm pies, then Bethany has us sit on two different sides of the room, girls on one side and guys on the other.

"You mean this pizza is free?" Tina says out loud and with astonishment as we take our seats at the end of a table.

"Yeah," I say quietly to her. "It's free. Eat as much as you like."

I nearly regret my words when she piles her second plate high with four large pieces of pepperoni while a tall boy from another school stands behind her with his empty plate then says, "There's only one piece of pepperoni left!"

Tina doesn't hear him. She is lost in her pizza and co-cola, and she's even grabbed two boxes of candy and put them in her purse.

Louisa, of course, picks at her plate since she's always trying to watch her figure. She eats the pineapple and the ham off her one piece of pizza then throws the rest in the trash behind us.

Bethany sets us up behind this long table opposite the guys, where there is a place for everyone with little strips of paper and pencils and little boxes of valentine candy. There are twice as many girls, so we sit on each other's laps or on the floor in front of the table.

The guys look a little nervous, and there are a few newcomers whose mothers must have forced them to come after all the announcements in the church bulletin about this new program.

LeBruce, the hyper kid, is in rare form—high from all the sugar I suppose, and he is comic relief for everyone. He even jumps on the table and does his howler monkey dance until Bethany and Stu have to suppress their chuckles and get him down.

"What's *that* kid on?" Tina says to me.

"He's just like that," I whisper back. "High on God, I suppose."

"Humph."

It feels so good to be here and to laugh out loud the way I do in this place.

"Thank you for this place," I say to the Lord, and my heart swells with love for Him.

Bethany gets Stu to whistle to get everyone's attention. Then she tells both sides to take a strip of paper and write down a general question we have for the other gender.

The guys put up a weak protest at her instruction.

"C'mon, guys," Stu says, walking over to their table. "This is your chance. What do you want to know about girls? What have you *always* wanted to know about them? This could benefit you immensely in the future if you figure some of this out."

They nod and nudge one another, then everyone goes to work writing down their questions on thin strips of paper and placing them in a heart-shaped box that Bethany has made for each table.

After a few minutes of chuckles, followed by one minute of serious thinking before everyone scribbles down their final question, Bethany picks me to be the designated question reader for the girls and Sasser for the guys.

She switches the boxes of questions and Sasser pulls out the first one from the girls to the guys, which reads "Why don't guys pluck their unibrow?"

The guys balk and offer an array of masculine explanations. And the questions continue back and forth as such:

"Why do gals go to the bathroom in groups?"

"Why does an eighty-year-old man marry a twenty-year-old woman?"

"What's with the hair?"

"'Why do boys hurt girls' feelings?'" Sasser reads, and I have a feeling that this one is coming from Louisa. No one says a word for a moment and Bethany clears her throat as if to signal us to push deeper.

"Why don't girls tell us about feelings?" barks a guy named Chandler, whose girlfriend just dumped him out of the blue.

"'Cause when we do, you don't want to listen," Louisa sounds off with a fury. She has wanted to tell this to someone for a long time, and her eyes are narrowing across the chasm toward the table full of boys. She is accusing them all with her stare.

"Not when you come at us like a screeching howler monkey, Louisa!" hollers LeBruce, and he stands up and does his howler monkey yelp in a high-pitched tone imitating a whiny girl's voice, and the whole place roars with laughter.

Bethany and Stu nod at each other as if to say, "Now we're getting deeper," and the questions continue to fluctuate between the meaningful and the trivial, but they all reveal the differences between the sexes. We continue like this:

"When something is wrong in a relationship, why don't girls tell us until it's too late?" Sasser reads, and I can't help but think of his mama. I wonder if he wrote that question himself.

"Because we want you to figure it out," a girl named Eileen retorts.

A few of the guys scratch their heads in disbelief.

"Why do you want us to figure it out?" Sasser asks. "Why can't you just tell us?"

The girls are stumped for a minute, and I don't really know how to answer that question, either. Finally, after no one says anything,

I see the yearning in Sasser's face for an explanation of this cruel truth and I say, "I don't know why we want you to figure it out, but I guess we shouldn't be that way. I guess we should help you along and tell you how we feel up front."

After Bethany asks us to write down our favorite childhood movies, further showing the differences between the girls who loved *The Secret Garden* and *Sleeping Beauty* and the guys who liked *Star Wars* and *Spider-Man*, she asks us to go over to the sofas, which we call the inner circle, where she teaches us from a book she just read called *Wild at Heart* by John Eldredge, which is about the differences between men and women and how these differences are all characteristics of our Lord and Maker. According to Bethany's summary of the book, we were both created in God's image as set forth in Genesis, and we fit together like two puzzle pieces that fulfill the desire of the other.

"But," she reminds us, "God's intention gets all perverted by this crazy world like everything else, so we have to look out for that." Then she goes over the three desires of men:

1. Like God, men desire a battle to fight for.
2. Like God, men desire an adventure to live.

When we learn that the third desire of men is to have a beauty to fight for, LeBruce walks over to Louisa and says, "Are you my beauty that I'll fight for?"

"Sit down, LeBruce," Bethany says, shaking her head while Lousia blows a bubble and pops it on his nose. Everyone chuckles; then Bethany breaks down the women's desires as follows:

1. Like God, women desire to be fought for.
2. Like God, women like to enter into the adventure with men.
3. Like God, women have a beauty to unveil to men.

Because of these desires, each of the sexes has three needs from the other. For men, they are as follows:

1. Men need to be trusted.
2. Men need acceptance for who they are and how they are.
3. Men need to be appreciated.

For women, it goes like this:
1. Women want to be cared for.
2. Women want to be understood.
3. R-E-S-P-E-C-T—just like the song says. Women want respect.

At the end of the night we break up into small groups to discuss Bethany's talk, and a lot of girls really open their hearts in our group.

Louisa recalls a memory of dressing up in an angel costume and dancing for her father in the kitchen while he ate his breakfast, hoping to get his attention, but he rarely had time to look up from his paper before darting out the door to the hospital. I feel a lightbulb ignite above my head: it's her busy surgeon of a father. He has never stopped to love her.

Tina talks about not having a dad at all and learning all that she thinks she knows about men from her mama, who has had one broken relationship after another.

I explain how it hurts my heart the way my old guy friends now treat me and the girls we grew up with. Sometimes I feel like we are just meat in a market and any old piece will do as long as we go along with their plan for the night, which usually involves drinking and making out.

Then I say with a tinge of bitterness, "I mean, I know it's hard for them with all of their raging hormones, but don't they remember who we are—that we're their friends who used to play kick the can and tag in the backyard together? That we're the ones they brought a cold glass of lemonade to in their mamas' gardens before sitting down beside us and asking us about our favorite music and if we wanted them to teach us how to throw a football? I guess I miss those innocent old days."

Most everyone nods in agreement.

☙

On the way out of town, Tina says, "DeVeaux, we forgot to go by your old house."

She insists on seeing it, so I turn the car around and we go down Tradd Street where my old house is lit up by the new family that fills it—two lawyers and their three children. They've added a newfangled gas lamp on the front of the house, and the whole place must have gotten a new coat of paint.

"Man," Tina says, "bet you miss those digs."

"I don't know," I say back to her. "I miss them, but not as much as I thought I would. I guess it's not so bad because I feel God is with me and I trust Him."

"Man, if I'd had a house like that and then moved to that small, run-down place where you are now, I'd cry myself to sleep at night."

I shrug because it's not all that bad and try to change the subject back to my mission. "So what did you think of youth group?"

"It was funny, I guess," she says. "I don't know, though. Most of those gals seem so innocent. Like they ain't ever gotten their hands dirty, you know?"

"Yeah," I say, "they have led fairly sheltered lives in comparison with the rest of the world."

"You know they're all virgins," she says.

"And that's a *bad* thing?" I ask back to her.

"Don't get your dander up, DeVeaux. I know you're one too. But at my school, you're a laughingstock if you're still one by graduation. It's just different."

"I guess it is different, but the thing is, it's God's will that's best to follow, not the world around you, whatever kind of world that is."

"Don't start getting all religious on me, now. I don't read the Bible, and I don't know about all of that God's-will stuff, and I'm not sure I want to."

"I'm not going to push, Tina," I say to her. "But you know, if there's something to it, which I believe there is, then why not take a look at it and then decide for yourself."

She knocks her head gently against the glass of the car window as if I'm boring her.

"I mean, just the other day you could have been in a *world* of hurt if that test had read positive," I say. "This might be the anchor that could give you and me both the security and love and protection we need, not to mention a whole new life after this broken, blink-of-an-eye one."

"I'll think on it," she says to me, and then, "Hey, you know that guy Floyd I told you I met the other day at the marina?"

"Yeah," I say in a defeated tone, because I know she's not listening to me. "Tell me about him."

"Well, he's older, around thirty I think, and he's a boat mechanic who lives in a trailer on Highway 174. I mean, Shane says we aren't going steady so I thought maybe—"

"That's *way* old, Tina," I say.

"Oh c'mon, DeVeaux," she says back to me. "He's real nice and Mama knows him, and she told me I could go out with him if I'd like."

"That's crazy!" I say. "I mean, that's asking for big-time trouble. You said yourself tonight that your mama isn't the best mentor for relationships, so you don't have to do something just because she gives you permission to."

"Well, he's coming by the trailer tonight to say hi."

"Shane the sleazy stallion and a thirty-year-old man?" I ask. "These are no bowls of peaches, Tina. Don't you think you should just get rid of both of them and start fresh with God?"

"DeVeaux," she says, trying to look me in the eye as I drive, "you're my new best friend, and when you moved out here to Edisto, I was real excited to have someone new my age to hang out with, but there are things that have gone on here for a long time before you came and will keep going on after you leave to go to college or wherever, and you just can't change it all in me with one trip to church. Okay?"

I guess I can swallow "back off" when I hear it and so I say, "Okay."

When I pull off the main road and into her driveway, Tina jumps out of my truck before I even put it in park.

"Good night," she says to me as she runs toward the trailer, and I can see a man lighting a cigarette through the thick curtains over the window of her home.

Tina fades into the blackness of the night between my car and her home, and I nearly begin to worry about her before she comes back into sight at the top of her porch steps. As she opens the door, I pull out of the driveway and make my way to Rose Hill guided only by my headlights.

I'm not sure if the night was a success or a failure in terms of accomplishing my mission. "She's in Your hands," I say to God. "And so is Louisa. Just tell me what to do next."

When I get home, I'm completely surprised to find the St. Paul's van parked by the fish shed, and then Sasser, who is sitting on the screened porch with Mama drinking a cup of her famous hot chocolate.

"How about a cup of cocoa?" she says to me as she throws the dishtowel over her shoulder.

"No thanks," I say, looking to Sasser. He hasn't been out to Rose Hill since we sold it, and I am a little embarrassed, even in front of him, at our shabby digs.

"I'll let you two be, then," she says to me, and I can hear Daddy's snoring when she opens the sliding glass door and heads inside.

"What are you doing here?" I ask as I sit down in a rocking chair beside him.

"I wanted to talk to you," he says. "I mean, tonight got me thinking. You know the pieces of the puzzle and all."

"I'm not sure I understand."

Sasser looks at me with his deep green eyes and says, "Tonight got me thinking about *you* in a 'more than a friend' kind of way."

"Sasser," I say, but I don't know what else to say after his name. He is my buddy, my spiritual mentor, and one of my last true ties to my old life. I have never thought of him in any other way than that.

Flounder is scratching on the screened door with muddy paws and I walk over to let him in where he takes his place right between Sasser and I, his belly cooling off on the concrete slab of the porch floor. Sasser pets the back of his neck and he begins to snooze.

"I want someone to be with, DeVeaux," Sasser begins again, his tired eyes staring me down. "It's like I've got this insatiable longing that won't go away."

"You mean you're lonely," I say, wondering how much of this is actually about his mother's leaving.

"Sure," he says, "I do feel alone. And I have this ache in my heart that's too painful to describe."

I reach out to take hold of his shoulder and say, "I'm flattered that you would think of me as someone you might want to be with, Sas. But don't you think this longing might have something to do with missing your mother?"

Now he puts his head between his knees, and I can see the blood rush to his temples. Sasser is always the strong one, so if he gets teary on me, I'm not sure if I can lift him back up.

Lord, show me how to care for my friend.

"Why did she leave?" he says, looking up at me. There is a thin vein in the middle of his forehead that is pulsing.

"It was an awful thing to do," I say to him, and I rub his back gently. "She abandoned you and your dad. I don't why she did it, but I know it was wrong."

"I keep going over it in my mind. I keep wondering what I could have done to prevent it."

"Don't," I say. "She made the wrong decision. It wasn't something you did."

He bites his lip and takes my hands in his.

"It's wearing me down," he says. "It's too heavy for me."

"I know," I say, and I truly do. For Sasser and me there is no escape from the pain in our homes. But I tell him what I know he would tell me—

"God will carry you through," I say. "It's a terrible thing you're living with, but He will not forsake you. That's the take-home message and you have to hold on to it."

Sasser takes a deep breath and pulls on my fingertips.

"I know you're right," he says. "Sometimes even I have trouble believing it."

Now this is a switch, and I have to laugh.

"You mean, you're contracting spiritual amnesia?"

"I guess so," he says and smirks through his red and clouded eyes.

"You know the cure for that," I say. "You've prescribed it to me many times before."

Flounder jumps up at the sound of a raccoon who just ran off the dock and plunked into the water.

Sasser doesn't notice any of it. He just looks to me and waits for the prescription.

"Just remember," I say. "Remember what God has done for you. Remember all of those ways He has touched you: from your physical healing to that conversation you had with Him at White Point Gardens just the other day to all of those brokenhearted people you have watched put their lives back together after a tragedy."

"You mean practice what I preach?" he says as he rubs his eyes with his forearm, and I can tell by the humor in his voice that he is returning to his senses.

"Exactly," I say, staring at his emerald eyes as the light rushes back into them. Now there's my Sasser. The lighthouse whom I adore.

"I'm sorry to come all the way out here, DeVeaux," he says. "I'm just a mess, and I just wanted to be near you."

"Sasser," I say, wanting to address his romantic notions from earlier. "Maybe there will be something more than friendship between us someday. But right now, both of our lives are completely leveled, and we'd best build them back with God as the other half of our puzzle and then go from there."

"You're right," he says, and he kisses me softly on my forehead. "What a girl you are."

And I can't help but blush when he says this. "You're so strong—bringing those two gals to youth group tonight in the middle of your own heavy stuff. You have handled all you're going through with grace and you will be rewarded."

Strength? Grace? Not exactly words I would use to describe myself these days. Or any day for that matter. But oh, how I have longed to hear them. So I take this as a gift of encouragement from the source of all light, and I commit it to my memory because I have a feeling I will need it when things get worse.

And as Sasser walks out to the van (he must have begged his father to use it for such a non-church-related excursion), he lifts up the bottoms of his shoes before turning back to say, lightheartedly, "Boy, it sure is muddy out here."

"In *every* way," I say, and I wave good-bye to my friend of faith as the St. Paul's van makes its bumpy exit on the dirt road of Rose Hill.

11

Sociable

When the Edings arrive for dinner, they are a half hour late.

Mama nudges Daddy, who is tending to the oysters at the grill beside the fish shed, and says, "Here they are!"

Daddy turns and watches the Edings consider a place to park. They drive a fancy white Range Rover. It is tall and hefty, decorated with mysterious tubes and gadgets, narrowing at the top like a wedding cake.

Mama has spent the majority of her week preparing for this get-together, which she calls the "midwinter oyster roast." She devoted one whole day to cleaning out the cobwebs and abandoned hornet's nests in the ceiling corners of the sheds, and she spent hours each morning on top of the tractor, surveying the yard and the avenue of oaks for dead limbs that Chambers scooped up and took to the dump. I was in charge of looking after Daddy, who acted as if nothing was going on. He spent his mornings working on the sailboat and his afternoons tending the fields.

Going on the theory that the scruffiness of Rose Hill, with its antebellum ruins and wildlife, was its charm, Mama went to the toolshed and hauled out the rustiest-looking trash cans she could find and placed them at the ends of the picnic tables where the Edings could hurl their oyster shells.

She also searched through the attic of the main house and found several old wool gloves and mittens, which she placed along with some old blankets in cardboard boxes beside the picnic table so people could huddle up together and keep warm.

She became nervous when the temperature rose to sixty-eight degrees yesterday, threatening to spoil the "winter cold" mood she'd envisioned. I thought she was either going to cry or yell at God when Chambers came over to the house to say that he spotted some buds on the azalea bushes in the gall.

"Oh, not yet," Mama says. "It's mid-February for heaven's sake."

But last night the temperature dropped and today it was cold again, hovering around thirty-seven degrees, and she said, "Thank the Lord" this morning while she watched The Weather Channel.

At the last minute, Mama decided that she should also invite the Davidsons, Dr. and Mrs. and Mary Margaret, as sort of a "Thank you for saving our tree; we're still civilized people and your neighbors" kind of a gesture. Daddy just shrugged when she asked him if this would be okay. He was as ready as he could be for the dinner, and it seemed to me that he thought Mama might as well combine all their social duties into one night so it would be over and done with.

So Mama called the Davidsons this afternoon and they showed up ten minutes early and have been sitting in the fish shed eating Mama's crab dip and watching the oysters as their hinges loosen beneath the croaker sacks, saying, "Those sure look good."

❧

Today, when Mama had me sweeping the dock, I noticed some movement on Otter Island, Daddy's failed development across the river. Bulldozers were knocking some pine trees around, and I thought this must mean someone else is going to develop it. I spent the rest of the afternoon worrying that Daddy would notice the activity over there, but he took a long afternoon nap and didn't come out to start the roast until after sunset. The island darkness will hide this bad news from him for the night.

It was funny to watch Mama carry on about this get-together, because Daddy used to be the one who was in charge of our dinner socials on Tradd Street.

And he never carried on or felt the need to create a "mood." Instead, he would just shuffle down to Mr. Burbage's Grocery on Broad Street, where someone would suggest to him a nice cheese and a bottle of wine. Then he'd dust off the semi-tarnished silver goblets and place them around the table in a shabby-chic manner. That was his charm.

During these socials he would guide the conversations from current events to politics and by the end of the night, he always settled back into a discussion about Charleston history and "the way life used to be." This was his favorite topic.

The Edings were regulars at these dinner socials. They are both from old Charleston families, and they always had a great deal to add to those conversations.

I remember one time when we, the children, were invited down for dessert at one of these socials where the guests were discussing the end of the Civil War. Dinks Edings had pulled out the diary of Edmund Seabrook Rose from Daddy's bookcase and they were trying to guess how it really was, his own slaves insisting on hiding his valuables in their bed quarters or in the woods while Sherman's troops marched dangerously close.

Daddy read the account out loud: "Benny, an older but strong worker, carried my dining room table and buffet back to the house after we received news that the troops were headed west toward Columbia. He had hidden some of our best pieces in the thick of the forest on the outskirts of the swamp, and together we pulled out the drawers of the buffet and checked for snakes."

"Those aren't the stories they will tell you in your history books, children," Mr. Edings said to us, as the guests sipped their sherry and the sound of the tourist carriages outside our window reminded us all of the strangers who were being hauled down our street, looking at our ancestors' leftovers.

❧

Now I notice Mama testing the temperature of the crab dip, which will be lukewarm by the time the Edings dig into it. (It's not that Mama wants to please the Edings so much as the fact that she wants to show Daddy what a good time he can still have even though things have changed some.)

After the Edings park, they pop out of their car. They are dressed appropriately in winter gear, duck boots, and goose-down jackets. "Hello, hello!" Mrs. Edings says.

Mama greets them. "Cornelia and Dinks!" she says. Daddy follows behind Mama.

Mr. and Mrs. Edings can't keep their eyes off Daddy, who has gained about thirty pounds since they last saw him. Several lines run across Mrs. Edings' forehead and Mr. Edings just gawks.

"You know the Davidsons," Mama says to them, "Dr. Allen and his wife, Nan, and their daughter, Mary Margaret, who grew up with DeVeaux."

"Why, yes, of course," says Mr. Edings, "the plastic surgeon." He reaches out to shake Dr. Davidson's hand.

"Not anymore," Dr. Davidson says softly.

"He's retired," Mrs. Davidson says.

"How romantic to be out at Rose Hill," Mrs. Edings says in the direction of Daddy as she bounces on the balls of her feet.

Mr. Edings breathes the cool air through his nostrils. "Many a cold morning and dusk Billy and I spent out here, sitting on stands, waiting for a twelve-point buck to walk into our range. Isn't that right, Billy?"

Daddy is quiet so Mama quickly responds, "Billy shot a twelve-point in January that we've been eating off of for weeks."

"How wonderful," Mrs. Edings says, and her eyes shake back and forth as if something is breaking loose behind them. She looks at each of us frantically and says, "I know you must love living in the wild."

I can tell Daddy is nervous because of his reserve. He realizes that he is expected to say something, but his mouth seems as if it has been wired shut. Finally Mr. Edings begins to pat him on the shoulder and then Daddy says, "In those hours that we spent in the deer stands at fifteen and sixteen, we imagined our whole lives by the time the hunt was over: who we would marry, how many children we would have, how many years of deer hunting were ahead of us."

"Ah, that's lovely," says Mrs. Edings, who smiles and rubs her husband's back. Her eyes calm down.

I smile with more than relief. *Daddy still has his charm*, I think to myself. It may be tucked so far down that it is hard for it to make its way to the surface, but it's still there. I am glad for him. Also, I am hopeful. This moment tells me that in time he may recover, and so will our family.

Then Daddy says to Mama, "Dee, show the Edings to the picnic tables while I go in and fix them a drink." He points to Cornelia and says, "Gin and tonic with a lime," and then to Dinks, "bourbon and water."

"That's right," the Edings say, "good memory."

Mama is about to jump out of her skin she's so happy that Daddy's warming up to his role as host. The stars are lighting up the clear, cold sky, and it looks as though the night is going her way.

Mama shows everyone to the fish shed while pointing out Orion and the Big Dipper.

"Oh my," Mrs. Edings says. "This is better than a planetarium."

"I can see the Milky Way," Mr. Edings says.

⁓

Within a half hour the first batch of oysters is ready. Daddy lifts the croaker sack and the sheet metal and hurls the shells onto the picnic table where everyone is anxious to dig in.

All of the couples are sharing blankets, and I am sharing a blanket with Mary Margaret.

Mrs. Edings is talking about her daughter, Martha Ann, who is getting married in the spring. She has just described her wedding dress in great detail and now is moving onto the description of the bridesmaids' dresses.

"Honey," Mr. Edings says, looking to Daddy and Dr. Davidson, "we don't need to hear *all* of the details."

Everyone chuckles and digs heartily into their oysters. The night is off to a good start.

About this time, Flounder makes an appearance. He comes running out of the house and circles the fish shed, then heads toward the dock.

"Oh, a Boykin spaniel," Mrs. Edings says. "What a beauty!"

"It belongs to Will," Mama says. "He decided to leave the dog with us until he graduates."

"What's his name?" Mrs. Davidson asks.

"Flounder," I say.

Mr. Edings yells, "Flounder," and Flounder does not turn around. He's just walking around the dock.

Daddy calls, "Flounder," and he still doesn't turn.

So I have to say it: "Flounder" (since I'm the only one who pays him any attention), and he turns immediately and comes running toward us. He hurries to each outstretched hand so that everyone can pet him.

When we finish the first bushel of oysters, Mr. Edings says, "We went through those like Sherman through Atlanta," and everybody laughs. Then Mama says, "We've got another batch coming, but in the meantime, come into the caretaker's house for a cup of beef stew."

While people head toward the house, I ask Mary Margaret if she wants to go on top of the fish shed to get a good view of the stars. She says yes so we climb up on the tin roof and stare into the night lights, which are framed by the dark limbs of the live oak trees.

This is the first time I've seen Mary Margaret since Christmas Day, when she and her dad returned our tree. She just looks at the stars and doesn't say much. She is a naturally quiet person, so I figure I better take the lead in our conversation.

"How's Cooper Hall?" I ask her.

"The same, I guess," she says, then she thinks for a moment.

"Remember Miss LaVan from seventh grade?" she says.

"Yeah," I say. "She was ancient and a little crazy, wasn't she?"

"Well, she's had to retire after she accused her class of breaking into her house on Limehouse Street and stealing her silver."

"What a loon!" I say. "Remember the time she lost our tests, then told us that we never took them?"

"Anyhow, they found out she has Alzheimer's," Mary Margaret says.

"Well, that explains a lot."

"Yeah," Mary Margaret says, then she takes out a tissue and blows her nose.

"So, who do you hang out with around here?" she asks me.

"Well, I've been hanging out with Tina Woodward, who lives down the road."

"That girl who wears a ponytail on the side of her head?"

"Yeah," I say, "that's her."

"Doesn't she live in a trailer?"

"Yeah, but you know, she's cool, and I work with her brother and he's cool too."

"Really?" she says. "I've seen that guy. Her brother. He fills our pontoon with gas at the marina."

"Yeah, that's his second job."

"He's kind of cute," she says, nudging me.

"I think so too."

We both wait a minute; then I say, "Hey, thanks for not telling everybody back in Charleston about the Christmas tree. That was really cool of you."

"Oh, don't thank me. Everybody has family stuff to deal with."

"I guess so," I say, then I hear Mama laughing with Mrs. Edings on the porch of the caretaker's house. It is a joyful kind of laughter that makes me feel safe.

"You know I still go to town to youth group at St. Paul's. You're welcome to come along if you want."

"Thanks, DeVeaux," Mary Margaret says to me. "I think that would be good for me. As pretty as this island is, I need to get away sometimes."

"Don't I know," I say, and we both chuckle.

Beneath the tin roof, I can hear Daddy setting up to roast some more oysters. Dinks Edings is helping him. While Mary Margaret stares into the stars, I try to listen to their conversation:

"Billy, sometime I need to talk a little business with you," Dinks says.

"Now's as good a time as any. Could you hand me that croaker sack behind the grill?"

"Sure," Dinks says. We hear the clank of Daddy throwing the oysters onto the sheet metal and the hiss of the steaming water.

Dinks begins, "Well, some developers out of Atlanta have bought Otter Island."

"Oh?" Daddy says.

"My company is investing a little in the project, and I'll need to meet you sometime soon to sign a few papers. Those Atlanta boys are pretty anxious to break ground."

I know this must be tough news for Daddy. I remember that it was Dinks' company who lent him the money to start on Otter Island. But when Daddy ran into big problems with the waterlines and the flood insurance, they had to pull out.

"What is the island going to be this time?" he asks.

"Similar to your plan," Dinks says, "twenty lots in the two-acre size."

"And a wildlife preserve in the center?" Daddy asks.

"Yes," Dinks says, "a wildlife preserve and a nature trail and a section of the beachfront blocked off for the sea turtles to lay their eggs." I can tell that Dinks is trying to contain his excitement, but he's not doing a good job.

"Sounds like a winner," Daddy says, trying hard to be enthusiastic. "Y'all could stand to make a killing."

"Maybe," Dinks says.

Then an owl begins to hoot in the forest behind us. When the owl is quiet Dinks says, "Well, it's great for you and Dee to have Cornelia and me out like this. Tell me how y'all are doing."

"Oh, we're doing good," Daddy says. "We're enjoying getting back in touch with our ancestors' way of living in the wild. Never a dull moment and the deer are everywhere."

"Glad to hear it," Dinks says, patting him again on the back. "Looks like the kind of living we all have a longing for."

"Yeah," Daddy says. "Why don't you go on in and get a cup of Dee's stew. And tell the others that the next batch will be ready in fifteen minutes."

"Sure thing, Billy," Dinks says.

I hear Daddy stoke the fire, and my heart sinks for him. He is more alone than anyone I know, and I pray silently, *Lord, let him feel Your loving presence.* Then Mary Margaret and I climb down from the roof and I go to give him some company. I put my hand on his back and say, "Need help?"

"I don't believe so, honey," he says, his eyes still on the burning logs beneath us. His face is glazed with heat. He steps away from my hand, picks up a pitcher of water and pours it on top of the burlap sacks. Steam rises like a wall between us. I can almost hear the tight shells loosen beneath the cloth, their hinges burning to softness. "Go on and help your mama," he says.

When we are shucking the second batch, Easy the cat jumps up on the table. She is sniffing her way around the shells. Daddy says calmly in the direction of Mama, "Get the cat down."

"I'll get her," Mr. Edings says. "Come here, Easy. Boy, you've gotten heavy," he says.

"Really?" Mama says. Mrs. Edings takes Easy out of Mr. Edings' arms.

"Yeah, boy. Is Easy going to be a mama?" she asks Daddy, who just grunts into his oysters and says, "Better not be."

Mrs. Edings looks at Easy's belly, and as she begins to rub beneath the fur, her charm bracelet knocks the picnic table. "Oh my, look at her nipples," she says. "She *is* going to be a mama!"

Dr. Davidson, the medical expert of the bunch, takes Easy from Mrs. Edings. As he runs his fingers along her belly, we all can see her bright red nipples.

"Yeah," he says, "looks like it won't be long. In fact, she's got quite a load in there. I'm feeling three on the bottom and there are probably at least three more."

"Well, I can't believe it," Mama says. "I haven't seen any other cats around here."

Then I picture that wild cat who was crying on our porch steps in the middle of the night last week.

Daddy does not like this news. He doesn't like Easy, and the thought of six more cats, even if we can eventually find homes for them, must be grating on his nerves.

I watch him pour the cup of melted butter over his shucked oysters. He keeps his head down while he eats them.

The next thing we know, we hear the sound of a young boy laughing. We look up to see Sagi running toward us.

"Surprise!" he says. He runs up to me, pats my knee beneath the blankets and says, "Miss DeLoach, will you take me to see the porpoises in the boat?"

Then Mrs. Shuzuki comes running after him.

"Oh, so sorry to interrupt," she says. "We decided to come down and check on the house renovations."

Talk about bad timing, I think to myself as I watch Mama and Daddy look back and forth at Mrs. Shuzuki and each other. The guests are also looking at one another. The Davidsons are peering across the picnic table at the Edings. Something in their eyes seems to indicate that they all *know* about the Shuzukis, though no one in our family has ever *told* them about the Shuzukis.

Mrs. Edings is the first to break the silence. She looks to Mrs. Shuzuki and says, politely, "Oh, the plantation house is being renovated?"

Proudly Mrs. Shuzuki says, "Yes, by Duncan Bell, a famous architect. You like to see it?"

We are about through with our oysters, and Mrs. Edings looks around the picnic table at us as if she has been elected to take control of this situation. She makes a fist on the table and says, "Why yes, I'd love to see it. What about y'all?"

The Davidsons wipe their mouths and say, "Yes, of course!"

And before we know it, we are making our way over to the main house. Daddy is leading us with his flashlight. We have to cross through the dark field and then the thick bushes and trees in the gall, but we can see the glow of the plantation lights just beyond the row of palmettos that Edmund Seabrook Rose planted along the entry paths.

From the outside the plantation house looks the same.

"I forget how majestic it is," Mrs. Edings says.

"Living history," Mr. Edings says. "You step back in time when you enter this place."

When we climb to the porch, Mrs. Shuzuki asks if we would mind taking off our shoes. We set them all outside the front door. Eight pairs of duck boots.

When we walk in, we see that the front side of the house has been entirely gutted, and what used to be the foyer, living room, and dining room is now one big den with shaggy white carpet and an enormous ivory-colored coffee table that is the shape of a shark's tooth. A modern couch the shape of a *U* outlines the coffee table, and a big conch shell with a pearl inside balances a large entertainment center, which contains a big-screen television and a stereo.

"Oh my," says Mrs. Edings.

I close my eyes then look again. I try to picture the house the way it used to be with the creaky floorboards that held dust from 1810 in their crevices, the grand staircase with its worn-in steps that carried guests like Lafayette to their bedrooms, and the layers of intricate molding that outlined the ceiling of each room and each window. I think about how many times Mee Maw Rose had people like the Edings over to the plantation house for her own socials. Mr. Edings grew up in and out of this house, warming up by the hearth on Edmund Seabrook Rose's ottoman.

Now I look over to Daddy, whose face is splotchy and damp. He must be fuming by now, but he's doing all he can to keep his composure.

Even Mama is downright embarrassed. Her head stays slightly tilted toward the floor as Mrs. Shuzuki leads us through the house: the slick-tiled kitchen with a Jenn-Air grill on a center island, the mirrored bedroom with its own wet bar and ice maker, and finally, the crow's nest on the roof, where the hot tub bubbles are accentuated by blue and red underwater lights.

Suddenly we hear Mrs. Shuzuki shriek. We look and see that her yelling is directed toward Flounder, who has just bounded through the front door and is now rolling around on the shag carpet in the center of her gigantic den.

"He is a filthy dog!" she says, and I run and catch him by his collar beneath the shark's-tooth coffee table and drag him outside.

꒰ꞋꞋ

On the walk home, Daddy is completely silent.

Mrs. Edings, in an effort to make conversation, says, "I was just looking at my latest *Architectural Digest* last week and I said to my cousin Dottie, who organizes the Historical Home Tour, I said, 'Modern furnishings are still quite popular, aren't they Dottie?' and she said, 'Yes, indeed.'"

"Would anyone like some coffee?" Mama asks without enthusiasm when we reach the caretaker's house, but everyone is quick to say that it is getting late and they need to get home.

Mary Margaret helps me fold the blankets in the fish shed while her parents collect their stuff. I'm too worried about Daddy to pay much attention to her. When we fold the last blanket she says, "Well, I'm around if you ever want to get together."

"Okay," I say. "That sounds good."

Then she says, "I'm an acolyte at Edisto Episcopal, and I'm the only girl in the youth group—there are five guys. Maybe you could come out with us sometime. We do pizza in Walterboro on Friday nights, and we're going to kayak in the ACE Basin next month."

"Sure," I say, knowing that a little old lady leads the group and that it is probably a very dorky scene. "Thing is, I work a lot of weekends, but I'll see."

She nods then turns to join her parents, who are flashing the lights of their Suburban in our direction. I watch as her gangly legs carry her through the mud to her car. Who'd have thought that I'd end up on this island with the nerd of all nerds from my days downtown? I chuckle to myself when I think of my social life options: pizza in Walterboro with Mary Margaret and the old-lady-led church youth group, or pregnancy tests in the Sears bathroom with Tina, or salty kisses behind the Dumpster of the restaurant with C.C. I guess I won't need to curtsy or waltz or use a finger bowl or a fifth fork like Mrs. Hillhouse taught me with such devotion and care. I may never even go to a prom or anything that might remotely require the use of my carefully honed social and etiquette skills.

❧

Later, I can hear Mama talking to Daddy in their bedroom. He says, "Well, Dee, we had *your* party."

"I'm so sorry, Billy," Mama says. "I had no idea that it would turn out like—"

"What kills me most of all is that you spent a whole week on this *disaster*," he says and then, "What a waste of energy."

"Honey," she says, trying to calm him.

But he will not hear her. He says, "Now, I'm getting real tired of you spending your time and effort on useless things. I want you to answer me a question."

"Okay," she says.

"How long have we been married?"

"Thirty years," she says.

"That's right," he says. "And have you ever held a job during any of that time?"

"A job?" she says softly. "No."

"So we've had thirty years of you spending your energy on unprofitable things while I've been working myself into a heart attack for this family. I think it's about time you start bringing some money into this house, Dee. *You* need to get a job."

Now Mama is quiet and so is Daddy. Eventually someone gets up to turn out the lights.

❧

When I wake up around midnight to the sound of Daddy on the creaky floors, I have an anxious feeling so I sit up in bed and listen to him walk onto the porch and out into the yard. I feel so desperate for Daddy. His suffering seems to go on and on like a terminal illness that will slowly infect us all.

Then I remember Bethany's words: *"This is not the end of the story,"* and they sustain me with their hope and strength.

In the distance I hear Easy meowing softly. She must be in the fish shed eating what was left in the oyster shells.

When I finally get up to see what is going on, I see Daddy walking toward the dock. I slip on my shoes and walk quietly out onto the porch. I can see him under the dock light. He is standing on the edge. It looks like he's holding something.

Then I hear a terrified "Meow!" and a splash, and I realize that Daddy has just thrown Easy into the creek. She must be moving quickly on the incoming tide because I can hear her cries fade as she sails away. Daddy stands there for a moment looking in the opposite direction, toward the Intracoastal Waterway and Otter Island.

❧

In a quiet panic, I slip through the yard and run down the dirt road of the avenue of oaks. I have to find help—someone with a boat. It's the only way to save Easy.

I consider going to find Chambers at Maum Bess's, but I am too frightened by the darkness of the swamp that I have to cross to get to their house.

Instead, I run out of the Rose Hill gates and down to Tina's trailer where C. C. is sitting on the porch smoking a cigarette. I am so relieved to see him. In a rush I tell him what's happened, and we jump in his boat with his flounder-gigging spotlight and start slowly riding down the creek.

We have to move carefully out of the narrow spit of water that backs up to C. C.'s house. Thankfully he knows the curves by heart and before we know it, we are connected to Rose Hill Creek, which is much wider with enormous mud banks that separate it from the waterway and the ocean.

"Cut off the motor," I say.

He does.

"Do you hear anything?" I say.

"No," he says as he pans the marsh with his bright light.

"Lord, help us," I pray as I follow C. C.'s light into the thick darkness of the marsh grass.

Suddenly, I hear a cry in the direction of Blue House Creek where our Christmas tree sailed. Then I imagine Easy dead in front of Mary Margaret's house, resting in a heap on top of their crab trap.

"Oh, how can we find her?" I say to C. C. through the lump in my throat, but I can tell that he already has a plan.

"She's probably up the creek on a marsh mound. This is going to be tricky because we need to go against the tide."

"Let's go," I say, and he hands me the spotlight as he starts the motor.

I frantically scan the marsh and the shoreline as we begin to move slowly against the tide.

Every few yards he stops the motor and we call her.

Nothing.

When we reach the bend just before my dock, we hear Easy. Her cries are coming from a mud bank.

The spotlight picks up her green eyes for a split second and C. C. throws out the anchor as I call her.

"She could be stuck in the mud," he says. "We might have to go into the marsh on foot to pick her up. Otherwise, the boat'll get stuck."

The look on my face shows that I am nervous about going into the marsh. I know it's the kind of place where raccoons and water rats and even alligators spend their nights.

C. C. calls the cat some more. She must be light enough to walk in the mud because we can hear her cries growing louder. He grabs the light from me, then he spots her, walking out to the tip near an oyster bank.

"Stay put," he says to me as he steps out of the boat. I see his leg sinking into the mud up to his knee, and he presses down on a sand bar to pull himself out. Easy walks out to the end of the mud bank then she jumps over to the sand bar and comes so close to C. C. that he is able to reach out and pick her up.

He hands Easy up to me then pulls himself back into the boat. I hold her wet, shivering body as close as I can while her muddy paws leave prints all down my sweatshirt.

"Thank you," I say to C. C.

"Well, we found her!" he says proudly before both of our teeth begin to chatter. Suddenly, we are freezing.

After looking around the cold night, C. C. says that it's too dark to make it back into his creek so we dock at the marina on the other side of the island and go into Coot's Lounge to find his mother for a ride home. (She whoops it up there every Saturday night.)

Together we walk into the bar. C. C. is wet and mud is up to his thighs. I'm still holding Easy, and I watch the Labradors, Muddy Girl and Cocoa, who are snoozing by the pool table. They slowly lift their heads and sniff in my direction, but they seem too tired to move.

C. C.'s mama, Hazel, is drunk. Larry, the doctor from Walterboro, broke up with her last week and she has decided to tie one on.

Tanner Strickland is holding her up. "You're just in time to take your mama home," he says to C. C.

Just then Sal and Jeeter come walking up to us. Sal puts his hand on my shoulder and says, "So have you and C. C. been rolling around in the mud?"

"Shut up, Sal," I say, even though he is my boss.

"I'm just kidding, Devo," he says. He starts to pet Easy. He says, "Poor ol' kitty cat."

"Yeah, Devo," Jeeter says, "let me buy you and C. C. a White Russian." He holds his coffee-colored drink up and slurps.

"You know I don't drink, Jeeter," I say to him.

"I might as well have one for the road," C. C. says to me. "It'll warm me up."

"I don't think drinking and driving is such a good idea, C. C."

He squeezes the back of my neck and says, "You're right. Bartender, make me a co-cola."

The bartender pours him a soda in a Styrofoam cup, which I carry in my other arm because Hazel is so bad off that C. C. has to literally pick her up and carry her out to her car.

In the parking lot, he fumbles through Hazel's purse for the keys then puts her in the backseat before offering me a sip of his drink. After a gulp, I realize that it is stronger than a regular soft drink, and I can tell that Jeeter must have spiked it with bourbon when no one was looking. I'm so tired of their antics and how nothing around here is as innocent as you think it is. As I pour out the drink so C. C. can't have it, my own head begins to spin.

Now I roll down the car window with Easy on my lap, and I look over to the sand dunes where I see one faint light, which must be the glow of a cigarette. C. C.'s headlights pan the dunes and for a split second I see a familiar figure, who stands up and makes a visor by putting her hands over her eyes. She squints into the lights. It is Cousin Eli. She's standing on the top of a dune looking in our direction. C. C. doesn't notice. He's concentrating on getting his mama home. He has done so much already that I feel too guilty to ask him to stop. My head is woozy now, and I just want to get some rest.

Tomorrow, I tell myself as I pet Easy, *I'll worry about Cousin Eli.*

When we get back to C. C.'s, I rest on the couch while he puts his mama to bed. I can hear either Baby Faye or Tina rustling beneath the covers in their bedroom.

When C. C. comes back into the den, he turns off all the lights except the one over the kitchen sink.

"Do you need to go home?" he says as he sits down on the couch next to me.

"I should, but I don't know what to do about Easy," I say.

He puts his hand on my cheek then puts a piece of my hair behind my ear. "Why don't you stay here and worry about what to do next in the morning."

Even though I know Mama will be worried and all, I can't help picturing Daddy on the edge of the dock, gently tossing Easy into the water. I can't go home to that. I turn to C. C. and say, "Okay, I'll stay here. On the couch. And you'll stay far away behind the closed door of your bedroom." He takes my cue and says, "Good night," before handing me a blanket and heading to his room.

As I lie on the couch listening to the deep breaths of Baby Faye, Tina, and C. C. on the other side of the thin walls, I think to myself that it's hard to believe I'm actually spending the entire night in a double-wide trailer, secretly, without my parents' permission. I wonder to my Lord, *How long will this story go on?* Then I smile when I recall that the first month of spring is just a few weeks away.

Now Easy, who has been snoozing on the floor, hops up on my stomach and I rest my hand on her belly, feeling the warmth of her thick fur and the lower three sacks that shift slightly beneath her skin.

12

Protection

The next morning I wake up to the sound of a truck barreling down the dirt road, just feet away from the front door of the double-wide.

I know that I have not slept well because of the night sounds, animal calls, and cold leaves breaking that seemed closer because of these tin walls. I think I was actually frightened once by a dog howling, frightened the way I used to be on Tradd Street when I was younger on those rare occasions when Daddy did not spend the night under our roof. He would be on an overnight hunt or a business trip and even with Brother Will in the house, even with the sound of Virginia snoring one door over, I would still slide down the wooden stairs and into the cold side of the bed, opposite Mama, where a loaded handgun rested in the drawer of the bedside table inches away.

One time, when Virginia was a teenager, some man with a husky voice called her in the middle of the night and whispered dirty things to her. I remember hearing her as she slammed down the telephone, jumped out of her bed and pounded on the floor above my parents' room, making the whole house shake. Since this was the signal for trouble, which Daddy had established, it took him less than three seconds to get upstairs. I can picture him now, flying past my room in his white boxers, a rifle in one hand and the flashlight in the other. I remember him carefully putting down his weapon and pulling her shoulders into his soft chest in the hallway, rocking her back and forth and saying, "I won't let anybody hurt you," as the bottom of her nightgown swept across the hardwood floor.

My next waking thought is of Cousin Eli, sitting alone on the sand dune in the dark, and I know that as soon as I get up, I have to go find her.

When I hear another rumbling motor, I clear my throat and C.C. walks out of his room in a T-shirt and pajama bottoms before lying down in the La-Z-Boy chair next to me. "It's early," he says as he pats my head. "Sleep a little longer."

I watch his chest lift itself up and down on the recliner, and in a few short seconds he's snoring lightly.

Before I fall back to sleep, I notice the faint sound of laughter from the television, which sits in front of us. Through my half-closed eyes, I see Baby Faye kneeling in her pajamas, inches away from the screen, watching cartoons with the sound turned down.

Suddenly, there's a tap at the window by the front door of the trailer. As I am about to rub my eyes, I hear my name. "DeVeaux?"

It is Mama's voice, and when I open my eyes I see her—nose pressed against the window, eyes squinting in the morning light. When she spots me on the couch with C.C. asleep on the chair next to me, she puts her hand over her mouth and gasps.

Quickly, I walk over and whisper into his ear, "Mama's here." His eyelids throw themselves back. He looks around the room like he's being hunted.

Mama taps the window with her knuckles and says my name again. This time it's a frightened-sounding question, and her voice breaks and wavers as she spreads the syllables out. "DeVeaux?"

Baby Faye looks back at me and to the window again.

I leap up off the sofa, hoping Mama can see that I am fine and in my right senses. By the time I get to the door, C.C. is standing up. I look back as he straightens his T-shirt and scratches the sleep out of his eyes.

Baby Faye walks over to him, pokes his thigh, and says, "I'm hungry."

When I open the door, Mama looks me dead-on. I glance at the truck, which is parked at an angle and running. "What in the world are you doing here, DeVeaux?" Mama says to me.

"Everything's all right, Mama," I say.

She peers into the trailer and sees C. C. looking down at Baby Faye.

I gently touch her elbow and whisper in a firm voice, referring to C. C., "I'm fine, Mama. I can explain."

She says, "I was getting ready for church, and . . ." Then she looks up at the Spanish moss that dangles over the tin roof like Indian scalps. She's searching for words.

As I wait, I notice that she is half-dressed for church. The slick black buttons of her teal green suit are all in place and the golden-colored Chanel scarf, which she inherited from Mee Maw Rose, is tied in a square knot around her neck. But she doesn't have on a drop of makeup. The puffy pockets beneath her eyes are unveiled, and her hair is still held up by an assortment of bobby pins and clips.

She collects herself and begins to speak again. "And I popped my head in your bedroom to see if you wanted to go and you were nowhere to be found." She takes a look at my rumpled, muddy clothes and says, "Now I don't know what has gone on here, young lady, but—"

Then Easy walks out the door and onto the porch where her tail curls around Mama's ankle.

"Easy?" Mama says like a clear question, as if the cat is going to have a better explanation than I will.

I hear C. C. just behind me. He clears his throat and says, "Morning, Mrs. DeLoach, ma'am."

Mama looks at C. C. and says, "Well, young man, I feel I must say that it is rather inappropriate—"

I grab Mama's elbow again and say, "Nothing *happened*. Let me explain."

Just then Tina comes out of her bedroom. She yawns and goes to the door. "DeVeaux?" she says. "What are *you* doing here?"

Tina looks C. C. up and down, then she looks at me and begins to grin. Just as she is about to speak, Hazel starts to rustle around in her room. In a whiny, country voice she says, "Tina?"

Tina says, "Yes'm?"

Hazel says, "How about fetchin' the aspirin bottle for your mama." She yawns loud enough for us all to hear. She says, "Lord, I'm in rough shape."

Mama's eyes grow wide. She bends down, picks up Easy, and says to me, "Get in the truck."

As I follow her to the car, I see streaks of mud on her calves and the heels of her black patent-leather shoes. A horizontal line of dirt has dried on the back of her skirt. She must have been in such a hurry to find me that she didn't maneuver herself over the muddy threshold of the truck.

As soon as she gets behind the wheel, the truck cuts off. It takes us three tries to start it up again and by the time we are pulling out of the dirt driveway, Tina, Baby Faye, and C. C. are standing on the front porch watching us.

When I look back at them, Tina mouths, *Call me*, while C. C. winks, his face still glowing with the glaze of sleep. And then Baby Faye starts to wave, dramatically, like she's sending off two dear friends after a long, satisfying visit.

❧

As we drive down the road toward Rose Hill, Mama says, "You have a lot of explaining to do."

I say, "Mama, I'll tell it all to you if you don't take us home."

Without hesitation, she turns the truck around and drives toward the beach to the Exxon station, the only place on the island that serves breakfast.

On the way, we pass Edisto Episcopal where an elder, dressed in his white robe, is cleaning one of the Tiffany glass windows beside the front door, and then we pass Mt. Zion AME where two men, Bibles tucked tightly under their arms, are setting a bouquet of plastic purple flowers on an easel outside the cinderblock sanctuary.

I look at my watch. It is 8:00 a.m.

At the Exxon, we take a seat in one of the three booths and order the special, gravy biscuits and a cup of coffee. As I fill my cup of coffee with heaping spoonfuls of sugar, Mama cuts down one of the cups with a plastic knife, making a little bowl. Then she pours a few of the half-and-half containers into it. She motions to the truck and says, "For Easy."

As I watch Mama wobble toward the truck in her Sunday suit, her inherited Chanel scarf blowing in the sea wind, I think of how Mee Maw used to take a trip to New York every winter where she would stay at the Waldorf-Astoria and buy a scarf from Chanel to add to her collection. She took every granddaughter the year they turned seventeen—two more years and I would have gone. When she died, I stood with Mama and Virginia in Mee Maw's closet as they divided up the scarf collection while Virginia reminisced about her initiation trip: the leisurely hotel breakfasts, a carriage ride through Central Park, the dressing rooms of Barney's and Bergdorf Goodman.

As Mama walks back from the parking lot, I look around the all-purpose gas station where I am surrounded by cheap postcards with generic pictures of sand dunes, cans of nonperishables, and refrigerator magnets with slogans that range from "Surf Naked" to "Jesus Saves."

A heavyset black woman sets plastic plates of gravy biscuits on our table. Out of the front pocket of her lard-stained apron, she pulls two plastic wrappers, each containing a thin napkin and a spoon with teeth.

She nods to two men, dressed in camouflage, who are seating themselves behind me. Deer season is over, and I wonder if they've been out there breaking the law.

As the lumps of sausage float in the gravy above the puffy biscuits, I imagine Mee Maw Rose again. This time she's in the dining room at the Waldorf-Astoria, her silver fork cutting into an omelet filled with caviar.

When Mama sits back down, I take one of her hands and say, "First, I want you to know that nothing happened between C. C. and me."

Mama nods her head and says, "You know we've never had our talk about s-e-x, but you know what I believe—"

"Yes, ma'am, I know." Mama, like Bethany and Stu, believes that you shouldn't have sex until God has brought you together in marriage, but her explanation isn't always as compelling as theirs.

Once, when Virginia was still in high school, she came home from a date well after her curfew, and I overheard Mama telling her about the blessing of sex after marriage and how God will bind her with her husband like concrete if she waits. Then Daddy interrupted and said sternly to my sister, "Let me be frank, Virginia. Why buy the cow when you can get the milk for free? Every young man wants the milk for free. And I ought to know because I once was one."

I remember being so terrified when I heard this. I was around eight years old, and for a year or so I was afraid to play with boys. But that was before I learned that Daddy isn't always right.

"So, start explaining," Mama says. I can tell she is relieved that what she believes is "the worst possible news" is out of the way, because she takes a hearty bite of her saturated biscuit, closes her eyes, and says, "Well, I'm already breaking my diet, but this is awfully good."

I take a bite and feel the cream and butter roll down my throat.

I know that I just have to go on and tell her so I say, "Did you hear Daddy late last night?"

"No," she says.

"Well, I heard him in the middle of the night. He got up and went outside and over to the fish shed where Easy was crying in the oyster shells."

Mama washes down her mouthful with a gulp of coffee and says, "What happened?"

"Mama," I say, leaning in so the two men dressed in camouflage in the booth behind us can't hear, "he picked Easy up, walked to the edge of the dock, and threw her into the creek."

"What?" she says, leaving her mouth half open like a hooked fish.

I tell her the same thing again. This time she looks down to her plate, which is now empty except for the leftover bits of sausage that swim in the gravy along the edges. Her eyes become soft and weary, and I know that she believes me. She seems more sad than surprised. She makes a mournful noise from the gut.

I look around the room and spot the back of a tall girl with thick dark hair at the register. Cousin Eli! But when she turns around to search the aisles, I see that it isn't. The girl looks younger than me, thirteen maybe, with braces and an unusually long neck. I watch her parents, both tall and thin. They come up to the cash register and stand behind her. The three of them remind me of the straight, narrow pilings, blasted by dynamite into the ground, that hold up the planks of the pier. The girl hands the mother her drink and a candy bar, and the father pulls his wallet from his rear pocket.

I decide not to tell Mama about seeing Cousin Eli last night. There must be some good reason Eli didn't want to tell us that she was here.

But I can't help but glance to the door each time it opens, to see if she'll come in to buy a pack of cigarettes. If she comes, Mama will see her, she will throw her arms around her, and I won't have to worry about keeping this secret.

Then Mama straightens up, looks out to the truck and back to me. "What happened next?" she says.

"Well, luckily the tide was coming in, otherwise Easy would have ended up in the ocean. But she was floating inland, and I was hoping she'd bump into a mud bank. So I went for help, without Daddy seeing me, and the first person I found was C. C. over at Tina's."

"Now I see," Mama says. She pats her forehead with her napkin and adds, "It was all my fault for forcing that dinner party on him. He had to swallow his pride before his old friends. I made him look bad, and I regret it so—but of course that's no excuse for him to do this. Well, go on and tell me the rest."

I say, "So C. C. got in his boat with his flounder-gigging spotlight, and we drove upstream until we heard Easy crying. Then C. C. jumped out of the boat to get her."

Mama says, "That could have been dangerous," then, "and it was so cold last night." She reaches across the table and puts the back of her hand against my forehead.

"No fever."

I notice that Mama is wheezing when she says the words "cold" and "fever." Now her lungs sound cloggy when she takes a breath.

"C. C. knew what he was doing," I say.

"But it's awful," she says, now in a whisper that she has no control over, "that you had to be out there like that."

"Mama, C. C. is real careful," I say, realizing that I'm trying to make him look good, which must mean I like him some. "He's a natural boatsman."

Mama nods then wheezes, "Well, go on and finish the story."

I say, "It was so late by the time we got home that I just stayed at C. C.'s house."

Mama shakes her head as she pulls out a fancy-duty contraption that looks like a mini snorkeler. She presses on it twice and quick bursts come out of it into her mouth.

"What is that, Mama?"

"I've got asthma, DeVeaux," she says.

"What?" I say.

"I went to the doctor last week, and I didn't tell you or Daddy because I didn't want anything to affect last night's party."

"Are you okay?" I ask.

"Well, yes, of course. I was actually having an attack on the way to his office so Dr. McCall got to see me at my worst. He had to put me on a respirator."

"Mama!" I say. I hate the thought of Mama in danger, and to think that I didn't even know about it.

"Don't worry," she says as she sucks in the air again. "Now I just have to blow on this thing when I get cloggy and it clears up my lungs."

"Mmm," I say. "Does it always work?"

"Yes, it always works—of course, Dr. McCall says to watch it. That there is a chance it might not on occasion."

"And what if it doesn't?" I say.

"If it doesn't, I have to go get on a respirator."

"Or what?"

"Or my lungs will close up."

"And you'll lose consciousness, then suffocate," I say. I know this because I saw a *60 Minutes* special on a little boy and a famous model who died that way.

"Well." Mama nods.

"Gracious, Mama! You should have told me about this. You can't keep something like that a secret. It's dangerous."

"There wasn't a right time last week," she says. "I was planning on telling your father tonight at supper, but I'm just dreading it."

"Why?"

"He doesn't know how to take in these things, DeVeaux. You know how he gets irritated when things confuse or upset him."

"But you *have* to tell him!"

When I hear Mama's familiar command of "Don't tell," I hear her voice throughout my childhood and all of the times she hushed my siblings and me into keeping quiet:

Virginia says, "Mama, I forgot to lock the door." Mama says, "Don't tell Daddy; just run home and lock it." Will says, "We forgot the safety jackets in the boat." Mama says, "Just don't tell Daddy. We don't need them." I say, "I spilled a jar of honey on the living room sofa." Mama says, "Don't tell 'you know who.'"

We four freeze wherever we are in the house as his car pulls up. Mama flutters, cleans, hide things. She says, "Daddy will not be able to handle this—just don't tell him." Will says, "The pot roast accidentally fell on the floor. Is it ruined?" "No," Mama says, "just don't tell Daddy. He'll want to throw it out." Cousin Eli trips and falls off the back porch, skinning her knee. "Shh," Mama says, "here comes Daddy. He doesn't need to know this."

Mama explains, "Daddy needs peaceful, calm waters at home. He has enough rockiness out in the world."

"But Mama," we say, "so do we."

As if she isn't listening Mama leans in and says, "I think it's best if when Easy has the kittens we keep them over in the teahouse, away from Daddy, just so he isn't running into them all the time."

"Boy, what a dysfunctional family we are!" I say and at this moment, I'm disappointed in my daddy. How has he become someone you can't even tell important, vital things to?

Now I have to know something. I say, "You know, Mama, I can think of so many good times with Daddy, but I can't remember when or how he's become the way he is now. I mean he's always had a short fuse, but now—I mean, what has changed in him?"

Mama says, "Oh baby, your father has not always been like

this." She says, "But the very beginnings of this started when he lost his sister, and since then he's had a kind of mad streak that comes and goes depending on how hard the times are. And these are the worst we've ever had."

"Mama," I say, and I look at her real serious because I believe that I have earned the right to know this as a participant in this recent family trouble, "how *did* Aunt Eliza die?" If I know this, maybe I can feel a new kind of sympathy for my daddy. Pull it from another source. Because as it is now, I can't will myself to feel sorry for him anymore.

Mama looks around the gas station. She looks back at me and rubs her thumb across my hand.

"Okay," she says, leaning in, "you're old enough to know this."

"Yes," I say, proud to have gotten somewhere with her, "I am."

She leans in farther and rubs her forehead. "It started when Mee Maw Rose had invited us out to Rose Hill for a picnic. It was early spring, and she wanted us to see the azalea buds in the garden because she'd just had fifty new bushes planted the year before."

Mama grins sheepishly. "I had just found out that I was pregnant with you at the time . . . And you know you were a surprise."

I nod.

"A wonderful surprise," she says, flapping her hand in the air like she's swatting away a fly.

Then her eyes focus on mine as she becomes serious again. She continues, "Anyway, your aunt Eliza and James Flint and Eli were living temporarily in the main house at the time. James Flint was working, writing some sort of a novel, and he needed to get out of Charleston. He was originally from Vermont, you know, never really received by Mee Maw Rose or Charleston. I think the town made him feel claustrophobic, but he adored Eliza and she did not want to leave."

I lean in to catch her words. This is the first time I've heard anything about James Flint, and I am fascinated. We never get to talk
about him around Daddy.

Mama continues, "I guess you could say that there was always a
bit of tension about Mee Maw Rose dropping in on Eliza and James
Flint without notice, invading the privacy of their home, which was,
of course, her house to begin with. And Daddy and James Flint were
always butting heads over this. Daddy wanted free rein of the fields
to hunt, and he wanted Mee Maw Rose to have her ladies out to
watch the flowers bloom anytime she pleased.

"So we were all out there unannounced for a picnic. And, it's
my guess that at the first glance at Daddy and Mee Maw Rose
driving down the avenue of oaks, James Flint decided to go on a
boat ride, to get out of our way, though he acted as if he'd been
planning one for days.

"When we arrived at the door, I could see him packing up the
boat and I could see Eliza making tomato sandwiches on the dock."

Mama pauses, puts her fingertips on her forehead and says, "I
can remember walking toward her on the dock. She said to me,
'You're beginning to show, Dee,' and as she smiled at me she then
said, kind of anxious, 'Tell Mee Maw and Billy that we're going for
a boat ride. Y'all can have the place to yourselves for a few hours.'
Then I remember right as she said this, Cousin Eli dropped down
from the roof of the fish shed and ran toward Will and Virginia.

"When I saw how glad the children were to see one another I
offered to keep an eye on Eli for the day and James Flint said,
'Fine.'"

❧

Now I try to picture the scene in my head. When I was a child, I
noticed that both Daddy and Mee Maw Rose had the same pic-

ture of Aunt Eliza on their bedside tables. In the picture, she is nineteen, dressed in her debutant gown—a simple, sleeveless, ivory silk dress, with long kid gloves that are pushed down below her elbows, revealing the suntan of her upper arms. Her thick, dark hair rests on her shoulders, ending where her arms begin. She is standing on the front porch of Mee Maw's house on Water Street, leaning against the railing, the thin, sharp leaves of the palmetto trees blossoming like fireworks in the background. Her hazel eyes are looking straight into the camera.

This is how I always picture my aunt Eliza when anyone tells stories about her, so now I see her standing on the dock in that long gown, the crumbs of the tomato sandwiches caught in the seams of her kid gloves.

❧

Mama continues, "After we had our picnic, your daddy wanted to take a nap and so I gathered the children up, and we went into the house for a long snooze. Mee Maw Rose had been inspecting the house most of the afternoon, and now she was sitting on the porch rocking back and forth, staring out into the gall, waiting for James Flint to return so she could have a word with him about his typewriter scraping one of the Rose family antique desks. She had Chambers fetch a card table from the hardware store for him to use.

"When it was time to head back to the city, late afternoon, Eliza and James Flint weren't back. We were concerned about leaving Eli so Mee Maw Rose said, 'Y'all head on back. Chambers can take me home.'

"By dark that night, Mee Maw had started to worry so she called your daddy and he called Chambers, who got the johnboat ready for a search. Late that night, Daddy and Chambers got in the boat and started channeling the creeks. They looked all night.

It was a clear night, too, but they didn't find a thing until a few hours after sunrise when they turned off Steamboat Creek onto that narrow cut-through to the Intracoastal Waterway. And there they found them. James Flint was all cut up from the blades of the motor and Eliza had drowned during high tide. Her legs were trapped beneath the front half of the boat.

"What they figured happened was this: James Flint must have run up on a mud bank that looked like deep water—you can never tell once the tide starts going out. He must have gotten out of the boat and tried to get the motor loose from the mud before the water disappeared, leaving them high and dry. He must have told Eliza to run the trim and try to raise the motor while he pushed the mud out of the blades, and it must have slipped out of neutral, cutting his hands and arms and throwing her forward where the boat jumped on top of her legs, then stuck back down in the mud. And there they stayed, watching the tide go out and come back in. No telling how long they were there. Conscious of one another. Both deep in the mud. One trapped beneath the boat. The other bleeding slowly to death."

Now the cream rises up in my stomach. I can't compare this feeling to anything I've ever had before. I am horrified.

Mama dips her head to catch my eyes. I look up at her and say, "So Daddy found them?"

She nods. "He picked them up, put them in the johnboat, and took them back to Rose Hill. Mee Maw was waiting for them on the dock when he rode up."

"I've never heard of anything so awful," I say.

Mama nods and says, "About five months later, when I was about ready to have you, your daddy started rustling the covers and screaming out in the middle of the night. Sometimes he would just shout or say senseless words. But one time he screamed Eliza's name twice in the pitch black of our bedroom on Tradd Street. He kicked the bedpost and punched at the mattress, and I was almost afraid he might accidentally hurt you and me, but it only lasted a few seconds and then he settled back into sleep.

"But the day after the night he screamed his sister's name, he came down for breakfast and had a kind of jumpiness in his eyes that I had never seen in him before. I remember that he was startled by Cousin Eli, who was sitting at the breakfast table with the other children slurping her cereal. He stopped in his tracks and stared at her. She looked so much like her mother in her eyes and in the way she held her body, and yet there was also a part of her face that looked like her father. I think it is the shape of her face, her square jaw and her high cheekbones. James Flint was a striking man. He looked German to me with his light hair and chiseled cheekbones. His face was strong and serious, and his chin jutted out, making him look like he was about to say something important. Anyway, Daddy stared at her a long time without her noticing. He watched her every move until she stood up and walked out of the kitchen. It was like he was afraid of her. Or afraid of the part of her daddy that was in her. Then he turned to me and said, "Things will never be the same.""

The waitress brings the grease-spattered check.

Mama says, "Cousin Eli is the only one besides you who knows how they died. I told her last summer after Mee Maw passed away. I thought she was old enough and that she had the right to have her questions answered."

"Good," I say, but in a way I hate that she has to know. The story must haunt her.

Mama says to me, "Now DeVeaux, you can't be bitter toward your daddy. You being bitter is just as bad as him being bitter about his sister's death." *This is a good point*, I think, *but how can I get rid of this anger? It doesn't just go away.* (Part of me knows that I've got to call Bethany or Sasser and ask them what to do about this, and another part just wants to go on being angry with him because he has earned my anger, distrust, and disrespect.) The voice of something dark even creeps into my mind and says, *"Just let this God thing go. Hate your dad and do whatever else you want to do. You've had it tough enough."*

Mama is waiting for a response.

"Yes, ma'am," I say, trying to agree with her, but suddenly I picture Daddy throwing Easy off the dock just last night. Then I picture his hand slamming down on the table when he tells Mama that he will not pay for Eli's college. I picture him snapping Will's uncleaned fishing rod in two the day after he gave it to him for his twelfth birthday. Will cried as Daddy said, "Now you won't forget to clean it."

I look to Mama and say, "But there are these heaps . . ." I stop and watch as she scrounges through her pocketbook, looking for her change purse. Then I decide not to finish my sentence. What I want to say is that the bad memories of Daddy pile up against the good memories, and I have to measure the two sides of what I have witnessed. I can't look at one without the other. He rescues. He endangers.

Mama must know what I'm thinking because she puts her pocketbook firmly on the table, looks straight into my eyes and says, "He is a good man, and I still believe God will work this all out in him."

As Mama writes a check for breakfast, I think how problems, even catastrophes, make some people worse and other people better. For example, Eli lost her parents, but she is not a bitter person. She is consistently good. She is always trying to reach out to something, to the deaf children she longs to teach and even to those stupid blue crabs who draw blood every time. And then there is Mama, who lost the daddy she worshiped and found herself in a marriage that was different from what she had hoped for.

Granted, she's not perfect, and a little fanatical, but who can forget her scrubbing those mud-filled ornaments last Christmas Day, salvaging what was left?

On our way back to the car we see that Easy is asleep on the seat of the truck. When I get inside, she stands straight up and walks into my lap and meows at us. It takes us a few times to get the truck started. On the third try, one of the men in the Exxon station comes out and says, "Sounds like you got a starter problem; best get it looked at."

"Thanks," Mama says to him as the truck finally starts, and we ride away from the beach. She looks at me and says, "As if we could afford to fix it." We both laugh, feeling the February sun cover us like a safety net.

As we drive home, we pass by Edisto Episcopal and Mt. Zion AME where an unusually large number of cars are parked, spilling out of the grass lots and trickling down the narrow road. There are large wooden crosses in front of each sanctuary with a purple cloak draped across each arm. The black women are in their glitter gold and turbans. The Episcopalian men are in their tweed jackets and bow ties. Behind both choirs, the minister drapes a black piece of fabric over the crucifix the acolyte carries.

"Is today the first Sunday in Lent?" I say.

"Yes," Mama says, looking back at the road.

Few things depress Mama, but I know that a Sunday without church does. The two best things in Mama's life are her weekly church and her diet. And here we are at the beginning of the week, at the beginning of the most sacred time in the spiritual year, and she's broken them both. It will be seven more days before she'll have a formal worship. I think of the handwritten note that is taped at eye level on the refrigerator door. It reads "Give us this day our daily bread," and below that she has written, "Lord, may I be filled and not hunger for more than my body needs."

After we pass the last row of parked cars, Mama says, "What a good breakfast." And I watch as she unbuttons her skirt for the rest of the ride.

"What will you give up for Lent?" I say, remembering all those years she and I gave up chocolate or co-colas or fast food.

"Anger," she says, looking at me out of the corner of her eye.

"I don't see how anyone could do that," I say.

"Alone, no one could," she says. And for a moment, I know what she is getting at, and I know that God is the answer to all of my problems, but sometimes I can't find my way back to Him.

"It will come to you, too," she says, and I think she means something more than just religion. I think she means something like the heavy light that came to Chambers in the Sea of Galilee and to her that day she raised her hand when the preacher asked who in the congregation was going to heaven. It's the Holy Spirit she's talking about. That's what Sasser says healed the ringing in his ears. That's what whispers to us when we know God is talking to us. Right now, I can't imagine the Holy Spirit wanting anything to do with me. But then I remember a verse from the apostle Paul's letter to the Romans: *"[Nothing] will be able to separate us from the love of God"* (8:39). And I think to myself, *Not spending the night on the sofa of a romantic interest. Not missing the first Sunday of Lent service. Not grappling with how you feel about your father.*

When we get home, I let Easy out over by the tool shed. Daddy is just returning from taking the Shuzukis fishing. He's cleaning a couple of croakers and a trout at the sink on the dock.

As the fish scales fall from his filet knife into the water, Easy walks directly onto the dock. When Daddy spots her walking toward him, he flinches almost imperceptibly. Then he goes back to cleaning like normal, separating gut from meat as she jumps up on the dock railing beside him, snags a fish head, and walks back to the yard.

I think Daddy knew there was a good possibility Easy would survive and come back, like the Christmas tree. He threw her like a chance. And luck was not on his side, as it hasn't been for some time.

The rules are the same as with the Christmas tree—don't talk about it. So, no one says, "Here's the cat you threw away. What do you think of that?" And no one says, "Here's the tree you threw away. What do you have to say for yourself?" But I think he knows, that we know—the things he wants to get rid of return to him like a boomerang.

The rest of the afternoon I stay out of his way. When we cross each other, things are tense on my end, but I don't think he has any idea that I saw what he did or that I rescued Easy last night. As I walk over to the toolshed to feed Flounder, he lifts his head from the Sunfish sailboat and says, "Some boy named C.C. called for you this morning."

"Okay," I say. "Thanks."

He keeps his head up and looks at me as if he has just seen me for the first time in ages. He cocks his head gently to the side and says, "Got a new boyfriend?"

"Not really," I say.

He shakes his head with a half smile and says, "Well, I guess my lastborn is growing up. I'll never forget that feeling I had watching you come out of that cabin at Camp Pinnacle. I knew then that you were on your way."

I have trouble returning his fond gaze. I look down and suddenly, I notice how much work he has done on the sailboat. All of the barnacles are scraped off, and now he is replacing the rotten wood in the hull.

"The boat's come a long way," I say.

"Yeah," he says, "it's getting there."

"A lot of history in that boat, huh?" I say.

"Yep," he says, "more than I can even recall." Then he sticks his head back in the hole of the hull and begins to work again while Flounder barks up at me for more food.

%

During dinner, croaker fish and corn muffins, Mama says, "Billy, I have some news."

Daddy looks up for a split second, then back down at his plate. "Good or bad?" I can tell he is still put out with her about last night and the Edings.

"I don't know," Mama says, her voice weary. "Bad, I guess."

He takes a deep breath. "Well, Dee, what is it?"

"Well, I went to see Dr. McCall last week for all of this wheezing, and he diagnosed me with asthma."

"Mmm," Daddy says as if he's thinking real hard.

I *want* him to understand the potential danger of this so I say, "She was having an attack on the way over, and he had to put her on a respirator when she got there."

"Is that right?" he says as he turns toward me. "You know about this?"

"She told me today," I say.

"Mmm," Daddy says then he turns back to Mama. "Are you all right?"

"Yes," she says. "I hate having to tell you, honey, to bring bad news, but yes, I'm fine. They gave me an inhaler that should take care of the attacks."

"Good," Daddy says, reaching into the basket for another muffin. He slices it down the middle and squeezes butter from a plastic tube onto each side. He takes a bite, then squeezes more butter onto the sweet, grainy bread.

"How about some good news," he says to Mama. "Have you thought about a job?"

"I'm going to make some calls tomorrow," she says, strong and sincere. She straightens up and pushes her shoulders back.

"Good," he says. "It will be a big help. I'm sure that your doctor bill was a doozy."

"Yes," she says.

When he treats her this way I wonder how she can stand it. She either has skin made of steel or she just doesn't care or God really is protecting her after all.

After dinner, he heads back out to the toolshed, turns on the light, and when we hear the scrape of the knife against the hull of the sailboat, Mama says to me, "Well that wasn't so bad."

"Nope," I say. I pick up the dirty plates and all I can think of is that story Daddy told me a few months back, of Aunt Eliza boldly setting his doves free from the cages. Surely something like that would have made him furious, but he laughed when he recalled it. He must have loved his sister so much that he forgave her for anything. Maybe, before she died, he loved other people that way too. Maybe he loved Mama that way.

Mama is already onto the next subject. "Now listen, honey, we never did talk about where you slept last night."

"But I told you . . ." I say.

"I know what you told me, but ladies don't spend the night in the homes of their potential suitors."

"I know, it's just that last night was so—"

"I know," Mama says. "I just want you to know that C.C. called when you were outside and I told him that if he wanted to see you that he should ask you out on a date and come over here and pick you up like a gentleman."

"Mama!" I say, mortified.

After the dishes are done Mama sits down to read, but she falls asleep within minutes. I sneak back to my room to change clothes. I'm going to find Cousin Eli.

I don't want to ask Daddy if I can use the truck and no one has driven the Honda since that day I took Tina to town, so I go over to Chambers and he lets me borrow his pickup. He says, "Don't be out too late now or your daddy'll have both our hides."

When I get to Suzanne's house (which is the best place to start to look for Eli), Suzanne is sitting in front of the television with her daughter, Becky, asleep on her lap. She's watching a made-for-TV movie.

I knock on the screened door.

She turns her head. "DeVeaux? Come on in."

I walk in and take a seat at her kitchen table.

"What are you up to?" she says.

"I'm looking for Eli," I say.

"Oh, Lord," she says, "did she get in touch with you?"

"No, but I saw her outside of Coot's last night."

"Oh," she says. "Well, I know she hasn't gotten in touch with you yet, 'cause she wasn't ready to tell your daddy that she's dropped out and all."

"Dropped out? What's she doing? Is she okay?"

"She's working on a deep-sea fishing boat that Tanner set her up on. She left this afternoon and won't be back until Wednesday."

Becky rolls over and moans. Suzanne says, "Bedtime, baby." Becky stands up on wobbly legs, rubs her eyes, and looks at me like I'm a part of her dream. As Suzanne helps her toward the bedroom, she turns to me and says, "I'll be back in a sec."

When she gets back, she makes two cups of hot chocolate with little marshmallows floating on top. She says, "I always drink this after Becky's in bed. I have to hide it from her or she'll want it all the time." And then, "I don't blame her, 'cause I want it all the time too." She chuckles.

I ask again, "Is Eli all right?"

"Yeah, sweetie," Suzanne says, "she's fine. She just ran out of loan money and then quit her job at The Gourmand after the owner locked her in the refrigerator when she wouldn't hook up with him."

"Oh no!" I say. "I didn't know that was why she quit."

"Yeah," Suzanne says, slurping her hot drink, "she just said, 'Forget this,' after your dad said he couldn't help her out. In fact, she never even went back to Columbia after the holiday."

"Really?" I say, and I feel both guilty and betrayed. Should I have pressed Daddy about loaning her the money? Did my spineless condition cause my cousin harm? Then self-centeredness gets the better of me and I ask, "Then why hasn't she called me?"

"She just wanted to get her feet on the ground, I reckon, before she told your family and all."

"But she could have called *me*," I say.

"Well, it ain't like she hasn't been looking out for you. I'm always checking up on you for her, aren't I?"

❧

By the time I return the truck to Chambers, it's late. He offers to drive me home, but I tell him I'll just walk, half-forgetting just how pitch-black it gets.

As I head through the dark fields, I think of my cousin Eli on a boat in the Atlantic Ocean. I picture her baiting the big hooks with lady fish and triggers. I picture her scrubbing down the deck and drinking strong coffee and laughing at the smell of the salt and fish in her clothes. Three whole days until I see her. I have already decided that I'm going to be waiting for her on the pier of the marina. I'll wave to her as her boat pulls up. She'll throw me a rope from the bow, which I'll catch and pull and tie quickly to the dock.

When I'm deep in the corn rows, I start to hear strange night noises: the crunch of dry leaves between my steps, the coo of the owl. Out of the corner of my eye, I see a pair of green eyes glowing on the ground at the far end of a corn row. I remember how Mee Maw Rose said that when she was a girl, she once spotted a panther out here at dusk, crossing the dirt road, yards in front of her. I start to run.

In the distance, I see the faint light of the toolshed. Daddy is still working. I know that if I stopped still right now, if I became too scared to go on, all I would have to do is shout out to my daddy as loud as possible, and he would come running out of the shed like a reflex.

I stop in the thick of the woods. I mouth the word without making a sound. *Daddy!* I could just yell it once or twice, and I know he would search the woods for me the way he ran, fully armed, up the stairs because of Virginia's signal, the way he searched for his sister in the winding creeks, back and forth along the rising water as the night gave way to morning.

13

Intersection

Wednesday morning I pretend to be sick so that I can skip school and meet Cousin Eli's boat, which is due in at 10:00 a.m. C.C. gave me that information from the marina schedule after I promised to let him take me on a real date. (Little does he know that I would have gone without a bribe.)

Yesterday, when Bethany called to check on me, she encouraged me to minister to Cousin Eli by just loving her and listening to how she is doing and asking how I can help her. I'm prepared to give her my tip money from the last week if she needs it, and I'll do anything else she says to show my love for her and help her.

Mama is too hurried to get to her job interview on time to worry about me. She looks in on me once as she runs from the utility closet to her bedroom holding several different shades of skin-colored panty hose.

"Going to be all right, sweetheart?" she says on her way by my open door and then, "I don't have time to take your temperature."

"I'll be fine," I say. "It's probably just this virus that's been going around school."

"I'll call and check on you later," she says from her bedroom. "Did I tell you that I have three interviews today? Two in Charleston and one back here on the island—Oh, I'll never get to town on time!" she says.

I sit straight up in bed and ask her, "What can I do to help you, Mama?"

It's funny how when you fake sick, it's like you've never felt better in your life. Right now I have more energy than I've had in weeks. I would love to bolt out of this bed and run around the house and out to the end of the cornfields. I bet I could do twenty-five push-ups without stopping.

"Oh, the truck!" I hear Mama say. "I haven't started it yet this morning, and it needs to warm up."

She comes running back to my room and stands on the threshold of my door as she unrolls her hair from the warm, spiked electric curlers that belonged to Virginia when she was in high school. She says, "I hate to have you get out of bed and go into the cold to start it, but—"

"Don't worry, Mama. It's practically seventy degrees. I'll be fine," I say.

"Well, okay. I told you how to do it, right?" she asks.

"Yes, ma'am," I say.

Then she hands me her Bible, the New International Version, as I'm slipping on my duck boots. She says, "Thanks, dahlin'."

Mama has found out that the Bible is the exact weight that needs to rest on the gas pedal to keep the engine revving as the car warms up. Each morning she goes out and places the Good Book vertically on the pedal and lets it run for ten minutes or so. If she doesn't do this, the car will cut off every few seconds on the way down the dirt road to the highway.

Yesterday, during breakfast, Mama went out to the car, Bible in hand, to start it up and I asked, "Why don't you just take the Honda, Mama?"

Daddy took his head out of the refrigerator and said, "No one is going to drive that car because I'm going to sell it back to the dealership next week, and I want as few miles on it as possible."

I said, "Yes, sir," and stared down into my bowl of grits so I could roll my eyes.

When I walk outside, I am struck by the smell of spring. Out of the corner of my eye, I see the buds on the azalea bushes leading to the gall. They are beginning to open, and I can make out their brilliant shades of pink and lavender. It's only mid-February so we're in for an early spring. Spring, already? I chuckle to myself with a hint of sarcasm. There's no happy ending in sight, but I'm not going to lose hope yet.

As I'm lifting my head up from the foot of the truck after getting it started, I see Chambers ride by in the tractor to pick up Daddy. Daddy shuffles out of the toolshed carrying a thermos of coffee and a box of oatmeal cream pies. I watch him step up onto the tractor and offer Chambers a pie as Chambers turns the wheel and drives them toward the fields. This week they're planting okra. They'll be out in the fields all day.

Their schedule fits well with my plan: I'm going to take the johnboat over to the marina around 9:30 when I know Daddy will be deep into the planting, practically fifty acres away.

Just two more hours until I see my cousin, I think to myself as I look up at the cloudless sky. Flounder, who must be picking up on my excitement, runs circles around me, barking and jumping. He follows me as I practically skip back into the house and force myself into bed for ten more minutes until Mama leaves.

❧

On my way to the dock, Sagi comes running out of nowhere and says, "Can I go for a ride with you, Miss DeLoach?"

"Not now, Sagi," I say to him. "Maybe later."

Flounder follows me into the boat, insisting to go.

"Please," Sagi says, "don't you want to show me the porpoises?"

Then I spot Easy walking slowly by. Her stomach is drooping low to the ground. She's bound to have those kittens anytime now.

"How'd you like a job, Sagi?" I say to him.

"Will you take me on a boat ride if I do a job?" he says.

"Sure," I say.

"How about keeping an eye on that cat there," I say, pointing to Easy. Then, "She's going to have babies any day now. I want you to watch her and if she starts to look like she's going to have them, put her in the cardboard box in the teahouse. It already has blankets and water. And don't worry, she knows what to do."

"Okay," he says. When I drive off, I see him following Easy closely behind, watching her every move. She turns around and meows at him with a sort of "Leave me alone" tone. He stops in his tracks until she proceeds forward then he follows closely behind her again. Even I have to admit, Sagi's a well-meaning kid.

⤸

As I turn from the creek out into the North Edisto River, I feel the fresh salt air brush against my face. The daylight flies across the marsh grass, coloring it an iridescent golden-green, and I am stunned by the way the sun lights up the murky water like sequins on a dark dress.

The sky is so blue it's almost startling.

Just behind me I hear the clink and clamor of Otter Island being developed. I look back around a curve in the river and see that the first house is on its way. The construction workers have laid the cinderblock foundation, and now they are stacking a layer of red bricks to cover the rough blocks. Some day we will have twenty modern houses with circular driveways and swimming pools facing us across the river.

When I get to the marina, C.C. meets me at the dock and ties my boat to the landing.

"You're just in time for breakfast, Devo," he says to me.

Flounder and I jump off the boat and follow him across the gas tanks and into the small, rickety building where the cash register is.

C. C. works here almost every day. He dropped out of Walterboro High School last year, but he's studying to get his GED. He attends night-school preparation classes in Beaufort two nights a week.

For breakfast he is having salt-and-vinegar pork skins and a Dr Pepper while he watches Regis and Kathy Lee on a small, portable television that sits on top of the vending machine. He spreads his arms out in front of the counter, revealing sweat marks beneath the armpits of his faded red T-shirt. I notice a grease mark that runs down the inside of his forearm. He says, "You can get anything you want out of the machines, Devo, because your ol' boy here's got the key."

I laugh at him and then decide on a pack of peanut butter crackers and a ginger ale. As he opens the machines I look out the window and into the bay, which leads to the ocean. C. C. hands me my drink and says, "They radioed just an hour ago saying that they were right on schedule. They should be here in ten minutes." As I open the can and let the sweet ginger bubble in my throat, I feel the hair stand up on my arms.

"Thanks, C. C.," I say. He walks over to the window, puts his hand on my shoulder and says, "Glad to help."

Thing is, even if C. C.'s not exactly my type, it is nice to have someone taking an interest in me.

When we spot the fishing boat on the horizon, I run out to the edge of the dock. Now the sun is lying across the water like a golden road. A passageway. And the boat is driving right down the middle of it, the large rods rattling in the wind and the great, brown nets blowing up like the bottom of a full skirt as the sea gulls hover above them.

As the boat turns toward the landing, I see my cousin Eli. She's sitting on the bow, her thin blue-jeaned legs hanging over the side of the boat. The bay breeze is lifting her thick, dark hair off her shoulders while the hood of her yellow rain jacket flaps up and down.

I wave my hands back and forth as they approach.

"Ahoy!" I shout.

Cousin Eli stands up and squints. She shouts through the wind, "DeVeaux?"

"Hi, cuz!" I scream out to her.

She starts to grin, but is overcome by a cough.

"You can get some nasty colds out there," C.C. whispers to me.

Then Eli runs to the side as they sail toward the dock and throws a rope first to me and then to C.C.

By now Sal and the other local restaurant owners are gathered on the dock behind me, right on time to buy fresh fish for their dinner specials. Sal is in his usual, flip-flops and a surf-shop T-shirt. He has parked his Trans Am as close to the landing as possible and since he left it running, we all get to hear the Steve Miller Band's "Jet Airliner" as it spills out his open windows.

The captain of the boat, a husky, middle-aged man dressed in camouflage and white rubber boots up to his knees, walks around the side of the boat while a large, mangy dog with knotted hair follows him. The captain blows his nose into his hands, coughs up some phlegm, which he spits out over the side of the boat, then hollers to the restaurateurs, "Yeah, we got 'em." Then he opens up a twenty-foot ice cooler and pulls out an enormous tuna, which he struggles to lift above his head.

As the captain turns his head back to the restaurateurs along the dock, I notice that the bottom half of his ear looks like it was cut straight off. And he has these narrow but deep wrinkles that crisscross around his neck. They are a lighter color than the rest of his thick, red skin.

Now the mutt paces back and forth and barks up at the fish in his master's hands. The captain looks down at him and shouts, "Get!" before leaning over to expel some more phlegm over the side. When the dog doesn't respond, the captain takes the toe of his boot and kicks the dog across the back of the boat. I feel my legs buckle as I watch the mutt land by the gas tank at the back of the boat and curl up in the corner beside it.

Sal walks toward the captain and says, "I'll take that one, Garrick, you salty old ogre. I don't care what the price is."

Eli leaps off the boat and gives me a firm hug. Her hair smells like salt and sweat and her nose is running. She says, "I'm not sure how you found me, but I'm glad you did."

"I don't understand why you were keeping this a secret from me," I say, and as I look at her face, I see that it is wind-chapped along her cheeks and forehead. Her lips are unusually pale, the same color as her skin.

She rubs a fish scale off my arm and says, "I'm sorry," then she presses the tips of her fingers hard into my shoulders. "I just wanted to save up enough money to be able to take care of myself before I told your parents, and I didn't want you to have to keep something from them." Then she brings her fingers to her dry lips, coughs deeply, and looks back at the captain. As I am noticing the dirt beneath her nails she says, "And I didn't want you to worry about me."

The captain jumps off the boat, leaving the mangy dog, who stands up and sniffs his way toward the cooler where the fish are. The captain looks back at Eli and says, "Friday morning at four, mate."

"Okay," she says as she looks at me.

He rubs the inside of his ear, and I see now that half of one nostril is missing, cut straight off like the ear. "You get paid after that," he says as he turns and shuffles toward the men, spitting once again over the side of the dock. Then we hear him say, "Let's do some business, fellows."

Eli looks back at me and says, "I'm so sick of that crude old man I could scream. Do you know he passes gas so loud the dog barks?"

"Let's get out of here," I say, nodding in the direction of the johnboat.

"I'll get my stuff," she says, and she jumps back on the boat and C. C. and I watch her climb down into the galley.

"That's some rough work," C. C. says to me. "Especially for a girl."

"No kidding," I say. Then, "And I sure don't like the looks of that captain."

"None of these captains are what you'd call gentlemen," C. C. says. "They're all salty dogs. Old Garrick is just slow, sick-smelling, and burnt to a crisp. He's got so much skin cancer, they've had to cut parts of his face off."

Then C. C. fills up my gas tank as Eli and I get settled in the john-boat. Before he unties us, he says, "Devo, how's tomorrow night?"

"Yeah," I say, "that's fine."

Eli raises her eyebrows and winks at me.

After we head out of the bay and around the bend into the North Edisto River, I stop the motor and say, "Where to?"

She holds up a bucket and a pint of Jack Daniel's and says, "First, to a crab trap—I'm staying with Suzanne, and I promised I'd bring her and Becky dinner. Captain Garrick is too stingy to give me a decent fish to bring home."

I nod and begin to scan the water for the floats that mark the placement of the square wire cages that rest all along the bottom of the river and creeks. The crab traps are marked by Styrofoam balls where the rope attaches to the cage. And there is an unspoken rule on the island with the crab trappers—if someone wants to take a few crabs, they can help themselves, as long as they leave a pint of liquor in the cage.

We stop at a trap on No Name Creek. We walk to the bow, spread our feet apart to catch our balance, and together we grab hold of the algae-covered rope below the Styrofoam marker.

Slowly we pull up the heavy cage from the muddy water. When we see the black wire surface, we give one large tug of the rope and the square container comes flying out of the water and lands on the bow. At least thirty blue and stone crabs are climbing all over one another in the cage, their claws pinching furiously at the air. Flounder jumps up beside us and barks viciously at the creatures while we unfasten the side of the trap and let a dozen spill out onto the bow. When Flounder sees that they are loose, he runs to the back of the boat where he stands on the seats, lowers his head, and whimpers.

Eli and I gently kick the creatures toward the bucket and some of them grab hold of our tennis shoes so we lift our legs up and dangle them over the plastic pail until they lose their grip and fall in.

As Eli reaches down to pick up the last few strays by their hind legs, I remember those times she used to stick her hands out to pet them. How they would pinch her until she bled.

"Quit flinching," she says to me. "I know how to handle these rascals."

Then Eli throws the pint of liquor into the cage and the remaining crabs knock their claws against it, the sound of fingernails tapping glass. She fastens the cage back together and hurls it back into the water, then she seems to collapse onto the bow with exhaustion.

"You all right?" I say to her as Flounder goes over to kiss her on the cheek.

"Yeah," she says. "I'm just tired, and I feel like I'm coming down with something."

"Maybe you should take the next trip off," I say as I walk over to her and put my hand on her forehead. "You feel kind of feverish."

"And let Garrick get away without paying me?" she says. "No way. I'm too close to getting enough money to get out on my own, and he's not the kind of guy who will pay me until everything I signed up for is done."

We anchor beneath a live oak tree whose lower limbs stretch all the way across the narrow creek. After I turn off the motor, I look across the boat to my cousin, who is cupping her calloused hands around a match to light her cigarette.

I notice her heavy, coffee-colored hair falling around her bony shoulders, and it occurs to me that she is the same age and shape as her mother was in that debutant photograph. Nineteen. Ready to be introduced to adult society. To be presented.

When Eli looks up at me and exhales, I see the Rose family eyes, hazel with gold flecks, just like Daddy's. But Eli's are completely calm. They rest on me.

Anticipating my concern for her health and her choices as of late, she says, "I know it seems crazy for me to drop out of college, but I just couldn't manage, DeVeaux. I lost my job and my loan money was running out and I couldn't ask Uncle Billy for more. I decided that it was time for me to go ahead and take care of myself." Smoke spills slowly from the corner of her mouth, and she reclines against a life jacket.

Then she scratches her chin and it begins to bleed like a scrape. "Windburn," she says as she pulls a tube of lotion out of her backpack and rubs white cream on her face.

She says, "I mean, this job's hard work and Captain Garrick is not exactly pleasant to be around, but the money is good and I'm only on his boat two more weeks, then Tanner Strickland says he'll be able to hire me."

A school of mullet skitter across the surface of the water and I say, "Are you safe out there? Not to mention you're sick as a dog."

"Yes," Eli says. "Garrick is just a slow, old mutt. And he knows I'll kick his rear into the Atlantic if he tries anything."

We chuckle and then I say, "But he's a lot bigger than you, cuz."

"Yeah, well, I've had to learn a little self-defense through the years, little one, so—"

As she says this I remember how she warned me about Sal and gave me tips on how to avoid him. Eli and I are probably the only ones in our family who have had to fend for ourselves. It's like my parents were just too tired by the time we entered the picture.

Then she pets Flounder and says, "And now for the $64,000 question, how *is* Uncle Billy?"

I just roll my eyes.

"Isn't he over Christmas by *now*?" she says. "I mean, the azaleas are in bloom, for heaven's sake!"

"He's just kind of got this mad streak is the best I can put it," I say. "He gets hurt or embarrassed and just gets crazy. In fact, he threw Easy into the creek just last week when we found out that she was pregnant."

"You're kidding me!" Eli says. "What did your mama do?"

"You know her; all she says is 'Have faith, and it will work out.'"

"Well, don't give her a hard time," Eli says. "She's just doing her best. And her faith has helped us *all* through some tough times. Your mama's done a lot for me. She loved me like I was her own."

"I know," I say. "She's been good to all of us, and I have her to thank for my own faith—getting me to church and all. But sometimes I think she's just crazy, too—to put up with him without protesting his temper tantrums, you know?"

Eli wipes a piece of algae off her rain jacket and says out of the blue, "DeVeaux, I always wondered, if my parents had stayed alive, if their marriage would have lasted. They loved each other, but I think they sort of drove each other crazy. I can remember them arguing with such passion over some kind of moral issue like race relations, each of them weeping by the end and saying, 'I love you, I love you.' It all seemed so desperate and painful, you know?"

"Yeah," I say. "I do know. It's enough to scare anyone away from commitment."

I watch her look intently out over the water as she spots two pelicans who swoop low over our heads.

"Now *those* are the greatest mothers of all," she says.

"Really?"

"Will once told me that when pelicans have nothing to feed their babies, they'll take their beaks and stab their chests, then they'll lean over and allow the birds to drink their blood," she says.

"No way!" I say.

"Yep," she says, "that's how come there are those carvings of pelicans at the bottom of the baptism tubs in St. Paul's."

"I never noticed," I say.

"Yeah, well you were the last one to be baptized. I remember watching Father Dan pour water over you. Your scream knocked all around the walls of St. Paul's, which made Mee Maw Rose comment to the neighboring pew that volume was a sign of a healthy baby."

Now I try to find the pelicans, who are like two tiny specks beyond our boat, heading for the ocean.

"That reminds me of Christ," I say, "the shed blood and all of that."

"Yeah," she says, "I'm just lately getting my head around that."

"What do you mean?"

"Well, when I was on the boat a few days ago, watching the sun rise and laughing to myself about something little Becky said a few days earlier, it just sort of hit me like a ton of bricks—God sacrificed His Son's life for *me* so that I could go to Him, and He could be my Father—and it's hard to explain, but it suddenly became *real* to me, you know? It's like all those Sunday school classes and Bible stories that your mama used to read to us before bed just finally sank in, and I knew it was right because it was the only hope I have right now, and it is plenty enough."

Before I can respond to her encouraging words, Eli outlines her plan. "After this next trip, I'll tell your parents I'm here because then I'll have enough money to rent a place of my own."

"But what about school?" I say. "What about teaching the deaf?"

"It'll all come in time," she says. "I'll get back to school somehow. I can even take long-distance classes in Walterboro once I have the money."

"I guess it makes sense," I say. Then I let myself imagine a time when Eli is living here on the island in a place of her own. She'll come over to our house for dinner and Daddy will welcome her with a hug. He will feel some relief since she is one more thing off his plate. And he will be proud of her.

I reach into my pocket and pull out a wad of just over fifty one-dollar bills from last week's work.

"Stop that, DeVeaux," she says. "I'm not taking money from my baby cousin."

"What I want is to get you home as soon as possible," I say, stuffing it in her anorak. "Don't you *dare* give it back!"

"Thanks," she says, and I hope I didn't embarrass her. She looks deep into the marsh and then back to me.

"So tell me about you," she continues. "I want to hear all about the restaurant and school and this marina boy you have a date with tomorrow night."

So I sit there in the boat and tell it all to Eli—about Sal and how he follows close to me when I'm busing tables, about Daddy being humiliated in front of the Edings, about Tina and the pregnancy test, and the night I spent on C.C.'s couch after he rescued Easy. She takes it all in and smiles and says, "Boy, I can remember times like that." She warns me in a softer way than Suzanne does about staying out of trouble, and that the island is different from downtown. Then I tell her about Bethany's words, about trusting God and waiting until the end of the story, and she says, "That sounds about right to me, DeVeaux."

Before I take her back to the marina, I ask if I can pray with her and she says yes. We bow our heads on the old johnboat, and it rocks gently back and forth as I put my hand on Eli's shoulder and ask the Lord to be with her, to protect her, to provide for her and to give her hope. When I say, "Amen," she looks up at me with the warmest smile.

"I needed that," she says. "Do that for me when I'm away."

"I promise, I will," I say.

When I take her back to the marina she promises that she will call me as soon as she gets back from this next week of fishing. She says, "We can hang out together," and, "I'll look after you."

Then I watch her long after she has told me good-bye and turned toward the road. I watch her carry the bucket of crabs down the dock, the water spilling over the sides onto her rubber boots. I watch her round the corner, nod at some fishermen who are cleaning their boats, cross the street just after a pickup truck passes and turn toward Suzanne's.

I'm starting to have a lot in common with Eli, I think to myself, and this makes me love her even more. We are both trying to survive. To make it out. Virginia and Will have already made it, but she and I are still struggling to find our way.

֍

When I pull up to the dock at Rose Hill after taking Eli back to the marina, Sagi walks by me, still following Easy. He glances at me and holds out his hands, palms up, as if to say, "Nothing yet."

On my way to the caretaker's house, I'm drawn by the color leading to the gall, this wild, overgrown garden full of hundreds of azalea bushes and magnolia trees between our house and the main house. So I walk toward the gall, pushing through the buds and bushes that lead to its center. When I get to the middle, I take a seat on the wrought-iron bench that sits just off the dirt path. Now I'm surrounded by a shock of color, hundreds of pink and lavender azalea blooms that must have just opened over the course of this day. I am amazed at the perfect shape of each petal. I look at one right after the other. They are flawless and making the air thick with their collective sweetness. Now I inhale them, knowing that they will only look and smell this perfect for two or three days.

I hear a scratching sound coming from above my head, and I look into a magnolia tree and spot a squirrel carrying a deer rack up to the top of the highest limb. It is the time of year that all the bucks who survived the hunting season shed their racks. They will grow them back in a soft velvet all summer long, and by autumn they are sturdy and grand again, making it easy for the hunters to spot them.

When the squirrel gets the rack in position, he begins to nibble on it. He will have enough food for days.

After I take the fresh, sweet smell of the garden into my lungs, I have the same surge of energy from earlier this morning, and I stand up, tighten the ties on my tennis shoes, and start to run around the bushes, in and out of the passageways as the petals brush across my arms and legs. I pretend that I'm running from something—play a game of chase by myself.

In minutes I can feel the sweat beneath my T-shirt, and my jeans begin to stick to my thighs. My heart is racing and it feels so good that I just keep going around and around. I know that my life will get better and better now that Eli will be here on the island with me, and I'm so excited I can't stop. "You have given me a new hope!" I say to God, and I think of Jeremiah 29:11: *"For I know the plans I have for you," declares the LORD, "plans to prosper you and not to harm you, plans to give you hope and a future."*

As I run back by the bench in the center of the gall, a voice behind me calls, "Feeling better?"

I stop in my tracks and look back to find Mama in her bright red interview suit that is another shock of color against the pink and lavender. She's holding a bouquet of azaleas and smiling. I wipe my brow and say, "Yes, ma'am." She laughs as she turns toward the house and says, "Good."

❧

That night at dinner, Mama announces that she's gotten a job as the assistant manager of the Piggly Wiggly grocery store. She's not crazy about the idea of working around all that food. She turns to me and says, "Constant temptation." But she tells Daddy and me that the hours are flexible and it's on the island so it will be convenient.

"I'm impressed," Daddy says. "You really followed through, Dee."

Mama is proud.

"What about the other two interviews?" I ask.

Then she tells us how the truck died on her way into town for the first two interviews and so she actually never made it to them. Thankfully, a garbage truck picked her up and took her to a "fix-it" station, where they charged her battery again and told her all the things wrong with the truck. She said that she told them she just couldn't afford to fix it right now and drove off.

❧

The next evening C. C. is scheduled to take me on a date.

Tina calls me twice during the afternoon. Once, when C. C. is not around, to tell me how excited he is. She says, "He's gonna blow a week's worth of work on you, gal! I watched him cash that check and put it all in his wallet." Then she calls back minutes later when C. C. is around to ask me what I'm wearing. I hear her as she closes her bedroom door and mumbles, "Now don't end up like me—the 'you know what' test and all."

"Tina!" I say in a "Get real" kind of way.

"Well, it's just that Shane's turned out to be such a jerk and all. Just yesterday someone at school wrote 'Shane says that Tina is a slut' on my homeroom desk."

Shane broke up with Tina last week. Tina said she cried and said, "But you were my first." And all he did was snicker and say, "Do all you girls say that?"

"Tina, remember what Bethany said," I remind her about youth group, "in a prayer you can be washed as pure as snow."

"But how can I forget?" she says.

"I don't know, but let's just pray some time next week, and we'll see how you feel then."

"Okay," she says. "I'll do anything to feel better."

❧

As I step into the shower, I hear Virginia's voice. Through the door I hear that she has come over to tell Mama she has a good hunch that Clayton may propose to her for her birthday next week. She guesses this because she actually spotted him coming out of Lacher's jewelry store on King Street with the owner, Mr. R. J. Lacher himself, when she was walking by on her lunch break. She had to hide behind one of the pillars of the customshouse while the two men stood on the street chatting. Then they shook hands and Clayton walked on back over to his law firm with Virginia trailing yards behind him.

After Virginia and Mama squeal at the thought of marriage and Virginia contemplates the possibility of quitting her job at the antique shop to become a full-time wife, I consider the fact that in our current state of affairs, there is no way my big sister will get the wedding she has always imagined: a candlelit church filled with large flower arrangements and a fancy reception at the Yacht Club with trays full of champagne and shrimp cocktails. But I decide not to dare bring this up and burst her bubble.

After a while Virginia comes into my room, her eyes gleaming like polished silver. With all this energy, she can't help but make fun of me as I get ready.

"I hear you have a hot date," she says to me as I'm slipping on the plaid wool skirt that Mama is making me wear. Then, "Don't go too crazy or you'll end up living in that God-awful trailer the rest of your life."

I don't have enough time to discuss her prejudices so I just sum up my thoughts by saying, "You're a stupid, snotty idiot!"

"That's right," she says to me, "go on and defend your gas-station man."

"Get out, Virginia! You must have no life if you're worrying about me going out to dinner with someone."

Then I slam the door behind her, and when I sit down on my bed I feel the wool prickle the skin on the backs of my legs. I think to myself (if I don't count John Henry escorting me to cotillion classes or having his mama pick me up and take me with him to a party or to tennis lessons) that tonight, with C.C., is my first real date.

When C.C. shows up, he is dressed like a gentleman, in a button-down shirt tucked into a pair of khaki pants. His hair is washed and slicked back.

Mama meets him at the door. She says, "Why hello, C.C. Don't you look nice."

Virginia is right behind her, and she says, "And where are you taking our DeVeaux tonight?"

C.C. says, "I thought I'd take her out to dinner and a movie."

"A classic date," Virginia says, "how smart of you." Then she swings around on the balls of her feet and heads back to the cheese and crackers that Mama has put on the dinner table.

As Mama tells us good-bye, I hear the sound of Daddy sanding down the sailboat in the toolshed. It looks like he's too busy to see us off, which relieves me because I can still remember his careful examination of Virginia's dates at our home on Tradd Street. How he would nearly bruise their fingers with his firm handshake and then sit them down and ask them extremely uncomfortable questions that ranged from "Now how do I know your parents?" to "Do you believe in wearing your seat belt?"

He doesn't think about that kind of thing anymore, I decide as I walk through the yard with C.C., stepping lightly so the mud won't clump beneath the heels of my shoes.

C.C. and I drive to town in his mama's Dodge Omni, which he has cleaned out, though it still smells a little like wet hay covered in Lysol. Of course, he doesn't open the door for me and note the way that I get in and out of a car, but I don't hold it against him. No one has ever told him about that.

Our first stop is at the Olive Garden, which sits in a strip mall in West Ashley. C.C. says that this is the best restaurant he's ever been to. He says, "Get anything you want, okay?" So I order chicken marsala and an iced tea, and he orders the fried cheese appetizer and a Dr Pepper with no ice.

Before the meal arrives, he smokes a few of his cigarettes as he tries to lead our conversation.

"So how do you like living on the island?" he asks.

"I'm getting used to it," I tell him, "but it would be good if my daddy weren't acting like a jerk half the time."

"Yeah," he says, "hope you don't mind me saying that your pop seems like he's got a screw loose."

I laugh because I know he's right. "Yeah, I guess so."

"I don't know," he says as he brushes a nonexistent crumb off his lap. Then he pauses before looking up, and I stare into the place where his part ends at the back of his small, round head. When he lifts his head, his thin lips form a perfectly round circle from which he releases his smoke. He says, "I guess it's better to have a loony pop than no pop at all."

I lean in, suddenly concerned about him. I say, "Have you ever met your father?"

"A few times when I was a kid," he says, "but he moved on down to New Orleans when I was ten."

"Oh," I say, keeping my shoulders toward the center of our table so the couple next to us can't hear the extent of C. C.'s tragic family life. Then my left elbow accidentally brushes against the bread basket and nearly knocks over the dessert menu, which stands upright in a plastic pouch and contains a cut-out picture of a chocolate brownie topped with vanilla ice cream.

C. C. continues, "He took a job on one of them gambling boats down there, and he hasn't got back this way since."

"Boy," I say, a little embarrassed for C. C. because he has never had much of a dad.

"Yeah," he says, "it's a shame."

When the food arrives, we don't say another word until C. C. takes the last bite of his fried cheese. Then he says, "How does *Star Wars* sound to you?"

"One of my favorites," I say encouragingly.

"Yeah," he says, "someone at the marina says they just reopened it, kind of like *Batman*."

"Sounds great," I say as I think of Brother Will, who used to collect all the *Star Wars* spaceships and figures when we were younger. I remember how he would stage space wars on the porch of our house on Tradd Street and whenever he couldn't find any boys to play with, he'd get Cousin Eli and me to go with him down to White Point Gardens by the Battery where he'd drape me in a croaker sack, which meant I was Yoda, then he'd ask Eli to pull her thick hair in front of her face so she could be Chewbacca, and the three of us would jump on the Civil War memorial cannons and shoot out into the harbor at our invisible enemies.

When we pull up to the theater, we realize that we are a half hour late. C.C. says he must have gotten the times confused and he blushes, but I pinch his shoulder and say, "Maybe there's something else on that sounds good."

As I stare at the other movie choices on the side of the cinderblock wall of the theater, I feel C.C. staring over at me. He suddenly starts the car and says, "I've got a better idea."

"Okay," I say and watch as we head over the bridge toward downtown Charleston.

"I was thinking that we could cruise the Battery," he says as he turns on his radio.

"Okay," I say, chuckling a little because the Battery is the tip of the peninsula and the most beautiful part of my old neighborhood, where the lavish city homes built in the early 1800s by the rice planters overlook the harbor.

I remember how much we used to make fun of the tourists and non-downtown residents who cruised the Battery. How I'd sit with my friends on their grand piazzas that looked out over the water and some parent or older sibling would say, "This is a priceless vista except for those dang rednecks who've got nothing better to do than cruise."

As we turn onto the Battery, C.C. rolls down the window and turns up the radio station, Country Rock 101.1, and we drive back and forth on the road between the grand houses and the bay while Travis Tritt's voice catches in the roofs of porches and corridors that lead to backyard gardens where I know that water trickles from stone fountains and baby-bud rosebushes are beginning to show their pale color.

For a moment I'm a little afraid that someone I know might recognize me, and part of me wants to slump down beneath the dashboard, but then I loosen up and enjoy the familiar ride.

On the third time down the road, C.C. puts his hand on my knee and smiles at me.

"Pretty nice, huh?" he says.

I smile sincerely at his true effort to make this a good date and say, "Yeah."

⅜

As I walk toward our front porch, I see that Mama and Daddy are on the couch. The fire is blazing and the television is on. Mama is curled up and leaning against Daddy. His arm is around her. They nod sleepily in my direction as I slip into the house.

When I'm crawling into bed I notice a new book by my bedside table. It has a big heart made out of the colors of the rainbow on the cover. The title is *Why Wait?: The Value of Saving Yourself for Your Lifelong Mate*, and it's published by one of those Christian groups out of Colorado. Mama has put a Post-it note below the title that reads: "I was going to give this to you for your next birthday, but I decided I better go ahead and give it now. Love you!"

I shake my head and chuckle a little. That's the *last* thing she needs to worry about with me. Then I fall directly to sleep.

In the middle of the night, I wake up from a dream to the sound of Daddy screaming my name.

"Deeeeee Veaux! Deee Veaux!" he shouts.

He's so loud the house shakes.

I say, "Yes, sir?" faintly, the sleepiness catching in my throat.

"DeVeaux!" he screams.

"Yes, sir?" I say clearer.

He says, "Get out here now!"

"What?" I say groggily, wondering if this is another nightmare.

"Get your rear out here now!" he screams.

I sit up, throw on some shorts, and say, "Yes, sir!" When I stand up and attempt to move toward the door, it's as if I'm walking through syrup.

"I said, get your haughty rear out here now!" he continues. "How dare you not come when your father calls you. How dare you!"

My limbs are weighted with exhaustion. I pull them up and shake them out as I scurry into the lighted den.

My mama is blue. She is standing in the kitchen wearing only a skirt turned inside out and her flesh-colored bra. She's leaning on the kitchen counter, her arms outstretched, her fingertips grabbing the counter. She's gasping for air while her back ribs heave, each one outlined like a starving child's.

She looks up at me, and her face is gray and hollow. Her head nods twice then it falls back down, dangling below her neck.

"DeVeaux!" my daddy says to me, grabbing my arm and turning me around. "You better come when your daddy calls you. You better obey the sound of your father's voice. Do you understand me?"

He's looking at me like he hates me inside and out. Like I am the hooch himself.

"Yes, sir," I say to calm him down. I think to myself: *This is how it happens. This is how real tragedy happens. My mother can't breathe.* My eyes move back to her.

He grabs my arm again. "Something's wrong with your mother," he says.

"Daddy, call an ambulance. She's having an asthma attack."

"What?" he says as though he has never heard of the condition before.

I say, "She told us that this could happen. Her lungs are closing, and she can't breathe. Call an ambulance. She needs help now!"

Mama whispers, "My doctor's number is in my address book."

I run back to her bedroom and find it. The commotion suddenly rouses Flounder, who leaps from my room and nips at my heels as though this is a game.

When I hand the address book to Dad, he dials the number and leaves a message with an answering service that assures him the doctor will call back. We wait for his call.

Whole minutes go by, and I want to scream in fear.

It is three in the morning.

In an effort to take control of the situation and get my mama help, I say to Daddy, "Let's call an ambulance."

He dials 911 and says, "My wife has a breathing-like condition."

"What?!" I say, wanting to grab the telephone away from him, but I'm too afraid of his reaction to go through with it. Am I gutless when it counts the most?

I say, "Daddy, she has asthma. It's called *asthma*."

"Shut up!" he screams at me and pauses to give me another hateful look.

I look at my mother. She's now lying on the kitchen floor.

Flounder is whimpering in the corner of the room as though even he knows what's at stake.

Daddy suddenly hangs up the phone in confusion.

"Please take her to the hospital," I plead.

He pulls Mama up by her elbows, and I drape her in one of his camouflage shirts that is lying over the couch.

As we walk off the porch I say, "Daddy, take the Honda. It will take the truck too long to start."

He looks back at me with a mean eye. "No!" he says. "I told you, we are *not* using that car."

"But Daddy," I say, "this is an emergency."

"Did you hear me?" he says.

"Yes, sir," I say, not wanting to waste another precious moment. "But she's in real danger here."

He ignores my plea and pulls my mother to the passenger door of the truck where he lifts her up over the muddy threshold.

It takes three tries for the truck to start, but it does. *It will take them nearly an hour to get to the hospital*, I think as I stand in the yard, suddenly aware of the damp leaves and twigs beneath my bare feet. I watch as they putt down the dirt road, the taillights of the truck fading into the pitch-black night.

When I walk back into the house, I lay down on the kitchen floor, still warm from my mother's bare back. I hear the sound of the shower. The drip of the coffeemaker. I see my mother's inhaler on the edge of the counter—a powerless prescription in this damp and musty place that is our home.

The phone rings and it's the doctor.

I tell him what's happened and he says he is on his way to meet them at the hospital.

I get down on my knees and pray wholeheartedly, trying to push my fear and anger aside. I say, "God, save her."

14

Freeze

It is 4:45 a.m. when I call the emergency room of the Charleston hospital.

"They made it," a nurse says to me. "Your mother is on a respirator now. She's going to be all right. In fact, Dr. McCall is with her."

"Would you like to speak with your father?" she asks. "He's in the waiting room. I could get him."

"No, ma'am," I say, "that's okay." He is the *last* person I want to talk to, but I don't tell her that. In fact, I'd very much like to throw *him* into the creek in the outgoing tide.

When I hang up the phone, I kneel down on the floor. I remember that my prayer has been answered and I say, "Thank You, Lord."

And then, like a typical human being, I move quickly from my grateful heart and shout out in anger so that the windows rattle, "*Why* is my father this way?"

❧

They putt into the driveway around seven in the morning. My teeth are chattering, and I'm exhausted because I have not slept a wink. I spent the remainder of the early morning hours stewing in anger toward my daddy and seeing, all too clearly, how easily bitterness can take root in one's heart.

"What a night," my father says to no one in particular.

"Hi, dahlin'," Mama says to me. She holds out her thin arms and I fall into them. Her soft, reassuring touch is on my back, and I feel her fingertips firmly trace my spine while she says, "Everything is okay now, love."

Daddy walks into his bedroom and closes the door. Then he opens it again and says, "DeVeaux?"

My back stiffens at the sound of his voice. This man whose pride seems more important than my mother's life. Who would have let her die while making a point about me being respectful in my sleep or about not putting sixty extra miles on the Honda so that he can sell it back for the highest price.

"What?" I say furiously, without turning back to look at him.

He misses my attempt to lash out at him and continues on with his order, "How about going over to Chambers and tell him I'm too tired to work today."

I do not answer. Instead I just walk out the door into the white morning light and head toward the swamp where Chambers lives.

On my way over, I have to cut through the gall and today I am stunned by the azalea blooms, their flawless petals, staring at me like an unkept promise. Spring is here, and I'm only sinking farther into this dark pit. Just the sight of the blooms makes my blood boil.

⁂

When I was in the third grade my classmate Laura Crawford's father was killed in a hunting accident in the woods of Jacksonboro. Another hunter had passed a rifle to him across a ditch, and it slipped between their hands and went off, shooting Mr. Crawford in the neck. Laura left school on a Monday and was back by Friday with a brand-new backpack and a set of high-tech colored pencils that her grandmother bought her. She sat across from me and for weeks I watched her out of the corner of my eye, as she waited for the words to appear on the blackboard, then took notes in multicolors.

During those same weeks I started a habit I had abandoned years before when my parents converted the attic into a rec room for the kids. I would sit with Daddy downstairs in the living room after supper, just in front of him, between his legs on his large leather chair and together we would watch the evening news. I would lean back into the small bulge of his belly, breathing his smell, a combination of coffee, ink, and sweat, as the weight of his arms rested on me.

And I would wake up suddenly at four in the morning as he quietly gathered his hunting gear and drove slowly out of our driveway. For the remainder of the night I would drift in and out of a light sleep and by the time I came downstairs for breakfast, he was back, sprawled out on the couch with heavy eyelids.

By the end of that semester the teacher wrote on my report card that I was often too drowsy to pay full attention in class and had dozed off more than a couple of times, which my grades reflected. So each night Mama gave me half a sleeping pill, and I didn't wake up early the rest of hunting season or anytime after that.

Now the thought occurs before I have time to recognize it, much less stop it: *I wish my father was gone.*

❧

When I get to Chambers's house, Maum Bess is sitting on the old porch reading the paper. Someone has put a fresh coat of bright turquoise paint on the shutters and trim of the porch to keep out the haints and other evil spirits. They have also relined the porch with screens and painted the cinderblock steps that lead up to the house a bright yellow.

I can't help but think of Mee Maw Rose when I see Maum Bess sitting there. She was in Mee Maw's kitchen cooking whenever I came over for dinner. And when I was little, she'd take me out in the hammock and swing me while the adults talked around the dining room table, and I can still recall the sweet, mossy smell of her dark, smooth skin. I'd plant my face right in the crook of her neck and smell her as we swung back and forth.

Maum Bess practically lived in Mee Maw's room the last six months before she died, straightening her blankets and feeding her her last bites of food before the cancer swallowed her whole.

I remember watching how Maum Bess fed my grandmother so gently, like a baby, lifting the spoon up between Mee Maw's lips so she would not have to work so hard.

I remember also in those last days, when we were all by her bed listening to her dry, thorny breathing, how Maum Bess took a Q-tip every half hour and dipped it in Vaseline and spread it gently across Mee Maw's lips and said, "That's better."

And how she called the afternoon that Mee Maw died. "It is over," she said to Daddy over the phone, and he walked briskly down Tradd Street and over to Water Street where Maum Bess stood on the piazza, her arms outstretched toward him.

Before I open my mouth she says through the screens dividing us, "You look bad."

"I was up all night. Is Chambers here?"

"No, he's already to work in the cornfield," she says.

"Daddy can't make it today," I say.

She swats her hand and says, "Chambers'll be back in a few hours and I'll tell him." Then she narrows her dark eyes and pats the plastic lawn chair next to her. "Come on in here, gal. I want to talk to you."

Without hesitating I open the porch door and slide into the chair next to her. I smell something like bacon and salt coming from the kitchen. Maum Bess's house is like her skin, warm and moist like moss. The floorboards of the porch slope beneath us, yielding to the weight of dampness and age, and I imagine a greenness thriving just below the wood, multiplying into forests of dank, slippery life.

She pulls a plastic glass out of a bag on the floor and pours some tea into it and hands it to me. I take a small sip. It is sweet and lukewarm and tastes a little old, but I rest it on my knee and pretend that I will drink more of it.

I haven't looked at Maum Bess this close up for a long time. She is dressed more casually than I remember. She's in purple sweatpants and a white sweatshirt with a picture of the Manhattan skyline topped with rhinestones for the stars above the buildings. Nearly all of her kin live in New York or Brooklyn, and she is proud of her daughter, who manages a hotel on Forty-second Street. And rightfully so.

Her face is round and wrinkled, long deep lines cross her forehead, her eyes, and where her cheeks meet her lips. Instead of making her look elderly and frail, these wrinkles have the effect of a kind of durability—like she's something that will last for a long, long time.

"What's goin' on at that house of yours, baby?" she says. "Something ain't right, and I want to hear it from you." As I look into her eyes, I see that even their color is loosening, the brown surrounding her pupils seems to be spreading out into the whites of her eyes, so that everything is soft and blurred.

"Well, Mama had to go to the hospital last night. She has asthma and she couldn't breathe." Then the tears start to come. Talking to Maum Bess is almost like talking to Mee Maw Rose, and it's hard to say what I really think of Daddy. I'm ashamed for him and I'm ashamed of how I feel about him. Truth is, I believe that if my mother had died last night, it would have been his fault.

"Daddy just didn't handle it right," I say. "He sort of blew up over it all, and I was afraid he wouldn't get her to the hospital in time. It could have been awful. I mean, she could hardly breathe, you know?" Though I'm ashamed, I feel relieved to tell her the story.

She makes a clucking sound to calm me and then, as if she were right there in the kitchen with us last night, says, "I knowed it. I knowed it. I knowed it."

Then she leans in and whispers, "The Lawd has been waking me up in the night, tellin' me to do something for your daddy. And so I been fasting and praying on him, trying to figure out what to do."

Of course I've never heard of God waking up anybody in the night except for maybe in the Old Testament, but somehow I am not skeptical of Maum Bess's words. She's got ties to our Maker that I'm not willing to question.

"I've got my gals at Mt. Zion praying for him and I know you saw me workin' on him Christmas Day after he threwed y'all's tree into the creek. I was sprinklin' salt around your house the way Elisha sprinkled it intuh the spring of Jericho's bad water, makin' it clean again."

"He's doing bad," I whisper, my head down in my lap. "It's hard to take him."

"Oh, baby, he has got tuh turn himself around," she says. "That's why I'm prayin' for his soul to be *seized* just like I did for Chambers. And I told the Lawd to do *whatever* it takes, you understand what I mean? *Whatever* it takes."

I nod, though I'm not quite sure I understand. If it means putting my mother's life in danger, then as far as I'm concerned it's not worth it, but what do I know about the way God works? I drink her lukewarm tea down while she tells me to go home and sleep.

But before I leave she says, "Now girl, *you* got tuh be patient with Him."

"Yes, ma'am," I say, though in my heart I'm thinking, *I've been patient enough! The flowers are in bloom, and I am over this story.*

She lifts her finger and warns, "Don't think *anything*, don't do *anything* without prayin' on it, hear? Don't let yourself get so far down on Him that you can't get back up?"

"You mean Daddy?" I say.

"Well, him, too, but I was talkin' about the Lawd. You've got tuh be prayin' too. We've got tuh all be prayin' that your daddy's soul will be *seized*. That the Lawd will have *mercy* on him. But you must beware, child"—and she lifts my chin so that I will face her again—"the enemy will use hatred tuh trap you and tuh keep you from Him."

Though I know what she's saying, I'm not ready to let go of my anger yet. The wound from last night is too fresh, and I want to nurse it some more. But, to appease her, I tell her that I understand, then place the glass down on the table.

As I head for the door with my back to her she adds, "You've got tuh listen for that still, small voice, girl. He whispers gently, and you have to *stop* tuh hear Him."

I don't respond, but I know that she knows I've heard her instructions—get rid of the hatred and listen for a quiet voice. I close the door behind me without looking back and walk out into the cornfields that are blowing gently in the wind. Down at the end of the row I can see the top of Chambers's gray hat and the big wheels of the tractor spitting up dirt.

I look and I want to listen for His voice, but too many thoughts are racing through my head, and I feel as though another barrier is going up instead of coming down as I had hoped.

I want to call Bethany and ask for her help, and I want to call Sasser and say, "I'd rather have my daddy leave instead of being trapped with him the way I am! You're in the better situation, Sasser!" But I know that would break his heart even more, so I won't dare say it.

In Maum Bess's worlds there are spirits everywhere. In the cornfields, in the night mist, in the form of a hot wind or smoke in the distance. And the Holy Spirit Himself is out there winning every battle for the kingdom.

And though she means well, and like I said, I'm in no position to dispute her experiences with God or the Holy Spirit, I can't imagine anyone or anything changing my daddy at this point.

Instead I settle into my thought from earlier this morning—wishing that he was gone. And I begin to imagine what life might be like without him, though I know it is a sick kind of pleasure, like raking my tongue over a sore tooth or pressing down hard on a fresh bruise.

But it is all too easy to picture the den in the caretaker's house with Mama and Eli sitting on the couch drinking coffee. They are safe and sound and laughing about some old story. They might sit there for hours, talking and watching the tide change from the front window.

As tempting as it is to go on with this daydream, I decide it would be more effective to get a gut and tell him what I think—that I hate the way he acted last night. And that he is endangering each of us with his crazed temper, and it is wrong.

Spring is here, according to the azaleas, and I'm going to take matters into my own hands. I'm weary of waiting on God.

When I go back to the house to find him, I stop to check on Mama, who is falling asleep on the couch with her Bible open and resting on her knees.

I watch her chest rise up slowly and fall back down. Her breathing is as clear as a bell. And I wonder if she has ever wished it too. That he was gone.

The Bible is open to Romans, a book that she studied for several semesters with her women's Bible study at St. Paul's. Once she wrote down one of the key verses on a torn piece of notebook paper and taped it to her bathroom mirror on Tradd Street, where its ends curled up and yellowed for over a year before she took it down. I remember it because that was during a stage when I used to sneak into her bathroom to play with her makeup. It was Romans 8:28: *"We know that in all things God works for*

*the good of those who love him, who have been called according
to his purpose."*

As I walk toward Daddy's room, I can hear the steady drone of
the television and him snoring. When I'm at the foot of his bed I
clear my throat and he opens his heavy eyes.

"Yes?" he says, slightly annoyed.

"Can I talk to you, Daddy?"

He rubs his eyes with the backs of his heavy hands and grunts
as if to say yes.

"Why did you stop and yell at me last night when you knew
Mama needed to get help?"

He snorts through his lips like a horse, then yawns. He looks at
me as though nothing I've said makes any sense. "Huh?"

(I must have inherited my amnesia from him.)

"Mama could hardly breathe," I begin, "and you took minutes
of precious time to lecture me about not waking up out of a dead
sleep quick enough."

"Mmm." He looks as though he has a faint idea of what I'm
talking about, but he can't quite place it.

"Your mother is fine," he says.

"But *every* minute counted," I say, and then I add silently to my
heart, *And I would have blamed you if she had died.*

I sense that he knows what I'm thinking, but he brushes me off
as he scratches the top of his head and says, "Did you find
Chambers like I asked you?"

"That's not what I'm talking about, Daddy. I want to talk
about last night. I was frightened and you—"

"It's over, DeVeaux," he says, and by the time he gets to my
name he's angry.

He adds with authority, "This is my home, and I expect you to
be respectful while you're living in it! Now answer me. Did you
find Chambers?"

"Yes," I lie.

"Good, now let me sleep," he says.

"Well, I wanted you to know how I feel about last night," I say.

"And I want you to leave this room, now," he whispers, and though it is dark in the room, I can see his face turning red.

"I'm leaving," I say, "but at least you know." And before I'm out of the room he rolls over and buries his head beneath a pillow—too weary to fight.

Funny how when you say what you really think to someone, you end up feeling worse than before.

❦

Without asking, I take the truck to go find Eli because she is the only one I can talk to about Daddy. When I get to Suzanne's house, little Becky comes to the door.

I look down at her through the screen and say, "Is Eli here?"

Then Suzanne appears behind Becky, the wrinkles of the sheets indented on her cheeks and a freshly lit cigarette in her hand. She opens the door, squints at the early spring light and says, "It's a school day for you, isn't it? Don't tell me it's spring break already."

I nod and say, "Where is Eli?"

Suzanne says, "She left around four this morning because Captain Garrick decided to take a two-week operation off the coast of north Florida."

"She went with him for *two* weeks?" I say.

"She needs the money," she says with her hand spread across the top of Becky's head. "She'll be back the third week in March."

Suddenly my limbs begin to feel like sandbags, and when I respond, I can't quite get at my voice. All of my tiredness from last night has caught up with me, and Suzanne leads me over to her couch.

She says, "What in the world is wrong, DeVeaux? Are you sick?" Then she holds her hand up in front of Becky's face to shield her from my germs.

"I needed to talk to Eli," I say. "Now she's gone for another two weeks with that mangy captain?"

"I know," Suzanne says, nodding, "but she'll be fine. After this job, she'll have enough to get on her feet, rent a place and all."

Now Suzanne sits down next to me and hoists Becky up into her lap. She says, "I've known your cousin for ten years now, DeVeaux, and what I've learned is that she can handle most anything."

Becky sucks her first two fingers and weaves her thumb in and out of a small blanket that is brown and stringy at the ends. She rubs the worn fabric in a circular motion against her cheek.

Suzanne says, "Don't you have to work tonight?"

"Yeah," I say, "and I didn't get a wink of sleep."

"Were you with C.C.?" she probes.

"No!" I say, sounding more defensive than I mean to, my voice betraying me.

"I've told you to be careful now, DeVeaux. I think it's about time we had a talk about . . ." I watch as she lets Becky down then slowly mouths, *sex*. The only sound in the room is a light smack as Becky knocks two Weeble Wobbles' heads together.

"Last night had nothing to do with C.C.," I say, too tired and embarrassed to explain about Mama's attack.

"What was it then?"

"Trouble at home," I say.

Suzanne scoots over to me on the couch. Then she rubs my arms all the way up and down like a mother and watches, trancelike, as my hair stands up on my goose bumps caught in the light coming through her window. She says sweetly, "Why don't you take a nap here before work?" And I nod and think how Suzanne understands what I'm going through. I know that her parents kicked her out of the house when they found out she was pregnant with Becky. From then on she just became a mother instead of needing a mother and now she takes pleasure in caring for me and Eli.

I follow her into the laundry room, Eli's makeshift bedroom, where Suzanne has set up a little cot by the ironing board.

After she closes the door behind me, I walk around the small space, inspecting my cousin's stuff. On the shelf above the washing machine there is a half-empty pack of Marlboro Lights, a pair of dangly lime green earrings, and two unframed photographs propped up on the windowsill.

One photograph is of her and a guy I've never seen. He's a few inches taller than her, stocky and handsome in a scruffy sort of way with thick dark hair down to his shoulders and a thin beard. They are on some dock in T-shirts and cutoffs, and she is holding up a large spot-tailed bass by its gills while his arm reaches across her back to the other side of her waist. It looks like he is gently pulling her toward him. I feel like a detective, turning the photo on its back to find the date—June 1995. Nearly two years ago. The summer before Mee Maw Rose died, and the summer Eli left our home on Tradd Street to live with Mee Maw in the main house at Rose Hill Plantation.

I realize once again that Eli may have many lives that I know nothing about. Pieces of her are spread out here and there, and she could have been abused or arrested or married and divorced for all I know. Or maybe she has simply fallen in love, just once, with the man in this picture, and her heart is still devoted to him wherever he is. How can I know?

The other picture is of me and Will and Virginia on the johnboat when I was just a little kid. We are dressed in orange life jackets, our hair wet, waving into the camera. I remember Mee Maw Rose and Eli standing on the dock of Rose Hill Creek as they took that picture. Mee Maw leaning over Eli's shoulder, steadying the lens while Eli peered into the glass, the bottom of her bathing suit still dripping with creek water as she pressed down the button.

When I turn this picture over, I see a smaller one connected to the back. I peel it off and see that it is of her mama and daddy standing on each side of her in the surf. She looks like she is about two, dressed in a yellow bathing suit that matches her mother's bikini top and swim skirt. Each parent is holding her hand, leaning in toward her for the picture while she digs her heels into the wet sand and leans back.

I rest the pictures back against the windowsill, but I hear them slide onto their backs after I have I taken off my shoes and slid under the covers. The springs of the cot sound off as I roll back and forth until I find a comfortable position on my side, facing the dryer.

As I listen to the sound of Becky's cartoons playing in the den next door, my muscles begin to slacken and my mind drifts. What I picture is the ironing board in Eli's narrow bedroom in our Tradd Street home where beneath her single bed Mama stored boxes of sewing tools and patterns. I recall the sewing machine with its multicolored spools that rested on a card table at the foot of her bed. And how on Saturdays we could hear the whir and chewing of the machine as Mama cut and sewed and hemmed, leaning large bolts of material against the corners of Eli's walls. I remember watching Eli shimmy around the bolts to get into the closet where her clothes hung against my daddy's old army fatigues, Mama's dusty prom dresses, and every ballet costume Virginia ever wore.

I'm ashamed when I think how I've been feeling so sorry for myself and my move to this island when my cousin has *always* lived in makeshift.

As I drift I think of Maum Bess and her prayers and the apostle Paul's words that Mama holds on to: "*In all things God works for the good of those who love him,"* and I wish I could believe them. I know I could pray for the Lord to take away my anger and tell Him that I trust Him, but I'm not ready for that again after what I saw last night.

If I could sit down with the apostle Paul or Father Dan I'd say, "If *all* things work for the good of those who love Him, then why is Eli poor and alone? Why did my father endanger my mother last night? And why did Aunt Eliza die, leaving us all in mourning?"

As I close my eyes, I hope that I'm not losing my faith. It feels like the barrier between me and God has only thickened over the last few days. I want to call Sasser or Bethany to pull me out of this spiritual slump, but I'm too exhausted to move. All I can do is lie here and listen to the muffled cartoons, the pitter-patter of Becky's footsteps, and the reeling noise of fear and anger inside my own head. Though I feel deaf and blind to the other world, the world of faith and the unseen, I can't help but say, clearly, to the still, small voice, "I want to hear You. Will You talk to me? Will You rescue me? I'm too weak to wait until the end of the story."

❧

I make it to the restaurant fifteen minutes late because the truck stuttered and died a half mile from the parking lot. At that moment, I had an urge to pull my hair out in handfuls and I wondered if Daddy's madness is seeping into me.

When I stepped out of the car into the matted grass of the roadside to wave down a ride, a gush of wind rushed under my khaki shorts and the sleeves of my T-shirt. It felt like the temperature dropped twenty degrees during my stay at Suzanne's. The wind was blowing the limbs of the palmetto trees so hard that they pointed down toward the marsh. When I jumped back into the truck to take cover from the wind, the engine decided to start.

At work I tell Jeeter to put me on the schedule as much as possible. I tell him I'll do anything—wash dishes, prep food—'cause I have to get out of my house more. He says he'll see what he can do. Thankfully, the tourists are going to roll in next week as spring break starts and business will pick up from now through the summer.

During the night I catch C.C. glancing at me as I run in and out of the kitchen carrying trays full of dirty plates, which he scrapes into one soggy pile of mush before taking the dishes over to the steam washer.

As I'm making a dessert, I watch him run around the kitchen pouring grits into the pot then sifting his fingers through the boiling hot silverware as Suzanne screams to him, "We're out of forks!"

When a customer doesn't finish their fried oyster appetizer, I secretly bring it over to him, and we walk out on the back porch and eat it together while our bare legs bump up from the gusts of unseasonably cold night air.

"Supposed to freeze tonight," he says, scarfing down an oyster as we look out over the marsh. "Winter's last show of the season, I reckon."

"Yeah, I feel like someone has just pushed the Rewind button," I say, feeling the goose bumps rise on my arms.

"Got to wait it out," he says. "March 16 is the first day of spring."

And I wonder if this is an inadvertent word of encouragement from the Lord. Or another detour on this wild-goose chase of a life I'm trapped in.

Now Mr. Lumpkin at the gift shop next door opens his window to look at us as his television lights up his dark den. His rifle is still propped against the porch for show, and I know he dreads the tourist season 'cause he has to continuously ask our customers not to park in his perfectly kept yard, where now the blooms of bright pink azaleas line his front porch and intricately landscaped patches of bright purple and yellow pansies span the length of the front of his house and circle his oak trees. C.C. nods to him, and he closes his window.

❧

As I'm putting the pecan pies in the freezer for the night, I see Sal in the back room with Tanner. They're sitting at Sal's desk beneath a picture of "Miss March," hunched over a piece of a mirror and knocking a credit card over white powder the same way Mama chops celery.

Sal looks up at me and says, "Want to join us in a line, Devo?"

Tanner knocks Sal's arm and says, "She's just a youngun."

I roll my eyes and say, "No way!" and as I head toward C.C., who is waiting for me by my car, Sal follows me outside, laughing and saying, "Oh, come on, DEEEE-VO! You're not too young! Heck, when I was your age—" Immediately, Mr. Lumpkin jumps up from his den, runs out on his porch and hollers, "Hold it down, Sal!"

"Give me a break, Lumpkin. No one's bothering you," Sal says.

"How about two cars trying to park on my property tonight? How about me having to get up from my supper table to tell them to move?"

Sal shakes his head in frustration.

Lumpkin adds, "And I'm not putting up with you or your customers' shenanigans this year. I've just spent seven hundred dollars re-landscaping this yard."

"Yeah, yeah, yeah," he says as he turns and walks back into the kitchen.

On the ride home I say, "So that was cocaine?"

"Yeah," C.C. says. "Rumor has it that one of Tanner's partners found a box in his shrimp net this week off the coast of Georgia.

They think it was a mis-drop from South America or something. Anyway, he was going to turn it in to the police but Sal talked him into keeping it. They've decided to horde it."

Now I picture my cousin on Garrick's boat in the middle of the ocean, lifting up the nets out of the dark water. When they open, the murky green catch splashes around her ankles, and she leans down to sift through the sea life, dividing it up into piles of sustenance or bait.

"So much for law-abiding citizens," I say, trying to feel out where C.C. stands on this issue.

He knocks my shoulder and says, "Can't change the world in a day, Miss Squeaky Clean, now can you?"

C.C. won't let me drop him off at the trailer. Instead he has me drive to the gates of Rose Hill 'cause he says he's fine walking home.

"You're going to freeze," I say as we watch the wind blow the limbs of the pine trees outside the car. "I'll be fine," he says.

When I stop the car just before the avenue of oaks, he immediately leans toward me for our first real kiss.

I move in to meet him, partly because I know he spent a week's worth of pay to woo me last night and partly because I just want to feel loved by another person.

As C.C.'s soft fingertips make their way, steadily, from my wrists to my shoulders, I can't help but think of Daddy, his firm grip on my arms, shouting at me last night. I sort of flinch, but C.C. gently cups both hands beneath my chin and I relax into the cushion of his palms as he directs my face back to his.

It is easy to see how one loses their virginity before they know what has happened. It must not be a decision to consummate a relationship, so much as indecision about saying no. Part of me wants C.C. to keep on kissing me because my heart is so numb that this is the only thing I can still feel, and it is all too easy to take comfort in it.

Recalling all of Bethany's "slippery slope" talks from youth group is like a warning bell that tells me to pull away from him, and when I do, he sighs and runs his fingers through his hair before saying, "Well, I guess this is good night, darlin'."

❧

I walk in the house and see Mama, half-asleep in her reading chair with her heels resting on Flounder's back. She's breathing clearly, but her split-body figure looks even more drastic than usual: Her ankles appear swollen, wrapped in wool socks and bedroom slippers, and the bulge of her hips is slight but noticeable beneath her long cotton skirt. But her thin arms seem skeletal and loose skin drapes her face, like someone let half the air out of a balloon. Like a ball of yarn that someone has taken the cardboard center out of.

She opens her eyes at the sound of the door closing lightly behind me. I walk over and sit on the ottoman next to her.

"All right, Mama?" I say, wanting her to say something about how Daddy treated her last night.

"Just fine, dahlin'." Then she sits up straight and says, "Have you talked to your cousin Eli lately? She keeps coming to my mind."

I stop and think for a moment, thrown to another difficult subject and wondering what my best response should be. "No, ma'am," I say.

"Well, I tried to call her twice today at her apartment in Columbia and I got a strange voice on the answering machine that didn't sound like her."

"Oh, yeah," I say, quick on my feet and wanting to cover for her. "I talked to her last week and she said that she gets a long spring break. I think she's gone with some friends down to Florida. I think I was supposed to tell you and I forgot."

She nods and mumbles, "I just can't seem to keep up with everybody." And we both watch Flounder as he rouses his neck from beneath her ankles, looks at me as if to say "hello" then puts his head back down again.

I look straight into Mama's tired eyes and say, "Last night was awful, wasn't it?"

She says, "Yes," with little reaction then perks up to say, as if our life were just a series of preordained hardships, "And now Daddy's come down with gout again—a bad case of it."

I give a defeated sigh, hoping she'll recognize my disappointment and say *something* about how he treated her last night.

I say, "Is it likely that you'll have an attack like that again? Because we need a better plan if—"

"Oh no," she says. "That's all under control. Dr. McCall gave me a more powerful inhaler and a breathing machine." Then she pats her stomach and almost chuckles as she changes the subject. "And Daddy and I had a craving for hot dogs and chili even though it's against his doctor's orders. Now I feel about as fat as a pig."

She puts her head back down toward Flounder and begins petting him. Is there anyone home in that brain of hers?

Now I realize that Mama isn't even concerned about last night. Her life is back to normal or it never has changed from normal and, in my view, she is foolishly perverting the idea of submission so she won't have to ruffle Daddy's feathers.

And as for me, I am all alone on this battlefield of domesticity.

As I turn toward my room, disappointed by her weakness, she calls out, "DeVeaux, you've got to help me get my diet under control before I start work next week."

"Yes, ma'am," I say with my back to her.

Then she adds, "And maybe we can get Daddy on it too. If only we could clean out his system, I just know he would feel so much better."

I turn back to look at her, but she is already digging in to another diet book.

Flounder follows me toward my bedroom, but changes his mind suddenly and heads down the hall to Daddy's side of the bed where beneath the hall light, I see a plate with a half-eaten hot dog on the floor.

C. C.'s smell, a combination of soap and food, lingers on me as I slide into my unmade bed.

Outside the wind whines, and I can feel the frozen air trying to push through the little openings of the house. A rush of large, bright petals float past my window. It is the azaleas. They are flying off their stems.

One lands against my window, already brown on the ends.

15

Spirits

As I open the lid of the washing machine and peer into the soapy wet lump of sheets and towels, I think of my cousin Eli. It's nearly mid-March, and it's been more than a week since she went out again on Garrick's boat with her bad cold and her new faith, and I haven't heard a word from her. I even called Will and Virginia to see if they knew anything, but neither one has called me back.

So she is on my mind as these spring days expand with sunlight, sending Mama and Daddy and me stumbling into another season.

Since the asthma attack, Daddy has been in and out of bed with gout, leaving Chambers to take care of the end of the planting. This last week, he barely emerged from the bed until suppertime; he ate quickly then shuffled out to the toolshed to finish up the restoration of the sailboat. I overheard him tell Chambers that it will be ready in a few days, but I can't imagine him actually using it. He hasn't been on the water—he hasn't done *anything*—in two weeks.

As for Mama, she hasn't had any more trouble breathing, though I've been trying to listen for that groggy sound in her chest. She's been working at the Piggly Wiggly grocery store on Highway 174 for three weeks now, and her work has been demanding from the start. She's in charge of everything from inventory to parking lot maintenance, so there is no way that she can keep everything running smoothly at home. She said this repeatedly on Sunday afternoon as she and I scrubbed the mold out of the coffeepot and changed the bedsheets.

To work Mama wears a red plastic pin with a giggling cartoon pig in a chef's hat that says, "I'm sticking with the Pig," above her name in capital letters: DEE DELOACH, Assistant Manager. And even though it's starting to warm up outside, it is so cold inside the Pig that Mama usually wears the pink wool cardigan sweater that she bought thirty years ago at Harrod's during her "London Abroad" semester in college. And I have seen her pulling it tight around her bulging hips as she strolls down the aisles, inspecting the expiration dates of canned vegetables or testing faulty wheels on shopping carts.

One of my several recent house duties is fixing supper since Daddy can't wait for Mama because she's often stuck at work until 7:00 p.m. So each afternoon I drop by her office on my way home from school, and she lets me pick out whatever I want to fix. One perk from the Pig is that Mama is allowed to take home anything that is nearing its expiration date at the store, and so she's always sending me home with things like nearly stale pound cakes, frozen-solid potpies, and ripe peaches, their juice already seeping onto the produce rack and attracting flies.

Now, Mama is still trying to diet, but I've caught her eating fried chicken and mashed potatoes from the Pig's hot lunch counter. And it seems like we've all put on a few pounds from this nearly unsellable food, even Flounder, who is now able to eat soft dog food in fancy cans whose time on the grocery shelf is up.

I think I'm the only one who is already sick of this endless supply of rotting nourishment. Each afternoon as I walk in the door after running Mama's errands, Daddy calls with enthusiasm from the bedroom, "What's on the menu tonight?"

I called it out to him a few minutes ago (red rice with sausage and Sweet Sixteen donuts), and now I hear him moving down the hall toward the scent of food as the red rice pops in the microwave and the donuts heat in the oven until the dough softens and the sugar melts into a warm goo.

I can't help but watch Daddy as he eats. There is a squirrel's nest on the back of his head where he's been lying in bed, which sends his thin brown hair shooting out in all directions. And he wears only his white boxers and a faded red golf shirt with a bleach stain at the tip of the collar. First he eats the donuts, and after a few bites of the red rice, he heads to the cabinet for a drinking glass and I realize that every glass or cup in the house is in the dishwasher, waiting to be washed.

"They're dirty," I say. He closes the cabinet, takes a can of Piggly Wiggly cola from the refrigerator and while he's opening it says, "Your mother is starting to let things go around here."

Caught off guard, I say, "Well, she works long days, Daddy."

He nods, then he begins opening the drawers, looking for something else, and I want to say, "She does have a full-time job, which is more than *you* can say . . ." but of course, I don't.

Instead I say, "What else do you need, Daddy?" I don't say this because I *want* to submit like Mama does. I say it because I *must* submit if I want to keep any peace under this roof.

I wait for his response as he rolls the drawers back and forth.

You would think these supper episodes might send me over the edge, but they actually pass with relative ease. For one thing, I usually go to work at the restaurant around this time, but the real thing is, I've got a plan to get out of here.

A few weeks ago, while running Mama's errand to the P.O. box, I received a new application to St. Mary's prep school in Richmond, Virginia, where I was supposed to go this past year until all of the money ran out. In this application there was an additional application for a new scholarship called "Renaissance Women" created for "well-rounded women who show an ability to balance academics and extracurricular activities." There was a letter written by Mrs. Stillwell, the admissions director, who interviewed me last year. In her handwriting at the bottom of the letter, she wrote, "Miss DeLoach, this scholarship is rather competitive, but I'd like to invite you to apply."

This, I thought as I sat in the steaming truck on that sunny day while a seagull perched on my hood, *may be my only legitimate out. Maybe I'm too weak to wait until the end of the story, and I haven't asked the Lord what He thinks 'cause I don't want to hear anything other than a "yes, go!"* I even got a checkup call from Bethany and Sasser that night, and when I told them what I hoped to do, they both said they would love to pray with me about it to make sure it was the right thing. I paid them the proper lip service on the phone; I even wrote down the verse that Bethany told me to look up, Isaiah 40:30–31, but no matter what it said, in my heart I knew I was going for it.

That evening after supper, I called in sick to the restaurant before locking myself in my bedroom to fill out the application.

I stopped only to look at the girl on the glossy cover. She was serving a tennis ball with the Blue Ridge Mountains looming behind the court.

I was overwhelmed by how badly I wanted to be there. With a dining hall and a dorm room. A satellite, just like Virginia and Will. Surrounded by strangers, with this island so far away in time and space that I may not even be able to picture the caretaker's house with its rusted pipes and cobwebbed corners. Or smell the dankness of the pluff mud or hear the *scrape, scrape* of Daddy in the toolshed as he strips down the sailboat, leaving small piles of barnacle and rot on the floor. Or see on the dirt road late at night, when I turn my head from left to right, the blackness that runs right up to me on all sides, as if I were already buried.

So the next thing I knew, I was flat out making up lies on my application in an attempt to impress the admissions office. I said that I was treasurer of my class (which I was, four years ago in sixth grade). I said that I was number two on the tennis team (though I've always been number five, and I didn't even play tennis this year, because my new school doesn't have a team). I even said that I created a peer counseling group called "Need a Friend," 'cause that is something Will did when he was in prep school.

I tossed and turned most of that night and I felt as though God was saying, "Why don't you trust Me? Why do you forget Me? Do you think that lying on your application is the way to go about this?"

Thing is, ever since Mama's asthma attack, I have been so desperate for a quick fix to my situation that I blocked out His voice when it wasn't what I wanted to hear, and in the morning, I drove directly to town and used my tip money from the weekend to Federal Express the application to Richmond, Virginia. I should get an answer in a few weeks. All my hope is resting on that answer.

❧

Last week, without much to-do, the kittens were born. Sagi knocked on the door at dusk that day and motioned for me to follow him. He led me to the teahouse, where we peered into the box and saw that Easy had six babies. Four were crying, warm to the touch and damp from the sacks they had just shed. But the last two were motionless, though Easy kept licking them over and over in an attempt to revive them.

Then I went and got a shoebox and lifted the two curled, cold bodies into it and Sagi followed me out into the fields near the creek, where the dirt is soft, and we dug a deep hole until it was moist, then we scraped away the weeds and roots and buried the box.

"You did a good job," I said to Sagi. "You deserve a long boat ride on the creek."

He nodded proudly, his hands full of dirt, and said to me, "Great!" Then he stood up to wipe his hands on his pants while his feet sank farther into the mud.

As we headed back through the fields, we crossed the swamp

where Maum Bess and Chambers live, and I could see the neon blue shutters through the trees. Chambers was sitting on the front steps peeling an orange.

Sagi pointed in his direction and said, "Why is their house painted bright like that?"

"It's to keep away the evil spirits," I said.

"You mean ghosts?" he said, looking back at the rickety house.

As I considered how to explain this to him a low voice came up behind us and a dry, brown hand clutched Sagi's shoulder. "No," it said, "there is an army of evil spirits, including the devil, that roam this land."

Sagi jumped, then cowered behind me. I looked back to see Maum Bess in her blue bathrobe and sneakers, her green and yellow turban tied tightly around her head. She was holding a bucket of blue crabs, and we could hear them fighting with one another as they attempted to climb the sides of the bucket.

Maum Bess looked us up and down, and I was suddenly aware of our muddy hands and knees and Sagi's death grip around my waist. As he began to stand up and come out from behind me, I saw that he had stained the sides of my shirt with his muddy handprints.

"Who are *you*?" Sagi asked Maum Bess.

"Now I should be asking you that, little one," she replied. "I've been livin' on this land for more than sixty years. I grew up and raised three kids here, and my own mama is buried round back of the swamp."

Sagi peered over and into her bucket. He said, "I'm Sagi, and I don't believe in spirits or the devil."

"Humph," Maum Bess said, then she winked at me. "I'm nearly ten times your age, Sagi, and I'm telling you that the enemy wants to make each soul his prisoner, and his plan for them all is death—just like those poor kittens you just buried. And the sooner you learn that you got to go to the Lord for the power to combat the devil, the better off you'll be, ya hear?" And with that she turned, shook the bucket so the crabs slid down to the bottom, then headed toward her house.

I could hear her muttering as she made her way down the path, "Jesus, have mercy on that one."

Sagi stopped me in my tracks and said, "How did she know about the kittens?"

I turned to him and said, "Sagi, I don't know. But what I do know is that somehow Maum Bess senses most everything."

"Do you believe there are spirits here, Miss DeLoach?" he said, and I pictured the spirits that Maum Bess used to tell me about, evil ones that were allowed to enter the island by the slaves who practiced voodoo, or the cotton planters who beat their slaves and split apart their families, or even ancient Indians who worshiped strange gods. She said they roam the fields in the pitch black, seeking a home to hook into.

"I can't say I've seen one," I said to him, "but I guess I wouldn't be surprised if I did."

Sagi kicked an oyster shell and shivered. "This place can be creepy," he said. "My mom gets scared sometimes when she hears a funny sound. The other night when there was a strong breeze, she screamed when the limb of an oak tree scratched her window. She made me sleep in her room."

I chuckled to myself, trying to imagine Mrs. Shuzuki in their remodeled fortress, with her state-of-the-art appliances and mighty iron gates, being frightened.

As we passed by the main house, Mrs. Shuzuki spotted us, then scolded Sagi in Japanese from the porch. She was obviously upset with how dirty he was. Her sounds were like a football hitting you in the stomach, grunty and guttural as if she were saying "ten hut!" over and over. She made him stop right there in the yard where she took the garden hose and sprayed him down with cold water.

Sagi shouted to me as I turned away, "What do those spirits do to you, anyway? If you run into one?"

I looked back to him and said what Maum Bess told me when I was little, "Aw, I don't know. But all you have to do is say, 'The Lord has won the battle, so in His name be gone!' and they'll leave you alone."

As I turned back he called again, "So you owe me a boat ride, remember?"

"Yes," I said without turning around.

"When?" he shouted, and as I began to walk through the trees of the gall I said, "Soon."

❧

Later, as I was making sure that all the kittens were getting to Easy's nipples, Mama came into the teahouse with a box containing fifty cans of kitten chow in assorted flavors.

"We lost two," I told her.

She nodded sympathetically then picked a kitten up, cupped it in her hands, and rested it against her chest. "Nature's way," she says.

Easy just looked up at both of us as though she was as confused as we were. Three kittens were nursing and she looked as though all she wanted to do was jump into one of our arms and be cuddled herself.

"Easy looks surprised to be a mother," Mama says.

"Yeah," I say.

Then Mama tells me a story about how when she had Virginia, she was so scared about being a mother that all she wanted to do was go home to Greenville, get in her own bed, and have her mama bring her chicken soup like she used to do when Mama was a child with a cold.

"How did you cope?" I said.

"Well, I just cried for about three days to your daddy, and called home every hour and begged for my parents to come and get me. Then one night Daddy brought the baby to me in bed and said, 'But Dee, you can't go home. *You* are a mother now.'"

We both laugh. Mama seems like such a natural nurturer to me, it's hard to imagine that she would have to make that kind of adjustment.

She put the kitten back onto Easy's nipple, then said, "DeVeaux, let's try to find homes for these soon, okay?"

And I knew that what she meant was that just seeing these kittens was going to eat at Daddy. It would be just another reminder of his heap of misfortune.

"Okay," I said. "I'll ask around."

Mama stroked the back of my head like she did when I was a little girl. "Thank you," she said, then, "It won't always be this way, dahlin'."

"What do you mean?" I said, probing for some hope.

"Your father will be better one day," she said.

As she said this I thought about Daddy in bed as a grown man and crying for Mee Maw to bring him some soup, rub his temples, and tell him he'll be well soon.

Together, Mama and I rose from the box, closed the door behind us, and walked toward the house where he was sitting on the porch in his boxers and a golf shirt, rubbing his swollen ankles.

❧

I guess you could say that C. C. and I are an "item" now. Everyone at the restaurant cracks jokes about us. It's hard to believe how much my tastes have changed since I moved out here, but I'm just trying to readjust to my new life. Also, I need an escape from home.

C. C. calls me each afternoon from the marina when I'm getting home from school, and I have been sneaking out occasionally to meet him, which I know is against the dating rules. Last week when Bethany asked me to tell her what C. C. and I did for fun, I just didn't have the heart to tell her about the sneaking out so all I said was, "We hang out for a little while after work at the restaurant." But I think she knew that wasn't the whole story.

Anyway, on those occasions when he invites me, I creep out of the house around midnight with a flashlight and my tennis shoes and walk through two fields until I get to the Rose Hill gates where he meets me.

Flounder usually comes along, too, keeping me company on those pitch-black walks. He hears sounds and smells that I don't notice, and I know he wants to run off after the scent of a raccoon or a bobcat, but he sticks close, and even attempts to conceal his whimpers.

As we walk quickly through the brush, I try not to think of the spirits that Maum Bess warns about, but I can't help but picture them with their feet turned backward, hovering over the fields as I pass by, hidden only by the thick darkness.

Sometimes, I'm spooked by a rustling in the trees or a sharp screeching and though it is too dark to see them, I know there are several bats soaring through the blackness that is their freedom.

For a few nights C. C. and I met a group down beneath the pier, but the local policeman found us one night and warned us not to come back. This happened around the same time Tina started to really go steady with the thirty-year-old boat mechanic named Floyd, whom she's been seeing off and on for some time now (against my wishes). If I want to see her, I have to go wherever Floyd is, so lately we've been meeting at his trailer that sits on the side of Highway 174. It's a dark gray single-wide with a gutted outboard motor for a mailbox. And his front yard is littered with boats of all sizes, propped on cinder blocks. Floyd usually has grease on his fingertips, but he's a bearable sort of guy, except for the fact that he wears his pants so low that you can see where his rear end begins when he squats to look up under a hull or pull something out of his mini-refrigerator.

Anyway, we usually listen to music at Floyd's or sit around while they drink beer (no, I haven't caved in to underage drinking, but I am more like an accomplice to a crime since I don't protest their choice to partake). I did take up smoking, and I always have a pin-prick of guilt in taking a drag since I'd been so good up until now, but there is a part of me that has learned to block out that guilt. It happened when I lied on that St. Mary's scholarship application, and I know I've got to rein it in before it reigns over me. Thing is, there is a part of me that just wants to push forward, hoping for some light at the end of this tunnel I'm in.

"Spring lasts for three months," Sasser said to me last week. "And we're only in March."

"I'm tired of waiting," I said. "I don't want to do it anymore."

Toward the end of these nights at Floyd's, C.C. leads me out to the bunk of a large sailboat in the backyard. There we sit on the narrow, lopsided berth and kiss as the occasional headlights from a car pass over us.

For a while C.C. hinted, although recently he has flat out told me that he wishes we could have sex. I was in shock the first time he said it, but at the same time it seemed like such a natural request to him that I took it in stride the way I do a lot of stuff with Tina and C.C., because I know that in many ways we are from different worlds.

My response was and still is, "I'm not ready. God says not to. I'm too young." And I know that all of this is true and right.

Sometimes I actually toy with the possibility of it, just for a moment. And when I do I come to the same conclusions: (1) I certainly couldn't go off to St. Mary's with a reputation. (2) Even though I'm pretty certain my siblings had sex by the time they graduated from college, there is still the voice of God making its way through the barriers, saying, "If you do this and it is wrong, you will regret it for the rest of your days." And I don't think I can muffle that voice. I mean, if there is a reason that God says to wait until marriage, shouldn't I consider that?

C. C. says, "Can I do anything to change your mind?"

"No," I say, and I know this is true.

Then he says, "It's your decision."

And I know he means it, that it is my decision, though I also know that every time we kiss, he's going to ask again, a question he poses with wandering hands, and I'm going to have to say no again by gently pushing him away.

But tonight we're not going to Floyd's. Sal has invited all the party folks of the island, young and old, over to his house. He says it's like a meeting, and many islanders are excited because they've always wanted to see the inside of his supreme beachfront house. Of course, several of the local women *have* seen the inside.

As we walk through the screened porch, C. C. and Tina and Floyd are gawking at the architectural feats: two-story windows that face the beach, enormous skylights that cross the ceiling, a spiral staircase that leads to a loft filled with a pile of pillows the color of red wine.

There are two stuffed blue marlins on opposite walls and in the center of the room there is a bronze statue of a mermaid with unrealistically perky breasts.

"Kickin' pad," Floyd says as Sal directs us to the bar.

Tina squeezes my wrist and says in the direction of our host, "You're rich as all get-out, aren't cha?"

Against Tina's suggestion, I order a grapefruit juice and sip on it like the teetotaler that I am as I look around the room at the folks of all ages. There are the waitresses and crew from the restaurant, the boys from the marina, and the older couple from California that run the hardware store. There is Kendra, the one and only hairdresser on the island; and Earl, the guy who owns the bike-rental stand.

As Sal directs us to take a seat, I begin to fear that I don't know what I'm getting myself into here. What is this all about? Just as I turn to C.C. to ask, Tanner brings out a small steel box, about as big as a paperback book, which he places on the dining room table. We all watch as he opens it. Inside are several small plastic bags that are filled to the top with packed white powder.

"If that don't beat all!" says Floyd while other people laugh nervously.

I look at C.C., and he must see the question and trepidation on my face so he cups his hand over my ear and whispers, "That's the cocaine, remember?"

As my throat begins to burn with fear and the aftertaste of grapefruit juice, Tanner hollers over all the chattering, "My crew found these when they were pulling up the shrimp nets about sixty miles off the coast of Savannah. Best we can figure is that it was a misdrop from South America or something." He pulls his stringy hair behind his ears and chuckles while he says, "I reckon some poor Latino boys are crying themselves to sleep."

Most everyone laughs, but I'm just looking for the door. *How do I get out of here without making a scene?* I think to myself. I could get in big trouble for being here. I could be arrested and never go to St. Mary's and my name could appear in all the news-papers that fall on the downtown piazzas of all my old friends, not to mention at Sasser's or Bethany's home. I deplore cocaine—or any drug for that matter. I'm afraid of stuff like that, and I know it could keep me from saving myself. From getting out of here. A lot is at stake in this moment, and I have to gain a spine and quick. Locked in anxiety I stay in my seat and begin to perspire, feel the burn beneath my arms, as Tanner continues.

He says, "So the point of this meeting is that we need to get rid of this stuff. And I was thinking that you all could help me enjoy it—'cause I'd kill myself if I did it *all*. So I want you to mark your calendars, hire your babysitters, whatever you need to do, 'cause next week we're going to have a lost weekend at Edisto Island— my treat!"

People look around the room. Some are grinning while others are fidgeting in their seats.

Sal says, "Who wants a sample now?"

And many people say, "I do."

Lord, help me get out of here, I pray. I'm so sorry that I've found my way into this situation. Please forgive me and protect me, Father.

After Tanner starts setting up lines on the glass coffee table, I motion to C. C. to go out on the porch. The beach wind blows my hair across my face, and I grab onto the railing and say, "I don't know about all of that, C. C. I mean, *I* don't want to try it, and we could get into major trouble. I feel like I'm in way over my head here, you know? I don't like this at all. I want to leave. *Now.*"

"Okay," he says as he cups his hands to light a cigarette. "Let's get out of here."

So we walk down toward the beach and along the dunes with Flounder trailing behind us. Then C. C. leads me behind a sand dune where he's spotted a catamaran. We sit on top of the boat, C. C. petting Flounder and me moving my hands along the black synthetic berth, which feels just like Louisa Townsend's trampoline in her backyard on Gibbes Street. We used to lie on that black circle, suspended, feet above the ground for hours between sessions of crack the egg, where one of us would curl up in the fetal position, holding our knees tightly to our chest while the other would jump all around the trampoline, over and on top and beside the opponent, in an attempt to have them release one of their limbs and surrender.

I think of this as C.C. unties his tennis shoes and leans over to kiss me. As he circles my ears and neck and face with his pecks, Flounder rolls around beneath the boat, then falls asleep in the sand beneath us.

After a while, I notice that C.C. is not acting like the gentle, tentative boyfriend he usually is. He pushes me down on the boat for a moment and plants himself firmly on top of me, his hands moving with a kind of aggression.

As I try to sit up, he pushes me firmly back down. Then with a strength from God, (whose hand is *still* on my life though I know I don't deserve it), I put my hand up to his chest, straighten my arm to push him away and say, "I said *no.*" The angry tone of my voice rouses Flounder, who leaps up on the catamaran and begins to bark at us as the wind carries the sand from his fur toward our faces.

C.C. makes a visor to shield the sand from his eyes and says, "Sorry, DeVeaux."

"That isn't exactly a nice feeling," I say. "It's more like an attack."

Then he puts his hand gently on the back of my head and says, "I guess I just get carried away sometimes. I'm ready to move forward, you know?"

"And I'm *not,*" I say, reaching for my shoes and heading back onto the beach. Before I know it, he catches up to me as we walk back toward the car. As he throws his arm loosely around my shoulder like nothing has happened, I begin to realize that C.C. isn't bothered by the things I am—sex with regrets, cocaine charges, never getting out of here—not to mention rebelling against God.

He seems as calm as ever, his feet digging into the sand, his head bobbing back and forth as his hair lifts in the wind, and I feel sad that we are in such different places.

"Are you going to do it?" I ask him. "The lost weekend?"

"Probably," he says. "Why not?"

And I see clearly now that C. C. is unlike me in many ways. It's not just that I am cautious, and I don't have any desire to do cocaine or any other drug, or that I need a sober mind to help me survive. It's that I'm not an islander like him. C. C. always has and always will go with the flow of island life. And island life, as I am now coming to realize, is different from downtown Charleston and probably the rest of the world. The fact is, we're isolated out here, and that means we are protected by our isolation. That is, we can get away with most anything because there's no one here to stop us. And it also means we are bored. So bored, any opportunity that comes along is worth the chance to quell the boredom. In C. C.'s mind he says, *What is there to lose?*

Lord, thank You for showing me that this is not Your best for either of our lives. Meet C. C. *where he is and reveal Yourself to him,* I silently pray as my heart forever leaves my island boyfriend on that beach in the pitch-black night.

And even though C. C. tries to pull me along with him as we head over the dunes, I step out from his arm and trail behind. I feel the sand he is churning up just a stride ahead of me as it hits my ankles and knees. I watch the casual way he swings his arms and tilts his shoulders from side to side. I know that he probably won't ever leave Edisto and this way of life. And he'll most likely decide to make the best of what comes along here. Whether it's a lost weekend, or a new girl from town, or a job washing dishes.

But the thing is, I'm not like this. I will leave here. Somehow I know this now as strongly as I know that C. C. will participate in the lost weekend. And even though he cares for me, he will eventually find another girl to be with, or even better, he will meet the Lord and forever fill the void of boredom and loneliness.

When he takes me home, he lets me off like usual at the Rose

Hill gates, and I say, "Good-bye," looking him right in the eyes, and I know he thinks it's over, too, because he doesn't make an attempt to kiss me good night.

As he drives off, taking with him the only light for acres, I am relieved to let go of him, and I trust the Lord to do His will in C. C.'s life. "That's over," I say with a lightness of heart before I shimmy between the wrought-iron fence and help Flounder slide under on his belly.

On the walk through the fields, I have a desire for the first time to bump into one of those night spirits. That is, I want to see if they exist, and if there is enough strength in uttering the name of God to fight them off. I turn off my flashlight and walk solidly through the blackness.

"Come out," I say to the darkness. "I'm ready to meet you."

And I am ready for an encounter with something greater than what I know. I want to see the unseen like Maum Bess. I want to have a conversation with the still, small voice of God. Hear Him wake me up from my sleep with His holy voice. It's time He showed me the climax of the story.

"C'mon," I say, "I'm ready."

But I don't see or hear a thing.

I look behind me, and down the rows of corn, but I don't hear a peep.

I look down at Flounder, who is watching my every move. He looks up at me, his eyes two iridescent marbles suspended in midair, and he is the closest-looking thing to a spirit out here so far. We continue to push through the black fields, feeling our way along the stalks and vines, half expecting a dark face on the other side of one of the rows. Half expecting God to say, "Well, here I am."

Suddenly, I trip on a vine, and as I land on my knees, a flock of startled bats flies up and over me. My skin crawls at the sight of them, but still I am willing to face my Maker. I want to hear and see and know what is beneath the exterior of this wild land. Right now I wouldn't be afraid if I bumped into the devil himself. I'd just say, "Get thee behind me!"

Still, nothing.

"Don't test the Lord," I remember from some old Sunday school lesson, and it dawns on me with certainty that the Lord has been holding me in His arms this whole night, protecting me from all of the dangers that could have had their way with me. "Thank You!" I say. "I know You are here!"

After walking ten or so more yards, I can see the porch light at the plantation house. I walk closer and see that Mrs. Shuzuki is on the second-floor piazza in her nightgown and robe, shivering as she directs the beam of a flashlight out into the darkness. As we walk closer she must be able to hear our footfalls. The vines are making a soft sweep across the dirt beneath our feet, and she must think that we are the spirits.

She shouts in our direction. It is Japanese so I can't make it out, but she sounds furious and tired.

I hold Flounder back by the collar and he begins to whimper.

We watch her for whole minutes as she reties the belt on her bathrobe and stares angrily into the darkness. The bats must have woken her up because they are circling the roof of her house, screeching. As they begin to descend and head back to the corn-fields, she shrieks when they fly by the piazza. Then she runs inside and slams the door. She turns off the lights in her bedroom and now the whole house is dark again.

I turn toward the caretaker's house, still looking, but by the time I get to the toolshed, I turn the flashlight back on. Not a spirit in sight for two whole fields.

In this quiet isolation, I can't help but picture my cousin, rocking back and forth in the vastness of the sea nights, waiting for enough fish to make their way into the net so she can rent her own place.

I pray to the Lord that He will take care of her the way He has taken care of me tonight.

❧

The next evening, as I'm warming up a frozen pizza for Mama and Daddy, Virginia comes tearing into the house, half hysterical, and leaps into Mama's arms, saying, "He broke up with me!"

Mama gives Daddy and me a frantic look, puts her arms around Virginia, and says, "It's going to be all right, dahlin'."

When Virginia eventually pulls back from Mama, I notice her feeling the flesh on Mama's sides. She looks into Mama's face then steps away, studies her body up and down, then says, "Mama, when did you get so *fat*?"

Daddy and I step back to get a good look at Mama, and for the first time I am struck by how much weight she has gained. I guess I didn't notice because it's been gradual, but now I see it all over: her widening hips that lift her skirt up on the sides, the thickening of her upper arms, and even the start of a second chin that is beginning to fill out below her jawline.

From the look of shock on Daddy's face, it seems he is just beginning to see it too.

"How in the world did this happen?" Virginia says. "It's just been a month since I saw you."

"You don't have to be so blunt," I say to my sister in a frail attempt to defend Mama. But even I can't mask the astonishment on my face.

Mama leans on the kitchen counter where she's just brought in a box of Piggly Wiggly cinnamon rolls.

"It's this job," she says as the wrinkles form across her fore-head. "I'm surrounded by food!"

Daddy plants both feet on the floor, then jumps over to his left foot because his right one is undergoing a severe bout of gout. He bends his knee to raise his foot behind him and says, "Well, baby, I guess it's time to get back on that diet."

Mama nods and says, "I'll call the church tomorrow."

Virginia sniffles and nods and I am shocked by how I could have been blind to this physical change in Mama. I wonder what else I have been missing, and I know that I've got to wake back up again and beg the Lord to give me eyes to see the truth, or who knows what else I'll miss. "Tear down any of the remaining walls that keep me from You," I pray to Him under my breath.

Virginia blows her nose and we all feel sorry for her. Here she thought Clayton was about to propose—Daddy looks nervously out toward the toolshed, and I know he wants to escape because he has no idea how to console his daughter. Then he says, "Well, I'll leave you girls to talk," and he walks over to Virginia and softly kisses her on the forehead, then jumps on his left foot out into the yard.

"Boy, he looks bad too," Virginia says; then she starts to weep again.

As Mama shuffles over to her reading chair and invites Virginia to sit down, I try to give them some privacy so I go to the laundry room to dry the sheets that have been sitting wet in the washing machine for three days now.

Through the thin walls I can hear Virginia relaying the particulars of her breakup. She says Clayton discarded her because he wants to go out with Gigi Heyward, a girl Virginia's age from a very old, still well-to-do Charleston family who have a house on the Battery and a plantation north of McClellanville where they host an annual polo match.

Weeping, she says bitterly, "Clayton just wants the best breed of Charleston girl," then, "and I'm not a breed at all anymore."

Mama hugs Virginia while looking nervously out the window, making sure that Daddy isn't heading back to the house because she wouldn't want him to hear this.

Mama commands Virginia in a whisper, "Don't let that anger in."

But Virginia pushes Mama away and says, "You're not even *from* Charleston, Mama. You don't even get it."

Later that night, after Virginia leaves with a roll of toilet paper for tissue and the box of cinnamon rolls, I'm sitting on my bed when I hear Daddy start to holler from the toolshed. First, he lets out a short yelp like he's in pain, then he calls Mama's name. I know it must be his foot. He probably wants her to help him back to the house.

He says, "Dee?" again, but she can barely hear him over the kitchen sink where she is washing the dishes.

"Dee!" he says louder. "Dee!"

As I leave my room to tell her that he is calling, she turns off the sink because she has heard him too.

"Dee!" he screams again, and she walks out on the porch as she throws the dishtowel over her shoulder and says, "Billy, is that you?"

"Yes!" he screams. "Get out here!"

"Coming," she says.

But he must not have heard her and he shouts, "Get . . . your . . . fat . . . rear . . . out . . . here, you idiot!"

Mama's body tightens at the sound of his harsh words. Her eyes move back and forth as if she's reading.

"Now!" Daddy screams.

Mama stands stone still for a split second. Then she walks directly back into the house and locks the sliding glass door behind her. She moves straight to her bedroom and shuts the door.

I close my door directly after her, letting her know that I agree with her 100 percent. A surge of energy goes through me because I am happy that she is standing up to him. I think to myself, *So Mama has her limit, after all.*

After a few minutes, Daddy hobbles back on one foot to the house and tries the locked door. He jiggles the handle back and forth in an attempt to see if the door is just stuck. Flounder barks from beneath the tractor as if Daddy were an intruder.

When Daddy realizes what's happened, he sits down on the picnic table, propping his head on his hand in the darkness. He clears his throat.

I just sit perfectly still on my bed, a part of me still secretly applauding Mama and another part knowing that she must be upset with herself because she's going against how she thinks she should be. Also, I can't help but feel sad for Daddy. I imagine him sitting there outside of his house, this caretaker's house, in the dark. It's weird to feel so many things at once.

No one says or does anything. And I am suddenly aware of the sound of my own breathing. It seems to fill the walls with a steady drone. So I look up the verses that are written on a scrap sheet of paper by my telephone from the last conversation I had with Bethany where I ignored her requests to pray with me as I prepared my application.

They pierce my heart with their truth: *"Even the youths shall faint and be weary, and the young men shall utterly fall, but those who wait on the LORD shall renew their strength; they shall mount up with wings like eagles, they shall run and not be weary, they shall walk and not faint"* (Isaiah 40:30–31 NKJV).

About forty-five minutes later, after I've memorized my verses and asked the Lord to forgive me for not waiting on Him to show me His way, Mama comes out of their bedroom and walks slowly to the sliding glass door and unlocks it. Then she goes barefoot out onto the porch. The dishtowel is still on her shoulder.

I sit up in bed and watch out my window as he remains seated, but turns slowly around at the table to face her.

She gets down on her knees in front of him and weeps into his lap. He gently strokes the top of her head back and forth.

He says, "Oh, baby," and she just whimpers in response. "It's okay," he says, and then, "I've been sitting out here on this porch thinking about poor Virginia. You know I couldn't have paid for a wedding anyway. I'm ashamed that I couldn't even pay for my daughter to have a wedding. I'm ashamed that I'm *relieved* that boy broke her heart instead of me having to do it." Mama doesn't talk, she just keeps her head in his lap and he continues to stroke it.

And then moments later he says softly but clearly, "Dee, I hate my life."

Mama just weeps in response, and he continues to stroke the top of her head back and forth while I think of Maum Bess and of her fasting and praying and patience, and I continue to simultaneously doubt and have hope in anyone's ability to rescue my father from himself.

I say to the God I've nearly abandoned these last few months, "Please rescue my daddy."

And when I pray this prayer, I suddenly have a love and a sympathy for my daddy that I haven't had for a long time. Who would have thought I could ever again have any positive feeling at all toward him? But God loves resurrection, even the resurrection of broken, hardened hearts, and this love for my dad is what I consider a miracle.

"Thank You," I say to the Lord as my daddy continues to stroke my mama's head.

My parents are out on the porch this way for longer than I can stay awake.

16

Lost Weekend

Today I owe Sagi a long ride in the boat, so I stop off at the gas station for fuel and pick us up a couple of Gatorades, some Tootsie Rolls, and a little bait 'cause I figure he might like to go fishing.

It is a bright day with a thin layer of clouds to shield us from the heat, and there's even a decent breeze coming off the water. I can see it gently lifting the Spanish moss from the arch of the oak limbs that shade the soft dirt road. As I pound the truck down the sides of the cornfields, cutting across the grass and creating a new road, it is suddenly peculiar to me that I have spent most of my life in the city, so tightly compressed with row houses and sidewalks, and the pervasive stench caused by the horse urine from the tourist carriages that boils on the black tar. It seems nearly foreign to me now—those curling one-way streets that take you three times as long to get to a destination that is, as the crow flies, just yards away.

Thing is, it has not taken me long to become accustomed to all this space, to drive directly to one's destination. In fact, I am accustomed to most all the changes that have occurred in the last seven months since we moved to the country: my run-down school, my restaurant job, Mama working at the Piggly Wiggly, my friendship with Tina, and my peculiar romance with C.C. I'm even accustomed to Daddy wearing his boxers at the dinner table and lying in bed half the time, though I'd be a fool not to admit that sometimes I'm afraid of what he'll do the next time he blows up. Or the time after that. Or the time after that. I guess no one can get used to being afraid.

With the exception of Sasser and Bethany, my downtown friends don't call as much, and I'm used to that. John Henry stopped writing two months ago, and Louisa calls only in desperate late-night fits when Peter Jenkins has shunned her for another girl. It is sad to see her so desperate about him, but I do my best to console her and try to point out other ways she could be spending her time. The only thing that hit her was when I suggested exercising and now she says she runs three miles every day and has lost ten pounds, which she did not need to lose.

"But Peter said my thighs are as big as his," she said when I cautioned her about losing too much weight. "That's absurd, Louisa!" I shrieked the last time she called me, and I have had this keen desire to write Peter Jenkins and give him a piece of my mind.

I rarely go downtown these days and neither does Mama, so I was surprised last week when Mrs. Davidson convinced her that Mary Margaret and I should attend the Junior Cotillion, a dance at the South Carolina Society Hall for Charleston teenagers.

"You've got to stay connected to your friends," Mama urged. "And I want you to be exposed to *gentlemen*," she added, her eyes narrowing, and I knew this was a subtle attack at my relationship with C.C., which she doesn't know is over. I was tempted to tell Mama about the slumber party episode a few months back and how the downtown boys are more boorish than the country ones, but I thought better of it and finally gave in.

I called Sasser the night before to see if he would meet us there.

"I can't this time, DeVeaux," he said with a great excitement in his voice, "Father Michael, the missionary who healed me a while back, is staying the night at our house on his way back to China after visiting some relatives in Savannah."

"What do you think might happen?" I asked.

"I don't know," Sasser said. "I'm just going to tell him that I want the gift of healing and see if he'll pray with me about receiving it."

"That's awesome."

"Yeah," he said. "Sorry to let you down, but you know I can't miss this."

"I wouldn't want you to," I say to him. "I'll be praying for you. Let me know what happens."

"Thanks, DeVeaux. I will!"

❧

The dance was a disaster. Mary Margaret was overdressed in a navy blue, sailor-style sundress, and I suppose I was underdressed and slightly out-of-date in a pair of Virginia's plaid pants and a yellow oxford shirt. Mary Margaret was embarrassed when her mother dropped us off at the entrance, because she saw that most of the town girls were in black miniskirts with bright silk sweater sets and chic, square-heeled black shoes. She stuck to me like glue as we walked toward the entrance, just slightly behind me with her head tilted toward the floor.

The chaperones were lax, and kids were spiking their punch in the bathrooms and getting tipsy quick. A dorky boy a year younger than me asked me to dance, and I felt terrible leaving Mary Margaret standing aimlessly by the punch bowl, but she told me to go on, that she'd be waiting for me right there, so I did.

As the boy led me to the middle of the dance floor I spotted Peter Jenkins dancing with a girl I'd never seen before, and I knew Louisa was somewhere nearby, her heart crushed once again. Then as a couple left the floor, an opening in the crowd formed and I saw John Henry Drayton dancing with Kendra Riddlehoover, his face buried deep in her chest and laughing a drunken laugh. "Oh well,"

I sighed, knowing that he must be home from spring break without as much as a thought of me. I danced with my back to them and hurried back to Mary Margaret when the song ended.

On our third trip to the bathroom for Mary Margaret to relieve herself after her nervous punch consumption, we found Louisa passed out on the floor beneath the sink.

Mary Margaret ran to grab one of the chaperones as I tried to revive her, and I was astonished as I became conscious of how tiny she had become. Her wrists were as thin and bony as a young child's, and her knees were knobby and out of proportion with her frail legs. And the worst part was her cheeks—they were empty and grayish, and I could see several thin blue veins in the hollows of them.

As she opened her eyes and said my name, I realized that she was starving herself for Peter Jenkins or maybe even her father, who never noticed her pleas for his attention. I pulled her close to me and cried, "Louisa, don't do this to yourself."

"Did you see him dancing with that girl from Wando?" she said to me in a feverish whisper just as a male chaperone stormed in, scooped her off the floor and said, "Time for you to go home, Miss Townsend. Your parents will be here momentarily."

Mary Margaret was substantially troubled by the evening, so she called her mother from a chaperone's cell phone and suggested we wait on the front steps of Society Hall for her to come and pick us up.

As we sat there, staring down Meeting Street into the night lights of downtown, listening to the muffled rock music in the hall behind us and the clod of a tourist carriage ambling by, John Henry suddenly stumbled down the steps on his way to someone's car, and as he glanced back, he caught sight of me and came shuffling over.

"DeVeaux," he said. "It's been a long time. How are you doing?"

"I'm fine," I said, and he sat next to us and told us how he just got kicked out of Woodberry Forest for smoking marijuana and that his parents might send him off to a military school next.

As Mary Margaret's Suburban pulled up, we told him good-bye, and he asked if he could call me sometime. When he asked this, Kendra came out onto the piazza and put her hands on her hips and said, "John Henry, I'm waiting for that drink."

He looked up at her, her voluptuous body outlined in the piazza light, and then back at me as we moved toward the car, Mary Margaret still like glue behind me.

"I'm coming," he said to Kendra, and he turned from me and walked toward the parking lot without even waiting to hear my reply (which was going to be "no thanks").

On the ride home, I sat in the backseat of the Davidsons' car and stared out the window as the city lights turned into suburban lights and then the country lights of nowhere. As I watched the darkness deepen, I gave thanks to the Lord for the blessing of not staying downtown my whole life. *Think of what I might have missed*, I thought to myself—*Tina, C.C., the island and its unspeakable beauty.* Of course I never would have been able to see this until now, that I could have ended up wasting away like Louisa over some boy who would drop me in an instant for a more desirable situation. That the highlight of my week could have been squeezing into a little black skirt, stuffing my bra, and drinking punch until I felt sick to my stomach.

I sigh with delight when I think that even now I can see the wisdom in what Bethany said to me a few months back on the way home from youth group. That I have to wait until the end to see the blessing, and I can't believe that this is already happening to me. I grin when I flip my calendar open to find that it is March 21. We are well into spring now.

Then I can hear Mary Margaret snoring as we cross the

Dawhoo River bridge onto the island, and I breathe deeply as we enter the mysterious darkness of my home, the gaping open mouth that has in its strange way swallowed me, protected me, and given me new sight.

᷎

When I pick Sagi up, he is waiting on the porch for me in a new neon-green life jacket with pink and yellow straps. He's got a little fishing rod that used to belong to Will, and he's got a pocketknife around the strap of his swim trunks. There are four construction trucks in the circular driveway and a man on the roof who is installing some kind of satellite.

Mrs. Shuzuki comes out onto the porch when she sees me drive up, and I can see slight circles beneath her eyes. I wonder if she continues to wake up at night and yell at the bats.

"Hello, Miss DeLoach," she says to me. "You will be very careful?" she asks as Sagi climbs into my truck. "Yes, ma'am," I say. "I've been doing this all of my life."

I notice two men digging a trench on the right side of the house, and I ask Mrs. Shuzuki, "What's going on?"

"Oh," she says, "my husband want to make this a more permanent residence. He move his business stuff here so he can communicate with office."

When she says this my heart sinks in disappointment for Mama and Daddy. The more the Shuzukis are here, the more my parents have to work, and the more Daddy is confronted with his losses.

Sometimes I begin to see the world the way Daddy does, a place where all the cards are stacked against him. Like everything is a conspiracy to undermine his efforts. Funny how when you think this way, it is almost like inviting your own miserable fate. I wonder if Daddy knows about the Shuzukis' plan. I hope I'm not the one to tell him.

"Let's go," Sagi hollers, and so I roll up my window and we drive toward the dock.

When we get to Peter's Point Creek, we anchor and I bait Sagi's hook and cast out his line. As we wait to feel a bite, Sagi says to me, "I've been looking for a spirit, Miss DeLoach."

I give him a side-angled glance. I laugh at him, even though there is a part of me that looks for them too.

"Yep," he says. "Like that old woman said. And I saw one in my dream two nights ago."

"Really?" I say.

He looks out toward his line, his small chubby hands clutched tightly around the reel. "I saw a strong man in farm clothes with a pale, mean face sitting on the porch rail outside my window. He was looking at the fields and then back to my room. I was scared, so I pulled the covers up to my eyes and pretended I was asleep."

"Mmm," I say to Sagi, "sounds creepy."

"Wait," he says, "I haven't gotten to the good part."

"Go on, then," I say.

"He kept staring at me. Then he even walked up to the window, put his big hands on the glass and leaned in to get a better look. I could see the lines on his face, he was so close! Then he tapped the window and said my name."

Now my interest is piqued. Maum Bess says that children have eyes to see what she sees, and so why couldn't Sagi spot an evil spirit?

"So what did you do?"

"I said what that old lady said to say. That God has won the battle, so get out of here!"

"And?"

"And for a minute he didn't move, just kept staring at me. But then an even bigger, stronger man, three times the size of the first one, came up behind him. I couldn't even see his face. I just saw his legs and they were as wide as the columns on the front of the house. So when the first man looked back and saw the second one, he turned away from my window, walked under the larger man's legs, climbed over the piazza onto the first-floor porch, and walked out into the fields."

With this he pulls his line and I help him reel in our first catch of the day. A four-pound trout. He shrieks with delight.

"Are you telling the truth, Sagi?" I ask as I reach for the fish.

"It was a dream, but that's how it happened, Miss DeLoach."

"So what about the other guy, the gigantic one. What did he do after the first one left?"

"Well," he says, "he stood there for a little while, then he put his hand over my window and said, 'He's gone and you are safe now,' and when he took away his hand, he was gone too."

As I take the fish off the hook, Sagi holds out his hands. I pass him the fish and it slides through his fingers and into the cooler.

He looks up at me and says, "Cool!"

I pat him on the back and say, "Cool dream." And we sit there for two hours more, reeling in two more trout, two stingrays, and one spot-tail bass.

It is dusk by the time we clean the fish, and after I show him how to fillet the first one, I am overwhelmed by a feeling of God's love for him.

"Sagi, do you believe in God?" I ask.

"I think I'd like to," he says.

As we clean the fish together, I tell him about God, that He made Sagi and all of us and that a long time ago we were separated from God because of the bad things that we and the people before us did. So He sent His Son to bridge the gap between us and God. And that if we believe this is true then we are back with God again and will also have eternal life.

"I believe it!" he says as he scales the last trout.

"You do?" I say, relieved and surprised. "We'll pray right now to let God know and that will be that."

"Okay," he says, "you do it."

So we lean over into the outdoor sink to pray, our hands coated with fish scales and blood. He is trying to be sanctimonious as he squints hard to keep his eyes shut. I pat his shoulder to let him know he's doing fine, and then I say, "Heavenly Father, Sagi believes in You and Your Son. He knows that he has done or thought things that made You sad, and he believes that Your Son paid the price for those things so that Sagi could be adopted as a child by You. Thank You that this prayer is his salvation. Amen."

"You can say amen now," I whisper to him.

"Amen!" he says, not sure if there is closure yet.

"It's done," I say, holding my hands palms up in a "Now, wasn't that easy," kind of way.

"Thank you, Miss DeLoach."

"You're welcome," I say, beaming with joy for Sagi's salvation and thinking that I can hardly wait to tell Sasser that I've had my first experience as an evangelist!

When I take Sagi home, Mr. Shuzuki is on the front porch talking on his cell phone.

He puts his hand over the receiver and calls to us. "How'd you do?" he says.

"Your son caught enough for your dinner," I say, holding the bag of fish.

Sagi grabs the bag from me and says thank you, then runs to his father to show him our catch.

It is still so peculiar that another family lives in the Rose Hill house. Mr. Shuzuki looks so strange up there on the porch with his cell phone and polished black shoes.

As I'm driving off the grounds I look up to the piazza just off

Sagi's room where the rocking chairs bobble in the wind. I think of the two men in Sagi's dream, and I picture the gigantic hand that went over the window, protecting him and opening his heart to the truth.

Mama says if you have the faith of a mustard seed, you can move mountains, and now I long for that much faith so I can move the mountain of my daddy's hardened heart and replace it with a softened one. I long for the great man in Sagi's dream to put his hand over the caretaker's house so that the darkness will no longer be able to make its way inside our home.

჻

Two afternoons ago I received an acceptance letter from St. Mary's School in Richmond, Virginia. I am one of the five girls to receive the "Renaissance Women's Scholarship." I was struck with a wave of guilt about lying on my application, then I prayed without waiting for a response, "Is this Your way of working all things for the good, even my lies, in order to get me out of here?" (Even though a part of my heart had a feeling it didn't work that way.)

They want me to attend the summer school session so I can catch up on part of the requirements that I missed this year. Summer school starts in May, just six weeks away.

I left two messages for Bethany and Sasser the day I found out, and at work that same evening I tried to tell Suzanne about it, but it was a busy night and most everyone was acting kind of crazy, a combination of the large spring-break crowd and the "lost weekend."

When I looked around the place it was like everyone was on fast-forward. Jeeter was running the customers to their seats, and Sal stayed right on my back as I bused tables. A couple of times he actually put his hand on my rear and tapped it while he said in a sharp whisper, "Quicker, DeVeaux, quicker." He made me nervous.

"Leave me alone," I summoned the courage to say, but he didn't respond so I don't know if he heard me.

Toward a lull in the night I started to look for C. C. to share the news with him. Even though we're not an item anymore, I thought maybe he'd like to know where I might be going in a few weeks. But when I found him, he had just come out of Sal's office with his eyes shooting in all directions. So I stopped and hid on the other side of the kitchen door, watching him run around the fiery stove like a madman, frantically scooping out grits and hurling shrimp into the fryer, which made the grease splash up, sending him reeling backward. Then he started to wash the dishes like that, too, jerking up the steaming box and pushing the plastic crates of silverware and glass through. When he lifted down the box and the boiling hot water spilled over onto his legs, he let out a shrill scream, then he laughed and started again, sliding through a crate full of dirty salad bowls.

Finally I went to Suzanne, who was sitting on the back porch slowly stirring some whipping cream into her coffee. Her last table had gotten their meal so she could relax.

As she lit her cigarette she said, "I'm just too old to be screwed up like them," and then with her instructional tone of voice added, "and you're too young."

"I know," I said, taking a seat on the back steps and nodding to Mr. Lumpkin, who was watering his pansies in the dark.

Last week he put up an additional No Parking sign at the edge of his yard and Sal went over and explained that this was a busy time of year for us so the parking may get a little out of hand, but we'd do all we could to keep it under control. Then Sal offered Lumpkin a bag of cocaine, which he actually accepted and said, "I'll try to bear with you." Ever since then Lumpkin's been up all hours of the night doing all kinds of chores at record speed: mowing the lawn, painting the fence, polishing the brass doorknob.

I said to Suzanne, "I'm not touching the stuff."

As Suzanne inhaled deeply, she said, "They've been snorting it for days now." She paused and licked the sweet cream off her lips and the smoke disappeared into her chest without reappearing as she exhaled, adding, "Jeeter's got *two* babies at home, and he *and* his wife have just been getting into the stuff. Now don't you think that's messed up?"

We both held our noses when C.C. came out to pour a trash can of mushy food into the Dumpster a few yards away. As the stench coated our throats, he hollered, "Man, life is good!"

"Yeah," I said.

Mr. Lumpkin jerked his head up from his garden hose, glanced at us, then settled right back into the watering.

As C.C. walked back into the kitchen, Suzanne looked back at me. She ashed before she needed to and said, "And C.C.'s not much better."

I leaned in and whispered, "Suzanne, I just found out that I got a scholarship to a boarding school in Virginia."

"That's great," she said.

"I guess," I said, "though I lied on the application to get in."

Suzanne made a spitting sound and sent her hand slapping toward me through the smoke-filled air between us. She said, "I say do what you *have* to do to take care of yourself."

"Thing is," I said, "I don't know if I should go or not. I've just started to get settled here and all."

"Settled?" Suzanne said. "In this godforsaken place? Not to mention your godforsaken father." She looked me in the eye and said, "DeVeaux, I say *get out* if you can." She nodded as she exhaled and added, "This place ain't goin' nowhere. Life here will always be the same—one minute boring as all get-out, the next minute crazier than any scene you've ever known. Sure, you may decide that you want to come back, later. But at least you will have had choices. You know?"

❧

After work that night, I was determined to tell my parents about the scholarship. I leaped out of the truck into the black night with a head full of steam, and I was happy to see they were both still awake and sitting in the den. But as I was walking toward them, we were all startled by a stream of light that suddenly lit up the waterway and poured through the windows that face the creek, illuminating the marsh and even the trees in our yard.

Mama and Daddy jumped up from in front of the TV to look out the window. There had never been anything other than pitch blackness out of all our windows this time of night.

When we couldn't figure out where it was coming from, we all walked down to the dock and saw that there was an electric glow that reached across the river and our creek, lighting the ripples of the outgoing tide.

The light was coming from Otter, the wild and beautiful island that Daddy was going to develop. The bulbs were spread out all over the palmettos and oaks, the whole island glowing from the inside out like a well-lit Christmas tree.

The first complete house was lit up, too. It is a large and modern house, shaped like a pentagon on stilts, and its front porch looks out over the river and onto our creek.

Daddy walked over to the porch and came back outside with a set of binoculars, which we passed among us every minute or so. Inside the new house, we saw the figure of a woman who seemed to be standing in front of a sink. Then we saw a man walking out of the front porch and toward his own dock where he had two boats, a large one for deep-sea fishing and a little johnboat for the creeks, both suspended in the air on one of those state-of-the-art boat lifts.

Until this moment Rose Hill Plantation had never been in direct view of any other people. In daylight, a boat could ride down our narrow creek and catch a glimpse of our house through the oak trees. One could even see the tops of our chimneys from the river, which runs parallel to the creek, but at night this land has always been hidden by darkness.

We watched the man for whole minutes. He checked his boats, lifted up his crab trap to count his catch, then he headed back through his yard.

When he finally walked back up the stairs into his house, we turned and walked back into ours, making our way to our separate bed quarters in silence.

৵

After that I hoped God was telling me to go to St. Mary's and get a fresh start. With the Shuzukis' decision to move down here permanently and now the successful development of Otter Island, I knew that Daddy was heading over the edge. And didn't I have the right to escape like my siblings? To keep myself from witnessing my daddy fall apart? I knew I needed to pray, but I sure hoped I wouldn't have to wait anymore.

As I turned out the lights, I tried to fall asleep imagining myself in the mountains of Virginia, carrying my backpack across the beautiful colonnade in St. Mary's campus square, nodding to handsome professors and happy groups of friends, but every time I rolled over, I was jolted out of my dreams by the lights from Otter Island making their way through my window, eliminating the Rose Hill darkness and the secrets of our land.

17

Resurrection

The next day when I get home from school, I prepare Daddy's supper and wait for Mama to get home from work so I can tell them about my scholarship. I know Daddy gets upset lately when family members take off, but somehow I think their lives might be easier if I weren't around. I've begun to feel the way Eli must have felt, that I am just another thing to take care of.

But before Mama gets home, Jeeter calls me and begs me to come into the restaurant.

"We've got 203 on the books, 'cause it's spring break for most of the public schools and every family in the whole dern state must have decided to head down here for the holiday."

"But tonight's a bad night for me," I say. "I need to talk to my parents."

"DeVeaux," Jeeter says, "heck, I'm so desperate here I'll pay you twice as much. C'mon, I really need your help."

"All right," I say, because when he puts it like that I feel sorry for him. And I don't see how they could manage with just Sal as the busboy, especially since he and half the rest of them are still on their lost weekend.

"But I want tomorrow night off," I say.

"Done," Jeeter says. "Now get your skinny rear down here and help me set these tables."

Since Daddy's asleep, I call Mama and she comes down from the Pig to give me a lift.

On the way I say, "Mama, I've got something I need to talk to you and Daddy about."

"Everything okay, dahlin'?"

"Yes, ma'am," I say. "It's good news, I think."

"Well, we could use some of that," she says.

As I'm getting out of the car Mama says, "DeVeaux, you've been so patient and you haven't complained at all since we've moved out here. I can't thank you enough for how you've handled all of this change. I can't imagine what your siblings would have acted like in your position."

I smile back at Mama, and I see that tears are forming in the corners of her eyes. It's the first time she's shown me her heart in a while. And in a way I feel relieved to know that she has felt the hardship too. That while she puts on her armor of optimism, there is something soft and vulnerable beneath it.

She doesn't look back at me, just puts the car in reverse and says, "I'll be back at midnight to pick you up."

"Come on, Mama," I say to her, trying to make my newfound hope contagious, "things can't be tough forever, right?"

"Lord only knows," she says, then she squeezes my hand. "Get to work."

Just then Tanner Strickland pulls up to drop Sal off. Sal gets out of the car with no shirt on and hobbles toward the back of the restaurant.

I wave good-bye to Mama as Sal stops to wait for me by the Dumpster. He's still high. I can tell by the way he's rapidly tapping his foot on the gravel as if he can't stop it. And his fingers are trembling at his sides. He says, "C'mon, Devo, we got a big night, girl."

After I set all the tables, refill the salt and pepper shakers, and fold the napkins, Suzanne meets me out at the Dumpster for her cigarette break.

She says she's expecting Eli home tomorrow morning. She called last night from a port in north Florida to say they were on their way home a little early because they've had some good catches, and they've both got some kind of god-awful flu. Garrick has paid her and she will start looking for a place to rent as soon as she gets back.

"Great!" I say because I can't wait to see my cousin and tell her my plan. I remember when she told me last Christmas that things would work out by springtime, and some already have. I *will* go to St. Mary's and ride out this family storm, and she *will* get her own place and start a life for herself. I feel an energy now. My mind is clear and my muscles are ready to be flexed, to pick up the loaded tray with dirty glasses, plates, and silverware and place it squarely on my shoulder and push through from the dining room into the kitchen. I'm ready to take on the hundreds of tourists that will blow through here tonight with their bright T-shirts, flip-flops, and constant demands for refills of tea and water. I'm ready for them to sniff the table water and screw their faces up. I'm ready to say, "It's deep well water. We are, after all, on an island. If you'd like, we have Perrier or I could bring you some lemons."

❧

The night is crazier than ever. My back hurts from lifting heavy trays and ducking under the tables to pick up food, silverware, and empty sugar packets. I set tables at least sixty times and when we run out of napkins I have to use Suzanne's car to drive down to the Piggly Wiggly and get some paper ones.

As the night winds down, everyone is so tired that they are punchy. Jeeter is handing out beers to all the employees except me, and Sal is telling an older woman he picked up how much the restaurant made tonight. Suzanne gives me a fifty-dollar bill for a tip out so I know that she has done well.

I drink coffee, of course, and I don't even partake in smoking a cigarette because the last thing I need is for Mama to smell tobacco on my breath the night before I tell her about my scholarship.

Everyone laughs at my decision not to partake, but I shrug my shoulders at them the way Suzanne would, and they leave me alone.

There is a general buzz because of the money we've made, and everyone decides to go down to Coot's Lounge at the beach to hear the local band, Trigger Fish. The older woman that Sal is hanging on says she has a van and could give some of us a lift.

Sal lifts his eyebrows and says, "Let's you and I save the van for ourselves."

She rolls her eyes, but keeps her hand on his knee.

C.C. and Tanner try to persuade me to come along, but I'm tired and Mama is probably on her way to get me. I watch them all trickle out one by one until I'm the only one left except for Jeeter, who has to lock everything up.

I'm sitting on the back porch when the truck pulls up. It is Daddy instead of Mama. He doesn't see me sitting there; he just honks the horn and I quickly run out to meet him.

When I get into the car he says, with a hint of frustration, "Well, Mama fell asleep on the couch."

"Oh," I say. "Well, thanks for coming to get me."

I can't help but recall those awkward times when on an occasion Daddy would pick me up from grade school when we lived downtown. With Mama I would giggle and tell her all about whatever I'd been doing and who had gotten on my nerves that day, but with Daddy I felt the need to make everything I'd done sound impressive. I'd recount what we learned and how I participated in class. I did this because I loved when he looked across the seat and said, "I'm proud of you." It was my goal in life to hear him say that.

The truck stutters and he starts it up again. Instead of asking me how my night was, he spots the fuel marker, pounds the steering wheel twice and says, "And she's nearly let this truck run out of gas."

I clear my throat and say, "The Exxon on the beach is open this time of night."

He grunts then turns the truck around and we head toward the beach.

I roll down my window to smell the dark night. It is one of those nights where the day's heat is lifting up from the ground and off the marsh in layers of smog and mist. The truck tries to slice through these layers, but they are malleable and make their way around us. After we pass through them, there's blackness everywhere.

As we drive, I look into the dense forest on either side, and I can see eyes in the depths of the curves ahead, green and gold glimmers caught by our headlights. There are bobcats and raccoons and deer everywhere. And I recall Chambers swearing along with Mee Maw Rose that once he also saw a panther on one of the back roads. He was riding in the back of a pickup truck, and he watched it slink across the road through the path of dust the truck had churned up.

Daddy is humming some tune I don't recall. He's probably making it up as he goes along.

From ahead of the curve, just before the beach, we see the blue lights of two police cars flashing. They're on the front and back of what looks like Tanner Strickland's truck, which is half in and half out of a ditch. He and his dog, Muddy Girl, are standing behind the truck talking to the policeman on the opposite side of the road. Tanner was just in the restaurant a few minutes ago. He was actually drinking coffee with me because he said he needed to nurse his hangover from the lost weekend.

A short, stocky policewoman puts up her hand for us to stop. Two other cars moving in the opposite direction pass slowly around the bend. It's Saturday night and all of the Edisto partiers are coming to and from Coot's Lounge.

"Just one car involved," Daddy says, in a tone somewhere between a question and an observation.

"Looks like it," I say.

"Poor guy probably hit another one of those deer," he says. "Boy, what a nuisance they are."

Before we can move farther, an ambulance sounds from the depths of the darkness behind us. I look in the rearview mirror and see its red lights ricocheting off the pine trees as it hurls towards us, sirens blaring. I imagine the chaos in the forest surrounding us—every creature ducking for shelter.

I think how it doesn't make sense to have an ambulance because Tanner looks all right. He wasn't driving anybody tonight since Sal hooked up with the van lady, and now the cop has him out of his car walking a line. The lost weekend is going to catch up with him now, I think to myself. And this is a good thing. These island Peter Pans can't go on living this way forever.

After the ambulance passes us and parks in front of the truck, the stocky woman motions for us to come on by.

As we move forward, my attention is pulled toward a ditch that runs alongside the road, and all of a sudden I spot a small duck boot at the top of the embankment.

When it's our turn to move around the accident, we see them loading someone onto the stretcher. The person is strapped down tight and appears to be unconscious. Thick brown hair falls over the stretcher. A bare foot peeks out from beneath the pants, and I recognize the conductor overalls that Eli had on Christmas Eve.

"Stop!" I scream.

Daddy swerves then pulls over to the side of the ditch.

"What in the world?" he says, and his eyes dart around the car then focus on me.

"It's Cousin Eli on that stretcher," I say. "Do you think she's been hit?"

Daddy jumps out of the truck and runs over to the scene where a policeman holds him back. I am behind him, and the policeman pushes us away as we watch the paramedics load her into the back of the ambulance.

"Stand back, sir," the stocky woman says firmly to Daddy.

Tanner is crying, pleading to a tall black cop, "She was passed out in the road, Officer. I swerved to miss her and I ran into the other ditch. I didn't hit her, Officer, sir—she must've just passed out there!"

Daddy says, "It *is* her."

He's blinking his eyes over and over as if he cannot focus them.

In seconds, we turn the truck around and follow the ambulance the fifty miles to the Charleston hospital as its lights flash and the siren whirs. The roads are nearly empty and we fly through the blackness of the island then onto the fluorescent Charleston roads where convenience stores and fast-food restaurants light our way.

Daddy stops once for gas and as I hear the fuel funnel into our truck, I try to recreate what could have happened to Eli. She must have been walking to the restaurant or even to our house. Something made her pass out right there in the road. I hope it's just the flu. Thank God Tanner didn't hit her!

Daddy gets back in the car and moans. When we're back on the highway he clears his throat over and over again but doesn't speak. I pray like I did about Mama when she had her asthma attack. All I can think to say as we fly down the road is, "Lord, please take care of my cousin."

When we get to the emergency room, all we can do is wait. I call Mama, who answers on the second try, then I sit in an orange vinyl chair that squeaks when I move, and I just watch Daddy, who stands trance-like at the glass door that leads into the hallway, his head following the nurses and doctors who walk by. His hair is matted in the back from where he must have been sleeping earlier in the evening and both of his duck boots are untied, their leather laces coiling across the slick, linoleum floor. I worry that he might trip and hurt himself.

Two hours pass and a Dr. Moore who works in the emergency room comes in to tell us that they are running tests because it appears that Cousin Eli had a seizure. The neurologist is on his way to examine her, and he's already ordered a CAT scan.

"From the flu?" I say. "I think she just had some kind of fever and head cold is all."

"It appears to be more than that," he says, looking more to my daddy than to me. "I need to get some questions answered because there is a chance this could be bacterial meningitis, and if it is, I want to ensure the safety of your niece and anyone else who has been around her."

Daddy nods in disbelief while the doctor continues.

"Does she live in your home?" the doctor asks Daddy.

"No," Daddy says, nervously pulling at his jaw, "she lives in Columbia and attends the university. That's why I don't understand—"

I know I have to speak up now, even though I still feel a little guilty betraying Eli's trust. But it's for her own good.

"No," I say to the doctor and Daddy, "she's been living on a commercial fishing boat the last several weeks, trying to earn some extra money."

"What in the fool are you talking about, DeVeaux?" Daddy spits.

"She was out of money, and she didn't want to go back to school after the Christmas holiday, so she decided to take a job with Captain Garrick to earn enough money to get out on her own," I say to him.

Dr. Moore says, "If the tests confirm bacterial meningitis, we need to find that captain and anyone else she has been around lately."

My mind races as I think about Becky and Suzanne, who were with her not too long ago.

Daddy nods, and he seems to be staring at something behind

the doctor. But there is nothing behind the doctor. Just a blank wall with more orange chairs. The doctor nods to the neurologist who has come briskly through the emergency room door in civilian clothes. The nurse is pointing in the direction of Eli's room with the chart in her hand, and he dashes off in another direction.

A loud sound goes off at the nurse's station, and Dr. Moore runs toward Eli's room.

"What's happening?" Daddy screams at a young nurse at her station.

"We'll let you know as soon as we do," she says.

"Seizure," Dr. Moore calls to the neurologist who is racing back toward Eli's room while he slips his arm through the sleeve of a white medical jacket.

Without warning, Daddy races to the trash can by my chair and vomits. The young nurse motions to another nurse, who scurries into the waiting room with a bedpan and together they try to help him up. As they pull up his torso, he begins to heave and snort with tears. Then he falls back into a chair and cries, "Eliza! Eliza!"

I run over to him and help the nurses usher him to his own little space in order to clean him up. One pats his back mechanically in an attempt to reassure him, and the other just stares at him for a moment as if he were a terrible riddle. Then she sits him on a cot, draws a curtain around us, and begins to wipe his face and hands.

"She's going to be okay, Daddy. She's going to be okay," I say as I rub his round back up and down. I assure him, "Now that she's here, the doctors can find out what to do for her." The nurse continues to pat his shoulder and she says, "That's right. Uh-huh."

Daddy doesn't respond and I can see that he has entered some other place in his mind, perhaps the place where he mourns the loss of his sister, and he cannot be consoled.

Moments later, he looks back at me as though he doesn't know me, but then a hint of recollection comes across his face.

"DeVeaux?" he says. "Yes," I say, "I'm here, Daddy," and I lean down so I can look him in the face. He starts to weep, long heaves and lots of breaths like a small child who has just been frightened for the first time. I rub his back again and let him bury his head in my neck as another nurse leans down and gives him a pill that relaxes him.

I pray, "Lord, have mercy," over and over as I hold him until he falls asleep in my arms. Then I sit back down on another orange chair and let my head fall back against the wall. I watch the ceiling, the grooves in it, as if it were the surface of another planet, and I weep for my cousin and my father and all the pain they have both endured.

The still, small voice of God's Spirit, which I have tried too hard to shrink over the last few weeks, whispers to me, *Their pain is more than you can begin to fathom.* And I know He speaks the truth.

By the time the neurologist and Dr. Moore are back, Mama has arrived on the scene and she and I follow the doctors into another, smaller waiting room, leaving my father to sleep away his old grief and his new fear.

The neurologist tells Mama and me the tests have confirmed that Eli has bacterial meningitis. She must have had a seizure on the Edisto highway and that is what caused her to pass out on the road. They are preparing her for a spinal tap so she can receive intravenous antibiotics, which have a 50 percent chance of getting rid of the bacteria. Normally the chances would be better, but her case has been going on for some time now and appears to be quite severe. They expect she may have another seizure, and she may be comatose for several days before, they hope, pulling through.

Mama, who saw a *Dateline* special about some college students who contracted this illness, says, "What about limb loss? My word, that can't happen, can it?"

"Yes, ma'am," says Dr. Powell, the neurologist. "That is a condition called bacterial sepsis that occurs in the most severe cases. It's when the blood vessels clamp down on the limbs so that all the blood is pooled toward the heart. If this happens, yes, it can result in loss of limbs, and it is good that you are aware of the possibility, but let's all hope it doesn't come to that."

"Let's pray it doesn't," Mama says.

"I can't think of a better idea than that," says Dr. Moore. "We'll know more over the next twenty-four to forty-eight hours, but the most important thing is for you all to be tested and contact anyone who has been around her recently so that they can be tested. Then you all should take Mr. DeLoach home and try to get some rest."

"One of us will stay here," Mama says.

"I'm staying," I say strongly to Mama. "You get Daddy a hotel room nearby and help him get some sleep."

Next Mama and I call Suzanne and tell her to get to the hospital now so that she and Becky can get checked out, and we ask Tina and C.C. to go find Garrick and see if he is sick too. Then we hold hands and pray with all our hearts for God to heal Cousin Eli.

After I help Daddy to the car, I race back in to call Bethany and Sasser, even though it is 5:00 a.m., and by 6:00 a.m. they are both here with Father Dan racing in behind them. Dr. Moore has already taken my test for bacterial meningitis, but he assures me that I was with her so long ago that he doubts I would have it. Before the doctor heads home, he tells me that we can go in and see her even though she is unconscious.

When we walk in, I stare at her for a moment, and she looks so worn out. Her lips are still chapped from the ocean, and her face is a grayish-green. As I begin to weep, Sasser asks a nurse if we can lay hands on her and pray, and she says, "Yes, but be gentle, and don't touch her head or face."

As we take our places around her and softly put our hands on her arms and legs, Father Dan takes the lead. His words are like honey and a healing balm as he asks the Lord to heal Cousin Eli and deliver her from this illness. I can feel a kind of heat moving through my hands as I touch Eli's leg, and I know it is the Holy Spirit moving in this room. Sasser begins to recite Scripture, beginning with John 11:3: *"Lord, behold, the one you love is sick"*; and continuing with Psalm 103:13–14: *"As a father pities his children, so the LORD pities those who fear Him. For He knows our frame; He remembers that we are dust"* [NKJV]. Then he ends with John 11:4, and he speaks with hope and conviction: *"This sickness will not end in death. No, it is for God's glory so that God's Son may be glorified through it."*

Then Sasser takes a little container of oil out of his pocket and anoints Eli's hands and feet with the sign of the cross, and together we all say the Lord's Prayer.

There is no obvious reaction from Eli, but I can still feel the heat and power in the room, and I know we have put her in the Lord's hands and that there is no one better to entrust her to. I kiss the top of her shoulder and lead them out into the hallway to thank them.

Father Dan hugs me and excuses himself because it is Sunday and he has to get to the 8:00 a.m. service. Then Sasser and Bethany walk me to the cafeteria and force me to eat some eggs and bacon, which does make me feel a little better.

"I'm so sorry all this has happened, DeVeaux," Sasser says to me while I sip my coffee. "What can we do to help you?"

"What you just did was the best thing you could do," I say. "You could just keep praying for her. And I'll keep on praying for you to get that gift of healing. Boy, I never knew how badly I might need you to have it."

We all laugh nervously and I start to get weepy again.

"We'll be here," Bethany says as she squeezes my hand. And she means it; she and Sasser are back that evening and early the next morning to pray for Eli again because she is still comatose.

Becky, Suzanne, and I found out that we didn't contract the illness, but Garrick was rushed to a hospital in North Charleston and seems to be responding better than Eli to the antibiotic. He has not lost consciousness.

On Tuesday when Bethany and Sasser come again, Daddy and Mama show up too. Daddy seems to be a little more in control of his emotions, but he is still taking those pills Dr. Moore gave him and his face is full of fear and anxiety.

Since we all are there at the same time, Sasser suggests that we go in and pray together. Sasser moves to the head of Eli's bed, lays his hands on her shoulders, and recites the same Scriptures as before. When he is finished this time, somehow I have this peace and even an assurance that she is going to pull through, and Sasser seems to have it too. He nods in my direction and I smile at him, and by that afternoon Eli wakes up while Mama and I are watching the news by her bed. The first thing she says is, "I'm thirsty, DeVeaux. How about some ginger ale?"

❧

Ten days later Eli is ready to be released from the hospital. Daddy and I went in last week for our caretaking orders, and the doctor told us she'd need to be in a wheelchair the first few weeks at home in order to regain her strength.

It took this good news and a few more days of that powerful medication for Daddy to come out of his trance of grief. But when his head became clear, he seemed to be overcome with a yearning to take care of Eli. He told Mama not to worry about work and all, that he and I would help her heal.

The first night that he was back at home he came to me and said, "Can we give Eli your room since it's so close to ours and to the bathroom? I was thinking you could live in the teahouse for a few months while Chambers and I build you another room on the back side of the house."

"Of course," I said with delight, because there is nothing I wouldn't do for my cousin. And I'm happy to have the chance to give her something.

So I cleaned my room top to bottom for a week, scrubbing the dusty corners and the gaps between the floorboards, vacuuming the curtains and relining the chest of drawers. And with my tip money I bought some magazines and books and filled my bedside table with them. Today I went and picked some late-blooming azaleas, which I put in a vase on the dresser so when she comes home this spring afternoon she will see their brightness and remember the beautiful parts of Rose Hill.

Now Daddy has gone to pick her up from the hospital. He's even taken the Honda because it would be too hard on them both for him to hoist her up into the truck. We cleaned the cobwebs off last night and took it to the car wash.

Will and Virginia came for Eli's homecoming, and we spent the morning catching crabs from the dock and catching up. I have decided not to go to St. Mary's because I want to be home and help with my cousin, and my siblings agree with my decision. Virginia said, "You aren't missing anything. That school messed me up more than it helped me." And Will looked out across the marsh and said, "I wouldn't choose anything over this, baby sister."

And I know that they mean what they say and they are right. Thing is, every place has its limitations and its benefits. And some children don't or can't follow the path of their siblings or the generations that came before them. Some traditions die, and that's okay. In the end, the only thing that counts is our relationship with God, and I've got all the time in the world out here to cultivate that.

We will not own Rose Hill again or our house on Tradd Street, just as Daddy will not get his sister back. And right now I belong here—in the caretaker's house, looking after my cousin, and the Shuzukis, and Flounder, and Easy and the kittens, and learning that mystery of hope Maum Bess and Bethany and Sasser possess—having faith in God and what His story for us will be. After all, it is already written.

※

When Daddy and Eli arrive I'm sitting on the fish shed reading. Virginia is in the kitchen with Mama cooking a huge meal that Daddy decided on: honey-baked ham, black-eyed peas, and rice and gravy. Will is casting his rod into the creek.

When they pull up, I slide down from the roof and we all move from our places and surround the car. Everyone is applauding my cousin, who can barely smile through the passenger-side window for all the medication, but she nods and waves her hands with the kind of exuberance and strength that belongs only to her.

Daddy gets out of the car, opens the trunk, and lifts out the wheelchair. We all stand back because he is the one who has been trained by the nurse in how to move her, and we let him do his work. He sets the chair on the ground in front of the passenger seat and opens it. Then he holds open the car door and reaches in and lifts my cousin out of the car and into the chair.

We all are applauding again and saying things like, "This will be a good workout for you, Dad." Then we get quiet because somehow we know this moment is important.

Daddy tries to roll the chair forward, and it rolls a few feet then gets stuck in the mud. He tries again, but once he makes it over the mud pile he hits another, and the front wheels sink into the black soil.

Will makes a motion to help, but Daddy gently holds up his hand as if to say, "I'll take care of this."

He reaches down, puts one hand behind Eli's back and the other just under her knees, and lifts her up. He pulls her toward him and she reaches her arms around his neck.

As they walk toward the house Will scurries toward the screened door to open it. Mama comes up behind them, folds up the wheelchair, and she and Virginia carry it inside.

I just stand still and watch as my daddy steps through the mud, one foot at a time, holding his niece tightly in his arms, her head resting against his chest.

There is a strength and pride to him as he does this, and just as they make their way through the screened door and onto the porch something catches my eye by the toolshed, over where the cornfields begin. I look out and find Maum Bess there, in a bright purple jumpsuit, and she stares in my direction. I wave to her and she nods once then turns and heads back down the fields, her round body shuffling between the stalks.

As she disappears I look around to find Flounder and Easy resting on opposite sides of the tractor. Then I hear laughter coming from my kitchen. As I walk toward the house, I feel a soft breeze like a whisper that rattles the leaves and lifts the hair off my forehead. And I know, surer than anything I've ever known, that Maum Bess has gotten her way. That the still, small voice of my Lord has prevailed, and it is making its way through the trees of this land and into our home in the form of a gentle wind.

Reading Group Guide Available
at www.westbowpress.com

Look for these other Southern fiction titles from WestBow Press

The Dead Don't Dance · Wrapped in Rain

by Charles Martin

Gardenias for Breakfast

by Robin Jones Gunn

A Song I Knew by Heart

by Bret Lott

Live Like You Were Dying

by Michael Morris

Savannah from Savannah

Savannah Comes Undone

by Denise Hildreth

Life Support · Life Everlasting

The List · The Trial · The Sacrifice

by Robert Whitlow

WestBow
PRESS

A Division of Thomas Nelson Publishers
Since 1798

visit us at www.westbowpress.com